*Tynan bent his head to hers,
and Lily's lips parted in anticipation.*

She had never wanted a man's kiss so desperately, so that her entire being seemed to vibrate with that desire. Tynan's long fingers deftly cupped her chin to turn her head to the side.

Lily made a noise then, a soft, frustrated moan that drew a chuckle from her tormentor.

"Patience, sweetheart," he admonished her, his gruff brogue more pronounced now. "Too fast and you'll spoil it."

Tynan trailed kisses down her jawline, the relative chill of his lips against her warm and sensitive flesh a shocking pleasure. Lily writhed in his arms, wanting to be closer, wanting some nameless *more* that she couldn't identify. But Tynan was relentlessly controlled. Lily heard his voice then, seeming to echo right inside her head.

Let me taste you.

Powerless to do anything but obey, Lily let her head fall back in submission...

DARK
AWAKENING

A Tale of the Dark Dynasties

KENDRA LEIGH CASTLE

FOREVER

NEW YORK   BOSTON

This book is a work of fiction. Names, characters, places, and incidents are the product of the author's imagination or are used fictitiously. Any resemblance to actual events, locales, or persons, living or dead, is coincidental.

Copyright © 2011 by Kendra Leigh Castle
Excerpt from *Midnight Reckoning* copyright © 2011 by Kendra Leigh Castle
All rights reserved. Except as permitted under the U.S. Copyright Act of 1976, no part of this publication may be reproduced, distributed, or transmitted in any form or by any means, or stored in a database or retrieval system, without the prior written permission of the publisher.

Book design by Giorgetta Bell McRee
Dynasty illustrations by Franklin Daley III

Forever
Hachette Book Group
237 Park Avenue
New York, NY 10017
Visit our website at www.HachetteBookGroup.com

Forever is an imprint of Grand Central Publishing.
The Forever name and logo is a trademark of Hachette Book Group, Inc.

The publisher is not responsible for websites (or their content) that are not owned by the publisher.

Printed in the United States of America

First Printing: July 2011

10 9 8 7 6 5 4 3 2 1

ATTENTION CORPORATIONS AND ORGANIZATIONS:
Most HACHETTE BOOK GROUP books are available at quantity discounts with bulk purchase for educational, business, or sales promotional use. For information, please call or write:
Special Markets Department, Hachette Book Group
237 Park Avenue, New York, NY 10017
Telephone: 1-800-222-6747 Fax: 1-800-477-5925

To my sister Kyra,
for always being my friend
and for putting up with the vampire Barbies.
This one's for you.

DARK
AWAKENING

THE DARK DYNASTIES
Known Bloodlines of the United States

THE PTOLEMY

LEADER: Queen Arsinöe

ORIGIN: Ancient Egypt and the goddess Sekhmet

STRONGHOLDS: Cities of the eastern United States, concentrated in the mid-Atlantic

ABILITIES: Lightning speed

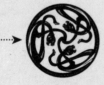

THE CAIT SITH

LEADER: None; considered lowbloods, despite the pure mark

ORIGIN: A Celtic line originating with the Fae

STRONGHOLDS: None; in servitude to the Ptolemy, or hiding in squalor

ABILITIES: Can take the form of a cat

THE DRACUL

LEADER: Vlad Dracul

ORIGIN: The goddess Nyx

STRONGHOLDS: Northern United States; Chicago (shared under an agreement with the Empusae)

ABILITIES: Can take the form of a bat

THE GRIGORI

LEADER: Sariel

ORIGIN: Unknown

STRONGHOLDS: The deserts of the West

ABILITIES: Flight is rumored due to their mark, but no proof

THE EMPUSAE

LEADER: Empusa

ORIGIN: The goddess Hecate

STRONGHOLDS: Southern United States; Chicago (shared with the Dracul)

ABILITIES: Can take the form of smoke

Prologue

THE BALLROOM WAS bathed in the soft glow of candle-light, and tiny flames danced, reflected in the eyes of those gathered for the ceremony. The young woman, the Chosen, stepped uncertainly into their midst, her bare feet noiseless on the dark and gleaming wood floor. Her eyes widened as she took in the sight of the lithe and elegant figures, pale-skinned and beautiful, who had come to witness this event, the most momentous of her life.

The last of her natural life.

Though she had caught glimpses of others like her lover before, she had never seen so many in one place. It was amazing, overwhelming...and just a little frightening.

Rosalyn. Her name echoed in a whisper all around her, though not a single mouth moved. Soon she would know their thoughts as well as they knew hers. These were to be her people, those who shared the ancient bloodline of a goddess, a pharaoh. They were the Ptolemy, and they were to be revered.

As instructed, she had come to this beautiful manor in the middle of nowhere, clad in nothing but a thin silk robe of purest white. Soon, Rosalyn knew, that would be gone. She would enter her new life as she had come into the first, bare-skinned and pure. Her eyes darted anxiously around the room, searching for her beloved. The one who had made all this possible, the one who loved her enough to want her by his side for all time. However, all she saw were unfamiliar faces, cold in their beauty, eyes glowing preternaturally in the semidarkness. Some watched her with interest, others with naked hunger. Not all were unkind, she consoled herself as she fought back a shiver.

But none belonged to her Jeremy.

Rosalyn shuddered in a shallow breath and moved forward, determined not to let her fear of the unknown get the better of her. Jeremy had gone through all the proper channels, and she had been questioned by an emissary of Arsinöe herself, gaining the all-important blessing of the queen and securing her permission to join the sacred House of Ptolemy.

She had spent the past week making her arrangements and, though her family didn't yet understand, saying her good-byes. Being born into this new life meant cutting ties with the old one, and she'd shed more than a few tears over it. But the loss was well worth the gain. No longer would she be just one of a vampire's stable of human lovers, kept (though kept well) for the willing and frequent gift of her blood.

Now she would be Jeremy's mate eternal. For the first time, they would feast upon each other. And when the ceremony was over, and her skin was branded with the mark that would forever bind her to the ancient dynasty that had been blessed by Sekhmet, Rosalyn knew she would walk into her new life with no regrets, hand in hand with her love. She would be Rosalyn of the Ptolemy.

But... where was Jeremy?

The small crowd of perhaps thirty witnesses cleared to form a wide circle around her, leaving her standing alone, exposed in their midst. They were unnervingly silent, as was the way of their kind, but Rosalyn had been admonished not to speak until spoken to. So she waited as silently as they did, keeping her shoulders back, her chin high. She had been declared worthy. She clung to that and hoped her looks reflected it. She had brushed her long, straight hair so that it gleamed like spun gold as it fell past her shoulders, and she'd left her delicate features unpainted, the way Jeremy preferred. After tonight, Rosalyn thought, her eyes flickering over several of the dazzlingly beautiful women in attendance, she'd never need cosmetics again anyway.

Vampiric beauty was incomparable, and eternal.

A soft murmur ran through the crowd then, and suddenly he was there, stepping into the circle with her. Tall, sandy-haired, boyishly handsome Jeremy. He stepped forward to take her hands in his, and Rosalyn shivered, as she always did, at the first touch of that cool skin on hers. But the warmth in his eyes, glowing deep blue with a light all their own, more than compensated. He leaned in close, and she could smell the faint musk of his skin.

"Ready?" he asked softly, his warm breath fanning her ear.

She nodded. "Always."

He smiled, and the light caught the sharp points of his incisors, gleaming white between deep red lips. He looked away for a moment, and between one blink and the next, they were joined by a third person in the circle, a tall, imposing man who stood ramrod straight in a severe black suit. His expression was solemn, and when he spoke, his voice rippled through the air with a power that signified great age, though he appeared no older than forty.

This was the master of the ceremony, one of Arsinöe's trusted emissaries sent to oversee and verify the ancient ritual.

His first question was directed at Jeremy. "By what name are you called, supplicant?"

Jeremy's response was immediate, and full of pride. "I am Jeremy Rothburn of the Ptolemy."

"And what do you ask of us on this full moon's night?"

"I ask to bring this woman, Rosalyn DeVore, into the sacred House of Ptolemy, to bind her to us with the dark gift and to share with her life eternal."

The emissary's pale eyes shifted to her. "And you, Rosalyn DeVore? What do you request of the House of Ptolemy?"

For one heart-stopping instant, she feared that she'd forgotten the words. But then they were there for her, rolling easily from her tongue. "I ask to join this house, to share in the glorious lineage of Sekhmet, the lioness, the warrior goddess; of Arsinöe, the eternal pharaoh; and of all fortunate enough to drink the blood of the greatest of the vampire dynasties. I ask to give of my blood, my life, to Jeremy Rothburn of the Ptolemy, and for his blood, his life, to be shared in return."

Jeremy squeezed her hands reassuringly as the master of ceremonies gave a solemn nod, acknowledging her request. Then he looked to the assembly. His voice rose, a powerful and compelling clarion call.

"All you gathered, keepers of the dark flame, honored bearers of the blood of the goddess, you have heard the petition. What say you?"

The resounding "Aye!" had Rosalyn's heart soaring. This was it. She'd been accepted. There was only one thing left...though the final barrier was the most frightening of all. Because she would see death before they were through, if only to turn away from it forever.

The emissary actually managed a ghost of a smile when he turned his attention back to Jeremy.

"Make her yours. Make her ours."

He stepped back then, fading away into the crowd until it was once again only the two of them in the circle. Rosalyn looked at her lover, feeling the importance of the moment, knowing she was drawing her final breaths as a mortal being.

Jeremy undid her robe with a flick of his wrist, leaving it to slide from her shoulders and pool at her feet. Then she was naked before him, before all of them, terribly, wonderfully exposed. His heart was in his eyes when he stepped forward, and Rosalyn quickly forgot about the crowd. There were only the two of them there, really. And all their eternity yet before them.

His cool hands slid over her skin, brushing against nipples that had hardened in the chill air. Fear and excitement pooled in her belly, along with an unexpected flood of desire. Then he was pushing her hair back over her shoulders, bearing the pulse beating rapidly at the base of her throat. His eyes began to change, turning feral and blindingly bright. His teeth shone like daggers as he bared them.

He had drunk from her before. She didn't fear his teeth or the pain that so quickly gave way to pleasure. But this time, he must take her to the edge of death. And he would bring her back by letting her drink from him for the very first time.

Rosalyn gasped as his teeth pierced her flesh, and she heard an answering sigh rise up all around them. Then she could see, hear, feel nothing but Jeremy, and the sensation of drowning in a rush of pleasure until all reality narrowed to a single bright point that glowed ever farther in the distance. Lethargy stole through her limbs, and still he drank, pulling her life out of her, taking it into himself. When she crumpled to the floor, he came with her, gathering her close in his arms while he continued to feed.

Her heartbeat slowed . . . slowed. From the pool of near blackness in which she wallowed, Rosalyn waited for the press of Jeremy's wrist against her lips. For the taste of his blood, so long yearned for, so that the ritual would be complete.

Instead, she began to hear the distant sounds of screaming.

At first it was only one voice, a startled shriek cut brutally short. Then another began, and another, picking up the cry until the cavernous room reverberated with the sounds of terror and pain. Rosalyn struggled to open her eyes as Jeremy's teeth tore from her throat, as he lifted his head to stare at whatever horror show her initiation had become. Above the screaming, she heard the sounds of running, of fists beating against doors that had been sealed shut.

And beneath all that was a wet, rending sound that could be only the tearing of flesh—a sickening splatter, then a rush of air as something, someone, was cast brutally aside for the next. And the next.

The thud of lifeless bodies grew closer.

"Where is it? I can't see it!" shrieked a terrified female voice. A window shattered.

Jeremy looked down at her, cradled in his lap, and if Rosalyn had had the strength, she would have cried out. For in his eyes she no longer saw the bright promise of eternal life.

Now there was only death.

"I'm so sorry," he said, an instant before his head was separated from his body with such force that it hurtled away from her, across the room. Gore spattered her naked flesh, crimson on white. Then she did scream, a weak, keening sound that was dredged up from the depths of her fading soul. But she couldn't run; she could barely move. The darkness was rushing up to meet her, and it seemed that for her, there would be no return from it after all.

Around her, amidst the fading screams, was the smell of burning.

And the last sound Rosalyn heard was the malicious gurgle of laughter.

chapter ONE

Tipton, Massachusetts
Eight months later

TYNAN MACGILLIVRAY crouched in the shadows of the little garden, listening to the mortals rattling loudly around inside the stuffy old mansion. He tried to concentrate on the scents and sounds of the humans, hoping to pick up any subtle change in the air that might indicate a Seer was among these so-called ghost hunters, but so far all he'd gotten was a headache.

This small-town gimmick was a long shot, and he knew it. But he'd been everywhere in the past eight months, from New York City Goth clubs to Los Angeles coven meetings. Anywhere there might be a whisper of ability beyond the norm. In all that time, he had found not the faintest whiff of a Seer or even a hint of anything paranormal at all. Just a bunch of humans playing dress-up, trying to be different.

He wondered how they would feel if they walked into an actual vampire club. Most of them would probably be too foolish to even be frightened for the few seconds their life would last in one of those places. But they might note that there wasn't nearly as much black leather and bondage wear in undead society as they seemed to think.

Ty got to his feet, all four of them, and arched his back, stiff from keeping so still in the bushes all night. His cat form was the gift of his bloodline, though it was of dubious help in places like this. The house he was staking out sat just off the town square, and there were only a few scrubby barberry bushes for cover. His fur was black, yes, and blended into shadow, but dog-sized cats didn't exactly inspire the warm cuddlies in passersby.

Hell. It's no good. Ty gave a frustrated growl as he accepted the fact that this trip was just another bust. He'd been reduced to combing psychic fairs and visiting what were supposedly America's most haunted places, hoping something would draw out the sort of human he so desperately needed to find. But soon, very soon, Ty knew he would have to return to Arsinöe with the news that the Seers had, in all likelihood, simply died out. For the first time in three hundred years of service, he would have to admit failure.

And the Mulo, the gypsy curse that was slowly killing those he was charged with protecting, would continue its dark work until there was no one left who bore the mark of the Ptolemaic dynasty, the oldest and most powerful bloodline in all of vampire society, begun when Arsinöe's life was spared by a goddess's dark kiss. No other house could claim such a beginning, or such a ruler. But if things continued, the other dynasties, eternally jealous of the Ptolemy's power, lineage, and reach, wouldn't even have a carcass to feed upon.

The invisible terror had attacked twice more, both times at sacred initiations of the Ptolemy, both times leaving only one vampire alive enough to relate what had happened. Or in the case of the first atrocity, one nearly-turned human woman. Rosalyn, he remembered with a curl of distaste in the pit of his gut. They had brought her back to the compound, bloody and broken, taking what information they could before finally letting her die a very human death. He doubted she had known how lucky she was.

Ty, used to fading into shadow and listening, knew that all in the inner circle of Arsinöe's court agreed: it was only a matter of time before the violence escalated even further, and the queen herself was targeted.

Without their fierce Egyptian queen, the House of Ptolemy would fall. Maybe not right away, but there were none fit to take Arsinöe's place, unless Sekhmet appeared once more to bestow her grace on one of them. If the goddess even still existed. More likely there would be a bloody power struggle that left but a pale shadow of what had been, and that petty infighting would take care of whoever the Mulo had left behind, if any. And the Cait Sith such as himself, those who had been deemed fit to serve only by virtue of their Fae-tainted blood, would be left to the dubious mercy of the remaining dynasties that ruled the world of night.

He could no more let that happen than he could walk in the sun.

Ty pushed aside his dark thoughts for the moment and debated heading back to his hotel room for the night, maybe swinging by a local bar on the way to get a quick nip from one of the drunk and willing. Suddenly a back door swung open and a woman stepped out into the crisp night air.

At first he stayed to watch because he was merely curious. Then the moonlight caught the deep auburn of her hair, and Ty stared, transfixed, as she turned fully toward him. Utterly unaware of the eyes upon her, she tipped her head back, bathing herself in starlight, the soft smile on her lips revealing a woman who appreciated the pleasure of an autumn night well met.

He heard her sigh, saw the warm exhalation drift lazily upward in a cloud of mist. For him, caught in some strange spell, it all seemed to occur in slow motion, the mist of her breath hanging suspended for long moments above her mouth, as though she'd gifted a shimmering bit of her soul to the night. The long, pale column of her throat was bared above the collar of her coat, the tiny pulse beating at the base of it amplified a thousand times, until he could hear the singular pulse and pound that were her life, until it was everything in his universe. Her scent, a light, exotic vanilla, drifted to him on the chill breeze, and all thought of drinking from some nameless, faceless stranger vanished from his mind.

Ty wanted *her*. And though a certain amount of restriction was woven tightly into the fabric of his life, he would not deny himself this. Already he was consumed by the thought of what her blood might taste like. Would it be as sweet as she smelled? Or would it be darker than she appeared to be, ripe with berry and currant? Every human had a singular taste—this he had learned—and it spoke volumes about them, more than they would ever know.

She lingered only a moment longer, and her heart-shaped face, delicately featured with a pair of large, expressive eyes he was now determined to see close up, imprinted itself on him in a way he had never before experienced. Ty's mind was too hazed to question it now, this odd reaction to her, but he knew he would be able to ponder nothing else later.

Later. Once he had tasted her.

When she turned away, when the burnished waves of her hair spilling over the collar of her dark coat were all he could see, Ty found he could at least move again, and he did so with the ruthless efficiency of a practiced hunter. Like a predator that has latched on to the scent of its prey, his eyes never left her, even as he rose up, his feline form shifting and elongating until he stood on two feet among the straggling bushes.

He breathed deeply, drinking in that singular scent with anticipatory relish.

Then Ty turned up the collar of his coat and began the hunt.

Lily rounded the corner of the house with a sigh of relief.

Probably she should feel guilty about bailing on the annual Bonner Mansion ghost hunt. Bailing before anything interesting happened anyway—so far, all she'd seen was a bunch of overly serious amateur ghost hunters who thought every insect was a wayward spirit. Oh, and that couple who had set up camp in a closet with the door shut, she remembered with a smirk. Whatever sort of experience they were after, she was pretty sure it wasn't supernatural.

Why she'd even let Bay con her into this was a mystery; their weekly date to watch *Ghost Hunters* didn't translate into any desire on her part to *actually* go running around inside a dark, musty, supposedly haunted house. Thank God the hottie from the Bonner County Paranormal Society had shown up when he had. Lily wasn't sure which had made her best friend's eyes light up more: the tight jeans or the thermal-imaging camera. Either way, she wasn't even positive the group had heard her when she'd claimed a brewing headache as an excuse to leave them there, but Bay's grin told her she'd be thanked for going at some point in the near future.

She lifted her wrist to glance at her watch, squinting at it in the darkness, and noted that it was about quarter to twelve.

"So much for another Friday night," she muttered. Still, it didn't have to be a total waste. Maybe she'd get crazy, stay up late with some popcorn and a Gerard Butler movie.

Wild times at Lily Quinn's house. But better, always better, than running the risk of sleep. She didn't need a silly ghost tour to scare her. Nothing could be scarier than the things she saw when she closed her eyes.

Lily crunched through dead leaves, then stopped, frowning at the unfamiliar view of bare trees and, a little farther off, the wrought-iron fence that bordered the property's grounds. Despite the reasonably close proximity to the town square, the Bonner Mansion sat back a ways from the road, and the historical society had managed to hang on to a portion of the original property, so there were still grounds to the place. But there was, as a nod to modernity, a parking lot.

And it was, Lily realized, on the *other* side of the house. She tipped her head back, closed her eyes, and groaned.

Her impeccable sense of misdirection had struck again.

After a moment spent silently cursing, Lily shoved her hands deeper into her pockets and set off on what she hoped was the correct course this time. Directional impairment was one of her defining features, right along with her inexplicable aversion to suitable men. If she could only find a well-educated, Shakespeare-quoting bad boy who still had a thing for sexy tattoos and maybe a mild leather fetish, she might at least have a shot at avoiding her probable future as a crazy old cat lady.

A long shot, maybe. But a shot.

At least it was a beautiful night, Lily thought, inhaling deeply. The smell of an October night was one of her favorites, especially in this part of New England. It was rife with the earthy, rich smell of decaying leaves, of wood smoke from someone's chimney, and shot through with a cleansing bite of cold.

Lily looked around as she walked, taking her time. In the faint glow from the streetlights along the road, this place really did have a haunted look about it, but not scary. More like someplace where you'd find a dark romance, full of shadows and sensual mystery.

She huffed out a breath, amused at herself. She taught English lit because she had always liked the fantasy of what could be, instead of the often unpleasant reality of how things were. Speaking of which, it looked like a little *Phantom of the Opera* might be in order for her Friday night movie. Even if the ending absolutely refused to go the way she wanted, she thought with a faint smile, no matter how many times she'd willed Christine to heal the dark and wounded Phantom instead of wasting her time on boring old Raoul.

It would have made for one hell of a love scene—

There was a sudden, strange tingling sensation at the back of her neck. Lily felt the hairs there rising as a rush of adrenaline chilled her blood. Someone was behind her. She knew it without seeing, felt eyes on her that hadn't been there a moment before.

But when she whirled around, stumbling a little in her haste to confront whoever was behind her, she saw nothing. Only the empty expanse of lawn, dotted with the skeletal shapes of slumbering trees, an empty bench, and beside her, the dark shape of the house. Nothing.

Nowhere even to hide.

Lily felt her heart kick into a quicker rhythm, and her breath became shallower as her eyes darted around, looking for a shape, a shadow, anything that would explain her sudden, overwhelming certainty that she wasn't alone.

Stupid, she told herself. *You're walking through a horror movie setup, and it's just got your imagination running, is all*.

Lily knew that was more than likely it, but she still wanted to reach her car and get out of here. Soothed a little by the thought that there were a whole bunch of people inside the house who would hear her scream if anything did happen, she turned to continue making her way out front, casting a lingering look over one shoulder.

Though the moon rode high in the night sky, nearly full, and the air was still rich with the very scents she'd just been enjoying, all her pleasure had vanished in favor of the insistent instinct that had kept humans walking the Earth for as long as they had: flight.

"Hey, are you all right?"

She gave a small scream before she could stop herself, jumping at the sudden appearance of another person in front of her when there'd been no sign of another soul only seconds before.

He raised his hands in front of him, eyebrows lifting in an expression that plainly said he was as startled as she was. "Whoa, hey, don't do that! I'm not a ghost or anything. You can start breathing again." One eyebrow arched higher, plaintive. "Please?"

It was the faintly amused concern he put into that last word that finally got her to draw in a single, shuddering breath. But she still shot a quick look around, gauging distance in case she had to run.

"Look, I'm sorry," the man said, drawing Lily's full attention back to him. "I needed to get out of there for a few. Too many people, not enough ghosts, you know?"

"I . . . yeah," Lily said, still trying to figure out how she should deal with this. Had he been inside too? She wasn't sure. . . . There'd been a cluster of people, and not everyone had shown up at the same time. It was certainly possible. But when she looked more closely at him, she was sure she would have remembered if they'd crossed paths.

"Let's start over," he said.

This time she picked up on the lilting Scottish accent in a voice that was soft and deep but with a slightly rough edge.

He extended a hand to her. "I'm Tynan. MacGillivray."

Yeah, it didn't get any more Scottish than that. Lily hesitated for a split second, but her deeply ingrained sense of politeness refused to let her keep her hand in her pocket. Tentatively, she slid her hand into his and watched as his long, slim fingers closed around it.

"I'm Lily. Lily Quinn," she said, surprised by the sensation of cool, silken skin against her own. But at the point of contact, warmth quickly bloomed, matching the heat that began to course through her system as she finally noticed that Tynan MacGillivray was incredibly good-looking.

Not handsome, she thought. That was the wrong word for what he was, though some people might have used it anyway. He was more ... compelling. She let herself take in the sharp-featured, angular face with a long blade of a nose and dark, slashing brows. His mouth held the only hint of softness, with an invitingly full lower lip that caught her attention far more than it should have, under the circumstances. His skin was so fair as to make him pale, though for some reason it only enhanced his strange appeal, and was set off further by the slightly shaggy, overlong crop of deep brown hair that he'd pushed away from his face.

It was his eyes, though, that Lily couldn't seem to avoid. Light gray, with a silvery cast from the moonlight, they watched her steadily, unblinking. She wanted to believe he meant her no harm. But there was an intensity in the way he looked at her that kept her off balance. *I should get moving, get out of here*, Lily thought, feeling like a deer that has picked up the scent of a predator.

But she was caught by those eyes, unable to look away. She shuddered in a soft breath as he stepped in closer. never letting go of her hand.

No, she thought, her eyes locked with his, her legs refusing to move. But then, right on the heels of that: *Yes*.

"Lily," he said, his voice little more than a sensual growl. "Now, that's a pretty name. Fitting."

No one had ever said her name quite like that before, savoring it, as though they were tasting it. Desire, unexpected, unwanted, but undeniable all the same, unfurled deep in her belly. She tried to think of something to say, something that would break this odd spell she was falling under, but nothing sprang to mind. There was only this dark stranger. Everything else seemed to fade away, unimportant.

"You're shivering," he remarked. "You shouldn't be out here in the cold all alone."

"No, I...I guess not," she murmured, mildly surprised that though she was shivering, she hadn't even noticed. She certainly wasn't cold anymore. And for some reason it was difficult to hang on to her thoughts long enough to form a coherent sentence. "I was...just going to my car."

His eyes, she thought, caught up in a hazy rush of desire that flooded her from head to toe, banishing any awareness of the temperature of the air. His eyes *were* silver, she realized as they grew closer. Silver, and glowing like the moon. Strange, beautiful eyes.

"Why don't you let me walk you?" he asked.

The words barely penetrated her consciousness. After struggling to make sense of them, she found herself nodding. Car. Walk. Yes. Probably a good thing. "Yeah. That would be great."

Tynan smiled, a lazy, sensual lift of his lips. It seemed the most natural thing in the world that, despite what each of them had said, neither of them made a move to go. Instead, he trailed his free hand down her cheek, cool marble against her warm flesh, and rubbed his thumb slowly across her lower lip.

Lily's lips parted in answer, and her eyes slipped shut as a soft sigh escaped her. She'd never felt such pleasure from such a light touch, but all she could think of, all she wanted, was for it to continue.

"Lily," he purred again. "How lovely you are."

"Mmm," was all she could manage in response. She turned into his touch as his skilled fingers slid into her hair, as he let go of her hand to slide his around the curve of her waist as he stepped into her. It was like drifting in some dark dream, and Lily embraced it willingly, sliding her hands up his chest and then around to his back, urging him even closer.

She wasn't sure what she was asking for—but at Tynan's touch, something stirred inside of her, some long-dormant need that arched and stretched after a long sleep, then flooded her with aching demand. She turned her face up to his, a wordless invitation. His warm breath fanned her face, and even through the strange haze that seemed to have enveloped her, she thrilled a little at the ragged sound of his breathing, at the erratic beat of his heart against her chest.

"Lily," he said again, and this time it was almost reverent.

He bent his head to hers, and Lily's lips parted in anticipation. She had never wanted a man's kiss so desperately; her entire being seemed to vibrate with desire. Her breath stilled as she waited for the press of his lips against her own. But instead of taking what she offered, Tynan's mouth only grazed her cheek, and his long fingers deftly cupped her chin to turn her head to the side.

Lily made a noise then, a soft, frustrated moan that drew a chuckle from her tormentor.

"Patience, sweetheart," he admonished her, his gruff brogue more pronounced now. "Too fast and you'll spoil it."

Tynan trailed soft kisses along her jawline, the relative chill of his lips against her warm and sensitive flesh a shocking pleasure. Lily writhed in his arms, wanting to be closer, wanting some nameless *more* that she couldn't identify. But Tynan seemed to be relentlessly controlled, the uneven intake of his breath the only clue that he might be as close to undone as she. Lily heard his voice then, seeming to echo right inside her head.

Let me taste you.

Powerless to do anything but obey, Lily let her head fall back in submission, baring her throat to him, willing him to touch more, take more. In some dim recess of her mind, it occurred to her that this entire situation was madness at best, suicidal at worst. But the harder she tried to hang on to any rational thoughts, the quicker they seemed to evaporate. And wasn't it so much more pleasurable to just give up, give in? As though Tynan wanted to illustrate just that point, he nipped at her ear, flicking his tongue over the sensitive lobe.

"Please," Lily moaned, moving restlessly against him, not even sure what she was asking for. Then he was drawing her hair away from her neck, tugging her head to the side to gain better access. He forced the collar of her shirt down, baring her collarbone to the cold night air. Lily allowed it all, her only desire to feel his lips on her skin again, to give him whatever he wanted. All the world had vanished except for Tynan. She could feel his hands shaking as his handling of her roughened, and she sensed his need was even greater than her own.

Suddenly he stopped, going stock-still as he expelled a single shaking breath. Lost in the deepening fog of her sexual haze, Lily gripped the thick wool of Tynan's coat harder and made a soft sound of distress. Why had he stopped? She needed . . . she *needed* . . .

All she heard was a softly muttered curse in an unfamiliar tongue.

Then, a ripple of air, a breath of chill wind. Lily slowly opened her eyes, only barely beginning to register where she was and what she had been doing. Her hands were fisted in nothing but empty air. She blinked rapidly, taking a stumbling step backward, feeling a crushing, if nonsensical, sense of loss. She turned in a circle, knowing that he had to still be here. He couldn't have left. It was impossible for a man to vanish into thin air.

But whoever—or whatever—Tynan MacGillivray was, Lily was soon forced to acknowledge the truth.

He was gone.

chapter TWO

Ty crouched silently on a tree branch, his silver eyes unblinking as he watched Lily Quinn slowly make her way to her car. She still seemed dazed, though by the time she reached the parking lot, the wobble had gone from her step and she'd quickened her pace, throwing a final, fearful glance over her shoulder before getting in and driving off.

He couldn't have seen what he thought he'd seen, Ty knew. It had to have been a trick of the light and his bloodlust-addled brain. Likely it was a birthmark, or even a tattoo, a wicked little surprise hidden beneath the classy wrappings. No mortal could wear a vampire mark, and Lily was most certainly mortal. But just as certain was that she was also . . . more.

Gods, had he ever reacted so strongly to the scent of a woman's blood?

The memory of her pressed against him, the feel of her skin beneath his hands, threatened to send him running after her to finish what they'd started. Instead, Ty clung to what control he had left, sinking his claws into the wood beneath him, the fur along his back rising in response to the ancient struggle inside of him. He needed to feed, and soon—even though it meant he would have to force himself to drink from yet another nameless, faceless victim.

Leave it to him to want a woman he would never be allowed to taste.

With a surly growl, Ty sprang from the tree. By the time he hit the ground, he was a man again, stalking off in the direction of the town square. He ought to be grateful that *something* had stopped him from sinking his teeth into Lily Quinn. If he had, he would have ruined what was likely his only chance at fulfilling his mission.

Still, it would have been nice if he'd noticed he couldn't catch even a hint of the woman's thoughts *before* he'd gotten so close that he could think of nothing but her neck. That impenetrable mind was the undeniable hallmark of a Seer. Lily's particular beauty was just a bonus, and an unfortunate one at that. To bite her would rob her of the ability he was in dire need of.

As the Americans liked to say, he needed to get his head back in the game.

Ty pulled his cell phone from his pocket and kept walking, his long legs eating up the distance with a speed that bordered on inhuman, and called the only woman he had any true allegiance to. His queen's favor had elevated him far above what any gutterblood like himself could normally expect; she had drawn him into her trusted inner circle, where his kind would never have been tolerated before—though in truth, he was only barely tolerated by the rest and had learned early on to rely on subterfuge to get what information he needed.

Still, right now, even having a vampire queen on speed dial didn't quite make up for the fact that he was alone. *Again.* And hungry in a way that he'd somehow have to assuage.

The phone rang only once before she picked up, and Arsinöe's honeyed tones could do nothing to disguise her agitation. The hairs on his neck and the backs of his arms prickled with it, warning him to tread lightly.

The woman was a force of nature. And when she was angry, she was apt to destroy everything and everyone in her path.

"Tynan. Calling to tell me of another fruitless adventure, I presume?"

Her voice was a smooth purr, and Ty could picture her reclining on her chaise, her kohl-lined eyes narrowed, her long red nails tapping on the fabric. She had always been kind to him, in her way, though he had seen plenty of her cruelty. One couldn't stay the ruler of the greatest of the vampire dynasties without it. But he had sensed a change in her lately, a strain and barely leashed fury that he attributed to the murders and her inability to stop them. Ty hoped his discovery of Lily could start to reverse that… provided she was, in fact, a Seer.

He could have been perfectly confident, were it not for that odd little decoration on her skin.

"Not this time," he replied, turning onto the sidewalk and heading for the lights of the city's old-fashioned downtown square. He slowed a little to give himself time to talk. No one else needed to hear this conversation.

"Tell me." The change in her tone was instant, sharpening with keen interest bordering on desperation. He wondered what more had happened since he'd last spoken to

Arsinöe. More death, likely. Ty found he couldn't dredge up much sympathy. He doubted he would have attempted to get close to many of the Ptolemy even if they hadn't given him a wide berth. His bloodline was known for producing cold-blooded killers, after all. The Cait Sith were gutter vamps, ruthless hunters with no leader and no conscience. This tended to give one an aura of unapproachability. Which was fine with Ty. Highbloods were a tedious lot, full of entitlement and fond of entertaining themselves by looking down on... well, on mongrels like him.

"There's a woman here," Ty said, keeping his voice low. "Her mind is closed to me. Can't hear a bloody thing, and you know I'm good at that."

"Yes, good, but can she *See*?" The angry snap in Arsinöe's voice surprised him, as he'd expected at least a modicum of praise for all these months of searching. But then, much about the queen had changed since the Mulo had come. Maybe, Ty thought darkly, some of it was permanent.

Or maybe it was always there and you just didn't want to see it.

He shoved the traitorous thought aside and focused on the situation at hand.

"I'm not sure yet," he allowed slowly, glad to be so far out of range of Arsinöe's stinging claws for once. "But she's the first I've found like her." He thought again of Lily's strange mark and nearly mentioned it. But something held him back. In his mind's eye, Lily's face appeared, innocent, open, her eyes closed and lips parted in invitation. For the briefest instant, Tynan felt an urge to protect her in a way that was borne of some deeper, unfamiliar instinct.

The kind of instinct, Ty thought as he ruthlessly snuffed it out, that could get a vampire like himself killed.

Still, he held his tongue. Another look at Lily's sexy little tattoo would doubtless reveal nothing. And if he was wrong...well, he would deal with that only if he had to.

"Tynan," said the woman on the other end of the line.

The weariness in her voice did pull at him now. He and Arsinöe had known each other a long time. There was, despite the class separation, some modicum of affection there. And the gods knew he owed her a great deal for all she had given him.

"I'm glad, of course, that you think you've found something," she continued. "But in the last week, we've lost fifty of our line, not to mention a number of priceless artifacts. The Mulo must be stopped, and I'm...*concerned*...that we are running out of time. I don't want possibilities—I need facts. Be certain before you bring her. I've no interest in another pretty toy when my people are dying. How long is this going to take you?"

"That depends," he replied. "Do you want her willing?"

"You should know by now that I don't give a damn about that," she said smoothly.

Again he felt that faint unease with the way things seemed to have changed back in the thick of Arsinöe's court. Something felt off, but he didn't know if it was her or if it was simply that he'd been out of the loop for so long now. It was one of the reasons he'd struggled with being chosen for this hunt: despite the way it had been presented, it felt like he was being eliminated.

She'd made a show of it, of course. Fawning over him, telling him how much more trustworthy he was than the others of his blood, how his skills were far better suited to finding this needle in a haystack than so many of her courtiers who had gone soft from easy living. Backhanded insults to his much-maligned bloodline that Ty was certain sounded like praise to Arsinöe's ears...but, of course, he was used to that. All Cait Sith were. All her praise notwithstanding, he had stopped being called, stopped being included. After all his efforts to prove himself over the centuries in her service, he could sense that Arsinöe had begun to push him out.

And the Ptolemy courtiers, who seemed to have grown more bitter and vicious over the years he had spent among them, gloated openly at his departure. They cheered at the purge of the gutterblood who had somehow infiltrated their rarefied little club.

He worried less about himself and more about what would become of his other blood brothers and sisters in his absence. Arsinöe had softened considerably over the years in her treatment of the Cait Sith she had conscripted, especially considering how dark things had been at the time of his own siring. But though the queen was strong, she was hardly immune to the views of the highbloods closest to her. And, gods, but he was tired of the politics.

"A week. Two, tops," Ty said after a quick canvass of his options. "I know nothing about her at this point. And setting people at ease isn't usually my strong suit. But as I doubt she just sits around having visions all day, I'll have to try and learn some people skills, I suppose."

He'd meant it as a little joke, but Arsinöe was obviously not in the mood.

"It had better be less than two weeks," she said, and Ty could hear the steel in her voice. "And if she is what you say, the woman will do as she is told. She will be well compensated, of course. Tell her she will be returned home. Tell her everything will go back to normal, will be set to rights if she does this service for me. For my *people*.

And throw in an offer of money if that isn't enough. That should do it. It always does."

"You would let her go after this?" Ty asked, surprised.

"Of course not. But that doesn't mean I won't keep her well. She may come in handy. One never knows. But it has little to do with you, Tynan," Arsinöe said, a casual dismissal that cut him to the quick. It had been many years since she had openly snubbed him for being less than her own blood.

His months away began to feel like years. What had *happened*?

But she seemed to have no intention of telling him, instead shifting gears smoothly into the role she often played with both servants and courtiers: the playful seductress. Ty could actually hear the sly smile in her voice when she asked, "Is she pretty, this new discovery of yours?"

Ty raked his fingers through his hair and looked to the heavens, a sky scattered with stars. *She knew.* Of course she did. The woman was ancient and had been born to rule, to manipulate people, to understand their motivations and use them. His three centuries on Earth, on the other hand, hadn't given him much artifice. Usually he didn't care, but he was surprised at how little he enjoyed having Arsinöe picking up on his interest. They had never been lovers, but she was a jealous creature by nature. She must be the only woman, even to her lowly pet hunter.

Easily done when no self-respecting vampiress would bed a Cait more than once.

"She's all right, I guess," he allowed, trying for noncommittal as opposed to a lie he'd eventually be caught in. No one could look at Lily Quinn and believe for an instant he'd thought her plain.

"Hmm," was all Arsinöe said. "Maybe I should send someone along to help you. So you don't get distracted."

Ty frowned, knowing full well that her teasing tone hid truth. "If you're going to send anyone, send Jaden," he said, referring to his closest blood brother, a Cait Sith only slightly younger than himself. He wasn't the most personable of vampires, either, but he was unusually trustworthy.

Arsinöe's soft laughter again stirred the hair at the back of his neck. She seemed to have other ideas.

"You *have* been gone hunting a while, haven't you?"

"Is something wrong?" he asked, gritting his teeth. He was in no mood to be played with tonight, and Arsinöe seemed to be in a dangerously changeable mood.

"You should ask Jaden if you see him," she replied lightly—*too* lightly. "But I doubt you will. He's left us."

Jaden, you fool. No matter how the Ptolemy valued their services, he and Jaden were servants. And servants did not have the option of quitting. That was the same as choosing death.

Yet another thing for Ty to worry about. Later. All that mattered right this second was that he wouldn't be getting help from any of his own blood—the only sort of help he might have tolerated.

As though she'd heard his thoughts, the queen continued. "I was thinking of sending along Nero. He'll deal with her quickly enough, one way or the other."

Ty's eyes narrowed in the darkness, and he came to a complete stop on the deserted sidewalk. A number of pieces clicked into place. *So*, he thought. *That's how it is.* Arsinöe had rarely taken lovers during his time traveling with the Ptolemy court, but each had presented some challenges. Nero, however, was more than just a challenge. Ty had long suspected the cold, calculating Ptolemy highblood wanted not just Arsinöe, but also the power she had at her disposal. And Nero had made no secret of his longing for the days when the Cait Sith were treated like slaves of the lowest order. For Arsinöe to bring him up this way could only mean Nero had finally caught her eye, which meant he had her ear as well. And whatever doubts she had already been having about Ty's presence in her circle would have been bolstered, agreed with, and amplified. For *months*.

Ty suddenly felt ill.

"Why would you send a highblood? You made it very clear you wanted a hunter for the job, and Nero isn't one to get his hands dirty," Ty ground out, barely managing to hold his tongue and lash out the way he wanted to. The queen might tolerate some insolence from him, but there were places one did not go ... and he was suddenly unsure of his limits.

"I did send a hunter," Arsinöe snapped. "And months later—countless precious lives later—I have nothing to show for it. There are tasks better suited to noble blood, Tynan. I have begun to think this is one of them."

His throat ached from all of the things he wanted to shout at her, things that would get a cat like himself killed in a heartbeat if said in the presence of a highblood—any highblood. But he had not made this world, he reminded himself. All he could do was survive in it. Which is what he would continue to do, no matter the unspeakable things it did to what was left of his pride.

"How long will you give me, Highness?" he asked hoarsely, reverting to the formality he hadn't used with her in many years. That finally seemed to touch her, for the little it was worth.

"A week, Tynan," Arsinöe said softly. Then with warmth she had thus far been lacking, "A week, and I give this to Nero. But I know you won't fail me. You never have."

He accepted what passed for an endearment, but when he ended the call and set off again toward the square, Ty was left with roiling anger and no outlet for it. He'd wanted to know what had happened in his absence, but in this case, knowing was no comfort to him. In a roaming court of bored vampire nobility who were as predictable as they were violent, one of the things you could always count on was the constant jockeying for position among the highblood hangers-on who served as Arsinöe's courtiers, advisers, and, occasionally, lovers.

Looked like Nero had finally made it to the top. And Ty couldn't begin to imagine how he might undo the damage the clever Ptolemy had no doubt already done.

Goddamn highbloods.

Tynan glared ahead as he zeroed in on a prime site for dinner, a seedy little bar called Jasper's where the occasional patron staggered out into the cold night and mediocre 80s power rock drifted from the darkened interior with each swing of the door. His hunter's mind saw all this, but the rest of his thoughts were consumed with Nero. He was well acquainted with the ambitious Ptolemy's "methods." Just as he had firsthand experience with Nero's feelings on lowbloods and what, exactly, they had been put on Earth to do.

Just get the girl and get home, he told himself. Lily Quinn would either manage among the Ptolemy or would not. It was nothing to him. What mattered was making sure that the handful of his kind who still lived under the thumb of the Ptolemy dynasty didn't end up like the rest: dead, or as good as.

As he stepped through the doors and was greeted by a blast of warmth and the scent of stale beer and cheap perfume, Ty allowed himself a moment, just a moment, to despise his own existence. He wished he had died that long-ago night. He wished his queen had never taken notice of him and left him to his fate.

But he had not, and she had. His lot was what it was.

And he had already been gone too long.

Hours later, at the time of night when the world seems to be holding its breath for the dawn, Tynan stood looking down at the woman who had already caused him so much trouble and who was, he feared, bound to cause him more before they were through.

His hunger had long since been sated by a homely little bleached blonde so drunk that she'd barely skipped a beat between the time he'd bitten her and the time he'd bundled her into a cab to go home. The blood, full of alcohol, had given him a pleasant buzz. But he found, with some dismay, that the scent rising from Lily's skin was quickly renewing the knife's edge of his eternal hunger. Feeding had done nothing to dull the odd effect she had on him.

He began to wish he had waited to come and find her here, asleep in the upstairs bedroom of the little old Victorian near the college where she taught. She had been so easy to find. He felt a moment's pity for her, for the way her life was about to be upended—however long her life lasted.

Lily shifted and gave a long, soft sigh, as though agreeing with him. She was curled on her side, knees drawn up beneath the quilted coverlet, the shape of her body making an S. Small hands were tucked beneath the delicate point of her chin, and all of the thick, shining hair he'd so admired in the moonlight seemed to pulse with a life of its own, bloodred against the white of her pillow. Long lashes twined together, and her lips, a feature he had tried with no success to get out of his head all night, parted gently in sleep.

She was beautiful, Tynan thought with an unfamiliar sinking sensation. And he needed to find a way to draw her in as quickly as possible. That he would betray her, likely hurt her, was a given. He didn't bother to rail against it much. If he didn't do what he was told, he would die, and that was one thing he'd really rather not do. He was out of the habit.

Before he could consider what he was doing, Ty reached out one long, slim finger to trail it down Lily's bare shoulder, finding her fair skin as soft as it looked. He sucked in a breath at the sensation that shimmered through his body at that small touch, curling through him, stirring him in ways that would prove very unhelpful if things continued this way. She shivered, too, as though sensing the direction of his thoughts.

He wanted her. But Lily, like so many things, was now forbidden to him.

With a frown, Ty lifted her hair away from her collarbone with a light, deft movement and bent as closely as he could without disturbing her. He didn't really want to see—it was as though a part of him knew he hadn't imagined it before.

A light green pentagram, entwined with a single snake, glittering faintly in the darkness.

Unconsciously, Ty lifted his other hand to rub at his own mark, the black Celtic knot of cats entwined with the ankh of the Ptolemy. When she had chosen him, the queen had branded him herself, allowing him but a single drop of her own blood on his tongue. She was so ancient, and so potent, that even a drop had been enough for him to manifest the ankh of the Ptolemy within his original mark, branding him forevermore as both minion and slave.

He was now the most fortunate, and most wretched, of cats.

Blood is destiny, Ty thought. The vampire creed. From the moment you were sired, your mark determined your path, the way you would exist, the circles you would move in. Your place in the realm of night, as fixed and immovable as the sun he would never see again.

There was no doubt in his mind now. Lily Quinn wore such a mark. But how and why and what it meant were all things he needed to have answered before he took her into the lion's den. He would not risk Arsinöe's wrath—not now, when he knew how much was at stake.

I will not have this woman torn to pieces because of my own mistake.

It was a foolish thought, rising unbidden and just as quickly pushed away with a faint feeling of embarrassment. Lily Quinn being ripped apart by a furious queen was the least of his concerns. And the gods knew he'd never try to protect humans again. Hadn't turned out so well the last time, that was sure.

After a moment, Ty drew Lily's hair back over the mark, casting a quick glance out the window behind him. He sensed nothing, but he would take no chances, not until he knew what this meant. He knew the marks of the dynasties, and of the lowbloods that served them, and all of the variations that marked the wretched nightcrawlers who lurked at the edges of society, who hunted as they were hunted.

This was nothing like those.

"What have you gotten me into, Lily Quinn?" he asked softly, rising again. But her sleeping face gave no answers. As the first hints of lethargy began to steal through him, heralding daylight, he left her, becoming a cat as he wound around the corner of her door and stole on silent feet down the hallway. The woman had a basement full of hiding places, and he had no intention of going far.

Even in sleep, he would guard her.

Because he had a bad feeling that Lily, before all was said and done, was going to need all the protection he could give.

In dreams, Lily wandered in a ruined temple that was still blackened and charred from the fire she had seen so many times. She looked for someone, but she knew not who; she knew only that they were lost to her forever. The fire, and the people, were gone.

In sorrow and confusion, Lily looked in vain for what would never return. A man's voice whispered on the breeze. Her name. She turned, feeling the simple word like a caress.

And the mark on her skin began to burn.

chapter **THREE**

B<small>Y THE TIME</small> her last class let out on Monday, Lily had to accept the truth: She was obsessing. And not just her usual, run-of-the-mill sort of obsessing either. She was a master at worrying over the most minuscule issues, but having an impromptu make-out session with a guy who'd managed to vanish into thin air didn't feel all that minuscule.

"Okay, that's it for today, everyone. Drop your papers on the desk on your way out, and start reading Spenser's *The Faerie Queene.* I hear groaning. There is no groaning in Intro to English Lit."

Not unless I'm the one doing it anyway, she thought, eyeing the growing pile of essays as the students filed past. Lily grabbed her cup of coffee off the podium she'd been lecturing at for the past hour and downed the last of it. Even with the aid of her superinsulated travel mug, it had gone pretty much stone cold, but she was hoping that eventually, when her caffeine levels hit critical mass, she could shake this weird, nagging feeling she was experiencing.

Tynan MacGillivray was probably a serial killer. A really, really hot serial killer. With beautiful silver eyes, and a mouth that felt like—

"My God, you look like death warmed over. Please tell me you at least had an attractive reason for losing so much sleep."

Lily jerked her head up, momentarily startled. While her imagination had gone wandering, the lecture hall had completely emptied.

And she hadn't even noticed.

This has got to stop, she told herself, but managed a smile for the woman making her way down the aisle toward her. Bailey Harper looked a lot like a pixie who had recently tangled with a werewolf, which meant she'd come straight over from work. Bay's wavy blond hair was desperately trying to escape the ponytail she'd wrestled it into, and the ancient jeans and T-shirt she wore were absolutely covered in a rainbow of dog hair. Lily's eyes dropped to Bay's sneakers, which looked as though they'd been recently chewed. Probably with her feet still in them, if Lily knew anything about Bay's clientele.

"Does every dog you bathe maul you?" Lily asked, frowning as she realized that there were indeed fresh chew marks on Bay's Nikes.

Bay narrowed her eyes as she came to a stop beside her. "Pretty much. And since you're avoiding my question, I guess I can assume there isn't an answer I'm going to like. Damn it, Lily, would you please get your ass to a sleep clinic before you just drop dead of exhaustion?"

Lily sighed and huffed an errant lock of hair out of her face. She had learned early on in their friendship that it was an exercise in futility to argue with Bay. The woman was very short, deceptively cute, and a human steamroller when she thought she was right about something, which was almost always. The only thing that kept Lily from wanting to clock her sometimes was that Bay's heart was permanently affixed in the right place.

"I'm fine, Bay. It's been a while since I hooked up with Prince Insomnia, so I guess he was due for a visit. He hasn't changed—all tease, no action," Lily said, deciding to go for humor in her latest attempt at defusing this ongoing argument.

"Ha." Her friend's look was bland at best. "Lily, I'm aware that I'm no fashionista, but those dark circles under your eyes aren't doing it for you. Or me, for that matter. I worry. You've seemed a little out of it since Friday night. Are you sure you were okay when you left the ghost hunt? Did something freak you out and you're just not telling me?"

Lily covered her discomfort with an amused snort. Bay was a lot closer to the truth than she liked, and she wasn't interested in talking about it yet, if ever.

"You mean besides having to listen to that couple getting it on in the closet? No. I still think they say that place is haunted just as a gimmick to add local color or something. Speaking of local color, how's the cute techno-geek?"

Bay pursed her lips and narrowed her eyes. "Another detour. We are not done talking about this, Lily Quinn. But since I have you to thank for it, cute techno-geek—otherwise known as Alex—is good. At least, I think he is. We couldn't manage to hook up this weekend, but I'm heading to dinner with him in"—Bay glanced at her watch, and her eyes widened in horror—"Jesus, an hour." She looked down at her dog-hair-covered clothes, then back up at Lily with a mischievous twinkle in her eye. "First date is way too soon for him to discover the real me, don't you think?"

"The real you is fabulous. I just hope he isn't allergic to animal hair," Lily replied. She leaned against the heavy metal desk that sat off to the side of the podium. Exhaustion, hovering like a phantom over her all weekend, seemed to be coming in for a landing. She'd been honest with Bay about one thing: It had been quite a while since her so-called insomnia had acted up. What Bay didn't know, and what Lily had no intention of sharing, was that her bouts of sleeplessness were entirely self-inflicted and born out of self-defense. Even this bone-deep weariness was better than falling into the nightmare about the woman in the temple, over and over and over…the nightmare she had spoken about only once and never would again.

In any case, the end result was the same. She'd managed less than five hours of sleep the entire weekend, and that was usually about the point at which her body and brain came to a consensus that it was finally time to hit the sack. But Bay, true to form, didn't seem inclined to just let this go.

Her friend's brows drew together, creating a stubborn little furrow between them that Lily was all too familiar with.

"Are you sure you're all right, Lily? I'm serious. You're way too pale."

Lily smiled with genuine affection. "You worry too much, Bay."

"Someone has to. I'll never understand how you managed so long without—" She stopped, snapping her mouth shut before the words came out.

But Lily knew exactly what they would have been. *Without a family. Without anyone who cared enough to take care of you.* Even unspoken, they stung. She had wanted a lot of things in her life that she hadn't gotten, but pity had never been one of them.

"I can take care of myself. I'd think that would be more than apparent by now," Lily said, her voice clipped. She didn't want to fight with Bay, didn't want to drive her off with a bunch of defensive BS either. But she wasn't in the mood to have a discussion about her family or lack thereof. Not now. Preferably not ever. She looked away, beginning to gather up her things with stiff little movements.

Bay's hand on her shoulder, the touch gentle and apologetic, made her pause. Still, she kept her gaze averted. She didn't want her friend to see the unshed tears that suddenly filled her eyes. *God, I must be exhausted*, Lily thought. It wasn't like her to let a simple mention of her crappy parental situation get to her.

But then, it was always when she was most tired that she had also felt the most alone.

"I'm sorry, Lily. I know you can take care of yourself. But it doesn't make me a bad person for wishing you hadn't had to for so long, does it?"

Lily sighed, her shoulders sagging. "No. I just hate being thought of as the poor little orphan no one wanted. It's pathetic."

"No. What's pathetic is adopting a kid and then dropping her the second Plastic Bimbo's baby factory starts working. What's pathetic is caring more about your image than your child."

Lily heard the icy fury in Bay's voice, and loved her for it. But it was time to end this conversation. She didn't want to expend any more energy thinking about the family that had cast her out—or the reason why they did it.

She blinked away the aggravating moisture in her eyes, straightened, and turned to look at her friend. "They don't matter, Bay. They haven't for a long time. But that doesn't mean I don't appreciate your burning need to kick their asses on my behalf. I'm just really tired, which means that Prince Insomnia has finally left the building. I'll be fine with some sleep."

Bay let her hand drop and stepped back, but that stubborn furrow in her brow remained. "You're sure?" Her big blue eyes were soft with concern. "We're good?"

"We're good. Promise. You go have fun, okay? Call me tomorrow with the gory details."

Bay lifted her eyebrows. "How gory? Like, sexy-time gory?"

Lily wrinkled her nose. "No, like if he lives with his mom and collects action figures gory."

They laughed together.

"You got it," Bay said, then threw her arms around Lily in one of the impromptu hugs it had taken her a while to get used to but were as natural to Bay as breathing. She envied her friend that, her comfort with physical affection. It had been in such short supply for most of Lily's life that it still startled her more than anything.

Except, of course, when given by a man who seemed to have been made entirely from moonlight and shadow.

"Be careful on your way home, then. I'd offer to drive you, but I know how far that would get me."

"You're finally learning." Lily gave Bay a quick squeeze and then drew back, frustrated that Tynan had reappeared in her thoughts so quickly. All she needed was sleep, she decided. Lots and lots of sleep. She could take care of herself perfectly well, just as she'd told Bay. And there was nothing *wrong* with her.

"I'll bring burgers by the shop tomorrow so you can tell me all," Lily said, forcing a cheerful note into her voice.

"Sounds good," Bay said with a nod. "I'll probably need the moral support. Moses comes in tomorrow."

Lily shuddered in sympathy. Bay owned a successful dog-grooming business, and a lot of that success had come because she loved pretty much anything with fur, even if it was ornery. She even loved Moses, the excitable Saint Bernard that, though friendly, seemed to have some kind of canine ADD. And he was a serious drooler.

"Burgers from Frank's it is, then," Lily said. "I'm sure we'll be able to find some tiny spot to eat that isn't covered with slime."

"Your lips to God's ears," Bay said. "And speaking of covered in slime, I guess I'll go get beautiful for the cute techno-geek. Wish me luck!"

Lily did, and watched Bay bounce back up the aisle and out the door. As the door clicked shut, Lily's smile faded. She turned to slowly finish gathering her things, feeling her fatigue weighing on her as though sandbags had been tied to all of her limbs. She wasn't even going to stop by her office. She was just going to get in her car, drive home with the window open so she was sure to stay alert, and then collapse into bed.

After that, well, she could only hope that her sleep was full of pleasant dreams, or at least unmemorable ones. Or even just dark oblivion. All of those options were far better than watching the woman with the red hair be slaughtered again, her blood turning her green silk dress black while her baby screamed somewhere in the darkness beyond and all the world went up in flames.

Better than waking up with her strange tattoo burning with white-hot pain.

It tingled even as she thought it, and Lily shuddered, pushing the visions from her mind and focusing on the tasks at hand. She slid the papers into her messenger bag, along with the notes she'd used for the day's lecture, then shrugged into the soft leather jacket that had been one of her splurges for the fall. The bag slung over one shoulder, her travel mug collected, she was off. A couple of her students waved at her as she exited Digby Hall and headed down the path that led to one of the smaller parking lots tucked behind the lecture halls.

She breathed in the crisp autumn air, surprised at how dark it was getting this early in the day. The sun was gone, and what light was left had turned the sky a deep bloodred that was rapidly fading in the west. Her steps were quick, the sound of her low boot heels clicking against the pavement in the quiet being punctuated only occasionally by the sounds of distant chatter. Lily watched a student hop into her car and drive off, the only other person in sight. Unease unfurled, quickly and unexpectedly, in her stomach. What was she trying to do, become a poster girl for how to get bad things to happen to you?

"I'm not the stupid girl who always dies first in horror movies," she told herself. "My boobs aren't big enough."

The thought made her smile a little, but Lily still sped up as she caught sight of her car, now surrounded by empty parking spaces. She was just pulling her keys from her pocket when she felt the hair on the back of her neck begin to rise. Her steps quickened. Instinctively, she knew she was no longer alone—and she was being very carefully watched. Every movement. Every rapid beat of her heart.

Lily swallowed hard, drew in a shallow breath. Without even looking, she knew who it was. Her encounter with Tynan MacGillivray might have sent her into a tailspin, might have left her in a fog that hadn't completely lifted, but she would never forget how his very presence had made her feel, as though she were nothing but a tiny, insignificant planet being pulled inexorably into the orbit of a powerful, and potentially deadly, star.

Over the last couple of days, she'd almost managed to convince herself that she was making too much of the strangeness of their meeting. But now, confronted again with the way every cell in her body tingled at his nearness, her normally iron will already softening and threatening to desert her, she knew her initial instincts had been right.

There was something very wrong about him. Something dangerous. And yet she found herself turning to where she knew he was, wanting desperately to see his face again.

He stood at the edge of the deserted parking lot, just outside the bright glow of the lights that illuminated the few cars, looking as though he'd been conjured out of her darkest longings and made flesh. There was little shadow to be had anywhere near the lights' fluorescent glow, and yet it seemed he'd managed to find some to stand in. Or, Lily thought as she drank him in, maybe men like Tynan simply created their own shadow. That was crazy—but no crazier than the rest of this.

"Lily. You and I need to talk."

His voice was just as she remembered, deep and slightly ragged. And at its sound, it took every ounce of her willpower to stay still. Every word he said seemed to translate to the same thing when it hit her ears: *come to me*. But this time, there was a difference. She'd had time to think about what he might be, what he might do to her before vanishing again into thin air. Things that would be worse than any nightmare.

Mentally, she dug in her heels, envisioning her feet encased in cement right where she stood. Whatever he was trying to get her to do, it wasn't going to happen, no matter how good he looked just standing there in his own little pool of darkness like some modern-day version of Dracula. She felt light-headed, almost a little drunk, and Lily dug in harder, pushed back.

A quick flash of emotion crossed Tynan's face as she concentrated, forcing the fog in her mind to lift a little. She saw both anger and bewilderment clear as day in the split second he let them show before schooling his expression into inscrutability.

Her blood turned to ice, but her fear, unwelcome though it was, anchored her that much more firmly in reality.

"Look," he said slowly, holding her gaze with his own. "I'm sorry for the other night. I wasn't trying to scare you, and I shouldn't have run off so quickly. But I didn't realize..." He trailed off, seemingly at a loss as to how to continue.

Lily just watched him silently, while in her mind she began gauging how quickly she could get to her car, open the door, and lock herself in.

He seemed to know.

Tynan sighed, an irritated little hiss of air through his nose. "You're not really hearing me at all, are you? It's always fight or flight with your kind, never any room in between." He closed his eyes for a moment, obviously grasping for whatever patience he had.

"I'm not a bloody negotiator," he muttered to himself.

Well, you don't look like one either, she thought, watching him warily as she began to edge toward her car, which was tantalizingly close, though not quite close enough. Without his strange eyes locked on her own, she felt freer to move again, more in control of herself. Right at that moment, all she wanted was to go home and forget Tynan MacGillivray ever existed. Because even now, when she knew he had *stalker* written all over him, she couldn't help but stare at him, appreciating the jagged, masculine beauty of him.

Couldn't help but want him.

It terrified her that she could feel this kind of desire for someone who was probably going to kill her in very short order. But she couldn't seem to turn it off any more than she had been able to banish the images of him from her mind since the night they'd met. Which meant only one thing for certain: she had to get out of here as quickly as she could and call the cops.

His eyes opened again to refocus on her with laser-like intensity. They were as silver as she remembered, and some trick of the light made them seem to glow faintly as he watched her, unblinking. As soon as his gaze touched her again, she felt her limbs go liquid, and a queer sense of calm tried to smother all of her misgivings and inhibitions.

"No," Lily said softly, the sound of her own voice in the thick, heavy atmosphere surprising her. But she could immediately tell that Tynan didn't like the simple refusal, so she shook her head and said it again. "No."

His eyes narrowed, and in that instant Lily saw clearly that beneath the dark, attractive veneer was something predatory. She took another step backward, testing her luck. He didn't move a muscle, but when he spoke, he didn't sound happy.

"If you haven't figured it out by now, woman, I'm not going to attack you. I could have ripped out your pretty throat a hundred times over by now if I'd been inclined that way. But you *are* going to hear me out, one way or another. There are some questions I need answered."

"We have nothing to talk about," Lily said. Another step. The night had gone still and silent around them, as though they were the only two people on Earth. Had he really just said he could rip her throat out? Who *said* things like that? And with every step away from him, from that strange pull he exerted, Lily felt reality returning, along with emotion undulled by Tynan's influence. Fear crept in, intensified. And began to pulse in time with her heart, which sped to a trot, then a full gallop.

It was then that she saw another emotion on his face, so raw and primal that it was all she could do not to turn and run.

Hunger.

"Don't," he said softly, his voice little more than a growl. "I don't blame you for your fear, *mo bhilis*. But you'll have to learn to hide it if you want to survive. Blood that runs so hot and fast is a temptation many won't even try to resist."

She stared at him, horrified, and this time Tynan couldn't hold her gaze. He looked away, a pained expression tightening his features.

I want to go home, she thought, her breaths shallow,

panic beginning to rush through her system like a drug. *I just want to go home.*

"I need your help," he said. "I don't have any more say in this than you do."

"I don't have any help to give." Her voice sounded thin, breathless, and she despised the weakness in it.

Tynan's eyes sought hers again, catching them, holding her captive.

"Oh, I think you do. In fact, I'm now sure of it."

"Well, you're wrong. And if you don't get the hell out of here in about two seconds, I'm hitting the panic button. They've got good campus security. And antistalking laws with actual teeth, if you think you're going to keep following me around."

For some bizarre reason, he seemed to think that was funny, which only confirmed to Lily that not only was this guy dangerous, but he was also crazy. His grin flashed in the darkness, as quick and beautiful as lightning in a summer sky. He was a terrible waste, Lily thought, hating herself for the hot twist of lust that coiled deep in her belly at that gorgeous, fleeting grin. Then it was gone, leaving no indication that he was anything but deadly serious.

"You can make this easy or hard, Lily. But the end result will be the same. Your choice."

"Then I'm choosing not to have this conversation," Lily replied, thumbing the panic button on her keychain. She knew she ought to just hit it and send him running, but something stopped her. Despite everything, despite her heart pumping like she had just run a marathon, some small, twisted part of her wasn't quite ready to let Tynan vanish again. But she had to make this stop, she knew. The stress, the return of her insomnia, and then the nightmare...

Somehow she knew it had all started again because of his appearance in her life. Whatever he wanted to say to her, whatever help he wanted, Lily needed to walk away from it now, on her own terms. Because all of her instincts were telling her that to stand here any longer was to invite madness.

She'd spent too long building walls against such things to let it in now.

"I'm leaving now, Tynan. If that really is your name," Lily said. "If you try anything, I'll set off the alarm. If you try to contact me again, I'll call the cops. Find somebody else to fixate on. I can't help you."

His dark brows drew together as she backed toward her car, not stopping now. Her heart still thundered in her ears, but she tried to keep her breathing steady, tried not to stumble.

"Lily," he began, his voice full of warning, and she knew she was going to have to push that button after all. But just as she felt the comforting bulk of her car against her back and began to grasp frantically for the door handle, Tynan's head snapped to the side, almost as though he'd heard someone calling his name. The movement was so abrupt, so unexpected, that even Lily paused for a moment to see what he had heard. Whatever it was, he didn't like it.

"Bloody hell."

When he looked at her again, the change in him was stunning. Lily felt a scream welling in her throat, trapped only because the look on his face had stolen her breath completely away. His eyes were as bright as the moon, filled with unholy light. His lips were peeled back in a feral snarl over teeth that glinted long and sharp. He looked like a—

"Go home. Now," he said, his posture tense, waiting, as though bracing for an attack—or preparing to launch one. "Lock the doors and windows. Let no one in. I'll meet you there."

She stared, astounded at the instructions. What kind of fool did he think she was?

"You actually think I'm going to—"

"I think you'll do as I say if you want to survive, Lily Quinn. There are far worse things stalking the night than me, and it seems I'm not the only one who's found you. If you want to live, do as I say. Go home. Now. And don't even think about running to anyone else, unless you want to be responsible for losing them."

Her legs trembled beneath her, even as her fingers wrapped around the door handle. She couldn't contain her sob of relief as she managed to pull it partway open. She turned, nearly falling to the pavement in her haste to get in. She couldn't think straight, couldn't think at all, really. There was only Tynan's voice, his terrible words, ringing in her ears. And coupled with everything she'd seen, everything she'd felt, they rang horrifically true.

The night had thickened around her to the point where any movement felt as though she were pushing through water. Even the lights, normally so bright, seemed to have gone dull and dim. As she threw herself into the car, shaking so badly she could barely disentangle herself from her bag enough to get the door shut, a low, menacing noise was vibrating through the darkness.

Growling.

She finally got the door shut. Lily slammed the key into the ignition and turned it, hearing her own shaking moan as the engine started only distantly, as though someone else were running her body and she was only an observer. She threw the car into drive, gripping the wheel so hard her hands ached. And still she couldn't stop herself from looking one last time at the man—the creature—who had just laid out a choice between letting him into her life or dying at the hands of who knew what. Probably something like him.

He had hunched his back, reminding her of a cat giving its last warning before attacking. His head was turned as he looked somewhere off to the side of her, out toward the athletic fields. And he was so still he might have been made of stone. But he must have sensed her gaze on him, because, although his eyes never left whatever he was tracking, he spoke, and the word he snarled was so loud he might have been in the car with her.

"Go!"

Lily slammed her foot down on the gas and tore out of the parking lot, tires squealing. This time, she didn't look back. Whatever lay ahead was bad enough.

chapter **FOUR**

T HE NIGHT AIR stank of death. And still, the coward did not show himself.

Ty didn't even turn to watch Lily leave; the squeal of her car's tires on the pavement was enough to give him some small amount of relief. But the rest of what churned within him was raw fury, all the more potent because it wasn't just a meal that some other vamp had decided to encroach upon. It was his mission, his *future*. And whoever had decided to try poaching was about to get a very nasty lesson in how to conduct oneself around a Cait Sith.

The animal within Ty stirred uneasily, reacting the same way any beast does to an approaching storm. Cold whispered over the ground, the temperature dropping twenty degrees in a matter of seconds. Even Ty's breath, though not as warm as a mortal's, escaped his mouth in a small cloud of vapor.

"Come on, you bastard," Ty growled, staring unblinkingly at the darkened sports fields where he knew the interloper was hiding. His cat's eyes picked up nothing, no hint of movement. But intuition, honed over long, hard years of experience, had never failed him.

Nor would it now, Ty thought, deadly anticipation beginning to course through his veins as he watched one particular patch of shadow divide itself in two, half of it pulling away into a shape that was unmistakably human. Even from this distance, Ty could see the red eyes glinting at him. Bright, murderous red. The sign of a vampire so hungry it was near starvation.

Ty fought the urge to recoil. There had been a time when such hunger was common to see. He had felt the knife's edge of it many a time when he was younger and newly sired, hiding in shadow, living in fear of being discovered and brutally destroyed. The memories were nothing he cared to revisit.

"Fight me, then," Ty snarled, his incisors elongating farther, his fingers hooking into claws. His stance was rigid, but his muscles were loose and limber, ready to spring. In truth, he savored the thought of making a kill. It was the only way he could think of to release the tension that had been building in him since he'd first seen Lily standing in the moonlight.

The red eyes watched him, glowing balefully, and the shadow tipped its head slightly to one side, considering him. Finally, a voice escaped it that sounded as though it had been dragged through gravel. The words it spoke were clear as day, delivered in a cockney accent that brought back memories of London's dirty streets long ago.

"It's not you I want, kitty cat. Don't fancy getting a hairball. The pretty one, though . . . she's quite the prize."

Ty's lip curled. "She's off-limits."

There was a harsh chuckle. "Says who? This ain't your territory. Your lot don't *have* territory. Gutterborn, bunch o' filthy strays. I've known many a good lowblood, but someone shoulda drowned *your* line at the first."

Ty let the words slide off his back like water. It was nothing he hadn't heard before. He wanted to get this done, to get the kill.

"This place is no one's territory, coward. And the woman is mine."

"The woman is worm's meat, kitty. And you will be, too, when I'm done with you." The breathing grew audibly harsh, and the man's voice changed then, sending a chill down Ty's spine that surprised him. "I'm just...so... *hungry....*" he wailed, his voice turning high-pitched and piteous, childlike, making Ty remember similar wails in darkened alleyways, the stench of flesh and garbage.

Enough, Ty thought. The past was best left in the darkness.

Ty crouched lower, sensing the impending attack before the other vampire moved a muscle. Then the gleaming red eyes were rushing toward him, and as the old blood-lust crashed over him, Ty opened his arms to receive his attacker.

The blow lifted him off his feet, surprising him with its strength and ferocity. Then the two of them were tangled together as they slammed to the pavement, becoming a rolling, snapping, hissing whirl of movement and sound. Ty fought the urge to gag as the other vampire's fetid breath mixed with the stench of rotting flesh, scents that were utterly overwhelming to his heightened senses. His eyes began to water, and the instant his vision blurred, jaws snapped together less than an inch from his nose.

It was enough to give him the focus he needed to finish it.

Ty threw all of his strength into one final roll, pinning his attacker beneath him in a fluid, lightning-quick movement, and used his claws to pin him by the throat to the ground. The move was an old one of his, well practiced, and Ty hissed, triumphant, when the other vampire stilled instantly beneath him. Claws pierced flesh, puncturing the tender skin just enough to cause intense pain but not true damage.

He might have just finished it then had he not gotten a good look at his attacker first. When he did, vicious pleasure turned to sick pity in one sluggish beat of his ancient heart.

"Gods, man," he hissed before he could think better of it. "Who did this to you?"

He had seen this sort of cruelty before, though it had been centuries. The vampire beneath him was a shell of a human, an animated corpse that had begun to decompose while he still drew breath. Waxy skin stretched taut over jutting bones. What hair remained on his balding head was patchy and fine. The body beneath him felt like a bag of bones, while the eyes that watched him bulged madly. Thin lips were peeled back over yellowed fangs.

No vampire would deny himself to the point where he became a hunger-crazed zombie, falling apart but unable to die, thinking only of food. But he had seen this done to vampires who had displeased their masters, chained in dungeons until they went mad with hunger for the crime of trying to subvert the order of things in the world of night. And, occasionally, those so-called gutterbloods who had been in the wrong place at the wrong time, who had crossed paths with bored, entitled, and incredibly sadistic highbloods, merited the treatment for no other crime but existing.

The practice had fallen out of use, Ty had thought. But apparently not all the way.

"Don't matter," the specter hissed, panting. "I smell your blood, kitty. It'll do. Give us a drop, will you? Just... a drop...ah, Lucifer's eyes, but it *hurts*!"

Wave after wave of revolting stench rolled off the pathetic creature that lay beneath Ty, but he forced his revulsion to the back of his mind. There was something *wrong* about this man, this attack. And before he put this creature out of his misery, which he would have to do, he wanted answers.

"Tell me who did this to you, and I'll see that you are fed," Ty lied softly.

The other vampire hissed out a laugh, part pain, part madness. But the trace of sanity that remained inside him seemed to emerge, if only briefly. "Lies. Pretty lies. He said you'd say that. But it's too late for me. I done what I was told. I'll kill you and feed, or die trying." The face contorted in agony. "I won't go back in the dark again... not in the dark, not in the chains..."

Ty's eyes narrowed, even as pity threatened to derail him. Pity had no place in his world, he reminded himself. The strong survived. The weak would always fall. And if a man wasn't careful, he could go right down with them for nothing more than a moment's compassion.

"He *who*? You were sent to hunt me?"

The sick grin was accompanied by a giggle that was near to weeping, and sanity departed again, likely for good. "Not you, stupid bugger. Stupid, stupid kitty. But I kept you busy, didn't I? No more dark dungeons for me, no more hunger. Stupid stupid stupid to leave the pretty thing aaaaaaaall alone..."

Ty sucked in a breath. *Lily.* He'd fallen right into such a simple trap. But how could he not have known he was being watched? He always sensed such things, always knew. However, he had never let himself get so preoccupied with a woman before, he thought with an unpleasant twist of guilt. Naturally, the one time he did, it could well cost him everything. Such had been the tale of his sorry existence.

It took all of Ty's willpower not to bolt right then, to run off into the darkness in pursuit of whatever else hunted Lily, for he had no doubt that he or she would be far more formidable an adversary than this miserable wretch of a decoy. But business left unfinished was business that often came back to bite you in the end. His grip tightened on the vampire's thin neck. On a whim, he yanked down the collar of the man's moldering shirt. The mark there was dark against the pale and waxen flesh, and it confirmed what his gut had already told him.

The Shades did not constitute a bloodline. Humans would have called them a *gang*, though a vampire would have found that description ill-fitting at best. The Shades came from all walks of the underworld, though mainly from varying levels of the gutter, trained to be masters at their illicit trades. They were the aristocracy of thieves and murderers, both feared and respected by even the high-bloods. This one seemed to have a dash of almost every lesser bloodline going, making for a fascinatingly intricate mark. But beside it, small and deceptively simple, was the telltale tattoo that was inked upon initiation into the Shades: a small black crescent moon. Blood did not create the mark of a Shade, but only death would remove it.

A voice from deep in his past returned to whisper from the depths of his mind: *"We're all killers, Ty. Why not join us and be revered for it? It's the only way a cat can live like a king."*

He pushed it away, locked it back in the recesses of his memory where it belonged. How disappointed the fledgling vampire who'd rejected that offer would be in what Ty had become, which was little different than all he'd denied, save for the dangerously thin veneer of respectability.

"You must have pissed off your masters terribly to be punished like this," Ty said aloud. "And someone big must have hired them—assassination is still one of the most expensive services at the House of Shadows, yeah?"

He didn't expect an answer, and he didn't get one. No matter how far gone this vampire was, he wouldn't tell. They almost never did. Bloody Shades.

"Peace, brother," Ty said as the other vampire began to thrash beneath him, making a final attempt to throw Ty off and gain the upper hand. Or perhaps he just wanted Ty to end it for him. If that was the case, his wish was quickly granted. With a flash of a blade that Tynan had carried with him from his first life into this one, head and body were sundered.

And by the time the decaying body burst into flames seconds later, Ty was nothing more than a black blur, streaking into the night. Praying to a god he no longer believed in that he wasn't too late.

Lily pulled into her driveway with no recollection of how she'd managed to drive herself home. The entire trip was like something out of a nightmare, her body on autopilot while all she saw in her mind was Ty's burning eyes and gleaming fangs, and all she could hear was that unearthly voice telling her to run.

She'd nearly taken a detour dozens of times, wanting to head for anywhere but where he'd told her to go. What stopped her was what Ty had said about being responsible for losing people. She wouldn't risk anyone else.

That didn't mean she didn't want to run...but there didn't seem to be anywhere to run to.

Lily got out of the car, shaking like a leaf. Somehow, though, she made it to the front door, where she fumbled around with her keys for precious seconds, alone there on her quiet street. And, of course, she'd forgotten to turn on her porch light. Again.

"Come on," she muttered, feeling terror trying to return in full force, tickling the back of her throat with icy fingers. Finally, she managed to drive the correct key home and turn it in the lock with a gasp of relief. The sharp click brought with it a burst of reassurance. Here was sanity. Here was some measure of safety. Quickly, Lily stumbled into the lit entry hall and slammed the front door shut behind her, then flipped the dead bolt.

I'm home. I'm safe. I'm home.

She turned, dropping her messenger bag beside the coat rack in the hall, and closed her eyes for a moment. She needed to center herself, to let the horror recede in the comforting presence of the familiar.

"I'm okay," she said aloud, her voice sounding thin and shaken. "Everything's okay now," she continued, more firmly. Then she opened her eyes, squared her shoulders, and moved toward the arched entrance that led to the open space of the kitchen and family room. Her footsteps tapped reassuringly across the wood floor.

With the return of normalcy, fear became anger.

Hell with this, she thought as her world began to right itself, and doubt about what she'd actually seen began to creep in. She was not a victim. She needed a plan. So the first step, the most logical step, was to call the cops. There was no way she was just going to sit here and wait for something awful to happen when there was a police station not two miles away. Tynan had obviously been stalking her. That much she knew for certain. Everything else, well...It was possible, even probable, that he'd been trying to scare her. She hadn't actually seen anyone else out there by the parking lot, had she? As for the glowing eyes and the fangs, someone clever enough, and sick enough, could have manufactured effects like that.

Humiliation twisted in Lily's stomach.

"God, I'm an idiot," she said. She'd been such an easy mark.

She reached to flip on the light, but as soon as the room brightened, she wished that she'd driven directly to the police station.

But it was far too late for that now.

He watched her from where he'd arranged himself in a chair at her little kitchen table, a bemused expression on a pale, handsome face that would have been the picture of friendly innocence but for the hunger that gleamed in eyes that looked blue one second, red the next.

"You're being a little hard on yourself, don't you think?" the man said in smooth, cultured tones that matched the elegant picture he presented. Crisp khaki pants, pressed button-down shirt, shoes that gleamed with polish. Not a hair was out of place. One foot rested casually on the opposite knee, and his hands, as pale as his face, were folded gently in his lap. A black wool overcoat was folded neatly over the back of one of the other chairs. He could have just come from a business meeting.

Apart from the fact that he was utterly terrifying.

When Lily said nothing, only stared at him with her mouth and throat going dry, he sighed.

"Not even a hello? Well. You may not be an idiot, but you're certainly lacking in manners."

He regarded her with those strange eyes, making her skin crawl. There was no emotion there, only dead cold. The eyes of a killer.

"Lily Quinn. I'm afraid you're in some trouble."

"Who are you?" Lily finally managed to croak. "I don't know you people, and I know I haven't done anything. I think you've got the wrong person."

The man chuckled softly. "People? Well, well. The queen's pampered pet has finally decided to show himself and make nice with you, yes? I'm surprised. Tynan was never gifted with many social graces." His eyes drank her in, up and down. "Though I can see why he changed his mind. He wants something, of course. Our kind rarely bothers with yours unless we want something."

Lily fought off a shudder. For whatever reason, this man had the complete opposite effect on her than Tynan had, though she had no idea why—it was a fair bet that they were the same sort of creature. But Tynan had given her the impression of power kept tightly leashed, tightly controlled. This one seemed more interested in toying with her, holding back from his hunger only until he grew bored.

She had a bad feeling it wouldn't be long.

Desperate to distract him until she could think of some

way out of this, Lily tried to keep the man engaged in conversation.

"Tynan. You two work together? He's a friend of yours?" she asked, trying to stay composed, stay cool. Inside, she felt something beginning to gather. The old, unpredictable darkness she'd kept at bay for so many years now. But she doubted it would be enough to save her, not when she'd deliberately locked it away for so long. And not helping matters, the question earned her a derisive snort.

"No, we don't work together. He's not strong enough to handle what I do—he never was. As for friendship, I don't believe he'd consider us that anymore either. I certainly don't. But I'm not really in the mood to explain."

He stretched a little, shifting position again as though he were tiring of this whole ordeal, and Lily was struck by his similarity to Tynan, despite what he'd said. They moved the same way, with a preternatural grace in even the smallest movements.

"You could explain who you are and what you're doing here, then," Lily said, wincing when she heard the bite of fear in her tone. But she couldn't hide it. He couldn't be real; this couldn't be real, any of it...

"I myself am no one," he purred with an inviting half smile. She got the sense that he was trying to pull her in, to lull her into the same trance that Tynan had been able to achieve with merely a look. And yet still, she felt nothing, only the same bright panic she'd felt when she'd first seen him. Her unwanted guest seemed to sense it, and after a moment, the smile faded.

"I'm just the hired help. *Expensive* hired help, but my employers have excellent taste. And as for you...it isn't what you've done, dear Lily, but what you *are* that's the problem."

"I don't know what you're talking about."

His gaze was unnervingly direct. "It doesn't really matter if you know or you don't. You can bury certain things, lovely Lily, but blood can't be denied forever. Trust me, it's a fact I live with every day. Well, night," he said, his mouth curving slightly. "I'm a vicious killer. And you are, shall we say, a woman of vision. Or at least, I'm assuming you must be, otherwise you wouldn't have had Ty sniffing at your heels for days." He cocked his head at her. "How sad. You really don't know what you are, do you?"

And the hell of it was, she didn't. She never had. As a child, she'd felt a power inside her that she didn't understand, but she knew that whatever it was, it made her different, and not in a good way. So she had buried it deep, so deep that it could manifest itself now only in nightmares. But the miserable affliction that had plagued her as a girl, that had left her alone in the world, had never truly gone. What on earth it had to do with this man, Lily couldn't imagine. And she wasn't at all sure she'd live to see the question answered.

"Are you going to kill me?" she asked. The truth in his eyes was unmistakable.

"What I'm going to do," the man said, "is be paid for a job well done. But I must say," he continued, his gaze traveling slowly over her, "the pleasure I'll get from taking you will be a welcome bonus. Such things are few and far between in my line of work. Still, it's a living. In a manner of speaking."

"What *are* you?" she asked hoarsely, every ounce of her common sense rebelling at the things she couldn't seem to blink away—the red eyes, the fangs, the pale and perfect skin.

His lips curved in a small, pitying smile. "My dear Lily, please. It's not much of a stretch to figure it out, even if you don't want to believe it. Would it help if I spoke in a bad Romanian accent? Not that knowing will matter while I'm drinking you dry, but I try to be obliging where I can."

He stood then, in one swift and graceful motion that caught Lily off guard. She took a step back. Horror rose in her throat. This was really happening. She was about to be attacked by a...*vampire*. And Tynan, if he'd ever really intended to help her, was nowhere to be seen.

"I don't want to die. Please. I'll...I'll give you whatever you want. There has to be something I can do!" she cried, hearing the desperation in her own voice. When it came down to it, she would beg for her life. Oh yes, she would beg. She would scream.

And that was exactly what this creature wanted.

He chuckled again, a sound that grated on Lily's ears.

"Dying is easy," he said, striding toward her. "Nothing to it. But if you want to run, by all means, do. It's so boring when your partner just lies there, don't you think?"

Lily felt the reality of the moment crash through her system at once. Staying still meant death. Running probably meant the same, but she had to try. She burst into motion, whirling back into the hallway, her feet barely touching the floor as she willed herself toward the front door.

She moved faster than she ever had in her life. Time seemed to crawl sluggishly, every second drawing out into an eternity. His laughter echoing in her ears.

He was toying with her. She was only human, no match

for the strength and speed he would surely possess. Still, Lily reached the door, all of her will focused on the dead bolt that she needed to flip, the knob she needed to turn. Her vision narrowed until they were all she could see, all that existed. A strange sensation shimmered through her that had nothing to do with fear. It felt electric, like the charge gathering in the air before a storm.

She remembered this, what to do with it. Shreds of those memories were still within her, locked away in the dark. If she could just tap into that current, make the door open . . .

At the instant before Lily gave all of her amassed energy the final push she both feared and needed, several things happened simultaneously that sent the world from grayed-out slow motion into Technicolor hyperspeed. The front door slammed open so hard it nearly came off its hinges. Something big, black, and yowling like a banshee came flying in from the night. Behind her, a hand slid into her hair and yanked her back so hard her teeth clicked painfully together. There was a rending sound as her shirt was torn down the front, baring not only her neck and chest, now scored by her assailant's eager claws, but also something else . . . something she had been taught at an early age to cover at all cost, now burning fire bright along her slender collarbone.

She saw her attacker's eyes go wide as they lit on her strange tattoo, a mark she had carried before she had any memories, before her parents were ripped from her and she was thrown upon the mercy of strangers. She saw the instant of horrified recognition, heard the hiss as his lips peeled back to reveal dagger-sharp incisors.

As though in a dream, she heard Tynan's voice.

"Damien! Lily, no—"

But she couldn't stop. All of Lily's focus, all of the power she'd drawn into herself, hit critical mass at that moment. With the door already open, its purpose lost, it had nowhere to go.

Nowhere but *out*.

She shrieked as power burst from her in a wave, tearing through the house with the force of a sonic boom. Lily felt her body bow sharply as the surge left her, her vision lost to a blinding flash of white. Pictures fell from the walls, glass shattered. The floor beneath her shuddered as though the Earth had moved. She was held rigid in the air for a single second, then dropped to the floor in a crumpled heap. The hands that had gripped her had vanished as soon as the power had let go.

Unfortunately, so had all of Lily's strength. She lay there, dazed, drained, eyes closed, listening to bits of glass dropping to the floor. All around her was silence. She knew, in a dim sort of way, that she should get up, run. Her attacker could be anywhere.

But all she could do was stay where she was. This sensation was one she also knew, though Lily thought she'd locked it away tight. She had experienced it only once, and as a much younger child. It had changed everything.

Ruined everything.

chapter FIVE

*S*HE KNELT WEEPING *in the middle of her ruined nursery, shattered toys littering the floor. A young, attractive woman watched from the doorway, eyes wide with horror, one hand resting protectively on her still-flat belly. A child of their own. An unexpected thrill. They wouldn't need her anymore, Lily knew. Not with a baby of their own flesh and blood. They would send her away, the little changeling whose oddities were becoming too numerous to ignore. An embarrassment. What would the press say if they ever found out? They would send her away, and she'd been so...angry....*

"Lily. You've got to get up, Lily. We don't have much time. He'll be back to finish the job. His sort doesn't quit until they're finished. Lily?" A pause. "You're not going to blow me all to hell if I touch you, right?"

There was a tentative, shuddering breath, then a gentle nudge at her shoulder to go along with that rough-edged brogue she couldn't ignore. She waited a moment to see if he'd go away, if this would all just pass. Because she knew that when she opened her eyes, her well-ordered little life, the one she'd always dreamed of, would be over.

The darkness would begin to seep back in.

And yet, what choice did she have? As much as she'd ever had, Lily thought bitterly as she slowly opened her eyes. Tynan crouched over her, closer than he'd been since the night they'd met, silvery eyes full of concern and... something else. Something wild, feral. Something completely inhuman. His mouth was set in a thin, hard line. No fangs were visible. But Lily was certain they were there just the same.

"Vampire." She whispered the word hoarsely, as much a statement as an accusation.

He nodded, his eyes never leaving hers. "Yes. Me and the other. I did warn you." He frowned, and the ferocity of it might have frightened her if she'd had any emotion left to give.

"Why?" she asked dully. "Why couldn't you have just left me alone?"

The unshakable conviction she saw on his face made her want to scream. He would not be leaving her here, and with that realization came helpless despair. She would have destroyed her house a hundred times over if it meant he'd leave her in peace.

"My queen needs your help."

"I don't have any help to give anybody."

He glanced around, at what Lily was sure was the complete mess she'd made out of her pretty little house. His voice was dead calm when he replied.

"You have something, woman. That much is certain." Then his eyes dropped to her tattoo—the snake, the star.

She waited, even hoped, for the same horrified look she'd seen on the other vampire's face, waited for it to drive him off. Instead, he focused on it with intense interest.

"What do you know about this mark?" he asked. "Where did you get it?"

She glared up at him, hating the disadvantage her prone position put her in. "It's just some stupid tattoo my parents put on me before they died, when I was a baby. Apparently, they were freaks. I'm not one. And if you're going to try killing me now, too, you should probably just get it over with."

He continued to study the tattoo. "Green," he murmured. "And see how it catches the light, how it shimmers. It's beautiful."

"It's just a stupid tattoo," Lily muttered, turning her head away as embarrassment bloomed. So she had a glittery, green tattoo. She assumed the artist had been some sort of psychedelic genius. And she wished he'd plied his trade on someone, *anyone*, else.

She sucked in a breath at the shock of Tynan's thumb, his skin cool against her warmth, as he rubbed slowly across the tattoo.

"It's not a tattoo," he murmured. "And Damien knew what it meant."

He seemed to be speaking more to himself than to her, but still his words reignited one of her deepest fears: that the glittering green symbol inked into her skin meant more trouble in her life, when she'd done everything she could to insulate herself from it.

"That's not—" she began, but stopped short before the word *possible*. If tonight was really happening, if Tynan was what he professed to be, then nothing was impossible.

Lily gritted her teeth and turned her head away from the searching gray eyes that lifted to look into her own. "Whoever you are—*whatever* you are—you need to call off the other creeps and get out of my life. I'm nothing. I'm nobody. And I repeat, *I can't help you*. I'm not going anywhere."

"The one creep, as you so accurately describe him, won't be bothering us again. The other will return before long." He shook his head. "There's no deterring a Shade."

The word sent an icy chill down Lily's back. "Shade?"

"*Shade* is an old word for 'ghost' or 'spirit,' and the ones coming after you are just as difficult to spot when they don't want to be seen. Shades are the most elite group of criminals in the vampire world. The most talented ones are filthy rich, and they're all a bit taken with themselves. Damien certainly is. The highbloods, our nobles, use them for all sorts of dirty work." He paused. "Like this."

The thought made her feel ill. Someone had gone to that much trouble...over *her*? "Well, since you're chasing me around, I doubt you're much better," she said flatly.

Tynan breathed out an exasperated hiss of air. "Do you really want to be here when Damien gets back?"

"What are my choices? Get eaten now or eaten later?" Lily asked, feeling as miserable and helpless as she ever had in her life. "Maybe sooner is better."

She heard him sigh, a hollow, unhappy sound that almost made her look at him. Almost. But Lily knew that if she did, she'd just get sucked in again, unable to think, unable to resist him. She could feel him studying her, those odd eyes searching her face for clues about her thoughts. She could actually *feel* him, lurking at the periphery of her mind, trying to get in.

All of the vampire pop culture garbage she'd ever

ingested—movies and books, some bloody and all a hell of a lot more romantic than her own bleak reality—came flooding back to Lily as she lay there. She wondered which bits of it were true, what she might be able to use to get out of this mess. She suddenly wished she had some garlic. Or some holy water.

Or a nice, sharp stake.

"Killing me wouldn't do any good, even if you could manage it, which you can't," Tynan said.

She glared at him. "Even if you can read my mind," she bit out, "don't."

Tynan's smile was grim. "It would be easier if I could. I've tried that already, though, and no dice. Your thoughts are locked up tight. Your expressions, however, are another story."

Silently, Lily cursed herself for having such a readable face, though she did take some consolation in the fact that he hadn't been poking into her thoughts, even though he'd tried.

"Why don't you think I could manage it?" Lily asked. "You saw what I can do. You don't know me at all. Maybe I like killing."

His faint, mocking smirk let her know that her statement sounded as ridiculous to him as it did to her.

"You're also a terrible liar. Anyway, even if you managed to get rid of me, which you can't, they'd just send another after you. Though with me gone, the Shades would get you first anyway. They'll be wanting their money. And shaking them off once is only going to make it uglier for you the next time." He paused. "Very ugly, knowing Damien. Someone's gone and paid for the best if he's involved."

She stared up at him, full of impotent rage. Even now,

with her house in shambles and her deepest-buried secret completely exposed, she couldn't ignore her simmering attraction to him. Having him this close, braced above her, completely focused, Lily saw that he felt it, too; she could see it in the way his breathing changed ever so slightly, the way his eyes, already intense, went to hot silver. So much of her wanted to stretch beneath him, to arch and invite him to put his hands on her, to melt under a touch she knew instinctively would be even hotter than his gaze.

Lily had to look away again. This was insane, and she needed to get a handle on it. *Now.*

"I'm going to sit up now," she said firmly. She might be a quiet girl, but she'd been taking care of herself for a long time. Growing a spine hadn't been an option, and she was glad to find hers intact in spite of everything. "You're going to need to back off."

Thankfully, he didn't ask why or argue with her about it. She tried to be glad of it as Tynan shifted and moved back from her with the liquid grace of a cat.

A cat... he had been a cat....

Lily struggled up to a sitting position, still feeling like little more than a hollow vessel from which all the contents had just been emptied. She glanced at Tynan, now crouching only a few feet away and watching her with guarded interest.

"I thought vampires were supposed to turn into bats, not big black cats," she muttered resentfully, lifting her hands to examine them for any cuts from the flying glass. Satisfied that there were none, she got her feet beneath her and began the arduous process of standing up without letting Tynan know how much it was costing her to manage it.

"Not all of us can turn into something else. It depends on the bloodline," he said, frowning as he watched her. And damned if he didn't get to his own feet and start to move toward her again, as though he wanted to help her up. Lily shot him a withering glare, and it must have conveyed what she wanted it to, because Ty quickly shifted back and stuck his hands in the pockets of his long black coat.

"Cats. Smoke. Bit of this and that. There are even a few who can turn into lions and jungle cats and things, though they've about gone extinct. And yes, bats. But turning into animals is usually sort of . . . frowned upon."

"Because?"

"Too much like werewolves. And vampires hate werewolves."

"I . . . oh." Lily tried to digest that, then just decided to pretend she hadn't heard it. The existence of vampires was enough for tonight.

"And that man who was here to kill me? Damien, I think you called him?" Lily asked, wrapping her arms protectively around herself as she made sure she was steady, then surveyed the damage she'd done. "Can he turn into anything else that I should be looking for?"

Tynan shook his head. "Another cat, I'm sorry to say, though you'll have to believe me that he's gone, at least for the moment. It's a shame that he's a Cait Sith," he said, pronouncing it *cat-SHEE*, a word that sounded Gaelic and mysterious as it rolled off his tongue. "He's a slippery enough bastard in his human form. All the Shades are, but he's special, even for them. The services of the House of Shadows are astronomically expensive for a reason. Theft, espionage, extortion—assassination. The Shades offer it all. And they're very, very good." He paused. "But Damien is in a class by himself. Easy to admire, when he's not being paid to kill you."

The sheer awfulness of what he'd just described to her was too much to take in, so Lily turned away from it, ignored the whole, and concentrated on the superficial.

"He mentioned you. I don't think the feeling is mutual."

"No, it wouldn't be."

Tynan didn't elaborate, so Lily looked at her bare walls, one of which had a massive crack running the length of it now. Her pictures, framed photos of places she'd been and people she'd enjoyed, lay scattered on the floor. Glass was strewn everywhere in the hall, and a quick look behind her told her that the kitchen was worse. The force of her energy leaving her had managed to fling open some of the cupboards, and it seemed she might not have any glasses left. Or plates.

She didn't want to look at any more destruction.

So she looked at Tynan, because he was the only thing here that didn't make her feel like her heart was being ripped out of her body. He stood, tall and dark and calm, in the middle of the debris, and once again Lily felt an inexorable pull toward him, toward his strength and steadiness as she felt her own façade threatening to crumble. But Lily knew, without a doubt, that she'd have to be a complete fool to give in.

He hadn't saved her, Lily told herself. He'd shown up while she was saving herself. And none of this would be happening if he hadn't been following her to begin with. Remembering that brought a welcome rush of anger to temper the confusing mix of emotions she was contending with. She pushed the memory of the look in Damien's eyes when he'd seen her tattoo into the background, where she could ponder and worry over it later. Though Tynan's voice still whispered that unthinkable word on a loop in her mind, over and over and over...

Assassination.

"So these Shades are trying to kill me. I don't suppose you're going to tell me why."

"Because whoever hired them would rather see you dead than have you help the dynasty they're trying to destroy," Tynan said. "Damien won't scare off so easily—he wants his money. My queen offers her protection in return for your help identifying her enemies."

He extended his hand, but she stayed where she was. She wanted so badly to just give in, to shift the burden of her safety onto someone else for a change. But she'd learned the hard way that the only one she could rely on for protection was herself.

She kept her hands where they were.

"Your queen, whoever she is, can go to hell."

Tynan pressed his lips together into a line of disapproval. "Don't be a fool, Lily. You're dead if you stay here. Let me help you," he said.

"Help me? You *caused* this! You said yourself you were careless. I would have been fine if you hadn't shown up!" Lily cried, outraged that Tynan thought she was so naive, so easily mollified.

He sighed, his shoulders sagging just a little, and Lily knew she wasn't imagining the weariness that flashed in his strange silver eyes. It made her feel for him, when she should have felt no sympathy at all. But the depth of the exhaustion she'd glimpsed was so great, and so much more ancient than what any human could muster, that it touched her unexpectedly. For just a moment, he had worn the look of a man who has struggled for so long that he has accepted it as a permanent state of being.

To a certain degree, it was a state she was intimately familiar with. Still she chafed at identifying with him.

"If you want to shout at me, Lily, go ahead," Tynan said gruffly. "But there's no changing what's past. What matters is now. And the choice is either myself and the protection of the most powerful dynasty of vampires in the world, or Damien and his creative methods of putting people out of their misery."

His sharp features now revealed nothing but determination. And any traces of vulnerability were gone... if she hadn't just imagined them to begin with.

"I want you gone. I want to be left alone. Tell your queen to find somebody else."

"There is no one else," Tynan replied. "Your gift is rarer now than it ever was. It took me months to find one Seer: you. And if it hadn't been me, Lily, another would have sought you out eventually."

Lily looked at him, feeling hopelessness threatening to consume her. "A *Seer*? Is that what you think I am? What exactly am I supposed to be able to see, huh? The future? Can't do that. The hearts and minds of other people? You've struck out there too. I'm not a mind reader or a visionary. And I think you've made a really big mistake." Her words tasted as bitter on her tongue as they sounded. But Tynan didn't seem the least bit put off. When he spoke again, his voice was soft but insistent.

"Maybe you don't think so, Lily, but you've got the out-ward signs—more, in fact, than I was aware existed—of the sort of human who can see creatures caught between

the living and the dead. It's not about prophecy but vision,
and you should be capable of that too. You may not know
how yet, but you can be guided."

She swallowed hard, hearing the dry click in her
throat. "So you're saying I should be able to see ghosts?"

"Ghosts, and other things. Vampires can do some incredible things, but we can't see beyond the here and now. Walking with death the way we do seems to rob us of our ability
to look beyond it." His voice hardened slightly. "Just be
glad I was sent by someone who cares what condition you
arrive in."

His words made her break out in gooseflesh. She'd
never seen a ghost—not that she was aware of anyway.
Her nightmare, though, was something else, something
more real than just a recurring wisp of an ugly dream.
She'd always known it, just as she knew there was something strange about the tattoo that throbbed and burned
upon waking. But the nightmare, vision, whatever it was
had never done her any good—it was just there, an unfortunate part of her. That her life now seemed to hang in the
balance because of it seemed hideously unfair.

"I can't see anything that would help anyone," she
insisted, pushing back against the beginnings of despair.
"And this"—she swept her arm around the ruins of her
hallway—"is this anything your queen is going to want from
me? What does this have to do with vision?" She gestured
to the tattoo she'd tried so long to hide, now exposed as half
of her thin sweater hung in tatters. "You wanted to know
how I got this, what it means. I don't know that either!"

Tynan's expression clouded as he looked at her mark.
"Yes. We'll need to sort that out first, I suppose. The
mark is...unusual. As are your abilities." He didn't sound

happy, and his honesty surprised her, but it was obvious that her objections had done nothing to deter him.

"Maybe I don't care," she said, though it cost her to even speak the lie. "Maybe I don't want to know what it means."

But within her, the energy she'd awakened so brutally still twisted and roiled, impossible to ignore. She didn't know how to use it, how to control it. She never had. And now that it had been unlocked, it would begin to look for a way out again.

"Damien doesn't scare easily," Tynan said softly. "But I saw fear on his face. Fear is only going to make him more dangerous to you, because what he fears, he'll work even harder to destroy. You need protection, Lily. Whether you like it or not."

"What if I flat-out refuse you?" she asked, trying to keep her voice steady.

He arched his eyebrow, and his gaze went to pure steel. "There is no refusal. I'd think you would have figured that out by now. If you continue not to see reason, then I take my chances that you're nothing more, or less, than a human Seer with a strange mark that looks oddly like something a vampire would have. I'll take you to Arsinoë by force, and you can see how far spitting in the face of a pharaoh gets you. Then you can find out what the Queen of the Ptolemy and her court think of your little symbol there without ever knowing yourself. And if you fail at what you've been brought for..." He trailed off, his voice dangerously silken.

She was glad he chose not to finish the sentence.

Lily glared at him helplessly. "But what if I'm nothing, Tynan? What if I can't have visions, or whatever it is you think I should be able to do, and I'm just some other variety of human freak show? Do you plan on letting this Damien know he can quit trying to kill me if that happens?"

Tynan shook his head slowly. "No. He'll consider tonight a personal affront. I'm afraid that regardless, you'll have to stay hidden until he can be taken care of. It may take a bit of time, depending on how much sense his masters are willing to listen to. But my queen promises you a return to your life, your home, no matter what happens. So long as you cooperate, this is an impermanent arrangement."

He had gone quite still, and his voice had a queer, flat quality to it, as though he were simply reciting something he'd rehearsed many times before. Up until now, Lily had found him an unsettling presence but strangely genuine. His honesty about who and what he was prevented her, oddly enough, from fearing him the way she had Damien. Until now, that was. His promise rang hollow and false. Lily stared back at him without flinching, her gaze direct. He shifted, but his gaze never wavered from hers. Still, she was sure he was lying. Maybe about a little…maybe about everything.

The hell of it was, it didn't much matter. The outcome would be the same.

"An impermanent arrangement?" Lily asked. "What is that to you, a hundred years or so?"

Tynan's eyes went arctic. "The alternative is to just give you to Damien once you've outlived your usefulness. He'd find you in a heartbeat anyway. Is that what you'd prefer?"

"How do I know I can trust you?" she asked, voicing her greatest worry. This stranger expected her to run into the darkness with him. She didn't want to be his next meal.

He smirked, but it was humorless, and Lily felt a chill as she saw just a hint of the remorseless killer in him.

"You don't, of course. But you have my word, for what it's worth," he said, extending his hand to seal the agreement. "I can't bite you, Lily. If you're a true Seer, vampire venom will rob you of your ability, and I've got a vested interest in preserving that. An invisible curse stalks the dynasty I serve, the House of Ptolemy. Without a Seer to show Arsinöe, the Ptolemy queen, who the source of the evil is, her people will cease to exist. And if I fail to provide that Seer, or even if the one I find turns out to be more a danger than a help, then I *also* cease to exist."

His words pulled at her despite herself, despite how little she understood. He looked so haunted in that instant that Lily was unable to resist the unfamiliar urge to comfort and soothe.

"I'm so sorry about your people," she began, but stopped short when something dangerous flickered across Tynan's face. It was a forceful reminder that whatever separated him from the creatures trying to kill her, it wasn't much. They were all vampires. Monsters, if even a handful of the legends about them were true.

"They're not *my people*," he said in a harsh growl. "I am no Ptolemy."

Lily blinked, confused both by his statement and his sudden anger.

"But I thought—"

"I'm a hunter, nothing more, though one with a very important job. Enough discussion. What we need to know won't be found close by, and I don't have much time. Damien ran off, but he won't stay gone for long."

She had no chance to either accept or deny it. Tynan

was at her side in a flash of motion, grabbing her by the arm to haul her from the room. He didn't hurt her, exactly, but his grip was like a vise, and the abrupt change in him surprised Lily into compliance. She allowed herself to be pulled out the front door, struggling to keep up with Tynan's long stride.

He paused on the little walk outside the door, tipping his head back to scent the air. Lily watched him with her heart in her throat. She wasn't sure which was worse: to have this over and done with now, courtesy of Damien the psychopathic vampire assassin, or to head for whatever was waiting for her. A vampire queen? A group of vampires who called themselves the Ptolemy? Ptolemy. That name pricked at her memory. She knew it from somewhere. . . .

"In the car," Tynan said, jerking Lily back to the present. He seemed satisfied with whatever he had (or hadn't) smelled in the night air. Panicked that this was all happening so fast, she tried to stall. But she'd already come too far.

"But . . . but I don't have my keys. . . ."

He dangled them in front of her face, glinting silver in the moonlight. "In the car," he repeated, looking pleased for once when she was speechless. It didn't last long.

"My purse," she began, taking a perverse sort of pleasure in his grimace even as he propelled her toward the car.

"There's nothing in it you'll need."

"But . . . damn it, Tynan, wait!" she cried, digging in her heels as he switched from pushing to pulling. Her efforts accomplished nothing against the strength he was exerting, and to her dismay, he didn't even look like he was trying. She whipped her head around to look at her house, the front door neatly closed, concealing the mess inside that would inevitably be discovered, and soon.

It would look bad, very bad, to whoever found it. They would know she was gone.

They would think she was dead.

Maybe she would be.

"I have no clothes, no money, not even a damned toothbrush. Tynan...*wait*!"

It was the anguish in her cry that probably stopped him. He turned to look at her, those silver eyes, so very feline in the darkness, gleaming with light that could only have come from within. Lily held out a moment's hope that he would see what he was doing, see how he was tearing her away from a life that she loved, a life that she needed, without even a moment to gather herself, to set things right—without even saying good-bye.

"You promise you'll bring me back," she said, desperate even for a believable lie. "This is all I have."

She didn't know why she'd said it, why she'd told a complete stranger the sad truth of her life. But there it was, laid out for him. And she saw something in the way he looked at her, some flicker of pity that made her want to weep. He might well betray her. But in that moment, she saw that he understood exactly how she was feeling.

"I promise you, I'll return you once this is done. But until then, you have your life, and you have me. Those things are all you'll need. Understood?"

Lily clung to that. She had to. "I...understand."

He moved in a blur then, wrenching open the car door and bundling her into the passenger seat before Lily could collect her thoughts enough to say another word. As the engine started and Tynan backed quickly out of the driveway, all she could think was that no matter what happened after this, the life she'd loved, that she'd so carefully built, was over as she'd known it. There was, however, the faintest glimmer of hope in all this darkness. She might get to know, finally know, what she'd been cursed with all these years. She might even discover how to contain it, control it, and, of course, use it to escape once she'd come up with a viable plan.

She stayed silent as they tore off down her street, leaving her house and all the trappings of her existence it contained behind them. In the rearview mirror, Lily watched it go, a single, treacherous tear escaping to trail down her cheek.

She was in the hands of a beautiful monster now.

And like it or not, she was headed back into the darkness.

chapter SIX

Ty's SLEEK BLACK Lexus slid through the night, racing down the highway at speeds that wouldn't have been possible without a very expensive, very illegal radar detector installed in the dash. They'd spent the day sleeping in some nondescript little city in Eastern Pennsylvania, and delayed leaving this evening so that Lily could pick up some clothing and essentials. She'd been impressively quick with her choices; he'd give her that. But though he wasn't a man who enjoyed a lot of noise and excitement, the chilly silence from his new charge had become nearly suffocating. Filling the wordless abyss of the last twenty-four hours with one-sided conversation fragments of his own had gone from odd to irritating, to just deeply depressing, very quickly.

It must have been the reason that Lily's voice, when she finally spoke, sent hot little sparks of pleasure coursing through his system instead of simple relief.

"So we're going to Chicago," she said without looking

at him, her voice soft and low. "To some woman you used to work with?"

"Her name is Anura," Ty said, sneaking a quick glance at Lily's fine profile, at the determined set of her jaw. He looked away again when those pleasant little flickers of heat turned a bit too intense for his liking.

"She owns a club in Chicago called Mabon. Has for over a hundred years now."

"A *vampire* club."

Now she just sounded disgruntled, and he fought back a smile. She would get used to blood drinkers soon enough.

"A vampire club," Ty agreed. "And a very good one. It's one of the few that manage to be neither exclusively highblood nor exclusively lowblood. A difficult balance, but she makes it work. I didn't work with her so much as she helped me out a few times when I badly needed it. Anura's a good woman. And with her background, I think she'll be able to identify your mark, or point us in the right direction if she can't. She's a highblood herself, and a very old one," Ty continued, remembering how different Anura's situation had been when he'd met her. "Even if the Empusae refuse to call her their sister anymore."

"Highbloods and lowbloods," she repeated with a sigh. "It all sounds a little...archaic."

The displeasure in Lily's voice quickly gave way to confusion, and a weariness that would pull at him if he let it.

"You're used to living in the daylight world, Lily," Ty replied gently, gladder than he should have been that she was finally engaging him. He knew he should be hard, cold, the sort of hunter and killer he'd spent years becoming. But sitting here, enveloped in her scent and all too aware of the pain he'd already caused her, Ty felt himself softening, responding to instincts he didn't even know he had.

"My world isn't anything like yours, though we walk the same streets, live in the same cities," he continued. "Where I come from, blood is power. Your mark is your destiny. And humans are either food, slaves, or pretty toys to be enjoyed and then thrown away. If you want to avoid becoming any or all of those things, then you need to pay close attention to what I'm telling you."

"Okay, see, you've lost me already," Lily said. "What do you mean, your mark is your destiny? What mark?"

In answer, he lifted his hand to his collar and pulled it down, exposing his right collarbone. He heard Lily's sharp intake of breath and knew she'd made the connection.

"Oh my God."

His mark had been a part of him for so long that he didn't even see it anymore when he looked in the mirror. But he knew it intimately—it was who he was, who his sire, the sadistic bastard, had dictated he become: the Celtic knot formed of stretching cats, midnight black. And in the background, large enough that the knot looked to be affixed to its center, the ankh of the Ptolemy. The first mark had made him an outcast.

The second had made him a slave.

"My sire was a Cait Sith," Ty said calmly, feeling the heat of Lily's gaze on his skin. From the corner of his eye, he saw her hand flutter to touch her own collarbone. He pulled the fabric back over his mark and returned his hand to the wheel. "It's a bloodline without a leader, with no centralized power. Tainted with Fae blood, it's said, and it may well be true. We have our talents, of course:

The cat-shifting is useful, and we're incredibly good hunters, even among creatures whose senses are naturally far beyond those of humans. But we're still considered lowbloods. Gutterbloods, many would say." He tried to keep the old bitterness out of his voice. He'd had to accept a long time ago that in the world that was the night's underbelly, there were some things that were simply beyond his control.

"And...how does the mark get there?"

He knew she was wondering about the intricate marking on her own collarbone.

Just as he wondered.

"When you're sired, which is to say when you're made a vampire by another one, part of the whole deal is that after they drink from you, you drink from them. At least if you want to keep living. Their blood brands you. I don't know how else to describe it," Ty said. "But the mark appears the moment your change is complete. It can be modified," he continued, remembering the way his blood had burned when the ankh had been added, the way his Cait Sith blood had rebelled against even that single drop of Ptolemy blood. "But it can never be removed. It's how we're known. It's who we are."

It was odd, talking about all of this to someone else. He had never sired another and had sworn he never would. He would never do to another what had been done to him, condemning someone else to a life with a mark that invited derision, fear, and often poverty.

It was as though she could hear his thoughts. Out of the corner of his eye, he could see Lily watching him with intense curiosity.

"And who are you, then, Tynan MacGillivray? You told

me you're not actually one of these Ptolemy you're working so hard to protect. So what does your mark say to other vampires?"

"The most important thing it says is that I'm a low-blood." He shrugged. "That makes me unworthy of notice to any *but* the Ptolemy, who tend to prefer my sort when they need people to do the jobs they don't want to do. Every dynasty has their preferences. But Ptolemy, Empusae, Dracul, Grigori, and a few other smaller dynasties tucked away here and there, they're where the power is. The highbloods, the ones from dynasties that can trace their roots all the way back to a specific god—or demon— are what you might think of as our aristocracy."

Her eyebrows shot up. "Uh, maybe I'm reading this wrong, but if these Ptolemy think you're so worthless, *why* are you trying to save them?"

Ty passed another car in a blur, noting that he was doing ninety and might want to slow down a little. He tried to relax, to force himself to loosen up. Lily was only interested in the answers, not trying to judge him, he told himself. Still, it was difficult. He wasn't used to being questioned. Loathed, yes. But not questioned.

"Because I'm a part of them, after a fashion," he said, baring his mark again briefly to explain. "The ankh there— looks a bit like a cross with a loop at the top—came a few years after my siring. Arsinöe herself gave me just enough of her blood to force the mark." He covered it again, unsettled by Lily's keen interest in it. "I'm the queen's personal hunter and am very good at what I do. I'm not supposed to save them, by the way. You are. I'm just facilitating."

"Thanks for reminding me."

He smirked at the testy note in her voice. "You don't

want the satisfaction of knowing that you've saved the oldest vampire dynasty, earning their queen's eternal gratitude?"

"I would have preferred to have a choice."

He felt a twinge of sympathy. "Sometimes you just have to accept the hand you're dealt."

"And sometimes you get abducted by some vampire bitch's pet cat."

Her words were unexpectedly heated, and they sliced through Ty even though he knew she hadn't intended them to. She was just venting and looked lost in her own thoughts. But she couldn't know how close her words hit to home. His animal side had condemned him to such remarks for centuries now: *filthy gutter cat, pet of the Ptolemy, worthless stray...*

"I'm no pet," he growled. He was suddenly compelled to make Lily see, make her understand. Why he should give a damn what she thought was beyond him, but being called a pet rankled. Hadn't Nero and his ilk said the same thing, time and again? He'd forced it to stop mattering to him. He'd thought himself immune.

And yet here he was, defending himself to this slip of a mortal. Ty thought for a moment, about how to explain it all to someone who had never lived in his world. Those who lived in the sun had, by and large, left the ancient caste systems behind. But in the darkness, the ancient world still lived and breathed. And so did their way of life.

"Look. When you're a lowblood, you either struggle or you work for a dynasty. I'd rather serve, to be valued and rewarded for my talents, than starve and scrape." He glanced at her. "Tell me you wouldn't feel the same."

Lily blew out a breath, shoved her hands into her hair. "I don't know. I'm not a vampire. But...yeah, maybe.

Maybe." Then she muttered, "Sorry about the pet thing. Bad joke. I'm just…I'm not okay with this yet. This Arsinöe is screwing with my life, Damien and whoever he's working for are trying to end it, and none of them even *know* me. Your queen can promise me whatever she wants, but for now, my life back in Tipton is in shambles. Still…I am sorry, for what it's worth. You've been really nice. For a vampire kidnapper."

It wasn't complete vindication, Ty thought, but it was something. He relaxed a little. Lily, for her part, seemed to be thinking. She was quiet a moment.

Then she said softly, "So tell me about these Ptolemy. What is that, ancient Greek? It's familiar."

This, at least, was more comfortable ground. "Arsinöe is the youngest sister of Cleopatra. The dynasty takes their family name of Ptolemy," Ty said. "Much of their lineage is Greek, which the average person seems to have forgotten."

He could feel Lily staring at him again, but not in the way he might have preferred.

"Cleopatra's sister."

"Yeah."

"You're yanking my chain."

"No."

"This is… Look, Tynan, as a dork who doesn't sleep enough, I admit I watch the History Channel, okay? I remember watching some show about this now. I knew I'd heard Arsinöe's name before. They did a show on her. Cleopatra took out any threats to her power, including her youngest sister. Woman was way more of a stone bitch than I'd ever realized."

"Trust me, it's still a sore subject," Ty replied, wincing a little as he remembered the last tirade Arsinöe had gone on about her celebrated, and very dead, elder sister. "And Cleopatra *did* have her assassinated. At least, she thought so. It was very bad form, to have high-value political prisoners of Rome killed. But as we all know now, Cleopatra was quite…persuasive. It's an ugly story, and one I won't recount, but as Arsinöe lay dying from her wounds, the gods took pity on her. Sekhmet gave her the dark gift, as the queen tells it. And in return, Arsinöe would keep the glory of Egypt's gods and goddesses from vanishing into the dust of time."

She wrinkled her nose. "I wouldn't say they'd really gotten their money's worth, then. Ancient Egyptian religion seems pretty dusty to me."

"Among the Ptolemy, it's very much alive. And that seems to be enough for the ones who made her."

Lily's voice sharpened. "And what about this whole highblood/lowblood thing? Branding servants? Treating people badly based on something they probably had no control over?"

Ty was torn between irritation that she'd decided to seize on that aspect of the situation and pleasure that she would be offended on his behalf.

"What about it?" he asked.

"Do these Egyptian gods and goddesses approve of *that*?"

"They must, I suppose," Ty said with a shrug. "As far as I know, no one's heard a peep in over a thousand years. Though even if they had…"

"Yeah, I get it. You're not in the club, and you wouldn't know."

He glanced over at her as they drove down the highway, past an exit where the lights of gas stations and res-

taurants glowed cheerily, beckoning as they lit up the
night sky. The fury in her expression surprised him, and
it suddenly occurred to him how young she was and how
old and cynical he had become. He barely remembered
what it was like to have the sort of fight in him that Lily
had now. Whatever she thought of the way things worked
in his world, though, it didn't matter. Vampire society
simply *was*. It was dangerous to question the power struc-
ture, to question why one mark should be venerated while
another should be spat upon.

Once, long ago, he had tried to rebel against the order
of things, but now he recognized his lot could be far
worse. He thought of the unlucky Shade whose punishment had been to be starved and then released as bait, and
knew he was doing what he had to do.

"I don't care what you think of the rules, Lily, because
I didn't make them. But there are plenty who enforce
them. My options are limited, and I've done the best I can
with them. Your mark is what matters in my world. And if
you fight it, you don't last long."

They lapsed into silence, Ty lost in his thought as he
drove. He had expected Lily to find his way of life odd,
even unpleasant. But he'd been surprised at how outraged
she was at what she saw as an injustice. He hadn't wasted
any time wondering what outsiders thought of vampire
society in a very long time, likely because the only times
he interacted with mortals was when he wanted a drink.

He needed to either get out more or not at all.

"Tynan?" Lily's voice breaking through the silence
was a balm to his thoughts, soft and sweet. It was the sort
of voice that could lull a man and leave him vulnerable.
He knew he needed to resist that, to stay on his guard.

He tried to separate himself from the closeness of the car, from the tantalizing scents of the soap and shampoo that overlay her own natural ones. His mouth began to water despite himself, his fangs lengthening in response.

Hungry. She makes me hungry for so many things....

"It's Ty."

He didn't know what had made him say it or why he was encouraging such familiarity with a woman who was a high-value mark, nothing more, nothing less. But the words fell from his lips before he could stop them.

"Ty?"

"It's what everyone calls me," he said, fighting not to hunch his shoulders defensively at the confusion in her voice. "It's, you know, less cumbersome. And doesn't remind me so much of my mother getting ready to box my ears."

Lily seemed to consider this a long moment, and Ty cursed himself for showing weakness. What did he know about interacting with humans anymore, much less human women who he had no intention of biting? Now she would ridicule him or simply ignore what he'd said. Yes...maybe that was best.

But her voice was considerably warmer when she spoke again, and Ty felt something, small but incredibly important, shift ever so slightly between them. A mistake, but one that nonetheless thrilled him in some dark and secret corner of himself.

"Ty, then. Has there ever been a regular human who was born with a vampire mark?"

"Not that I've ever heard."

"Can vampires have babies?"

He tried to picture bloodsucking babies. "Fortunately, no."

"Oh." Her voice was small and quiet, and Ty felt another

ill-advised tug of sympathy for her. He might not have a lot going for him as a vampire, but at least he knew what he was and where he stood. Lily obviously did not. And he had begun to get the distinct impression that she never had.

"I just wish I knew what this thing meant," she said, tapping her collarbone and the intricate design that was hidden beneath her shirt.

"Well," he said as the car rushed deeper into the night, "that's what we're going to try and find out."

chapter SEVEN

H OURS LATER, as the sun neared the horizon and the sky went from black to a dull, dishwater gray, Lily sat in a dimly lit room in some mom-and-pop motel in western Ohio. She perched on the edge of the room's sole, king-size bed, more tired than she'd ever been in her life and yet unable to relax enough to sleep. She ought to, though. She was going to need all the strength she could get.

Instead, she found herself watching Tynan. No, *Ty*, she corrected herself, trying to look like she wasn't fully absorbed in every graceful feline movement he made, fascinated by both his preternatural beauty and the paradox she was already discovering him to be. Lily had no problem believing Ty was as much a killer as Damien and these Shades who were after her. He was probably all sorts of things, she thought as she watched him in the faint reflection off the television. Probably most of those things were unspeakably awful.

And yet, he had been kind to her when he didn't have

to be. He had talked to her, really talked, painting her a rudimentary picture of a vampire society that functioned in a way that was utterly alien to her. And despite Ty's cool veneer, she had seen flashes of humor, of hurt, even of pity that made her want to know more of him.

The two of them had forged the beginnings of a connection. Lily knew she should turn away from it now, before it got any stronger. He was an ancient killer who had ripped her away from her home! And she...she was just Lily. A little strange, a little unfortunate, and yeah, a little telekinetic, but still just Lily Quinn.

She slid her eyes back to Ty's most excellent backside and sighed. Easier said than done. A *lot* easier.

There was a soft rustle of fabric as Tynan finished preparing the room for daylight. Fortunately, he seemed oblivious to the fact that he had such an attentive audience. He'd been too busy jury-rigging the bed's comforter over the curtains, ensuring that no light would enter the room. Extra pillows were pushed up against the crack at the bottom of the door, and a DO NOT DISTURB sign hung on the doorknob outside.

The light of the single lamp illuminating the grubby little room was already dim, and then vanished altogether when Ty turned the knob on it as he finished making the room into a cave for the day. Lily's heart tripped in her chest as the room was plunged into blackness, and her eyes, unaccustomed to it, blinked sightlessly. Her breathing grew gratingly loud in her own ears. Ty made no sound at all.

Then the bed dipped beneath his weight.

"Give me your hands, *mo bhilis.*"

His voice scraped deliciously over her nerves, like fingernails over velvet. Against her will, Lily felt her awareness of him heightening. He smelled of moonlight, and the very nearness of him made her skin tingle in anticipation.

"Why?"

"So I can tie them, of course."

"You're going to tie my hands again?" Lily asked, hoping the pang of hurt she felt wasn't obvious in her voice. How could he tie her now? Yesterday she had hated it, but at least she had understood. Now, though, he had opened up to her, at least a little. He'd made her feel like she was something more than just a pawn in all of this. And her reward for responding to his kindness was to be bound like a prisoner?

"You don't need to do that this time," she said firmly. "If I was going to try anything stupid, I would have done it by now."

"Glad to hear it," Tynan said, his velvet voice far more soothing than his words. "Still, I'm sure an intelligent woman like yourself would agree that, given the situation, a little insurance is in order. What would I do if, for instance, you decided to get up, have a peek out the window, and wound up incinerating me? Or you could just decide to murder me in my sleep. Stranger things have happened." His voice was infuriatingly reasonable.

"I'm not like that."

"I don't know you," he replied, his soft purr now edged with warning. It shouldn't have bothered her. What did she care what this creature thought of her? And yet his casual assertion that she could do something either stupid or homicidal if he left her untied rankled.

"I'm not an idiot," she said, sounding a little more snappish than she'd intended. "I told you that I want to know what my tattoo means. Besides, didn't we already establish that if I run, I'll still have an assassin after me? And I don't have any wooden stakes on me. I'm no Buffy. I'd be toast."

She heard his snort in the darkness and realized she'd managed to amuse him. Knowing he thought she was being funny didn't exactly make her feel any better.

"What?" she asked irritably.

"You can't kill us with stakes, sweet. You'd need a blade. Think you've got the strength to cut off a man's head?"

She kept her voice deliberately sweet when she answered him. "If you're that curious, I'm willing to try."

This time he laughed, and the silken sound of it sent a shiver of pleasure down Lily's back. This was ridiculous, sparring with him, deliberately egging him on, though the information about how to kill a vampire was at least useful, if completely nauseating. But she was glad to have pulled Ty back out of cold-blooded vampire minion mode and glad it hadn't even taken much effort.

"You've got a mouth on you, woman."

She could hear his smile in the words, turning the insult into a sort of backhanded compliment. Lily felt her own lips curving up in return, felt her tense muscles beginning to relax with their easy banter. Ty's eyes lit as he watched her, cat's eyes glowing a soft silver through the thick darkness that surrounded them. They were all she could see.

"My mouth is part of my charm."

"Aye. That it is." There was a rough edge to his words, and tension flooded back into Lily's system, though this time it was of a very different sort. She knew he was looking at her lips. They felt warm, as though his gaze were a sort of kiss. Desire, unwanted but undeniable, fluttered nervously in her belly. Disconcerted, Lily tried to shift the conversation back into safer territory.

"Look, Ty. The point is, I won't mutilate your corpse, and I won't fry you. I won't even run up the telephone bill. But you're not tying me up again." She paused, wondering if an appeal to his better nature was worthwhile. But the heat in his eyes decided for her.

"Being tied up in a hotel room all day while you sleep, or whatever, really creeps me out. I only managed to sleep yesterday because I was exhausted. Today, I'll just be sitting here. Please don't do that to me."

He hesitated for a moment.

Then his hand brushed hers. Lily pulled away with a jerk, startled by the sensation of his skin against hers, by the way her lack of sight seemed to have intensified her sense of touch. Caught entirely off guard, she could only utter a single word.

"Please," she said, her voice little more than a whisper.

His voice was soft, husky, and strangely soothing. "Give me your hands, *mo bhilis*. I won't hurt you," he coaxed. "I can help you, I think. If you let me."

It was so appealing, the thought of letting another soothe her, of giving over just a bit of control so that she could rest. And as strange as it was, she felt certain that Ty was sincere in his offer. Just another puzzling piece of what was shaping up to be a very appealing whole.

"Are you still going to tie me up?"

"I can't take the chance of leaving you free, no matter how small the possibility of you escaping. But it won't matter to you if you sleep. Let me help you, Lily. I don't have many gifts, but this is one I'm glad to share with you. One I promise you'll appreciate."

She relented. It was an offer she knew she'd be a fool to refuse. Lily wordlessly held her hands toward him, where they were caught in a grip that was surprisingly gentle. He began to wrap a length of what felt like thin rope around her wrists, binding her hands with a knot that felt intricate even without seeing it. She dipped her head, trying to watch what her eyes struggled to pick up in the darkness. Each subtle brush of his skin against hers was a torment to her, but not because he repulsed her, Lily found to her chagrin. Memories of their first encounter came flooding back, and she felt heat rush into her system as she recalled what it was like to have those hands in her hair, his body against hers.

His lips on her skin.

"Don't look at what I'm doing. Look into my eyes," he said. His voice was low, hypnotic, pulling Lily's gaze right where he wanted it. Her breath caught in her throat at the way his eyes glowed, as bright as twin moons. There was such power there, the sort of strength and ruthless determination that no human could possess. Unnerved, she tried to look away, but she was caught, seemingly unable to move. Panic bloomed quickly in her chest.

"No, no, don't do that," he murmured, and again his voice was a balm to her frayed nerves. "Relax, Lily. Just look at me, and let everything else go. Just for now. No more worry. No more fear. Just you and me, here and now. Let go."

Her breathing slowed. Ty's words felt like a caress, and she found that it was easy, so wonderfully easy, to focus on the moment so long as she kept her eyes locked with his. As his hands moved over hers, winding the cord, she found it harder and harder to care about him tying her up. His touch was gentle, and Lily relaxed into it. His words echoed in her mind like a chant.

Just you and me... you and me... you and me...

Tynan finished securing her wrists, but his hands lingered on her skin, his flesh cool against her own warmth, maintaining the connection that seemed to sizzle and snap between them the longer it went on. Through her blissful fog, Lily was suddenly very aware of his nearness, of the intense focus that was now entirely on her.

It seemed so natural, so right, to let the peace Ty had given her shift shape and form ever so slightly to become need. Something deep in the recesses of her consciousness wanted to struggle, but Lily turned away from it, wanting nothing but the sanctuary of Ty's silver gaze. The horrors of the night fell away, leaving nothing but the moment. Her breasts felt fuller, tighter, and desire twisted into a pleasurable little knot deep in her belly.

Long, elegant fingers caressed her hands, and an errant thumb rubbed across her knuckles, sending shivers of sensation up her arms. Lily's breath grew shallow as Ty's hands slid up to her elbows, cupping them as he moved closer, slinking forward as smoothly as the cat he could become. Lily drank in the energy he seemed to radiate, the wild scent of him. Her lips parted in anticipation.

The long, seductive sound he made as he moved in, as she felt herself leaning in to meet him, vibrated all the way through her. Lily's breath caught on a gasp as moisture pooled between her legs, that knot of desire twisting tighter and making her throb.

She had made him purr like that.

"Lily," Ty said, exhaling her name like a prayer. "Just a taste. One taste, and no more."

She had the fleeting thought that he was making a promise not to her but to himself. However, an instant later he'd slid over her, pressing his lean, rangy body against her own, and Lily could no more hold a thought than she could push him away. He eased her back against the mattress in one swift, fluid movement. Then her arms, the only barrier between them, were extended above her head, and Lily was fused against a form that seemed designed to mold perfectly with her own. One of Ty's hands skimmed down the length of her, and she arched beneath his touch. In this moment, it seemed pointless to deny the connection between them. All Lily could do, all she wanted to do, was revel in it.

His hand returned to cup one aching breast as Ty rose above her for a breathless second, the lips she had imagined countless times but never tasted barely an inch from her own. And his eyes, glowing in the dark, were beautiful, burning...

Then he plunged in, taking her mouth in a slow and drowning kiss, melting into Lily until thought gave way to pure sensation, until she didn't know where she ended and Ty began. Her body rose beneath him, restless with the need for *more*, *now*. Waves of pleasure flowed through her, over her as Ty's mouth, surprisingly soft, moved against her own. He tasted her, tongue rubbing against hers in lazy strokes that deepened as Lily moved against him.

"Sweet," he whispered against her mouth. He sounded as dazed as she felt.

Yes, was all she could think as his breathing roughened, as that tight, lean body surged more insistently against hers. Lily shifted, capturing him between her thighs so that the rigid length of him was nestled firmly against the part of her that was now slick and swollen with pure need. He pressed his hips into her once, almost tentatively, on a shuddering breath that caught on a moan, and Lily felt something within her, something dark and hungry, rear its head.

It wanted to bite, to claw, to take. To *feed*.

It was like nothing she had ever felt before. But it felt good, felt right, to give over to it here in the dark. She surged upward against him, turning the kiss rough, demanding. Her pulse quickened as she began to lick and nip, catching Ty's lower lip between her teeth and pulling it before letting go. She heard him growl in response, a sound utterly inhuman, and it only fueled the wild need that was pushing her on.

In Ty, even her darker side had found its match.

His hand tightened on her breast, giving it a rough squeeze, then delivering a sharp tweak to the taut bud of her nipple. Lily quivered at the pleasure, the bit of pain that only made it sweeter.

"Shall I take you there, Lily?" he asked hoarsely. "I can feel how close you are.... Ah, gods..." He breathed a word she didn't understand, Gaelic, she assumed. It was sensual coming from his mouth no matter the meaning. Then Ty rocked his hips into her again, beginning a grinding rhythm that had Lily's breathing going ragged. She clenched her fists and twisted into him, wanting nothing more than to have her hands on him, to have his hands on her bare flesh. Pressure began to build deep inside her, pulsing in time to Ty's movement as he continued to devour her.

His breath, shallow and catching, only incited her. His head dropped forward on a raw moan, and she couldn't think, couldn't recall anything that had ever existed outside of this. The fact that she was at his mercy gave her a dark thrill that would have shocked her had she been able to do more than just feel. As did the knowledge that in a way, he was just as much at hers.

She wanted him buried inside of her, wanted to put her hands on him, to explore him without these clothes that chafed roughly between them.

Even then, it might not be enough.

She could feel his heart racing, pounding in time with her own. Could feel him trembling like a man at the edge of his control.

Then he was gone, flinging himself with a furious curse onto the other side of the bed with a force hard enough to nearly send Lily bouncing off her own side. The rusty old bedsprings squeaked in protest, but Ty said nothing. All she could hear was his ragged breathing. And all the lovely oblivion of Ty's gift, the removal of everything but pleasure and the immediacy of the moment, vanished. A hollow and insistent ache was all that remained in its wake. Soon, it was accompanied by Lily's confusion and her shame. She had let go, opened up.

And he had rejected her.

Outside, the sun was doubtless on its way up into the sky, the world growing light. But in here, it was time for the vampire to sleep. And despite the toxic swirl of emotions roiling inside of her, Lily decided she'd be damned if Ty was going to pass out without saying *something* to her about what had just happened. Her head was still spinning, and she ached in places she wasn't even aware could ache from sheer pent-up, unfulfilled sexual energy. Half of her wanted to punch him for taking such complete advantage, and never mind how accommodating she'd been.

The other half of her was seriously considering crawling over there and having her way with him. That was the half that frightened her, the half she was trying very hard to ignore. But Lily had seen, without a doubt, that she wasn't alone in this odd bond she felt with him. It was Ty's reaction to it that had her cheeks burning in the dark.

"Well?" she finally asked, her voice a hoarse whisper. "Aren't you going to at least say *something*?"

He did. Ty's ragged brogue couldn't conceal the contempt, the utter disgust, in his tone.

"Damn you, woman," he said.

"What?"

"You weren't supposed to like it."

Her mouth dropped open. In an instant, everything he'd made her feel withered and dried into something twisted and repulsive.

Never again, Lily thought, though the taste of him still lingered on her lips, and her mouth was deliciously swollen from his tender assault. She had trusted him. She'd made a mistake.

"You're a bastard, *Tynan*," she said by way of good night.

"I am," he replied after a moment, his voice tight. "And you'd do well not to forget that."

It was the last he said before his breathing turned deep and even, solving at least one puzzle for Lily about the nature of vampire rest during the day. The man wasn't dead. He was just asleep. The asshole.

She lay there for quite some time, seething and listening to the slow and steady rhythm of Ty's breath. Eventually, though she hadn't thought it possible, Lily drifted off as well.

And dreamed of fires in the darkness.

chapter EIGHT

I$_T$ HAD BEEN YEARS since she'd been to Chicago.

Lily found she barely remembered it, though really, most of her young memories of trips were little more than mental snapshots of the insides of opulent hotels and an ever-changing sea of nannies. Even if she had gotten out enough in the city to form clear memories of the place, Lily was pretty sure she wouldn't have been in this part of town, except maybe by accident. She looked around, trying not to gawk at the fascinating sea of people wandering around her. She saw hair in every color of the rainbow, piercings in places she had never considered sticking a sharp object through, and lots of leather and vinyl. And rubber. And metal.

Every face was deathly pale.

Ty walked beside her, looking far less out of place than she felt. She looked like, well, normal, she guessed. Cute and boring. Ty, on the other hand, looked like a modern-day Heathcliff, stalking the city streets instead of the moors.

His long black coat coiled around his legs as he moved, and it was a struggle to keep up with his long stride—not that Lily would ever have admitted it.

"Stop staring. It's slowing you down."

His tone was dry, but Lily thought she detected a hint of amusement. She slid a heated glance at him, set her jaw, and just kept moving. There was no way he was getting a reaction from her. Not after what he'd done, and after all the angry, awkward silence of the drive here from the motel.

Of course, all the anger seemed to be on *her* part now, Lily thought. Ty ran hot and cold. Caught up in her brooding, she had to dodge quickly to avoid a bald-headed woman, at least six feet tall, who seemed to have an unhealthy affection for safety pins and who looked a lot like Pinhead from *Hellraiser.*

The wind had a bite to it tonight, and it chilled the tip of Lily's nose, which was full of the scent of smog and the promise of rain, along with whatever they were cooking at a little Chinese place across the street. Her stomach growled pitifully. She was pretty sure Ty had forgotten that she needed to eat regularly, but pride wouldn't let her whine about it. Not yet anyway. The doughnut and soda she'd grabbed at the 7-Eleven a few hours ago would have to do.

"Watch it," Ty warned her as her head swiveled after another strange character, making her stumble over a bit of heaved sidewalk.

"I'm not *staring*," she hissed, even as she goggled at a guy about her own age who was pretty cute, actually, and who'd managed to get his hair into foot-long liberty spikes all over his head. He winked at her, and Lily couldn't help the answering smile, despite everything, before blushing and ducking her head. An instant later, Ty had silently caught her arm and looped it through his own.

"I'd thought it would go without saying, but flirting will *also* slow us down."

She glowered at him and tried to pull away. "I'm not flirting. Not that it's any of your business if I did."

He gave her a quick look, and the intensity in those eyes made her want to melt into a puddle right there on the sidewalk. *Stupid*, she thought, her anger bubbling back to the surface.

"*Mo bhilis*, I thought I told you. For now, everything about you is my business." His grip turned to iron, and she very nearly dug in her heels to let him try and drag her down the street. The strong suspicion that he actually would was the only thing that kept her walking.

"Don't call me your stupid little pet name," Lily muttered. "And don't talk to me. I just want to get this over with."

Ty blew out a long breath beside her, and his quick stride first slowed, then stopped. Lily reluctantly looked over at him as people flowed around them, unconcerned. Ty tipped his head back, looking into a sky too bright to reveal its stars. He was silent a moment, but Lily held her tongue, interested despite herself in what he would say.

"Look. About this morning…"

Lily watched his face and found that she didn't have it in her to slice into him with a comeback. His uncertainty, and his sincerity, were both too real and too raw. After a moment, he lowered his head to meet her gaze with a look of grim determination.

"I shouldn't have touched you. It isn't like me to take

advantage. Not like that. I don't expect you to believe me, but that much is true."

Lily tipped her head to one side, genuinely curious. "Then why did you?"

Ty pressed his lips together, looking at the ground with a frown. "I don't know, Lily. Something about you... It doesn't matter why," he said, cutting himself off with a frustrated shake of his head. "What matters is that I started to lose control with you, and that can't happen. Not when the most important thing is keeping you safe. Too much depends on it."

"I wasn't safe?" Lily asked, remembering the way she had felt in his arms, beautiful and powerful and as safe as she had ever felt in her life. Ty lifted his gaze to lock with hers, and the barely leashed hunger in it was stunning— and darkly thrilling.

"When I touch you," he said softly, "I want my teeth in you. And that would mean the death of an entire dynasty. I can keep you safe from anything else—Damien, an entire army of Shades, anything that walks the night. I hadn't realized I would have to work quite so hard to keep you safe from me."

She was unused to blunt honesty, but it touched her in a way no other apology might have. Lily nodded. "Apology accepted. And...thank you."

His dark brows winged up. "For?"

She gave him a small, tentative smile. "For explaining. And for bothering to apologize at all."

"Oh. Well." He ran a hand through his hair and found something interesting to focus on somewhere off to his left. "We should get going. Mabon's not far, and I'd like to get there before the place is completely packed. The earlier it is, the better the chance we'll be able to get a moment with Anura."

They set off again, and this time Lily let her hand rest easily in the crook of Ty's arm. Maybe it was foolish, but Ty's uncomfortable honesty had made her only more certain that if she had to be dragged into the vampire underworld, he was the right man to keep her safe.

As they made their way down the street, Lily's thoughts turned to Bay and the lunch date they were supposed to have had. Maybe she could find a way to call and just let her friend know she was okay, if she could ever get away from Ty long enough to do it. She had no doubt that Bay had discovered the mess left behind and had already assumed the worst. Knowing that this was causing her friend— who had one of the best hearts she'd ever encountered— pain was a terrible feeling.

One more thing to worry about. Though she supposed her parents would revel in it if she made the news, jumping at the chance to play the grieving victims. Finally, she'd done something that might please them.

Sighing, and annoyed at herself for the bitter turn her thoughts had taken, Lily tucked a lock of hair behind her ear and narrowly avoided another collision. Ty seemed to be navigating for one, not two, in his hurry to reach the club.

"I had no idea how many of you there were," she said, throwing Ty's "no staring" rule to the wind and craning her neck to take in everything she could. The neighborhood was a little dingy, but fascinating. And even though it was a Wednesday night, the streets were alive with the denizens of the underworld. There were a few regular people like her scattered about, but not many, and they stuck out like sore thumbs. Did they know what they walked among? Lily wondered. Did they care?

"Hmm?" Ty glanced at her absently. He seemed to be looking for something, and Lily could see, when she looked more closely, that he was scenting out the place too. Weird and kind of...cool, she decided. She would much rather be able to turn into a cat at will than be able to toss furniture with her mind.

"I didn't know," Lily repeated, and when he looked at her blankly, she realized he hadn't heard a word she'd said. He stopped, arching an eyebrow at her as though she was speaking a foreign language. Lily sighed, glanced around to make sure no one was listening, then stood on tiptoe to reach his ear and whisper, "All of these vampires. I didn't know there were so many of you!"

When she drew back, Ty finally seemed to understand, and amusement flickered across his serious features.

"Humans have the most ridiculous ideas," Ty said as they walked, a bit more slowly now. "Those aren't vampires. All mortal, I'm afraid."

Lily frowned over at him. "Then where *are* the vampires?"

"Going about their business quietly, and probably stopping to laugh once in a while at the spectacle around them. Mabon was here before this crowd moved in, but I suppose it does give it some atmosphere." He glanced around and snorted. "Fools, the lot of them. They sense us. They want what we have. They've no idea what they're inviting."

A group of college-aged girls swept by them, looking dark, gorgeous, and like they'd happily eat the heart of any man who crossed their path. Ty looked unimpressed, but Lily felt a pang of envy as she watched them go, imagining how drab she must seem in comparison. She'd always longed for the confidence to live completely out loud. Instead, she had become the quiet watcher, guarding her secrets, protecting what was hers. Blending in.

"You're prettier," Ty said, and she realized he'd been watching her, along with every transparent emotion that had crossed her face.

Lily looked at him, then away, flustered. "I thought you said you couldn't read my mind."

"I can't. It's right there on your face."

Damn.

"It's nothing," she said. "I just feel a little weird. This is like...like the prairie schoolmarm visits Wes Craven's imagination. I look ridiculous wandering around here."

Ty considered her as he steered her around a corner. "In my experience, the tastiest morsels require a bit of unwrapping. You shouldn't worry so much. Queen Cobweb back there isn't anything *but* wrapping. And trust me, she'd taste terrible."

The icky face he made, so sincere, made her laugh.

That was, until she realized he'd steered her around the corner into a darkened alley. She tried to slow him down, but it worked about as well as it had the night before, which was not at all. Her heart began to hammer in her chest. They were, as she recalled, here because they planned on actually meeting more vampires. She just hadn't counted on it happening quite so soon.

Not *ever* would have been preferable, but that ship had sailed.

About halfway down the alley, which was shrouded in darkness, Ty stopped and turned to face her. Lily saw the tension etched onto his features, and her own stress immediately went through the roof.

"Oh, God, don't tell me. Is it Damien? Were we followed?" Her voice was shaky, and she felt only marginally better when Ty shook his head.

"No. It's just...there's something you need to put on before we go down."

He dug in his pockets and pulled out a wad of fabric. Lily stared, confused, as he undid it, revealing a length of crimson velvet ribbon. She watched his fingers work, fascinated by the graceful elegance of them. She didn't understand what the big deal was about the ribbon, but it had to be something worth worrying over. She hadn't seen him this agitated since he'd scented whatever had been stalking them at the college.

Curious, nervous, Lily simply waited for him to explain.

"Lift your hair," he said. She did, beginning to understand what he was going to do, if not the purpose of it. His skin brushed hers lightly as he looped the ribbon behind her neck, then tied it in a small bow at the side. He had to get close to do it, close enough for Lily to feel his breath on her face. She fought back a shiver, both wanting and not wanting his gentle ministrations to continue and remembering his warning.

He finished quickly enough, though Lily could swear his fingers lingered just a moment longer on the quickening beat of her pulse. In that instant, his eyes changed again, and she saw that terrible hunger, that longing. The beauty, and the sadness of it, took her breath away.

What happened to you? she wondered, recognizing unhealed wounds. After all, she had a few of her own.

Then it was done. Lily licked her lips, wishing for a bit of moisture in a mouth that had gone as dry as the desert.

The tiny flicker of her tongue drew Ty's attention for an instant, but she saw his jaw tighten as he looked away.

"What's this for?" she asked, her voice sounding unfamiliar to her. Husky. Inviting. It was hardly on purpose, but the dark desire he'd stirred in her early this morning, that unfamiliar midnight creature she'd felt herself become beneath his talented hands, seemed destined to rear its head whenever he got this close.

"It means you're a *sura*." His voice dropped to a low murmur. "That would be a vampire's—in this case my—uh…concubine."

The ribbon suddenly felt tight enough to choke. "C-concubine?"

He didn't look any happier than she felt, though it was small consolation.

Ty blew out a breath and shifted restlessly. "Look, there's only one reason a mortal woman would be in a vampire club. She'd have to belong to someone there. Some keep only one human lover. Those who can afford to have a bit of variety in their lives have more. It makes sense," he continued, a little defensively, "to keep a willing blood donor on hand, rather than risking your life with the hunt every night."

"Uh-huh," Lily said, glowering. "Then why do you look like you want to throw up?"

"This club we're heading into, Mabon, is a bit rough. As I told you before, it's a mixed club, which means plenty of lowbloods looking for a good time and a handful of highbloods slumming it and looking for women, trouble, or both. Don't act shocked by anything, and for God's sake, don't stare. I don't want the wrong vamps taking notice of you. Anura was never one to hide in the shadows, so let's hope we find her quickly."

She did hope. If she was risking her life by heading into a place full of people who might want to eat her, it would be nice if it weren't for nothing. And anything that delayed her meeting with Arsinöe the vampire queen was welcome, since that was an event in her life she still hadn't really wrapped her mind around. Still, this concubine business...

"So I'm supposed to, what, make goo-goo eyes at you and walk around like I've been partially lobotomized?"

He looked irritated. "That's what a good thrall looks like, yeah. And if I could get one to work on you, believe me, I would. But as it is, you're stuck acting. Think you can manage it?"

If he could get one to work on me... Lily remembered that intense pull she'd felt toward Ty that first night, the fuzzy-brained compulsion to throw herself into his arms that had taken her completely by surprise. She guessed that was what he was talking about, along with the fact that she seemed able to throw it off, though barely, where he was concerned. Damien had tried and she'd felt nothing. What he'd done to her this morning probably counted as some sort of mild thrall, but he'd needed her full cooperation, and it had hardly been mind control. Still, she'd need to be on her guard. Just in case.

"If there's one thing I can manage," Lily said, "it's acting." It might not have been in her blood, but it had been a big part of her life for a lot of years. And not in a good way.

But though she would never admit it, a night spent fawning over Ty wouldn't be much of a chore to manage. At all. She might even get to paw at him a little.

Oh, she was a sick, sick girl. Lily hunched her shoulders a little and sighed, which Ty seemed to take for resignation. That was fine with her.

"Come on, then," he said. "It's the next alley over."

She started to follow. "Don't worry about me," she said. "I'm not that noticeable. I'll blend."

Ty didn't look at her, but his voice was grim. "The hell you will."

chapter NINE

MABON WAS HIDDEN out of necessity, and it was cheap because its patrons insisted it be and grungy because it always had been. The club's only entrance was down a small alley, through a nondescript door. A flight of stairs led down to what had once been the basement of a sprawling old building from the turn of the century, and despite its questionable reputation, the place was always packed with vampires looking for one of two things: blood or trouble.

Often, the unwary found both.

Lily was plenty wary by the time she and Ty pushed open a heavy metal door and entered the cavernous, dimly lit club. He'd told her not to stare, but it was hard not to be a little shocked at first glance. No wonder he'd chuckled over the human wannabes up above. Because it looked to her like vampires, real ones, were far more apt to make wardrobe choices as unobtrusive as her own. There was only one noticeable difference between them and the rest of humanity: these people were freaking gorgeous.

Eyes that shimmered and glowed faintly in the half-light turned toward them as they walked in, full of little more than polite curiosity. Two bouncers, muscular and intimidating, lounged just inside the entrance. One wore a sleeveless T-shirt, and a tribal tattoo, intricate and beautiful, coiled all the way down his arm. His eyes, a luminous blue, flickered over Lily with interest, and she saw him take note of the ribbon around her neck.

"Evening, beautiful," he said with a lazy half smile. "Welcome to Mabon."

"She's mine," Ty growled beside her, drawing the bouncer's attention away from her.

Lily flushed at the hot possession she heard in those words. No one had ever sounded that way when they'd talked about her. She kept her eyes on his face, hoping she looked enamored enough.

"Humph," the bouncer grunted. "Bet she's not by the end of the night. Your mark, stranger."

She watched Ty's jaw tighten, saw the dangerous flash in his eyes. "Since when does Mabon check for bloodline? All used to be welcome here. Has that changed?"

The bouncer just glared at him, and it was obvious he wasn't budging, so Ty bared his mark with an angry little jerk of his hand. She saw the other man's surprise—and more than a hint of displeasure.

"It hasn't changed as long as you're not here to make any trouble. Anura told us to start checking marks after a few ankh-wearing assholes came in a couple of weeks ago and made a lot of trouble for her—and us. Ptolemy aren't welcome here right now."

"I'm not Ptolemy," Ty said flatly.

"No? Looks to me like they own you. And cats don't

usually get to keep a *sura* like this unless they've been behaving real well for their masters." The bouncer leaned in close, his voice dropping. "In fact, I've never seen a cat keep a *sura* at all. I know who you are, hunter. Tell your queen he's not here, and go away."

Lily's heart began to pound as she felt the level of furious male testosterone go right through the roof. The other bouncer, who was just as huge as the one accosting them, was watching very closely. And she could see, out of the corner of her eye, that they were starting to generate some interest from some of the vampires near them.

Ty kept his voice just as low, and just as dangerous. "I don't know who you think I'm looking for, but I'm not here on behalf of the queen. I came to see Anura, actually, for reasons that are personal and therefore none of your damned business. But if you'd prefer I make a scene, I assure you, I have no problem shedding some blood to get in, and it's going to be yours. My reputation is well earned."

They stared at each other for a long moment, and Lily worried that the bouncer wouldn't back down, though she found she believed every word Ty said. But finally, she saw the bouncer's shoulders relax as he stepped back. Still, his eyes were frigid.

"Fine. She's dancing. But I'm warning you, if I catch wind you're sniffing around for deserters, it's your head. The Ptolemy have no power here," he sneered. "The Dracul are in charge of Chicago, and they let the Empusae think they have a hand in running things, but all the Ptolemy can do is watch from a distance and dream about what they can't have. No matter how much they want it." His eyes shifted to Lily. "Take my advice, honey. Do some flirting, trade up. You can do way better than some gutter cat, no matter whose skirts he gets to hide behind."

Though she was sure that was going to be the last straw, that Ty would stand and fight (not that she would have blamed him), he merely dragged her into the club with little more than a threatening, feral growl at the bouncer, who leaned back against the wall, satisfied.

She gripped his arm, hard, trying to get his attention. When he didn't so much as look at her, she moved in front of him, and remembering what he'd said about appearances, pressed herself against him so that she could look enamored while whispering furiously in his ear.

"What the hell was that about? Why did you let him talk to you like that?"

He slid his arm around her waist, pulling her closer. It was an intimate embrace, completely at odds with the anger she heard in his voice.

"Would you rather I'd ripped out his throat? I told you, Lily, things work differently here. I need to find Anura and find out what's going on, if she'll talk to me. Just stay close. And don't look at anyone."

He drew back with a warning look and then turned, grabbing her hand to lead her through the crowd.

It was telling, she thought, that he hadn't even mentioned the fact that the bouncer had treated him with undisguised disgust. In fact, if she wasn't mistaken, that wasn't even what was bothering him about the encounter. He'd told her that his line were considered "gutterbloods," but still, actually seeing it and Ty's acceptance of it filled Lily with outrage. The only consolation was that the bouncer seemed to have a healthy amount of respect for Ty's prowess, even if he had none for him as a fellow vampire. Otherwise, she was pretty sure they'd both be back outside right now trying to decide on next steps.

As it was, Lily found herself getting her first look at a vampire's idea of a good night out, and even though Ty had told her not to stare, she found it hard to do anything else.

It was decadent. She didn't know how else to describe it. Somehow, a vast expanse of concrete basement had been turned into a den of ragged opulence and open debauchery. The floors had been covered in hardwood, which still gleamed despite years of feet and who knew what else on it. A massive circular bar dominated the center of the space, though Lily wasn't certain she wanted to know what was dispensed into the heavy crystal goblets that hung suspended above the bartenders' heads and that they continually plucked to fill with whatever was hidden behind the wall of people obscuring the counter from view. Music throbbed and pulsed, blending with the rise and fall of the many voices as the vampires chattered, flirted, and fought. And Lily was pretty sure she caught a glimpse of a dance floor at the far end of the room. It was almost funny: a club like this existing, unknown, in the middle of a neighborhood full of humans who seemed like they would be hunting for just such a place.

The walls were covered in silken fabric, shimmering in the light of hundreds of candles. They were everywhere, flickering in sconces, dancing on the tall, glass-topped tables scattered randomly about, making what should have been a dark, dank place seem to glow. Concrete pillars had been encased in wood, in marble. Gilt-edged mirrors reflected the feral eyes of the crowd. And though Lily found herself stunned by the place, it was the crowd that she couldn't look away from.

At first glance, she'd thought they looked like beautiful mortals, some dressed impeccably, others in jeans. But to look for more than a few moments was to see the truth. Their eyes danced with light that had nothing to do with the candles, and each mouth that opened to speak, to laugh, to snarl, revealed a pair of shining fangs. Many wore clothing that bared their marks, and some seemed to have incorporated more tattoo work, as the bouncer had, to showcase and enhance the signs of their bloodlines. They moved like dancers, quick and graceful, and the collective sound of their voices was as musical as the song that throbbed sinuously throughout the room. And as far as throbbing went...

Ty squeezed her hand tightly and gave her a quick yank when he caught her gaping, wide-eyed, at two incredible-looking men sharing a pretty blonde who also had a ribbon at her throat. One was behind her, one in front, and both had their teeth in her neck. The blonde, however, didn't seem to mind. Her eyes were closed, her face contorted with pleasure, and her skirt had been hiked up to accommodate—

"If you don't want to be invited to join them, then quit bloody *looking* at them," Ty growled in her ear. Lily could only swallow hard and nod. She managed to tear her eyes away, though she couldn't seem to catch her breath. She'd had a taste of what that woman was feeling, she realized. But seeing that, seeing how it could be, imagining how it might be if Ty decided to push her up against the wall...

She stumbled a little as Ty dragged her forward, and she caught sight of another couple locked in a similarly erotic embrace. It didn't seem to bother anyone; a few watched, casually interested, while most ignored. There were no boundaries here, Lily realized, or at least not the same ones that applied in most parts of the human world.

Her chest suddenly felt tight, her skin too sensitive. And her palm, clutched in Ty's hand, went slick with sweat and heat. Her entire life had been about control and, to a certain extent, denial. To be thrust into a place where it seemed to be encouraged, even celebrated, to have neither was more than a little overwhelming.

And surprisingly tempting.

The air smelled like incense and wax, and Lily wondered whether she'd ever be able to smell either again without being swamped by lust.

Then Ty's breath was feathering her ear, sending hot little shivers over her skin, and she knew she wouldn't.

"There," he said. "I can see Anura, in the white, dancing. If she asks you anything, don't answer—let me do the talking. Things have changed here. I'm just not sure how much."

It struck Lily that Ty didn't seem to be affected the way she had. If anything, he seemed more tense. She looked past him, into the crowd, and immediately saw the woman he meant. Lily got only a fleeting glimpse of a dark-haired beauty dancing with an abandon Lily had only ever dreamed of, before another voice sounded, dangerously close.

"Well, well," murmured a voice into her ear. "How did a gutterblood ever get his teeth into you, beautiful? I think it's time you moved up in the world."

Lily stiffened. Tynan growled. She was fairly certain that the night had just gone completely to hell.

chapter TEN

DAMIEN TREMAINE LEANED casually against the building not a block from Mabon, watching the stinking sea of humanity mill blindly around him. It had been so long since he had been one of them; he really had no memory of it. Oh, he could recall various things he had done, people he had known, places he had seen, but the memory of what it had truly meant to be human, to live and breathe with the knowledge of his own mortality, had vanished.

He would never be part of "good" vampire society, would always wear a mark that kept that from him. But he had worked for many of them and had picked up quite a few of their attitudes, particularly about the limited uses for mortals. And why not? The House of Shadows was its own sort of aristocracy, Damien reasoned. It could provide a good life, if not an easy one. And fortunately for the Shades like him who had built formidable reputations of their own, there was no possibility that they would be driven out or disappear.

The highbloods, vicious, weak-minded fools that they were, had forgotten how to exist without them.

The cell phone in his pocket vibrated, and Damien took the call. It was nothing he wanted to deal with, but it had to be taken care of. Hell had no fury like an unhappy customer.

"Tremaine."

The voice on the other end of the line was so cold Damien could almost feel the chill air oozing from the phone.

"Damien. Tell me, what exactly am I paying you for? Because despite the fact that I'm out a fairly large chunk of cash, I do seem to have forgotten *why*."

The voice was calm, subdued, even. But Damien had learned that beneath the calm veneer was the sort of monster one rarely encountered anymore among his kind. Most highbloods were pompous cowards, looking for others to do their dirty work for them. Not this one, though. Behind the beautiful mask, this one was pure darkness.

Damien fought the urge to squirm. He could handle this. He'd been requested specifically because he could.

"The woman's not what we expected." He remembered the mark that had glittered on her collarbone, the shock of it. He might not have believed it, except for what she had done. Except for the power that had ripped through him like a force of nature.

"I think you'd better explain yourself," the voice hissed. "Because a Seer is just a squishy little mortal with a better-developed mind. And to have it take this long is *unconscionable*."

Damien suffered a moment of indecision, a rarity for him. But he pushed through it quickly enough and relayed, in hushed and urgent tones, what he had seen and all that had occurred. After all, it had little to do with him. He was being paid for a service. Best to just provide that service and get on with his own business.

Besides, this one would be a dangerous enemy to make, should he suddenly decide to grow a conscience. This one, Damien felt sure, would *know*. Then he'd be the one disappearing.

When he'd finished, there was a long silence. Damien waited, very still. It was one of his gifts, his stillness, and one that had contributed greatly to his abilities as a killer. Tynan had learned much, but he'd never learned that. He'd always been brooding and restless, and loyal enough to make him just a little bit foolish. Damien had sometimes wondered whether it would ever catch up with his old friend.

Seemed it finally had.

His employer eventually spoke, and the tone was thoughtful, deliberating, and full of a dark pleasure that managed to stir a bit of pity in Damien's breast for his pretty mark. Truly, she had no idea what was after her. She'd never had a chance.

"You're certain she's mortal," the voice said.

Damien remembered her scent, the terrified beating of her heart. They stirred him, despite himself. He'd wanted her, to feel her in his arms as she went under, to taste her. And he was suddenly certain that the pleasure was about to be taken from him.

"She's as mortal as she can be," Damien replied. "And no control over what's in her. The blood might not have died, but the knowledge that went with it seems to have. Lily Quinn is an orphan," he said, relaying the bit of pertinent information he'd dug up on her. "Parents disappeared under mysterious circumstances when she was just an infant. No next of kin, no extended family. She was adopted, but she doesn't appear to have any contact with the family. No trace of them in her house anyway. Not a picture. There's a story there, I'm sure. I can dig that up for you, if you like. Just take a little more work."

"No. No more delays. This is taking too long as it is. MacGillivray was never supposed to find anyone," the voice said flatly. "The damned cat was supposed to be an afterthought, not the center of this. But since he's put himself there and found such an interesting prize. Really, I should have known. He does seem to have an uncanny knack...."

Damien felt a muscle in his jaw twitch. No, he would not be getting the woman as a perk. That was certain.

"Well, there's no reason to waste such a fascinating creature," his employer finished. "And that the blood still has so much latent power...useless to someone like her but imagine the possibilities in the right hands...yes," the voice said, and Damien could hear loud and clear the one thing he'd found all highbloods had in common: greed.

"Kill the gutter cat. Bring the woman to me. I'll want her drugged and bound, of course. She had enough control to throw you, and I'd hate to have to kill her so quickly. Once you have her, I'll give you the location. I'll want to keep this private." The tone sharpened. "Does he know what she is?"

"No. But he wouldn't have come here first if he hadn't decided to try and find out."

"Don't let him. Those who would remember are few and far between, but I won't have word getting out."

Damien could hear the smile, and it chilled him to the bone.

"Such decisions, Damien. There are so many ways to destroy, so many ways to rule. What do you think, you mercenary little gutterblood? What would you do?"

Sensing that any answer would be both inadequate and dangerous, Damien took the high road. "I'm not interested in ruling anything but myself. Do what you like. You can, after all."

It was the right thing to say.

"Patronizing, but true. Be quick about it, Damien. I haven't got much time. And if you hold me up, you'll have even less."

Damien ended the call without a sound, looked at the phone for a moment, then tucked it back in the pocket of his overcoat. He was suddenly very, very tired and felt every minute of the centuries he'd spent just like this, stalking the prey of some spoiled noble who wanted more than they ought to have. In this case, a whole lot more.

But he was a Shade, sworn to it body and soul until the two were sundered. A man only had so many choices with a mark like his, as he'd told Ty long ago, and even fewer good ones. And as he'd told Ty before they'd parted ways with a fight that still ranked among the most bitter Damien had ever been involved in, you either chose a profession where you made the highbloods beg for your mercy or you wound up at theirs.

He had made his own destiny.

People continued to come and go in the October night, oblivious to the fact that the man by the building seemed to vanish in the blink of an eye.

Just as no one noticed the large black cat that stood in his place for only an instant, then turned a corner and vanished into shadow.

chapter ELEVEN

T Y TOOK ONE LOOK at the brawny vampire in the expensive suit and knew they were in trouble. He couldn't see the man's mark, but he didn't need to; he knew highbloods when he saw them. And this one had clamped a hand on Lily's shoulder with a grip that left no doubt as to his intentions.

Lily had gone completely still, but one look in her wide eyes told Ty she wasn't any happier about the situation than he was.

"I like it where I am, thanks," she said, trying to slide away. Ty saw the grip tighten and groaned inwardly. So much for being innocuous. But then, he'd known that having a sexy redhead on his arm would bring him trouble. He just hadn't counted on it quite so quickly.

"Please," the other man said, never even bothering to so much as glance at Ty. "I knew he was a gutter cat the second I looked at him. You can't have been with him long, honey, or you would have realized right away that you're looking at a serious difference in quality here. I'll be happy to demonstrate."

Ty felt the hairs along his neck prickle, a warning sign of a serious flare of temper. He'd learned long ago not to let these assholes and their ignorance bother him. But this particular asshole had his hands on Lily.

"She said she's happy where she is. Show the lady a bit of respect," Ty said, his voice low and raspy. It was all he could do to keep himself from growling. That got the high-blood's attention, and Ty could see right away that this one was in a fighting mood. Probably been drinking the high-test O-neg spiked with expensive vodka. He'd be ridiculously easy to take down, this egotistical stuffed shirt with his pretty face and his rheumy, red, drunken eyes.

The problem, of course, was the group of his buddies watching very intently just a few feet away. They always ran in packs, just like the werewolves they hated so much.

"Respect, huh? I think that's something you need to learn," the vampire said, his eyes narrowing as he stepped forward. "No stupid cat is going to talk to a Dracul that way. What are you gonna do? Scratch me?" His mouth split in a wide, sinister grin.

Oh, hell with it, Ty decided. He could take them, but it was probably going to be ugly. The alternative, however, was completely unacceptable. He saw a flash of understanding, then irritation, cross Lily's face.

"I thought you said you didn't want to cause a scene," she muttered.

He ignored her.

"I think I'll show you that bloodline has nothing to do with being able to kick someone's worthless ass, you piece of—"

Lily cut him off so neatly he never saw it coming and never managed to finish. She spun, as graceful as a dancer, and cozied up to the other vampire, whose curled lip left no doubt that he'd be happy to take Ty up on his offer. The sudden change in her attitude was enough to surprise both men into silence, and when she spoke, her voice was as sweet and smooth as warm honey.

"Oh, Tynan, look! Your friend is coming over to see you." She waved merrily at someone behind Ty, and a quick look showed him that a wary-looking Anura had spotted the impending scene and was on her way over. He opened his mouth to ask Lily whether she'd lost her mind, but the daft woman continued speaking, and this time it was to the man she'd snuggled up to.

"Maybe you're right," she cooed. "Maybe I should broaden my horizons a little. Do you dance? I *love* to dance," Lily purred, resting one hand lightly on the vampire's broad chest and looking deeply into his eyes.

Ty stared, completely gobsmacked. He felt a number of things in that moment, and none of them were pleasant. She couldn't possibly be thralled, could she? But then, Ty thought as invisible steel bands seemed to encircle his chest and squeeze, he had little to do with the Dracul, whom the Ptolemy hated on general principle. Maybe they had some kind of special technique...maybe he was just losing his touch.

Or maybe the woman had gone stark-raving mad.

But in any case, Lily's about-face had soothed the pompous Dracul's ruffled feathers in no time flat. Ty found he couldn't blame him. If Lily had been looking at him that way, he probably would have stopped being able to think altogether. Something ugly coiled itself into a hot knot deep in his belly.

"I'll dance as long as you're my partner," the Dracul said, just as Anura's voice sliced into the conversation.

"Ty MacGillivray. I'd say welcome back, but I've had just about enough of anyone wearing an ankh."

The Dracul looked at Anura, who was every bit as gorgeous as a goddess in high dudgeon, and then flicked a smug look back at Ty. Lily, who appeared to have lost her mind, simply gazed up adoringly.

"Oh, you're one of Arsinoë's little pets. MacGillivray...I've heard about you. Uppity gutter cat, but plenty good at killing, right?" He shrugged. "Explains the gorgeous woman, but you should have known better than to bring her out." He leaned in close, and Ty could easily scent both booze and simmering anger.

"You tell your bitch queen to keep her dirty spies out of Dracul territory. We've earned our right to be here. She keeps it up, she'll be as dead as the dust she came from," he hissed, softly enough that only Ty could hear. Then he pulled back to look at Lily. "Come on, gorgeous. I like this song."

"'Kay. Just let me say good-bye," she cooed. She leaned in to give Ty a quick peck as he stood there, wondering when the hell he'd stepped into an alternate dimension where lesser dynasties openly insulted, even threatened, the Ptolemy queen, and how exactly he was going to get Lily out of Mabon before she became some Dracul's *sura*.

Her furious whisper went a long way toward righting his universe, though he had a sudden urge to throttle her.

"I can keep him busy for a little while, but if your conversation with her takes too long, I will figure out how to cut your head off along with a few other pieces, and I am *not kidding!*" She pulled back with a placid smile, but this time he didn't miss the steely glint in her eyes.

"Later, Ty. It's been real."

She waggled her fingers at him and swept off with her new admirer, leaving Ty staring after her, thinking murderous thoughts. Anura's impatient voice quickly dragged him back to the present.

"Why are you here, Ty? I don't remember you being such a glutton for punishment, bringing your women out so they can be swiped from under your nose. Then again, I don't remember you bringing women out at all. You used to be discreet. What happened? Have the Ptolemy started punishing their servants by hitting them in the head?"

He turned to her, needing to look away from the sight of Lily sliding into another man's arms and slithering right into the song's sinuous beat.

"Anura," he said, keeping his tone as friendly as he could manage with the hot rage now boiling in his chest. "You haven't changed a bit."

She hadn't, apart from the hint of weariness around her dark, almond-shaped eyes that he didn't remember being there before. Other than that, she was still knock-you-on-your-ass stunning, every inch a Mediterranean goddess. Her long, dark hair was partially pulled up and fell to frame her face in loose curls. The rest tumbled down her back. She wore white, her favored color, and the simple one-shouldered dress was bright against her olive skin.

And she was pissed off. That was also familiar.

"Sure I have. I've got even less patience for Ptolemy bullshit than I used to." When he simply waited, used to her bluster, she huffed a curl out of her face and rolled her eyes. "Damn it, Ty, this isn't a great time for you to be here. Did *she* send you? I already told the others, I don't know where he is. I don't know anything, except that another bloodbath is really going to kill my business." Her eyes hardened. "He must have some pretty good dirt on them, for them to call out the big guns on one little Cait Sith."

Ty tried to hide his surprise, though tonight was testing his capacity to keep his reactions to himself.

"I'm here on my own time, Anura. I haven't even been at court in nearly a year."

Now it was her turn to look surprised. "Oh? Did you finally decide to run too? I wondered if you'd get tired of it eventually—though, like I said, this place isn't as ankhfree as it used to be, and way less than I'd like it to be."

She cocked her head and looked up at him, studying him, and Ty knew she'd likely see what most couldn't. She should still have been a full Empusae. She belonged with that dynasty, had been among the best of them. But her mark showed the taint that she had taken upon herself out of love, ill-advised as love could be. Her sisters had cast her out, as was the custom.

And Anura, as obstinate as she was beautiful, kept her mixed mark—a torch, the flames coiling along her collarbone like elegant scrollwork—proudly bared even now, long after the one who'd made it had gone. And wrapped around the base of the torch was a large, sharpclawed paw.

He remembered the lion who had given it to her. But the Rakshasa had been hunted to ground long ago, and Rai's blood had been shed with most of the rest.

Ty shook his head, knowing that if she caught any hint of his pity, Anura would toss him out on his rear end. "No, no, I've been…on assignment, I guess you could say. It's taken me longer than I'd thought to finish."

Her eyes darkened until they seemed almost black. "This is about the attacks."

This time he couldn't hide his surprise.

Anura nodded, her expression grim. "Yeah, word has leaked out, Ty. A little here, a little there, but you don't have a Gypsy curse rip up that many of your young and keep it completely quiet. She's done good damage control—I'd expect nothing less—but she needs to rein in her thugs until she's got some proof about who's to blame. There are way too many Ptolemy around here lately. And to say they've got a bug up their asses about the Dracul would be a serious understatement. You and I both know that relations between those two dynasties are just a tinderbox waiting to go up, and it seems like everyone's itching to light the match."

"I didn't know it had gotten so bad," Ty said, and was sorry he hadn't.

"Well, that's obvious," Anura replied.

He wondered whether she'd throw him out anyway, but instead she quirked him a half-smile. Old friendship, no matter how long neglected, trumped her worry over his presence. For now.

It made him feel like a heel for having neglected it for so long. Anura had always been generous to the castoffs. It occurred to him all at once that he had never really repaid her kindness.

"So what brings you here, Ty? And don't feed me a line. You may be a cat, but everyone knows you're the queen's man these days."

It rankled, the casual comment. More because he'd

only recently heard the same thing from Lily, the implication that he somehow *belonged* to Arsinöe. He'd always mentally separated what he did from who he was. But it seemed he'd missed the fact that no one else had. It came to him, and it bothered him more deeply than he might have imagined. But then, how long had it been since he'd even come around here? Ten years? Twenty? And even then, Ty realized, he'd been neck-deep in court business.

"I came for advice, and for information," he said, hearing the defensiveness in his own voice. Reflection was not something he cared for.

Anura's eyebrows lifted in surprise. "Advice? Well. That is flattering. Of course, I'll tell you what I think, Ty. As for the information," she continued, guarded, and he could see that things had, indeed, been rough lately, "that depends on the subject. If you came here sniffing around for Jaden, I'll just tell you what I told the others. I don't know where he is."

Jaden. The pieces fell into place, and suddenly he understood. "They came here looking for him. That's who you were talking about when you came over here. But why would they look in Chicago, of all places? He's the last person who would go hide in a herd of Dracul."

Anura frowned, looking puzzled. "Where have you *been*, Ty? This is one of a dozen Dracul strongholds where Ptolemy have shown up over the last couple of months, making their presence known, starting trouble. We had a damned bloodbath in here a couple of weeks ago that started as a shoving match between a Dracul who was minding his own business and a bunch of Ptolemy who decided to make an example of him. Insulting his bloodline, calling the dynasty illegitimate, and I won't even go into what they said about the Dracul himself. Stuff that Arsinöe would never have allowed in the past, no matter whether she agreed with it in private. A lot of highbloods have said that and worse about the Dracul, but still, this is their city." She wrapped her arms protectively around herself, eyes piercing. "*My* city. And more people than just me are beginning to fear the worst."

She meant war, of course. One dynasty against another, until one was wiped from the face of the Earth, its leader dead, its remaining members subsumed by the conquering dynasty. Such a thing hadn't happened in Ty's lifetime, but he'd heard whispers that it had been far more common in ancient times—that the very first dynasty, in fact, had fallen that way.

He didn't relish the prospect. But he also understood that sometimes it was kill or be killed.

"If the Dracul are responsible for the mass murders of Ptolemy, Anura, they deserve to vanish," Ty said. "You don't know the whole of it." He hesitated, then decided he owed her a bit of the truth. "Someone's gone and set a Mulo on them. Whole initiations have been wiped out, the bodies dismembered, the houses burned. And it's not just the young being killed anymore. Each time, whoever controls this thing ups the ante."

Anura closed her eyes, and he knew she was thinking of the purge that had claimed her beloved. For that, there had been no justice and never would be.

"Mother above. No wonder." Anura shook her head. "I appreciate the warning, Ty, though you must believe me when I say you don't know all of what's been going on either. *If* the Dracul are responsible, you may be right that they deserve all this. But without proof, this looks like an ancient and arrogant dynasty has finally found the perfect excuse to take care of the upstarts and grab a little more power while they're at it. And it seems too obvious, too easy, that they would use the Romany magic all over again to conjure a curse like a Mulo. Vlad Dracul is a lot of things, but he's no fool." She shook her head and looked out into the crowded club. "Of course, it's not like they've shared the secrets of how such things work with just anyone. Who else could it be?" She sighed heavily. "I don't know. All I want to do is run my business and be left alone."

She looked so miserable that Ty found himself in the unfamiliar position of wanting to offer comfort. The hell of it was, he had no idea how. Awkwardly, he reached out and gave her bare shoulder a tentative pat.

"Well. You'll be all right, Anura. You always are."

It didn't work exactly how he wanted, but at least Anura looked bemused.

"Oh, don't get all mushy on me, Ty. I wouldn't know what to do if the most badass Cait Sith I've ever known went soft." She brushed off his hand and glanced back out onto the dance floor.

Suddenly, he remembered Lily. She'd been dancing with that prig for three songs now.

He looked over to see Lily glaring daggers at him from over the big vampire's shoulder as they moved to the beat, plastered against each other. She could move, he saw with a hot flare of jealousy. Why was it always the prim little things who had the ability to get out on a dance floor and suddenly start oozing sex? Her partner looked like he was in seventh heaven, but a dancer he was not. And Ty recognized the way he was starting to nuzzle at her neck. Her new suitor was hungry, horny, and eager to reach the next stage of his evening with the lovely Lily.

"Do I need to rescue that poor girl?" Anura asked. "I assumed he'd managed to thrall her away from you, but she looks like she's having buyer's remorse."

"That's no thrall. She went with him because she's got odd ideas about the acceptability of me shedding blood in public places," Ty growled. "Though she threatened to shed mine if I didn't figure out a way to get her out of here peacefully in fairly short order. She knew I needed to talk to you."

Anura's laugh was low and throaty. "Tough to thrall and a little violent? I like her already. Though considering how picky you are, I shouldn't be surprised you'd settle on a good one when you finally decided to choose a *sura*." She looked at him curiously, though Ty barely registered her expression. He was too busy staring at the placement of Lily's partner's hands.

If they went any lower, he was going to make everyone very unhappy, despite Lily's best efforts.

"Ah, she's not yours yet." It was a statement, not a question. But then, Anura had always been maddeningly perceptive. He could see no reason to deny the truth, especially when he needed information from her.

"She's not mine at all," Ty said simply. "She's a Seer."

Anura paled so much that even Ty could tell in the candlelight. "Oh, by the goddess, Ty, you brought a Seer here? Why? Why would you risk her? I wasn't even sure there were any of the blood left!"

"Well, that's the problem," Ty said. "I'm not quite sure what her blood is or isn't. Long story. I'll explain, but we'll need to get her out of here first, before I make another mess in your fine establishment."

She was all fury and fear. "I'm no expert on those humans unfortunate enough to be psychic, Ty. I don't want this. Get her out of here. Get her to Arsinöe, do what you must, but go away. If she's not truly a Seer, then at least you will have delivered the queen an appetizing snack."

It wasn't like her to be so callous, but Ty could see how agitated he'd made her. Still, the thought of Lily cut down so easily sliced right through him.

"I need your help."

Anura bared her teeth. "You bring an unbitten mortal into my club and risk inciting a blood frenzy, and for what?"

"Anura, do you know of a mark that looks like a pentagram? A snake curled around the outside of it?"

She stopped short, her lovely face going completely blank for a moment. Then he saw the understanding dawn, and he had no doubt. Relief coursed through him.

She knew.

Anura looked at Lily again, more closely now. "Of course," she murmured. "Of course." Then she looked back at him, and Ty could see that whatever Anura had just realized, it was deadly serious business.

"We still need to get her out of here," she said. "Now. But I will help you. I swore I would, though I never thought I'd see the day." Her pupils, already huge, dilated until they turned her eyes black. "Blood of the goddess, Ty, what else have you brought down on me?"

That was when he smelled the smoke.

chapter **TWELVE**

IN A SINGLE INSTANT, Mabon descended into pandemonium.

Lily found herself quickly released from her partner's embrace, which would have been a lot more welcome if she hadn't been surrounded by shrieks of "Fire!"

"Come on," he said. "I'll get you out of here."

Lily shook her head and took a step back, though a quick look for Ty had shown her nothing but a crowd of people all rushing to the door. He was there; he had to be in there somewhere. He wouldn't leave her—not willingly anyway. Not after all this.

"No."

He didn't look happy about it, but he didn't reach for her either. "Suit yourself," he said, and was gone.

Despite the grayish smoke that began to coil around her ankles and the unmistakable scent of burning, Lily focused on only one thing: finding Ty. She shoved past panicked patrons, all of whom were headed toward the single exit. There were no windows, and she worried that the air would quickly become difficult to breathe. The music played on over the escalating sounds of shouting and fighting.

She knew, without a single doubt, that this was happening because she was here. Somehow, Damien had caught up, and more quickly than she could have imagined. But then, Ty had warned her.

Suddenly he was there, one hand on her arm, shouting to be heard above the din. His quicksilver eyes reflected nothing but steely resolve, and it steadied Lily the way nothing else could have.

"Come with me," he said. "This way."

He took her hand and pulled her through the crowd, heading in the opposite direction as everyone else. They headed to a large mirror that was taller than Ty and twice as wide, hanging on the wall opposite the bar. After he felt along the side of it, Lily heard a faint *click*, and the entire thing swung outward like a door. No one paid any attention as they rushed by.

Ty motioned for her to go in ahead of him, and so she stepped in, hearing him shut the door behind her. Lily coughed as she looked around her at an opulent office now hazy with smoke. Inside were two people: Anura and another man she didn't remember seeing inside the club, though she supposed she could have missed him. She doubted it, though. He could have been Ty's younger brother, with his chin-length black hair tucked behind his ears and the same guarded expression that she was already so used to seeing. Jet-black eyeliner rimmed bright blue eyes that warily watched the two of them enter, and on one of his forearms, a tribal black cat stretched.

Ty's reaction surprised her, but she thought it surprised the other two even more.

"Jaden!" he cried, one of his rare smiles lighting up an otherwise serious countenance. He strode forward, grabbed the younger man, and pulled him into a quick, tight embrace. "I worried you were dead, brother. You should have tried to find me."

Jaden stiffened for a moment but then seemed to accept the spontaneous show of affection. One fist pounded Ty's back a couple of times, and then he was released. He didn't return Ty's smile, but Ty seemed too preoccupied to really notice. Instead, he rounded on Anura, and Lily could see the confusion and anger in his expression.

"I expect you to explain this. You lied to me about it even when you knew I hadn't come for him."

"I couldn't be sure," Anura replied, spreading her hands before her. "Much hangs in the balance, and your loyalties are divided. We couldn't be sure which side you would come down on. I told you . . . you don't know all of it."

"We?"

The pain in Ty's eyes when he looked back at Jaden was so deep that Lily could feel it herself, a knife in the belly. She didn't question why it hurt her so, didn't have time. All she knew was that she didn't ever want to be the source of such anguish for him.

"You're blood, Jaden. Everything I've done, I've done for my blood. I protected you when no one else would have. We are *brothers*. How do I not deserve your trust?"

"Weren't you the one who told me to rely on no one, to trust no one, but myself?" Jaden asked, though Lily could see that Ty's words had affected him. On his pale cheeks there was a faint pink bloom that looked like shame. Jaden glanced away, and his voice dropped so that she could barely hear.

"In truth, brother, it was safer for you not to see me. You risk enough. You always have. I worried you would risk more, once you knew the way of things. It would be better if you hadn't come here."

Anura sighed. "As my club is on fire, I would have to agree. But what's done is done."

"So...this is your brother?" Lily asked, glad for Ty that he at least had family that had followed him into his life as a vampire. She hoped to do something, anything, to distract him from whatever emotions had put such an expression on his face. Her effort didn't amount to much, but he did, at least, answer her.

"Jaden is my blood brother," Ty said, tearing his accusing eyes away from the other two. "He's of the Cait Sith, like I am. And he and I have done plenty of running together for the Ptolemy over the years." There seemed to be a wealth of meaning in just that one sentence.

"Not anymore," Jaden said, his voice soft and slightly rough.

"No, not anymore," Ty replied, his tone hardening. "What the hell are you doing here, Jaden? You know what they'll do to you if they find you. What's happened?"

"That will have to wait," Anura said tersely. "You three need to get out of here. Now. The entire damned stockroom is already in flames, and this place was never brought up to code because it isn't even supposed to be here. This may all be gone by tomorrow. Someone is trying to smoke one or both of you out. Take my stairs. Jaden, you take Ty and Lily to the apartment. I'll meet you when it's safe for me to do so, but it could be a couple of nights. You can't be seen leaving here. And I can't be seen leaving with you." She glanced at Lily, and it seemed there was an ancient sadness that lingered in Anura's eyes. "There is more at stake than you know."

Jaden looked sharply at Anura. "Are you sure you'll be all right?"

Anura smiled, though it was humorless. "I've always got a backup plan or three. I'll manage. Be careful," she said, looking first at Ty, then at Lily. It was the strangest sensation, looking into Anura's dark eyes. Lily felt the room waver the moment their gazes connected, and the smell of smoke seemed to vanish in favor of the scents of incense and night-blooming jasmine. For just a moment, Lily could hear the wild song of flute and pipe, and a vision flashed before her eyes of white-robed women dancing, hand in hand, in a circle beneath a full summer moon.

She blinked, and reality roared back. Someone was banging on the mirror door, and the smoke was thickening.

"Anura! Are you in there? Anura, we need to get out of here. We can't save it!"

Lily recognized the voice of the bouncer who'd given Ty a tough time at the door. She sucked in an acrid breath and immediately started coughing again. Ty, seemingly unaffected, looked at her worriedly, and Anura strode to open a door on the opposite wall. Beyond it were stairs leading up.

"Go!" she commanded. "As you can see, I'm not without protection. Not that I need it, but it's nice just the same."

Jaden gave a quick nod, then headed in. Ty put Lily in front of him and nudged her forward. She went, but paused at the threshold where Anura stood waiting for them to go. The pounding against the door intensified.

Without understanding why she did it, Lily reached

out and clasped Anura's forearm. Instantly, she felt the warmth of the connection, the truth of the bond. She just didn't know what it meant. But she could see that Anura did, and her gaze was warm.

"Be safe," Lily said, feeling like an idiot, wanting to say something. She had so much to ask, but the opportunity was being stolen. The disappointment of it was crushing.

Anura, who had clasped Lily's forearm the same way, gave her a smile that was both sad and sweet. "Blessed be, little sister. You stay safe too. We have much to talk about."

Lily caught only a glimpse of Anura's physical form vanishing, turning transparent before dissolving into a column of pure white smoke. Then they were gone, rushing up the pitch-black stairs as the world filled up with fire below them and sirens wailed above.

And not long after, the three of them emerged into a cold night dotted with indifferent stars.

chapter THIRTEEN

IN HER DREAMS, she was back in the fire.

Lily stood in the empty club, watching the fire slowly consume Mabon. The only lights were those of the flames, but though the heat grew steadily more intense, the smoke didn't fill her lungs. She drifted through the club, watching the fire lick its way up the walls and curl around the wood of the bar. The door to Anura's office hung open, but all was blackness beyond.

It was there she was drawn, and though part of her knew she was dreaming, Lily still felt sick dread coiling in her stomach as she approached that blank space on the wall. It seemed to yawn as she drew closer, but she knew it was useless to resist its pull. This was where she needed to go.

"Look inside, daughter. See the past. Our past."

The voice was all around her like a sigh, warm and familiar. Lily knew she'd heard it before, perhaps in other dreams. So she stepped forward, hesitating only a moment before her foot crossed the threshold.

It was a step into madness...but a madness she had seen many times before and knew well.

She stood in a beautiful temple, white marble columns soaring above her. And all around her rang the screams of the dying as the floor ran red with blood. Lily stumbled forward as the battle raged, as men and women garbed in red and gold forced their way through the crowd that had gathered, fangs bared. Their silver blades flashed like lightning as they came down, again and again, like the Reaper's scythe.

Vampires, Lily saw. But not only the aggressors. The innocents had fangs as well, visible with every battle cry, every dying scream, and they fought valiantly though it was obvious they had been taken by surprise. This had been meant to be a celebration. Lily knew it, in the way that the reality of dreams seems certain to the dreamer. Instead, it was a massacre.

At the head of the temple, a woman stood, both a part and not a part of the scene. She was the most beautiful creature Lily had ever seen, with wild red hair that tumbled over the shoulders of a simple, one-shouldered gown made of jade-green silk. Her skin was alabaster, her lips as red as blood. She watched the horror with sad and ancient eyes that rose and then locked with Lily's, as green as the dress she wore.

Around her upper arm, a golden snake was coiled. From her neck hung a pendant shaped like a star.

"So fell our people," she said to Lily, her voice echoing as Lily approached her up the long central aisle, drowning out the screams. "So fell the first dynasty, the bloodline of the Mother."

In the woman's arms, Lily realized, was a baby, swaddled in rich cloth. Lily could hear its cries rise above the din.

"You are all that is left of me, daughter. In you the blood will be reborn or will vanish forever. Do not let them take it. They will try. Better we are gone forever than corrupted by what coveted our power. Our sisters will carry on as best they can, though most have forgotten the promise that was given."

The woman turned and handed the baby to another woman wearing a long cloak. The baby was hidden beneath, the woman's hood drawn so that no features were visible. They clasped forearms, the woman and the goddess, before the one with the baby rushed off, cloak flowing, looking like little more than a wraith. It was fitting, Lily thought as she moved more quickly toward the red-haired woman. This was a haunted place. Panic rose in her throat, telling her that the end of this dream, so terrible and familiar, was nigh. She started to run, feeling the evil in the air pressing in on her, all around her. Something horrible was going to happen. She didn't want to see.

But she knew she had to.

The power crackled in the air around her, and it was then Lily realized that the men and women fighting for their lives were fighting not only with their hands and blades, but also with something that emanated from within them. She looked to her left, and a bloody but triumphant vampiress hurled a red-clad intruder away from her as a flash of light burst from her hands. Another look around her, and Lily saw it was much the same everywhere. After the initial shock of the ambush, the temple vampires had rallied.

But for every attacker who was beaten back, two more took his place, and these were strong and lightning fast, so quick that their movements were only flickers.

If only they had been prepared, Lily thought. If only they hadn't been taken by surprise, they would have triumphed.

The goddess-woman was gathering her own power. Lily could feel it, as she'd felt the same sort of power gathering in herself the night she'd left Tipton. Lily rushed toward her, hoping the woman would be triumphant but knowing that the worst was to come. And then she saw her, slim and dark, her lips peeled back in a snarl and a glittering, curved blade held high above her head. She moved into position directly behind the red-haired woman, whose eyes were closed, readying for the final burst of power that would scatter her enemies to the four winds.

"Bride of the demon! Whore! You'll destroy us all with your madness!"

"No!" Lily shrieked as the blade came down, slicing right through the long, ivory neck.

The world flashed bright red, bursting into flames, and then went dark as Lily's scream rang painfully in her ears. A baby cried. A woman screamed her command, though it echoed as if she were hearing it from across a great distance.

"Find the child! Where is the child? It must be destroyed!"

"Break his chains, free our blood. No house can stand alone." It whispered through her mind as Lily jerked awake. Ty was shaking her.

She gasped in a breath of blessedly clean air, not a trace of the acrid smoke of her nightmare remaining. Her lungs expanded painfully, and her body surged upward as though she were surfacing from underwater.

She was okay. It hadn't been real. In some ways, it

was the same scene she had witnessed dozens of times since she'd been a child. But in others, it had been utterly new.

The woman had never looked at or spoken to her before tonight.

Ty's eyes gleamed above her in the darkness. His hands gripped her shoulders tightly.

"Lily, damn it, are you all right? Wake up!"

She tried to focus, to come all the way back. "Yeah. Yes. I'm here." Her voice sounded gritty and rough. It took her a moment to remember where, exactly, "here" was. Then, slowly, it came back. The burning club. The ride to a decidedly more upscale part of the city, which had been marked by the uncomfortable silence between the two men she was with. And then they had come here, to a loft in a converted warehouse where it seemed Jaden had been staying.

Jaden. Lily's eyes darted around the darkened space as she thought of him, but she and Ty seemed to be alone. There was a vulnerability in Jaden that she hadn't seen in Ty, and it made her worry about where he might have gone, even though she'd only just met him. Though he'd stayed guarded with Ty, he'd been nothing but solicitous of Lily. He'd even fed her—some wonderful pasta and sauce he'd had in the fridge. At her surprise, he'd given her a tentative smile and replied, "Just because we don't have to eat regular food doesn't mean we can't or that we don't like to occasionally. I've always enjoyed cooking."

The food in her stomach, coupled with the excitement and the radical change in the hours she was keeping, had made her logy. She knew she must have drifted off while Ty had stepped out for a moment, and Jaden had busied himself cleaning up. The leather couch was comfortable, and the apartment, with its high ceilings and exposed brickwork, was cozy and inviting despite the strangeness of the evening.

One minute she'd been brooding over what, exactly, Ty had gone out to do—she was fairly certain of what the meaningful look he and Jaden had shared meant, and the thought of him with his teeth in some random woman provoked a wave of irrational and somewhat violent feelings in her that she'd rather not explore in-depth—and the next minute, darkness.

Then the temple, and the woman, and the fire.

And now there was just her and Ty. From all appearances, alone.

The sudden warmth that fleeting thought provoked was unwelcome, and Lily pushed it away, shuddering. Someone had covered her with a blanket, she saw, strangely touched. And there was a pillow beneath her head.

"What time is it?" she asked, noticing that Ty kept his hands on her. She knew she shouldn't be glad of it, but the connection, however small, was still a comfort.

"About three a.m.," he said. "You've been sleeping quite a while. I was going to wake you before I went to sleep, just to tell you where we are and where you'll want to stay during the day. But you screamed, and I was wor— I thought you'd probably slept long enough. You really do need to get adjusted to sleeping when we do."

He was worried about her. Lily found that simultaneously sort of sweet and a little hard to believe. This was, after all, the man who had tied her up so she couldn't run away, despite her promises that she'd stay put. But his flustered expression and sudden refusal to meet her eyes gave his near-confession the ring of truth. It pleased her, even as it made her uneasy.

"Just a bad dream," she said quietly. "It was nothing."

"What do you dream about, Lily? You seem to have a lot of nightmares for someone who's lived, from the looks of it, a quiet life."

She frowned, and now that her eyes had adjusted to the lack of light in the apartment, which was not pitch-dark but illuminated by the light that came in through the high windows, she could see him quite a bit better. And he *looked* worried. Another surprise.

The memory of eyes, green and full of sadness, and the woman raising the dagger to close those eyes forever, flickered through her mind, and Lily shuddered. They weren't just dreams, and she knew it. But she didn't know what to do about them, what they meant. And she certainly had no intention of sharing them with Ty, who for all his efforts to decipher her mark was not exactly working in her best interest. He had his own agenda.

Break his chains, free our blood. Now, what was she supposed to make of that? She almost wished the woman hadn't spoken to her. At least before, Lily had always been able to chalk it up to some sort of symbolic vision. Though being abducted by an honest-to-God vampire had messed with the "symbolic" portion of her interpretation almost immediately.

"Lily?" he repeated.

She knew she wasn't imagining the concern in his voice. She needed to ignore it; otherwise, thinking he actually gave a damn was going to mess with her head. Attraction was one thing, but she knew she shouldn't get in any deeper. It would only hurt her. She forced herself to focus on the present.

"How do you know I'm prone to nightmares?" she asked, then frowned and shook her head to ward off whatever Ty might say. "No, never mind. I'm assuming the answer is going to be creepy and stalkerish. I'd rather not know."

"I could say you're right. But that's not an answer to my question," he prodded with a light squeeze.

Lily considered Ty watching her while she slept, and the very thought of it made her flush with heat that had nothing to do with the temperature in the apartment.

"I'm just ... I don't know. I just have nightmares, okay? Maybe it's some kind of psychological leftover from being orphaned as a baby. I don't remember my parents, but I'm assuming I was around when whatever happened to them happened. I think some of it must stem from that." It was crap, of course, but for a time when she was younger, that had been her working theory. Maybe Ty would buy it.

"Ah. Very analytical of you," Ty replied.

Then again, maybe not.

He removed his hands from her shoulders then, though the motion was reluctant, and he skimmed his hands down her arms before pulling them away. He sat very close to her, perched at the edge of the couch, his hip pressing against her own, and it seemed she could feel the sensation from that one point of contact vibrating through her entire body.

It was, at least, a distraction from what Ty wanted to talk about, which was nothing she had any interest in canvassing with him. But as distractions went, this one was fraught with its own sort of danger.

"Yeah, I'm full of deep thoughts," Lily said wryly. She pushed her hair away from her face with one hand and swallowed a yawn. It suddenly occurred to her that he'd said something about where she would be allowed to go during the day.

"So, what, no tying my hands today?" she asked.

He shook his head. "I'd rather your hands be free if we need to make a quick exit. It's not safe here. I'm sure you've surmised that the fire tonight had a little something to do with us being at Mabon."

Lily nodded, remembering Anura, hoping she was all right. "Damien?" She hated saying the name, as though just that simple act might summon him out of thin air. And from what she'd seen so far, the idea of that happening wasn't so far-fetched.

"I would assume. We didn't have any time to talk to Anura, and I'm sure that was the point. I can only hope she managed to avoid him on her way out. I've often thought that smoke is a much handier form than a cat, but beggars can't be choosers. In any case, we'll have to be very careful while we're here. I don't want to stay any longer than we need to, but…" He trailed off and turned his head away, frowning.

"But?" she prompted.

"Things aren't right. Nothing is right."

She heard the bewilderment in his voice, and it tugged at her. She wasn't familiar with his world and couldn't say she much liked what she'd seen of it so far. But he'd been living in it for a long time, and it certainly seemed like things were in a state of flux.

"I was sent to look for you because of the attacks. Simple enough, right?" he asked, surprising her when he kept talking. But he seemed to need to, and she didn't interrupt, just nodded. She wasn't sure he was really talking to her, anyway, so much as working things out for himself.

"But then it wasn't simple at all. I wind up wandering in the boonies for nearly a year, too busy to get involved with the usual dynasty bullshit. I find you, and you're... not what I expected. We've got the Shades after us, courtesy of whoever wants to decimate the Ptolemy. And now I find out that not only is the damned dynasty in danger, but they're also making it awfully hard for anyone else to feel sorry for them. I can't even begin to guess why the Ptolemy are provoking the Dracul this way. It's easy to suspect them, but I was under the impression that Arsinöe actually wanted proof before they incited a bloody *war*."

He gave a frustrated groan and shoved his head in his hands. Lily watched him, mulling over what he'd said. Some of it was new to her: he hadn't mentioned these Dracul before as the suspected source of the trouble.

"I've been cut out completely," he said. "And hell if I know what to do about it."

"Why them?" she asked. "Why would the Dracul go after the Ptolemy?"

Ty scrubbed at his face with his hands, then looked at her. He looked tired. Appealingly tired. She tried not to notice.

"Bad blood, simmering ever since the Dracul petitioned the Council for recognition as a dynasty in their own right. They're the youngest, and I suppose you can imagine how rare it is for a new bloodline to show up anyway. Vlad had to prove he was the first to wear his mark, and since he swears it was given to him by an ancient and rather dark goddess, the proof was... well, I understand it was quite an undertaking, but he managed it. Still, there were lots of roadblocks the other dynasty heads threw up, trying to stop them. They're the ones who can turn into bats, you see," he said with a wry smile. "The only highbloods with an animal form. And the most famous, which pisses everyone off. They weren't going to have him no matter what he did. Vlad's a wily one, though. By the time he petitioned, he was already well organized and backed by plenty of muscle. He was selective, and smart, about who he turned. There were too many of them. The Council couldn't say no. Especially when someone set a Romany curse on a couple of very vocal opponents."

"The invisible thing," Lily said with a frown. "The Dracul are Gypsies?"

"Some of them," Ty said. "And the curse is a thing called a Mulo. A flesh-eating spirit that sleeps in its corpse during the day. How to create one is not exactly common knowledge."

"I still don't get why he'd try to take out the Ptolemy. Especially not with something so obvious."

Ty shrugged. "You play to your strengths. And he and Arsinöe *hate* each other. She made it very clear what she thought of the Dracul, their penchant for elevating gutter-bloods into their ranks. She was the lone 'no' vote on their acceptance, and when the two camps aren't avoiding each other, they fight. Maybe Vlad's decided to go for the brass ring, Lily. I don't know. It's highblood business. I don't think like they do, and I don't particularly want to."

She'd noticed this before, his way of separating what he did from those he did it for. The way vampire society worked, Lily decided, was something any medieval tyrant would have been proud of. And it was telling that the word *gutterblood* rolled so easily off his tongue, when it was something she herself had heard him called. He was so used to it . . . and that made her sad.

"But you allow yourself to be a weapon of the Ptolemy," Lily said as gently as she could. Did he truly not see this? "Doesn't that make you about as involved as it gets? I mean, don't you care that you're contributing to the problem? It sounds like Arsinöe is one of the worst ones for wanting to keep highbloods and lowbloods separate."

She could see the shutters come down over his eyes immediately.

"The problems," Ty said gruffly, "are not of my making. And if it weren't me, it would be someone else. I don't have the luxury of choosing my path. I'm just a weapon, not the hand that wields it. And I owe the queen."

"Yeah, you mentioned that," Lily muttered, looking away. "But if you're so important to her, you'd think she would have mentioned all of this other stuff. And what about Jaden? Can't be all that great if he ran away from it."

"I don't know. He won't talk about it, and he's gone... out." She saw the flash of anger, though he quickly buried it. "Maybe he's gone out to see Anura so they can talk about you and me. Maybe he's working with Damien now and has gone to plot our untimely demise. Hell if I know, Lily." He sighed heavily, and Lily again felt that reluctant tug at her sympathy. "Jaden's my blood brother. Something happened to him, but I can't help if he won't trust me. I won't apologize for what I am, what I do, but I've never betrayed blood."

He looked so vulnerable, sitting there in the dark, that Lily felt herself opening to him. Her instinct was to comfort him, perhaps because he was the only man who had ever tried to do the same for her. Ty was a difficult and moody man. That she had seen from the first. But it was something to know that he could be hurt by a friend's lack of faith. That he considered himself worthy of such faith, at least when it came to his own blood. There was some code of honor he ran by; she just hadn't figured out what it was yet.

Nor if she fell under any of it.

"What about me?" she asked softly, unable to help herself. "Will you betray me?"

It was obvious he didn't care for the question. "I thought we'd established that I was trying to make sure you stay safe, Lily. I've been up front about why I sought you out."

"No, I mean when it comes to Arsinoë. What if she decides my mark means I shouldn't exist? Or what if I'm made as much a slave as—" She barely stopped herself from saying *as you.*

He watched her, a hint of regret in his expression. That, and all it implied, frightened her more than almost anything she'd been through since she'd met him.

"There's a saying among vampires," he said softly. "*Blood is destiny.* Your blood, Lily, brought you here, and brought you to me. I believe that. And as long as you're in my care, I'll protect you. Beyond that, your blood will take you where you're meant to go. And it will get you home. You'll have to trust in that, if nothing else."

She shook her head. "I don't believe in fate, Ty. I've made my own. And so have you, right? You aren't supposed to even be looking at a queen, much less be so valued by one. You made that happen. Not some weird blood destiny."

He gave a humorless little chuckle, and she hated the bleakness in his eyes. It was the look of a man worn down over many years, to the point where he had no hope left. What came after that, in another hundred years? Maybe it would be the coldness she'd seen in Damien, the complete lack of feeling.

But Ty was different. And so utterly alone.

"Who protects you?" she asked suddenly, and saw his surprise.

"I'm going to try not to be insulted you asked me that. I can take care of myself."

Lily sighed and tried again. "What I mean is, you seem to carry plenty of responsibility. You've been entrusted with me, which I know is more than you bargained for. But who stands for you, Ty? Would the Ptolemy jump in if you needed it? Who has your back?"

"I..." He trailed off, and she could see he was uncertain about how to answer.

For her, that was the answer. She wanted to tell him that she understood, that she knew what it was like to go through life with no one but yourself to rely on. What she didn't understand was how he could tolerate being little more than a slave, no matter what he called it. Ty said this queen had saved him. What on earth had she saved him from that was worse?

Blood and destiny. It was nothing short of appalling to her that such a little thing as a mark could determine everything. She rubbed at hers, feeling it tingle and burn with its slow, undeniable heat as she thought of the dream, of her strange moment of connection with Anura. Lily wondered if she had any choice in anything at all, if she ever had. But no...she refused to believe she was powerless.

Ty looked lost, in this moment, here in the dark. It had been a long couple of nights, and she was certain he'd had more before that. Her world had been utterly upended. But it seemed like his had been, too, in his absence from the center of his dynasty's power. It made her feel for him, and she was too emotionally exhausted to fight it off.

It might not be the usual sort of thrall, Lily thought, but when she was in his presence, Ty never stopped calling to her.

Knowing she would regret it later, she gave in.

chapter FOURTEEN

LILY REACHED OUT to stroke Ty's face, marveling at the coolness of his skin, the rough feel of stubble along his jaw. Ty closed his eyes and turned his face into her touch, though his expression was one caught between pleasure and pain.

"You shouldn't," he murmured.

Don't I know it, she thought. But she continued her gentle exploration of him, threading her fingers through his hair. It was soft, silken, as she stroked it, and she lifted her other hand to do the same. He tipped his head back slightly, giving in, just a little. A soft thrumming sound reached her ears, and it took her a moment to place it. When she did, she chuckled softly, and his eyes opened to look at her warily. Even now, she realized, his first thought was that she would mock him somehow. He didn't trust her...didn't trust anyone, she imagined. It made her want to change that, though it would serve no purpose.

Maybe it was because she understood so completely what it was to be alone.

"You're purring," she said with a smile. He tried to pull back then, but she tightened her hold in his hair to stop him. The power of it slithered through her, dark and sensual. She had never had a man at her mercy, had never grasped control. But something within whispered that she could, if she were brave enough to take it.

"I've never made a man purr," she said. "I like it."

He didn't try to pull farther away, but he didn't lean in closer, either, instead letting her resume stroking his hair, his face. His eyes slipped shut again as the purring resumed, and Lily figured out then that it was a reaction he didn't have much control over. And it was, hands down, the sexiest noise she'd ever heard a man make.

"We shouldn't do this," he rasped.

"Didn't stop *you* before," Lily said, rubbing her thumb across the mouth she'd grown so fixated on. The skin there was soft, making her remember how it had felt pressed against her own lips. She sucked in a surprised breath when Ty's lips parted and he took the thumb into his mouth, flicking his tongue against it, sucking it lightly. And the entire time, he watched her. Lily had no doubt he could see her flush, even in the dark, could hear her breath catch each time she inhaled. Her lower belly clenched into a hot and pleasurable little knot that sent little shock waves of sensation through her entire body.

Ty gave her fingertip a soft kiss. "Be careful what you invite, Lily. It's late, and I'm tired of pretending I don't want to take a bite out of you tonight."

She felt like someone else, someone far more confident than she had ever been, and could hardly believe what she heard herself saying.

"What if I don't want you to pretend?"

The light in his eyes sparked, and Lily found that she didn't fear it, this side of him. Maybe she should have, but she knew instinctively that Ty would never intentionally hurt her. It just wasn't his way. She had no doubt he'd done things that would make her blood run cold. But there was, buried in the vampire, still a man. Still a heart. Lily could see both, even if no one else seemed to.

Even if no one else wanted to.

"You don't understand," he said. "When I saw that bloody big Dracul with his hands all over you tonight, it was all I could do not to take his head, Lily. It's not normal, the way I want you."

"Ooh," she murmured with a smile, stroking his hair back from his face. "Deviance. Tell me more."

But he grasped her hands and pulled them away, squeezing her wrists tightly as he held them still. His expression was deadly serious, though there was no mistaking the terrible yearning in his eyes.

"It's not normal, Lily. I barely managed to keep my teeth out of you the last time, and that would be the end of everything. But your blood, your scent...I can't think straight. You have no idea what I want to do to you. What I've wanted to do since that first night at the mansion."

She met his gaze steadily, and with no fear. "I'm assuming it's the same thing I want to do to you. You're not the only one who feels that pull, Ty. I don't know what it is, either, but I'm no vampire, and I still find myself thinking about sinking my teeth into you."

He made a soft, strangled sound that was almost a groan. "I have nothing to offer you, Lily. I've got chains on me that you couldn't possibly understand, and no matter what happens, I have to return to Arsinöe."

"Is that what you want?"

"It doesn't matter what I want," he said. "It never has."

She looked at him for a long moment, knowing that he was right, that he was being truthful. It would be pointless, change nothing. And yet, all her life, she'd been pushing things away. For once, she wanted to take something she wanted, in the moment she wanted it, without having to ruin it with endless consideration. Maybe it was better that it couldn't last. Then she would have no illusions.

"It matters to me," she replied.

He said nothing. But he slowly released his grip on her wrists.

"I don't know if I can keep it under control," he said, and there was a raw vulnerability in his tone that she had never heard before. He had so many defenses. It felt good to have managed to get through at least a few of them.

"You can," she said. "I've never met anyone as strong as you."

His laugh was bitter. "You must not have met very many people, then."

She decided that further talking was useless. It wasn't what either of them wanted anyway. As they had sat like this, touching, so close to each other, the tension in the air had thickened to the point where it could have been sliced with a knife. Whatever existed between them wove its dark spell around them once again, blocking out the rest of the world until there was nothing but the two of them.

Lily shifted, rising up on her knees and gently pushing Ty back so that he was fully seated on the couch beside her. He watched her with naked hunger but did as she bid him. Maybe he was still afraid to touch her, she thought. Or maybe he simply wanted to see what she would do.

Either way, it came to the same. And this was how she needed it, at least at first. Before, he had been in full control, and she'd wound up angry and confused. This time, she wanted to be the one to lead, to take.

To give.

She slid over him with a liquid grace that she hadn't known she even possessed, straddling him so that they were face-to-face. Immediately, she knew he was as affected as she: He was nestled, rock hard, against the apex of her thighs. It made her feel empowered, bold.

Never taking her eyes from him, Lily arched and pulled her shirt over her head, exposing creamy flesh and her simple black silk bra.

Simple it may have been, but the effect it had on Ty was anything but.

His hands were skimming up her torso as she discarded the shirt behind her. She leaned back slightly, moaning softly as he filled his hands with her. She heard his breath leave him on a single, shuddering exhalation.

"Be sure, *mo bhilis*," was all he said. "Be sure."

For once in her life, she was completely certain.

Without a word, she grabbed Ty's T-shirt and pulled it over his head. He didn't object, helped her, in fact. Then his hands were on her again, roaming hungrily over exposed flesh. Ty pulled her hard against him, and Lily ran her hands into all his soft, dark hair before dragging his mouth to hers.

They melded together, mouth to mouth, body to body, fitting together as though each had been the missing piece of the other. She moaned low in her throat as their lips met, as Ty took her mouth hungrily, completely, plundering her with his tongue. She could sense a need in him that was just shy of desperation; it shocked her to realize it matched her own.

Lily gasped when he moved, rising suddenly with his hands gripping her backside to keep her in place. She wrapped her legs around his waist and nibbled at his ear.

"Bed," Ty said hoarsely, moving with preternatural speed toward the stairs. "I want to be on you . . . in you . . ."

A sudden worry occurred to her. "Isn't the bed Jaden's?"

The expletive-laden reply about what Jaden could do with himself if it bothered him made her laugh, though the laugh turned to a moan as he lay her down on the vast expanse of bed that occupied the loft. Ty covered her with himself, and the feel of his bare chest against her, of the weight of him pressing down on her, was pure pleasure.

He made short work of her bra, neatly unclipping it and tossing it on the floor. In between hot, increasingly demanding kisses, they managed to remove every article of clothing that remained on them and threw them to join the bra. Then it was Lily who found herself making a sound that was awfully feline as Ty slid against her again, this time nothing between them but heated flesh, skin against skin.

He felt . . . incredible. Her thoughts scattered and refused to reorganize into anything that made sense as Ty stretched above her, against her. The thick, hard length of him pressed against her thigh as he moved with her, and Lily reached between them to wrap her hand around it. Ty stilled, eyes closing. He looked caught somewhere between pain and pleasure.

"Lily," he said, softly exhaling her name. "That feels . . . ah . . ."

She stroked him, and he seemed to lose whatever he'd wanted to say. His reaction was quite enough for Lily. His head dropped forward, and he groaned, a low, sexy sound that had lust tying her in knots. He allowed her to continue for only a few moments, however, before his hand stilled her exploration of the velvety-soft skin of his shaft.

"I'm not going to last if you keep that up, sweet. And I want to make this good for both of us."

She smiled. "Feels pretty good to me already."

He returned her smile with a wicked grin that set her heart pumping even faster.

"It gets better. I've wanted to taste you since the moment I saw you," he said. "Think I'll find out if you really do taste as good as you smell."

He silenced her flustered reply, born of a sudden attack of self-consciousness, with another delicious kiss. But his lips strayed quickly, trailing down her jaw, down the sensitive skin of her neck. Lily's eyes dropped shut, her head arched back to give him better access. Then he drifted lower still, swirling his tongue over her flushed skin and then fastening on one tightly budded nipple with a suddenness that made Lily give a sharp little cry.

"Ty," she murmured, tangling her fingers in his hair as he began to suckle her in long, languid pulls that she felt at her very core. Her hips moved restlessly against him, seemingly of their own accord, as something within began to wind tighter and tighter, sending off white-hot sparks of excruciating pleasure every time his teeth grazed her tender flesh.

He gave equal attention to each breast, until Lily thought she might just lose her mind over the sweet torment. And then, as she knew he'd intended, that wickedly talented mouth moved lower still. Hot kisses made her belly jump, made her quiver.

"Open for me," he purred, and the sight of him settled there between her legs, his silver eyes shining in the dark, pushed her that much closer to the dizzying edge of wherever he was taking her. She felt her legs parting for him, seemingly of their own volition. She felt boneless, helpless, completely under his spell. It felt lovely to give over control, if only for these moments. To feel instead of think.

The first time his tongue laved the sensitive nub hidden beneath her auburn curls, though, Lily couldn't think anymore either.

Her body jerked up off the bed as his tongue flickered against the most sensitive part of her, alternating between rapid and lazy strokes, seeming to know exactly how to push her right to the edge of sanity and keep her teetering there.

"So sweet," he breathed against her. "So very sweet."

When he slipped a finger inside her, Lily came in a flash of blinding, intense light, her body bowing beneath Ty. And the fact that she could feel him watching her, could feel his breathing grow rougher as he watched the effect he had on her, only made the orgasm that much more intense.

And yet still, as the waves of pleasure ebbed, Lily knew there was so much more, if only she dared to reach for it.

He moved back up her body, positioning himself over her. Lily hooked a foot behind his legs, though, and flipped Ty onto his back so neatly she would have wondered if he'd wanted it that way, but for the surprised expression on his face.

"My turn," she breathed, her heart pounding as her

pleasure went from ebb to flow, and she began her ascent again.

Ty's hands went to her waist, but she swatted them away, feeling the dark thrill of the power she had over him. She slid up the front of him, their bodies now slicked with sweat, and Lily smiled over the fact that as cool as Ty often seemed to be, she could make him hot enough to glisten like this. He groaned when she pushed away his hands a second time.

"I need to touch you, woman."

She rose up enough so that her hair brushed over his chest and regarded him with a sly little smirk. "You can— as soon as I've tasted *you*. Turnabout is fair play, you know."

His eyes widened, and she laughed, low and throaty, as he realized she meant to turn the tables.

"Didn't I tell you I wanted this to last? I don't...I don't think..."

But his voice trailed away as she licked her way down the front of him, and soon Lily was completely absorbed in the feel of him, the scent and taste of him. Her hands trailed over a chest as hard as rock, lovingly exploring every angle and curve of him. He smelled of candlelight, of smoke and darkness. She loved feeling his muscles bunch and jump the lower she got, until finally she reached what she'd been after.

He nearly came off the bed when her mouth closed around him.

There were no feelings of awkwardness, no self-consciousness as Lily gave herself over to the wonder of pleasuring Ty. He was wonderfully responsive, his body shifting and rising beneath her, and every broken moan was seductive music, each note reverberating deep within her until she was quivering anew with need. At some point, his hands slid into her hair, but she didn't push him away.

He tasted of the sea.

Finally, when his body had grown as taut as a bowstring, Ty pulled her away. "Now," he gritted out. "Now."

He was all lean feline grace and ferocity as they tangled together and rolled across the bed, each vying for supremacy. Lily's blood pounded through her veins as she wrapped her leg around him, feeling him press against a place that seemed to have gone to nothing but liquid heat. She'd never felt so alive, or so free, as she did tonight in his arms.

He pinned her beneath him and drove hard into her in a single swift movement, filling her completely as he buried himself to the hilt. Ty hissed with pleasure, his head falling back. Lily could only open her mouth in a wordless cry, buffeted by intense waves of sensation. Her nails dug into his back as he began to move within her, sliding out, then pushing into her again with exquisite slowness.

Lily felt the aftershocks from it spiral all the way from her toes to the top of her head.

"Ty," she sighed. "More."

She fastened her hands on his hips, guiding his movements until the bed shook with the force of their lovemaking. She wanted it harder, faster, *now*, and told him so in breathless, barely coherent bursts of words that only seemed to make Ty hotter. His eyes, his skin, all burned with the heat of what they'd created between them.

Then she was rushing, rushing toward a shimmering point of light as everything in her focused on reaching that peak.

Her orgasm was a slow implosion of sensation, unfurling like the petals of some dark, night-blooming flower. Lily clenched around him, a tight, hot fist, as she went higher, then higher again, until finally riding waves of feeling that left her limp and shivering. Ty could only last through one such ebb before the next wave took him over the edge. He came with a hoarse cry, stiffening as he emptied himself into her. Lily could feel every pulse, every throb, and it only fed her own wild climax as she bucked against him once again.

He chanted her name like a prayer as they clung to each other, as Lily rode out the storm, trembling, welcoming all of it. Ty buried his face in her neck, but Lily could feel his own shaking and knew that at least for now, Ty was a man first and a vampire a distant second. She was in no danger from him—no physical danger, at least.

Had she thought he seemed invulnerable? Lily wondered as Ty raised his head and, sleepy-eyed, brushed her lips with a series of kisses as sweet as his others had been heated. He murmured something in a language she did not understand, but the words touched her heart because of the tone in which he said them. And she knew then that he might be an immortal hunter but that his solitude, which she'd sensed so often in their short time together, was a vulnerability all its own. She could only hope that what she felt, this new and surprising wholeness, was something he shared. For the moment, he certainly seemed to. But it couldn't last. He'd told her it couldn't last....

Stupid though she knew it was, Lily felt her eyes sting suddenly with unshed tears. She was a fool. But wasn't it better to allow herself this little slice of heaven with the only man who'd ever made her feel this way, as short as their connection was destined to be, than to never have it at all and always wonder how it might have been?

She truly didn't know.

All she knew was that she was now in serious danger of losing not only her life, but also her heart, and to a man she wasn't at all certain had a heart he would or could give in return.

"Lily. Beautiful Lily," Ty purred, nuzzling her hair as he wound himself around her and settled down to sleep. "My Lily."

Yes, Lily thought, giving over to the simple wonder of being held by a man who had just made love to her, who had worshipped her body in a way she'd never before experienced. She was in deep, deep trouble.

And this time, she had no one to blame for it but herself.

chapter FIFTEEN

SHE WASN'T EXACTLY sure where she was when she awakened.

That seemed to be a trend lately.

But she knew exactly who the arms wrapped around her belonged to, and that was quite enough for Lily as she slowly drifted up from sleep. Her rest had been deep, dreamless for the first time in a very long time, and she felt wonderfully refreshed. Her body felt pretty amazing, too, Lily thought with a languid smile. And that had nothing to do with sleep.

Ty's breathing was deep and even against her as they lay tangled together in bed like a pair of kittens, and his heart beat slow but true. She could hear its eternal rhythm as her head lay on his chest. Her legs were tucked between his, and he'd pulled the blanket over them before they'd finally slept.

Well, at least, after the last time he'd awakened her with his purring and nibbling and licking and . . .

Lily felt heat suffuse her just at the memory. She was just as hungry for him now as she had been last night, before he'd even touched her. And for Ty, *hunger* hardly seemed an adequate word to describe the edge of what she'd felt coming from him; yet, as wild as their lovemaking had been, there had been a tenderness to it that had prevented Lily from seeing it as a purely physical act. He could have left her alone, but instead he held her in the dark while he slept. Even now, she could feel his fingers wound in her hair. There was so much more to Ty than what he presented to the world. So much more she wanted to know about him. If only they'd met differently, if only he were mortal and she were normal. If only...

Lily nuzzled into Ty's chest, breathing in his scent, hiding from the truth. It figured that she'd finally met the perfect man for her, and he turned out to be a cat-shifting vampire with issues. And that was before she even started to take her own problems into consideration.

She lay there a while, as her euphoric sexual haze turned to brooding. She tried to get back to sleep but to no avail. Finally, she got so sick of herself that Lily decided she ought to get up and do something, even if that something was merely to hunt up some coffee and wait for her companion to wake up.

Make that companions, she thought, wondering if Jaden had come back. Oh God, she hoped he hadn't arrived during one of the louder portions of the night. Lily's cheeks grew hot thinking about it, but there was nothing she could do now. If she'd been an accidental exhibitionist, so be it. At least the loft had screens, though that would have done nothing to muffle the soundtrack.

Gently, she set about extracting herself from Ty's embrace.

At first she worried that he might wake up, but after a few minutes of struggling with dead weight, it seemed clear that vampires slept while the sun was in the sky, whether or not they wanted to.

Finally, she got her hair free, which was the trickiest part. Breathing a sigh of relief and rubbing a little at her smarting scalp, Lily drew away from Ty. She looked down at his sleeping form, giving herself a moment just to ogle him. He looked different when he slept, Lily thought, her eyes drinking him in. He lost the wariness he wore like armor, and his sharp, handsome face was so much more open, more innocent. In sleep his figure was loose, relaxed. And as she looked, Lily felt her heart begin to ache in a way she knew she could not assuage.

She forced herself to turn away and slipped out of the bed.

Lily pulled on some clothes from the open duffel on the floor, patting herself on the back for having so quickly picked up the art of dressing in the dark. Then she padded quietly across the floor and down the winding stairs.

A breath in the blackness below gave her pause, until she realized that Jaden must be on the couch. And as it turned out, the vampire who reminded her a great deal of a sexy, sullen rock star was a snorer. Light, but unmistakable.

Lily made her way down the stairs, worried once or twice that she was going to fall.

She felt only a moment's guilt about fishing in Ty's pocket for money. She was no thief, but he hadn't exactly made it easy for her to pay her own way, and she desperately needed coffee. He'd mentioned letting her out in the light before they'd found other avenues to discuss, and a frou-frou latte sounded like heaven right now.

Then there was the other thing. He'd kill her if he found out, but it had to be done. He operated under his own code, Lily knew. And so did she. There were some things she just couldn't countenance, no matter how hard she tried.

Even though there was the sound of breathing (and snoring), the place was a little too tomblike for Lily's taste. She hadn't realized how much she'd needed to get out of the apartment until she slipped out the door, grabbing the key from the small wrought-iron key holder hanging just inside of it and then locking up behind herself.

She strode quickly down the hall, feeling lighter with every step even though there was no hint of natural light until she hit the front doors; whoever had chosen this apartment had chosen well. The building was a cave. Then she was pushing through the heavy glass front doors and heading out into the sunlit world, blinking as her eyes adjusted to the brightness of it all.

After spending the last few days as a nightcrawler, it was like walking onto another planet. The sky was partly overcast, with clouds scudding across and intermittently obscuring the afternoon sun. There was a biting wind, and it smelled like a cold rain might be on its way in. Lily inhaled the scent of it, along with the smell of exhaust and the faint aroma of food. City smells, she thought and, after a moment's indecision, headed right. She hung a left at the corner, following her nose, and after a couple of blocks found herself standing in front of a small greasy spoon called Santo's. Just a couple of doors down was a coffee shop called Brewing Grounds, which she expected would be a great place to grab that latte.

But first there was the matter of what stood between them: a pay phone.

No one paid any attention to her, a pretty red-haired woman eyeing a telephone booth—which she felt lucky to find in the age of cell phones—like it was a hungry beast that might turn and attack her. However, Lily felt like every eye was on her. She'd been told not to involve any-one else. But this didn't exactly count, and she didn't want to cause her best friend any more hurt than was necessary.

She made the call collect.

Bay's assistant, Anna, readily accepted the call, but she must have been standing right by Bay, because it was the latter whose shaking voice Lily heard once the charges were accepted.

Guilt coursed through her. She should have done this earlier, even if it would have been hard to manage.

"Oh my God. Lily? Is it really you?"

"It's me, Bay. I'm…Look, I can't tell you much, but I want you to know I'm okay."

"Okay?" Her voice was only slightly below the level of a shriek. "Where the hell are you, Lily? Has someone taken you? What happened? I went to your house after work Tuesday when I didn't hear from you, and it looked like…I mean, broken glass, furniture thrown around, blood on the floor. You're all over the local news, and the cops don't seem to have anything to go on, except that it looks like foul play."

"Blood," Lily murmured. It had to have been Damien's, shed when she'd thrown him. It would give the police no answers, and that was safer for them, she decided. No one who went looking in the quarters she was now running in would find anything good.

"Yes, damn it, *blood*, Lily! Where are you?"

She considered how to answer this and wished just

a little that she'd considered this a bit more before she'd picked up the phone.

"I'm safe, for now. Look, I can't really talk, Bay. There's stuff going on that I can't even get into, and you wouldn't believe me if I did. But just...just don't worry."

"That's insane," Bay said, and now she sounded just as angry as she was afraid. "This whole thing is insane. I thought you were dead. I pictured you being chopped into pieces in some psycho's basement. And now you're calling me from somewhere, telling me not to worry? What do you think I am, *stupid*?"

It shamed her to have caused this, to not be able to tell Bay where she was. Though it hadn't been her choice to be dragged into all of this. Bay had been the truest friend she'd ever had. She owed her more than a crappy phone call like this.

"Okay," Lily said. "In a nutshell, then. The reason I hate my adoptive parents? They tried to have me institutionalized as a kid. Repeatedly. But it never stuck, because I'm not crazy. I'm, um...well, I'm psychic."

Bay was quiet for a moment. "Ah. Okay?"

It was Lily's turn to bristle. "You wanted the truth— you're getting it. It's why I have problems sleeping. The stuff I see in my dreams...Well, that's not important. The things I can do can be destructive, and as a kid, I didn't have much control. When the last hospital dismissed my parents as nutjobs who just had it in for their kid, my folks sent me to boarding school so they didn't have to deal with me. They paid for my schooling as long as I steered clear of their fabulous, camera-ready life as often as I could, and since they made it uncomfortable for me to be around, I obliged them. We don't speak. End of story. Well, that story."

"I wish you'd told me," Bay said quietly.

Just that simple, no doubt in her voice. And at that moment, Lily realized just how much her friend meant to her.

"You believe me? Just like that?"

"Lily. You're my best friend. You're also one of the sanest people I know. And in a weird way, this all actually makes sense. I always knew there was stuff you weren't telling me, but I let it go because I figured you'd tell me when you were ready, and that must have been painful. But that still doesn't explain why you're gone and your house looks like a crime scene. Is there, like, a secret government agency after you?" Suddenly, her voice was more animated. "Have your parents sicced the Feds on you? Like, they want you to use your powers in a covert program to weaponize psychic powers?"

Lily closed her eyes, torn between amusement and dismay. Leave it to Bay to take all of this to the next level. Though the actual truth, Lily thought, was probably on a level even further out than that.

"Uh, no, Bay. It's actually weirder than that. It's... um..." She blew out a breath, knowing it was going to sound insane no matter how she phrased it. Finally, she just blurted it out. "I'm with a couple of vampires."

Bay snorted. "That's not funny, Lily."

"No, really. Apparently vampires can't be psychic, and they need me to help them find a murderer that none of them can see but me. It's... complicated."

The line crackled for a moment as Bay mulled this over. "Are they feeding you drugs?"

"No. I could use some coffee, though."

The skepticism that had been blessedly absent before

was now in full effect. "Where are these vampires now? It's daylight."

"They're sleeping back at the apartment. It's a little different than in the movies. They're breathing and everything. But I don't think I'd be able to wake them up."

"And they let you out to just wander around during the day?"

Great. She's going to decide I'm crazy now too, Lily thought. Still, she'd started this truth-telling business. Might as well finish it off right.

"Look, Bay. You don't have to believe me, but I'm telling you the truth. This didn't start off being anything I wanted, but things are a little different now," she said, thinking of Ty, sleeping peacefully back in the bed she'd shared with him. "There's more going on with my abilities than I thought. I'm going to wind up dead if I take off— you wouldn't believe how complicated vampires are and how many of them there are, considering everyone thinks they're fictional—but I don't even really want to take off anymore. I want to know what I am. Can you understand that?"

"So you *are* in trouble," Bay said.

"Yes," Lily replied, still unsure which parts Bay believed and didn't believe but feeling like a weight had been lifted just by telling someone about all of this. "And no. I'm pretty well protected."

"Hmm. When are you coming back, Lily?"

"I . . . don't know. Hopefully once I take care of whatever they need me to take care of. We're not there yet."

Bay's voice went to steel. "Not good enough. I don't know who these so-called vampires are or what they've been doing to you, Lily, but we need to get you out of there. Tell me where you are. We'll get you protection. We'll make sure no one hurts you, but you have to tell me where you are."

"Can't, Bay," Lily replied, knowing she was going to wind up hurting her friend but still certain it was better than the alternative, which was Bay thinking she'd died some horrible death. Not that it couldn't still happen, but so far so good.

"Damn it, Lily, let me help you! I don't want to lose you again!"

Lily heard the anguish and the fear, and felt guilt and misery twist themselves into a knot in her chest. But there was nothing to be done for it. She'd done what she'd wanted to do when she'd picked up the phone. Bay knew she was alive, and that was the best she could do.

"Bay, you can't help me. And don't go looking for me—that would be a great way to get hurt or killed. I'm not even supposed to be calling you, but I couldn't stand you thinking I was dead somewhere. I will get this sorted out one way or another, and the vampire I've been traveling with...he's really strong, really savvy. He's not going to let anything happen to me."

"Oh God, Lily, have you gotten involved with one of these nutcases? Please tell me you haven't. You know what Stockholm syndrome is—be smart enough to recognize when it's happening to you. Get the hell out of there and come home!"

"Bay," Lily said, "I have seen things in the last few nights that would blow your mind. Please, trust me enough to know the difference between the imaginary and the real. This is real. These people are ancient, and powerful, and dangerous. I don't have a choice in helping them, but in cooperating, I do have a chance to answer questions I've always had about myself. Try and understand that."

"I don't understand any of this," Bay said, and once again she sounded on the verge of tears. "I'm scared for you, Lily. I want you to come back."

"I will if I can. And hey, whatever happens, don't let my family take my stuff. My will is in the office safe. Everything is yours."

"Oh, Lily..."

"Yeah, well, I want it all back when I come home," she said, knowing Bay was now openly crying back in Tipton. Her own eyes began to water and sting, and she knew it was time to end the conversation. Nothing more could be accomplished. All that was left was causing more pain, and she didn't want to do that. She'd just try to focus on the good. Bay knew she was okay. That was the important thing.

"Take care of yourself, Bay. I love you."

She hung up before she could hear Bay's response and wiped at her eyes with the sleeve of her jacket. Apparently, she hadn't managed to do that as calmly as she'd thought she could. Still, it was done.

Talking to Bay, and hanging up the phone, had felt like saying good-bye to her old life, like breaking a tie instead of reaffirming it, when the latter had been her intention. But there was no changing what was or what she had to do. All she could hope was that she came out the other side in one piece.

And despite everything he'd said, despite knowing it was probably impossible, Lily hoped that that "other side" somehow managed to include Tynan MacGillivray.

Because it was becoming clear to her that she was falling for him, hard and fast, and she had no idea how to make it stop.

Her mind full of impossibilities and burdened with a fresh set of worries, Lily trudged into the coffee shop and hoped she hadn't just made a grave mistake.

When he awakened, the first thing he noticed was that he was alone.

Following rapidly on the heels of that was the jarring realization that this state of affairs wasn't at all what he wanted. He'd drifted off wrapped up in Lily's warmth, in the luscious scent of her. Never, in this life or his last, had he lost himself so completely in a woman. And yet joining with Lily had been like tapping into some lost piece of himself he hadn't even known he was missing.

It was dangerous stuff, Ty thought, slowly sitting up in the large, empty bed. Lily was dangerous to him in ways he hadn't even thought possible. And blaming it on the lure of her blood was no longer an option. It would no doubt have enhanced things, but the pleasure he'd experienced with her had already been so intense that after a certain point, biting her had ceased to cross his mind.

Dangerous. And yet... all he could think of was seeing her, being with her again.

Ty dug his fingers into his hair, pulled up his knees, and sighed. Somewhere in all this mess, he'd gotten in over his head. And he was pretty sure he'd been up to his neck at least the very moment he'd first seen her.

Sleeping with her had been an incredibly bad idea.

So naturally, he'd gone right for it.

Jaden appeared like some malevolent spirit at the edge

of the screens that hid the bed from view, as though he'd
been drawn by all the negative energy Ty was currently
producing with his thoughts.

"I never thought I'd say this, Ty, but you're going to get
yourself killed if you keep this up."

Ty looked up balefully, not at all in the mood to be
accosted. "You'd know a lot about that, Jaden, being a
deserter and all. That's having a death wish if I ever saw
one. And what, exactly, am I doing that you find to be so
bloody dangerous?"

Jaden didn't crack a smile, though that wasn't something anyone saw on him very often anyway.

"The woman. If you truly have any intention of bringing her to Arsinöe, which I personally wouldn't suggest,
then you know how futile getting involved with her is. If
the Ptolemy even let her live past her shining moment of
usefulness, *you'll* never be allowed to see her again. Especially not if things stay as they are."

Ty shrugged, a careless gesture that was forced far
more than he would ever let Jaden know. "She has no illusions about me. And I see no reason not to enjoy some
aspects of my job while I can."

Jaden gave an incredulous snort. "Right. I wish you
could see the way you look at her, Ty. And she at you.
You're both in far too deep."

"I don't look at her as anything more than a job with
some interesting benefits," Ty snapped, hating the way the
words sounded, harsh and unfeeling, even as he tried to
convince himself they might be true, could ever be true.
Especially since the instant they left his mouth he began
to worry that Lily was close by, had heard them, and
would get the wrong idea about his feelings.

Feelings. Oh, hell, he wasn't having an attack of *those*, was he?

Ty's head began to hurt. Gods, he needed a drink, and it wasn't even seven.

"Where is Lily, by the way?" he asked, trying to keep his tone casual. But he knew, from the knowing flicker in Jaden's blue eyes, that his simple question had only confirmed everything the other vampire had just insinuated.

It rankled, even as Ty realized there might be just a bit of truth in Jaden's accusations.

"She's having a shower downstairs, so don't worry, she can't hear the bullshit you just spouted at me. Lovely girl. Much too nice for you. Shame you ever found her, really, and I'm going to guess you've thought the same thing a time or two."

Ty glared back silently, because Jaden was right, and he knew it.

"And as to how you look at her, you look at her like you want to drown in her," Jaden continued flatly. "And that's what you're doing, the both of you. Drowning. But don't let my pesky observations spoil your fun. I'm just the guy who had to wait until the sun was headed into the sky before I could safely come back to crash on the couch."

Ty shifted uncomfortably. "Ah. Sorry about that."

It was Jaden's turn to shrug. "Don't worry about it. I had a few things to see to anyway."

"Wait," Ty said as Jaden turned to go, and saw his old friend's back stiffen. He wondered if they *were* still friends, and what might have caused things to change so completely.

"Jaden. What happened to you?"

Jaden turned his head to look at him warily, but there

was more there now than just the sullen shield he put up for the rest of the world to see. There was a weariness that had never been there before, the same sort of weariness he'd seen in Anura. Ty knew Jaden to be a competent, ruthless hunter when he needed to be, though sometimes frustratingly idealistic. But he'd been plenty cocky before too.

Ty saw none of that old arrogant spark now.

"Why does it matter?" Jaden asked. "You're going back."

"You know why it matters," Ty replied. "I need to know what I'm walking back into. I need to prepare. And I need to know if I can help the others, if they need it."

Jaden just shook his head sadly, with a wistful little smile that Ty found both infuriatingly condescending and unnerving.

"I don't think there's any helping left, Ty. Nero's brought out all Arsinöe's worst impulses, things I forced myself not to see for too many years. Not that it would have made any difference, my seeing them, though maybe I would have gotten out sooner, consequences be damned. You think you're helping, bringing Lily to her." Jaden's voice dropped, became urgent. "But all you're doing is condemning her. The decision has already been made, Ty. The Dracul are going to be wiped from the face of the night. All the rest of us can do is take cover and hope the fallout isn't too bad."

"How do you know this?" Ty demanded, feeling a cold sliver of fear slip into his heart. "Did you hear her say it?"

"I didn't need to," Jaden said simply. "Nero speaks for her now. And his actions speak more loudly of his intentions than his words ever could."

"Bull," Ty snapped. "Arsinöe makes her own decisions. She always has."

"Then she is more a monster than we had ever imagined. Do yourself a favor, Ty. Go into hiding. If you care at all for Lily, turn her, because we both know she won't have any chance at a normal life after this. But steer clear of the Ptolemy. They're thirsty for blood, and you're not going to get in the way. You'll go back, and they'll treat you like any other animal. That's all we are to them: animals." His voice turned bitter. "I should know."

"I can't believe that," Ty said softly. "The others—"

"Are beyond help, Ty," Jaden finished. "You've been gone a while. Do yourself, and especially your unfortunate lady friend, a favor and stay gone."

"That's a bit hard to do, I'm afraid, with the House of Shadows tailing us. The Ptolemy need Lily. They can protect her."

Jaden's dark brows winged up. "And you?"

"I can take care of myself. And I refuse to accept that things are as far gone as you're saying, Jaden. I don't know what they did to you, and I'm sorry for it, but the queen will see reason. Once I bring her the key to solving this—"

"Spare me the idealism," he spat. "You never were big on it before, but you've always had too much faith in a woman who would just as soon squash most of us than look at us. Who did, in fact, squash most of the ones who wouldn't submit. Or have you forgotten we're an endangered species outside of the compound walls? You bring Lily, and maybe she'll throw you a bone. Or maybe she'll smile and then let Nero throw you in the dark with the rest. You'll be safe enough from the Shades at court, I suppose." He shrugged. "But a useful pet, Ty, is still a pet. The Cait Sith can do better. You sure as hell can."

Ty's temper flared. "The gutter isn't any damned better!"

"It's better than a lot of things," Jaden said quietly. "But suit yourself. I'll do what I can for you while you're here. She's a sweet one, your Lily. But I'm not going back, and I hope, as a friend, you'll honor that."

"I'd never turn on a Cait, Jaden," Ty said with a sinking feeling in the pit of his stomach. He shouldn't feel such trepidation about fulfilling his mission, not now. But everything Jaden had alluded to only raised more questions for him, more concerns.

"Yeah, I know you wouldn't," Jaden said, and for a moment he was the man Ty had known for a couple hundred years now, with half his mouth quirked up in a wry smirk. "We gutterbloods have to stick together, right? It *is* good to see you, brother. Despite everything."

He turned and retreated without another word, and Ty was left to stew in his juices, which, he imagined, was exactly what Jaden had intended.

chapter SIXTEEN

THE CITY STREETS were wet with rain when Ty finally left the apartment a little before midnight. Jaden walked slightly ahead of him, while Lily was at Ty's side. He preferred she stay there, and not just because her presence seemed to soothe some of his ragged edges when he could little afford them. Knowing she'd been out earlier made him uneasy. He hadn't specifically forbidden it—and in fact, he'd been on the verge of telling her to go ahead and get some air and sun if she wakened too early, as long as she kept fairly close.

She wasn't the type to screw and run. He knew it, and hated himself a little for being glad of it on a level that was purely practical. But still, there it was. She wouldn't be running from him now unless he hurt her. And hurting her was no longer an option, if it ever had been.

He hated himself a little for that as well.

In any case, though, something had been nagging at him all evening, something he couldn't quite put his finger on, and it had him on edge. It wasn't exactly like being watched, though he was fairly certain they *were* being watched. It was more a sense of lurking and imminent danger, like something was going to fall out of the sky on their heads and there was nothing he could do about it.

Lily was unusually quiet. It had taken him some time this evening to realize that it was shyness, a marked contrast to the wild thing she had been with him in the darkness. Things had changed between them, and on a level deeper than he'd intended. In the end, Ty knew it would change nothing, could change nothing.

So he let Lily be quiet and slightly awkward, because he had no idea how to deal with it, either, and the relative silence allowed him to avoid having to try.

Nothing, however, could prevent him from being enveloped by her scent, sweet and incredibly female, stronger and somehow even more enticing than before. Ty tried to focus on something, anything, else. Because though she had made him forget all about blood while their bodies had been joined, in the aftermath, his desire to drink from her seemed only to have grown worse.

On a normal night at this time, he'd be hungry.

Tonight, he was damn near starving.

"Are you sure she won't come to us? It's her apartment. And she seemed very sincere," Lily said, managing to keep up with him even though his stride was twice as long as hers. Ty was glad she hadn't complained—they had little enough time, and he needed as much speed as he could get. He swallowed his thirst for the time being and focused on the situation at hand. He only hoped she didn't look too closely at his eyes, for fear of what she might see.

"Sincerity doesn't always equate to a follow-through,"

Ty replied. "Mabon won't be open for a while, though I'm glad they managed to save the building. She'll rebuild, reopen. There's been trouble in the past, and Anura has weathered it. But we don't really have time to wait. Especially not if she's been forced underground."

Lily's gaze sharpened, and he looked away. But he wasn't the cause of her concern.

"Forced underground?"

"Possibly." He cocked his head at her. "You're awfully concerned about her. You only met her for a few minutes. What does it matter to you?"

He saw right away it had been the wrong thing to say. Her blue eyes flashed fire.

"Oh, I get it. I should only worry about what people can do for me, right? Not the people themselves."

Ty shrugged uneasily. "It's a more practical way to live."

"It's a sad way to live. How would you treat me if I wasn't useful to you?"

"I wouldn't treat you any way at all," Ty replied. "Because we never would have met."

Lily blew out a breath, and he could tell she wasn't pleased with the answer. He was just glad he had an answer that made some sense and wouldn't cause her to tear him a new one. He didn't think.

She was tiptoeing perilously close to territory he had no interest in canvassing with her.

Fortunately, her next comment made it clear she didn't have much interest in fighting right this moment.

"What is she anyway? Anura, I mean. What's her mark about, the torch and the paw?"

Yes, she was interested. A little overly interested, Ty decided. He thought he had seen it in Anura, too, that flash of recognition when the women had said good-bye. And he knew he needed to understand it.

It irritated him that Lily hadn't told him about whatever silent understanding had passed between them. It irritated him more that he couldn't just pull it out of her head. He concentrated and pushed at her, anyway, trying to at least get a sense of her emotions. Humans were so much easier when he could see what they thought, what they wanted. And what they were trying to hide.

Immediately, he felt her shove him back, along with a blast of her annoyance.

"Don't do that," she said.

She was strong, Ty thought. So much stronger than she knew. He had tasted the edge of her power the night they'd left Tipton, and even when his mind grazed hers, he felt the simmering electric charge of the energy she carried in her.

"I wouldn't do it if you'd just be up front with me. Why the interest in Anura? Something happened," he said, and saw from Lily's face it was the correct guess. The woman was as transparent as glass. He hoped she'd never have to lie about anything important. Then he thought of her having to deal with Arsinöe, who was as adept at practicing deception as she was reading it, and felt a sinking feeling in his gut.

"I just...I felt something from her. Saw something. When we touched," Lily said, not looking at him as they followed Jaden down a seedy street in the outer limits of the city. They passed, in rapid succession, a strip club with blacked-out windows, an X-rated movie and toy shop, and a place that was both a pawnshop and a bail bonds dealer. Lily didn't see the pair of scruffy men leering at her as

they lounged by a bar on the other side of the street, but
Ty did.

Mine, he thought, pushing it at them with vicious force.
They would know it without understanding why, would
feel it in their marrow. And so it quickly was, as they scur-
ried back toward whatever dank hole they'd crawled out
of, throwing fearful glances back at him as they departed.

It was satisfying. Even if the sentiment wasn't altogether true. Still, she was his, in a way. For now.

"Saw something," he repeated, returning his attention
to the matter at hand. His temper began to flicker. She
was holding back, he thought, hiding things. They always
did where he was concerned. It made him wonder what
else she hid, what else she would keep to herself because
she found him untrustworthy or too damned stupid to
understand.

"You might have mentioned it," he said, barely managing to keep from showing his teeth. Anura was so obviously highblood, despite her fall from grace. Of course
Lily would want to wait and speak to her, pour out her
heart. But not to him.

Not to a cat-shifter who could only slink among the
mighty.

His thoughts were a storm, the dark clouds of them
rolling in quickly and threatening a downpour. And it
was then Ty realized he was feeling something he hadn't
thought himself capable of anymore. Something that he'd
longed to be rid of, that roiled and cut and stabbed: hurt.
She had hurt him with her secrecy.

He very nearly stopped walking to turn and run for the
hills instead. So quickly he had begun to let Lily in where
he'd let no one for centuries. And if she could cut him so

easily, he didn't want to imagine what she might cause him later....

"I wasn't sure how to describe it," Lily said. "I'm still not quite sure it was real."

He could see how oblivious she was to his turmoil, and that was best.

"You still should have told me," Ty said flatly. "Every little thing could help us figure out what that mark means. And if there's more you haven't said, you'd better do it now. I won't look like a fool in front of the Cait Sith."

"Yeah," she allowed with a nod. "There's a little more you should probably know."

Such a simple admission. And yet it floored him completely, taking the wind out of his sails. His anger dissolved as if it had been nothing, replaced by bewilderment. He wasn't at all used to getting his way so quickly. And when he did, well, he had cause to be wary.

But the same something that was still prickling with unseen danger from an unknown source told him that Lily was being sincere.

She sighed, tipping her head back to look at the sky as she collected her thoughts, and Ty was reminded forcibly of the first night he'd seen her, standing in a moonlit garden. The innocence of her that was so much on display then was still there, but he also saw weariness that hadn't been there before.

He had never had anyone so unspoiled, had never had a woman give herself to him without wanting something in return. And yet here was Lily, beautiful, slightly shy, yet with nerves of steel, still by his side after last night. She asked for nothing.

Something hit him then, welling up and then crashing

over him like a wave, feelings that he had locked away for centuries because to allow them was to invite only pain. But he couldn't stop it, couldn't lock it down again. Ty stopped short on the sidewalk, giving in to the overwhelming impulse that gripped him. He saw Lily's surprise as he grabbed her hand, as he pulled her into him.

"What?" she asked, eyes wide.

Then she was in his arms, fitting against him as if she were his other half, and he took her in a kiss that said everything he couldn't express in words. Instantly, she melted into him, meeting his tongue stroke for stroke, gripping his shoulders as though he were the only thing anchoring her to this spot. He could feel the wild thing stir inside of her, and his own body responded accordingly.

It was a little taste of hell to have to pull away, but if he didn't, he was going to put on a show he'd rather not do in public.

Lily's eyes were pleasingly blurry when he pulled back, her lips full and swollen from the kiss, her skin flushed.

"What was that for?" she asked, sounding bemused.

He smiled to cover the new turmoil that he was grappling with just beneath the surface. "I have impulse-control problems. Didn't I mention that?"

Her smile was slow blooming, and exquisite. She opened her mouth to respond, but Jaden's voice cut off whatever she might have said.

"Hate to interrupt," he called over his shoulder, "but I think someone's expecting us."

It was the story of her time with Ty: moments of bliss, hours of irritation, and the occasional life-threatening event.

This appeared to be yet another one of the latter.

Lily turned to look at where Jaden stood, stock-still in the middle of the sidewalk. He glanced back over his shoulder with a look that was unsurprised and maybe just slightly anticipatory. She wondered if that was a Cait Sith thing, a vampire thing, or if Jaden and Ty were both just a little off that way.

"Incoming," he informed her and Ty, and then grinned.

It was telling, that this was the only thing he'd smiled about since she'd met him.

Up ahead, a trio of vampires peeled away from the wall they'd been leaning against and headed for them. Two were men, tall and broad-shouldered, and the other was a woman, small and sharp-featured. All wore black, more what Lily would have pictured as "traditional" vampire gear. Though she guessed that vampire society must have members who played up that angle of their existence.

These three looked like fighters, especially as evidenced by the bloodthirsty gleam in their glittering eyes. She didn't shrink back. In fact, she'd spent the afternoon pondering how she might be able to help if this sort of thing kept happening to her, which seemed fairly certain. Her dream had been at the front of her mind, namely the things she had seen the red-haired vampiress's people do. If it was more than a dream, an actual vision, Lily thought it might be possible to use what she had inside of her the way she had with Damien.

It was an experiment, and risky. But Lily figured that if it worked, it proved a few things about what she came from, as crazy as it might sound. If Lily could do it, then the woman who had led the "House of the Mother," as the woman in green had called it, was directly tied to her.

She straightened her back, inhaling deeply.

"Stay behind me," Ty instructed her as they headed up to join Jaden and wait. She shot him a sharp look, but he wasn't paying any attention. All of that was focused on the three vampires who sauntered up and stopped right in front of them, their postures exuding both competence and confidence.

She placed herself at his side and could actually feel his disapproval. But there was nothing for it now.

"Evening, everyone," said the tallest man. He had an olive complexion and a curly mop of hair the same color as his dark, expressive eyes. His accent was vaguely foreign, but Lily couldn't place it. Nor could she place the intricate design of the tattoo that coiled from beneath his shirt to adorn the side of his neck. It looked a bit like a flower. Or a bat.

It was then she remembered what Ty had said about animal-shifters and who could do what. These were Dracul. And this was their territory.

"Something we can do for you? Or are you just out for an evening stroll?" asked Ty.

Lily was struck by how relaxed he seemed. Then again, he was probably used to people wanting to kill him. For her, it might take a while to get used to.

The man smiled, and his companions chuckled. "We're as much on a stroll as you are. I'm sure you're aware there are better parts of town this time of night. Unless, of course, you have more exotic plans for the night than most people."

His eyes flicked to Lily for a brief instant, and Lily could feel his mind trying to slip inside hers. With Ty, it was just irritating. With this man, it felt like a violation. She shuddered and reflexively pushed back at the feeling, at *him*.

She saw the flash of triumph in his eyes and knew she'd done exactly what he'd wanted her to. It seemed the impenetrability of her thoughts was always going to be a dead giveaway. A fight was now inevitable, though she was fairly sure it had been from the beginning.

"What do you want, Ludo?" Jaden asked, sounding bored. "This is a great little reunion and all, but I'm sure you have better things to do. I know we do."

"Actually, I'm doing exactly what I was sent to do," Ludo replied. "Vlad caught wind you were in town a while back, Jaden. Too bad for you, because he would have left you alone if you hadn't taken back up with MacGillivray, here. The Dracul have no interest in Ptolemy deserters. In fact, I would have said good move. But you've got shitty taste in friends."

"Unlike yourself, of course," Jaden replied blandly.

The woman bared her teeth at him.

"I'm honored to have generated such interest," Ty said. "But I don't see what Vlad would want with me. I may work for the Ptolemy, but I'm just a cat, after all."

"A cat with something very interesting in his possession," Ludo said, and this time he made sure to catch Lily's eye. "Vlad has great interest in this woman. And in what she's doing here, when one would think you'd deliver her right to Arsinöe. That's what this is about, yes? Finding a human, a Seer, who can reveal the source of the Ptolemy's woes?"

"We've got some pretty good ideas about that already," Ty growled, and Ludo's face darkened.

"Your ideas don't interest me. They're obviously wrong. But, of course, the exalted Arsinöe would like to think otherwise. We're an affront to her. Animals. Like you."

"We have nothing in common," Ty snapped. The two men faced off, drawing closer to each other, and Lily felt her muscles tense. She was just waiting for someone to make the first move, because violence was thick in the air.

"We have more in common than you think," Ludo said, his voice soft and deadly. "But it matters not. You're blind. Why didn't you go south, to the court of the queen? Why seek out Anura?"

"Why ask me questions you know I won't answer?" Ty responded.

Ludo looked at Lily again, and this time, Ty and Jaden both hissed, ferocious sounds of warning. Something, however, made Lily want to hear him out. There was more going on here than she'd thought.

"What is it?" she asked Ludo. "What do you know?"

"He knows nothing!" Ty snarled.

But Ludo's eyes stayed locked with hers. "Our leader, Vlad, has a keen interest in vampire history and lore. Did you know?" he asked, his voice silken.

"There seem to be a lot of things I don't know," Lily said. "I'm no vampire."

"You're no Seer either. According to Anura, that is."

Jaden swore. "Damn you! What have you done to Anura?"

"She came to us of her own free will. Vlad respects her, even if her own people couldn't be bothered with her," the woman snapped. "This woman will be used as a weapon against our dynasty. Anura was right to come to us. And you're going to give your prize up, unless you want to lose your heads."

Lily looked between the two camps, and it was clear neither side had any intention of backing down. In this case, she knew she couldn't avoid the bloodshed. Which was a shame, because what Ludo had said to her was beyond intriguing. It could all be a lie. But then again, the man who could explain what she was to her could well be the one Ty was trying to protect the Ptolemy from.

Damn it, why couldn't anything ever be easy? But she needed to stay with Ty. More, the Dracul were unknown to her. It was a chance she couldn't take.

"If this Vlad wants to talk to me," Lily said, "he can come and find me himself."

"It doesn't work that way, *gadje*," Ludo said. "But if it did, trust me, you don't want Vlad Dracul hunting you down."

"Just the same. If it were that important, he'd have shown up," Lily replied. "So I think I'll stay put."

Ludo sighed. "You know I'm going to take you anyway."

"Don't talk to her," Ty said. "Not another word. She stays with us. And Vlad Dracul can go to hell."

"Have it your way."

Lily saw the flash of pleasure cross Ludo's face as he began to circle them, along with his two companions. He'd been hoping to fight, she realized. But then, he'd known she wouldn't be given up. Lily pressed into Ty's side. He and Jaden, in contrast to the trio of Dracul, were as still as statues, though their eyes missed nothing. They were also utterly silent, though Lily suddenly heard Ty's voice in her head as loud as anything.

Stay close. I'll protect you.

Apparently he could make her hear him, even if he couldn't hear her. Lily didn't bother to retort that she could protect herself. She figured she'd try and show him instead, though she was a bundle of nerves. Could she defend herself? Did her abilities even work this way?

It seemed that if she wanted to know, this was the time to find out.

She was just beginning to gather her power when Ludo lashed out, drawing blood with a slash across Ty's cheek. He made not a sound, though she knew it must have hurt. Ludo, on the other hand, chuckled.

"First blood, cat. Be prepared for a lot more."

And just like that, the power was *there*.

It occurred to Lily, a split second before she returned fire, that all it seemed to take with her was fury. It might have frightened her a little had she been capable of seeing anything but the blood dripping down Ty's cheek.

"Don't touch him," Lily spat, and the power was a flood, rising, rising within her until she knew it was going to come pouring out. It was terrifying, and exhilarating, and oh God she couldn't stop it if she tried. . . .

When the second vampire made a grab at her, all she had to do was grab a fistful of his shirt and give a mental *push*. There was a flash of light, a screech, and a body flew through the air to slam into the pavement halfway down the street. In the moments afterward, when all the others had turned to stare at her, Lily took full advantage. She gripped the female, lifted her off the ground with both hands fisted in the front of her shirt, and hurled her in much the same manner as the first vampire, who was now struggling to his feet. All she could think of was the dream and the way the temple vampires had fought.

Red haze drifted over her vision, and in her ears rang the cries of the doomed. Her people . . . her people . . .

She smelled fire.

She saw Ludo, and knew only that he was the enemy. In her head, she could hear the woman shouting at her, and the words poured from her own lips in a voice that was both hers and not hers.

"You will not take what is mine!" she cried, and this time light flashed from her hands as she reached for Ludo. But she did not throw him, only held on as the power tore through him, whipping his head back and forth. A wild wind came up out of nowhere, screaming along with her. She began to speak in a language that was not her own, that her conscious mind didn't understand.

The rational part of herself that had not been subsumed could only watch in mute horror.

I curse you in the name of the Mother.

I curse you in the name of the blood eternal.

She felt the world at her fingertips, the night opening within her like a dark flower, full of possibility and fully, eternally hers. She was a child of the Mother, the one most favored. The only one left.

The pentagram and snake burned her skin like white-hot fire.

"Lily!"

Somehow, she heard him shouting her name, and the storm, both within and without, stilled. Lily came back to herself all at once, and it was nearly overwhelming. She had been adrift in some dark and raging sea of power and anger, and then she was simply herself again.

Lily blinked as she looked around, bewildered. The street was empty, though garbage was strewn around it as though there had been a particularly windy storm. Jaden and Ty were staring at her and looking even paler than usual.

And she was still clutching Ludo's shirt. The vampire was barely on his feet, and she could feel his trembling. Even as she realized he was there, he began to fall. Without even thinking, Lily moved to take his weight and was mortified when he flinched at her touch.

"Don't!" he wailed. "Get away!"

Lily watched helplessly as Jaden stepped forward to take him.

"I've got it," he said, and Lily hated the wary way he looked at her now. What the hell had happened to her? She wrapped her arms around herself protectively and shivered, but not from the cold. She didn't even want to look at Ty, didn't want to see the horror she was sure was there.

"You going to be all right?" she heard Jaden asking Ludo. The Dracul vampire's voice was weak at first but quickly gained strength. That, at least, was encouraging.

"I'll be fine," Ludo snarled, shaking away from Jaden to stand on his own. He looked at Lily balefully, his eyes spitting dark fire. "You're right. The Dracul can come after you himself. I want no part of this." Then he looked at Ty, just behind her shoulder. "Take her to the Ptolemy. I hope she kills every last damned one of them."

Then he was simply gone. A small winged shape flickered into the air and vanished. Lily watched it go with a heavy heart. Even among freaks of nature, she was considered a freak. And here, she didn't seem as able to control it. She was slipping, and she didn't know why.

All she knew was that wherever she had gone, Ty's voice had brought her back.

Jaden's voice claimed her attention then. "Holy God, woman. What got into you?"

She opened her mouth, but nothing came out. What could she say? Slowly, reluctantly, she turned to look at Ty. His expression revealed nothing, but she *knew* that he would take the first opportunity now to deliver her to Arsinöe and run. Just as anyone who had ever seen one of her "episodes" had run.

She didn't really blame them. But that didn't ever make it any easier.

"Lily," he breathed. "What happened?"

The world began to swim as the reality of what had happened landed on her with immense force. The power was a high, but the comedown was an awful bitch. She swayed but didn't reach for Ty. She knew better. He wouldn't be wanting to touch her now.

"The red-haired woman from my dreams," Lily said, having to force herself not to slur her words. "The priestess, or whatever she was."

Ty frowned. "Priestess?"

Lily shook her head, and wished she hadn't. The motion was nauseating. God, it had never been this bad before. But she'd never thrown so much force before. "Vampire priestess. I don't know. I could hear her in my head. And then it wasn't me anymore."

She was stunned when she felt his hands on her, though she thought it was only to prop her up. She was sliding fast. Too much output, not enough energy to keep going afterward.

Crap.

"Who's this woman, Lily? What are you talking about? What have you seen?" He sounded almost frantic, but there was little she could tell him and even less she could explain. Besides, she was sliding toward the darkness now, warm and welcoming. There was no time for small talk.

"She rules the House of the Mother," Lily said, and saw Ty's face change. "But she died, a long time ago. Her people were slaughtered. And she says I'm the only one left. I carry her blood. Somehow..."

He looked stunned. But Lily had no time for it.

"That's not possible," Ty said.

"Yes, it is," Lily replied, feeling her legs buckling, relieved that she was going to get to escape if only for a little while. "But you're going to have to catch me while you figure it out, okay?"

The last thing she felt was his arms around her as consciousness slipped away.

chapter SEVENTEEN

SHE HAD NO IDEA how long she'd slept, only that she awoke to a comfortable bed and delicious warmth.

Lily opened her eyes slowly, finding herself in an unfamiliar room. It was small, tidy, and lit with only a single flickering candle that had burned almost all the way down. Her shoes had been taken off, but everything else remained. However, she had been tucked neatly beneath a soft and faded quilt. And the warmth, she saw, came from the enormous black cat lying up against her.

Ty. She knew it was him immediately. He was sleeping, drawing in deep, even breaths. Despite the fact that Lily thought it was likely daylight outside, she moved carefully, not wanting to disturb him.

So this was the form that made him a vampire outcast, Lily thought, fascinated that the animal beside her could be the man she'd been with all week. He hadn't changed form around her, though she wasn't sure what he did on the occasions he vanished to get the sustenance he needed. She'd only seen him like this once, and then it had been fleeting.

One thing was for sure: just as no one would ever mistake him for a domesticated male, he was never going to pass for a house cat.

He was long and sleek, stretching half the length of her body. His fur gleamed black in the flickering light, and his frame was muscular, more like a wildcat built for hunting. Which he was, Lily knew. She lifted her hand, momentarily uncertain.

Oh, what the hell, he's passed out. He's not going to know if I pet him.

Tentatively, Lily ran her hand down his side, fingers brushing over silken fur. She stroked lightly at first, then more assuredly, soothed by the feel of him as she began to turn over all that had happened and ponder what was to come. She let her hand travel over his flank, his face, pausing to rub velvety ears.

She smiled a little when a low vibration began to thrum beneath her touch. She didn't know what he was like with other people, but he seemed to be a purrer with her.

Her smile faded when she thought back to what had happened in the street. She'd lost control. Why she'd ever thought she could grab her particular tiger by the tail and make it obey was beyond her now, though how could she have expected what felt like possession? She shouldn't have cared, but the sheer terror on Ludo's face was going to haunt her.

It was the look her adopted mother had had on her face when... when...

Lily pushed it from her mind. There was no point in revisiting something so far in the past. What was done was done. She needed to figure out what to do going forward. It was a complete mess. Anura had run to the leader of the Dracul. She still had Damien out there somewhere, hunting her. And Ty still seemed determined to take her to Arsinöe, who was probably going to be disappointed at best in her ability to produce the sort of vision she needed.

She stroked, unseeing, lost in thought.

And suddenly realized that she was no longer stroking fur but taut, silken flesh.

Lily sucked in a breath, jerking her hand away instinctively. It was now Ty lying alongside her in the form she was used to, wearing nothing but jeans and a sleepy, heavy-lidded look that made her want to press him back down on the bed and crawl on top of him. Immediately her troubled thoughts stilled, replaced by her need for his body and by a longing, one she couldn't quite articulate, for more than just the physical.

"You should warn me before you do that," she said, hearing the shaken sound in her voice and knowing that it had nothing to do with what had happened earlier. It had everything to do with him.

He rested on his side, up on one elbow, watching her with his steady silver gaze. The hazy expression had vanished almost as soon as she'd noticed it and was now as sharp as ever. He didn't smile, only seemed to be searching her face for something.

"You're all right," he said. There was something strange in his voice, something she hadn't heard before.

Lily slowly nodded. "Yeah. I guess ghostly possession is one of those things that doesn't have any lingering effects."

The crack appeared to fall on deaf ears.

"I wasn't sure when you'd wake up. *If* you'd wake up," he said. "Jaden and I carried you here. Fortunately it wasn't far."

Lily found it hard to tear her eyes away from Ty's, but curiosity made her take another look at her surroundings. The room was small and simple, with an iron bed, a nightstand. The wooden floor was bare. There were two doors, both shut, and one of them was dead bolted.

"And where is 'here' exactly?"

"It's a safe house. Every large city has them, and there are others scattered about. Good places to hide if you're a lowblood in trouble. This is actually where we were headed when we ran into Ludo and...everything. It's run by an old friend of mine. Another Cait Sith." Ty looked away. "I'd thought he might know where Anura went, but we already have the answer to that question."

Lily nodded, troubled as she remembered. "Why would she have run to the Dracul? I still don't understand why she would have told this Vlad about me. She seemed so..." She trailed off, but a number of words came to mind. *Warm* and *wise* were two of them. Descriptions completely at odds with what she had done.

Ty looked less surprised than she felt. "She's protecting her interests, no doubt. Vlad Dracul is a powerful vampire, if not the most beloved, and though the Empusae have a presence here, it's really his dynasty that tolerates them being here and not the other way around. She smells war, Lily, and she's probably not wrong. Anura is just shoring up her protection. I don't like it, but it wasn't personal. Even if she is on the wrong side."

"And you're on the right side?"

He sighed. "It'll be the winning side. Makes it right

enough, in my opinion. I don't get to sit this one out, so I'd rather stand with the Ptolemy." He shook his head. "Doesn't matter right now. What matters is that we're in some serious trouble." He looked at her closely, hesitated, and then brushed a lock of hair out of her face with a tenderness that surprised her.

"You're sure you're all right?"

"As all right as I'm going to be. I'm not exactly sure what happened."

Ty's brows drew together. "You were talking about the House of the Mother right before you passed out. Do you know what that is?" he asked.

Lily shook her head, pushing away memories of fire and smoke and screams. They had come upon her so quickly in the street, overwhelming her. "Not a clue. But I think the woman I see in my dreams, the one in my, well, I guess they're visions, of a sort...I think she's the head of it. She's got red hair, same color as mine. And she's always wearing this one-shouldered green dress that looks Greek or Roman or something. I always see her in a temple, and there's a huge fight. Seems like an ambush, actually, with the other side in red." Lily closed her eyes and saw it so clearly. "It's a bloodbath, at least at first. The ones attacking are so fast."

"Like lightning," Ty murmured, but she barely heard him.

"But then things start to turn around. I've never seen people fight like that, throwing things with just a touch. Flashes of light. It's pandemonium," she said, swept up once again in the thought of it, the intensity of the scene that she'd stood in so many times. "I always think she might manage a victory, pull it off. But every time, she dies."

"Dies?" His voice was soothing but far off. Lily could smell the smoke again, and the distant echoes of the cries of the doomed began to echo in her ears. She didn't want it, but she felt herself slipping, falling down into the dark place again where she knew someone else was lurking— someone who had already risen up to use her body, her voice. Someone incredibly strong. Her mark tingled ominously.

"There's a woman, beautiful and dark, with a knife," Lily said, struggling back up from the encroaching darkness. She opened her eyes, banishing the vision that wanted to claim her again. "She comes up behind the woman in green, out of nowhere. Calls her terrible things. And after...you know...she wants to know where the baby is. That's always the last thing I hear, this dark-haired woman demanding to know about the baby."

Ty was watching her closely, his expression unreadable. She didn't want to be telling him this, was afraid he'd think she was as crazy as her family once had. But she knew she had no choice. This time, it was important.

"Lily," he said, "are these people you keep seeing vampires?"

She nodded. "Yes. I could see their teeth. And the abilities they had are definitely not normal."

"Then I don't see how there can be a child. Vampires can't have children. And all things considered, that's probably best."

Lily shrugged and looked away, frustrated. "I know. Maybe she'd kidnapped it." Except that wasn't right, she knew. She'd seen the tenderness on the red-haired woman's face, seen the way she'd held the baby. It was hers. Somehow, it was hers.

"In any case," Lily finished, "the baby was important. But she handed her off to another woman before they could take her away."

"Her. It was a female child?"

Lily frowned. "I... Yeah, it was." She knew it was true. It felt true. Even though she realized at that moment that she'd never heard anyone in her dream refer to the baby as being a boy or a girl. Still. She knew.

She looked at Ty, an oasis of silent strength standing just outside of her own whirlwind, and tried to use his outward calm to center herself. "I don't understand it, Ty. What happened out there... it's like I wasn't myself. There have been a couple of incidents over the years. But this time was worse. Or maybe not worse," she qualified, remembering the thrill of the power that had rocketed through her like a drug, the seductive edge of what she had wielded. "More dangerous," she decided. She could have killed Ludo. She'd felt his life in her hands, the pulse and beat of it. Why she'd stopped, she didn't know. She could only be grateful that she had, because she'd also known as soon as she'd touched him that he was no match for her.

The sole heir to the House of the Mother. Whatever that was.

"This has happened to you before?" His voice was quiet, calm, but she could see the worry in his eyes. "Before Damien, even?"

Lily hesitated for a moment. If she was telling him everything else, then what was this one thing more? Ty wouldn't think she was crazy, at least. Actually, she didn't know what he would think.

She nodded. "Yeah. I was adopted. I think I mentioned

that, or maybe you already knew. Anyway, they were very well-to-do, very impressed with themselves for having snagged an attractive baby to adopt. Bought, I should say. Everyone knows the adoption system in this country works a little differently for the wealthy. She—my mother, Elizabeth—told everyone she couldn't get pregnant, but she really just didn't want to lose her looks. She told me that when I was young. Who tells their kid that?"

Lily's stomach clenched as she remembered what it had been like growing up in that house, where nothing was to be touched and no one ever let her forget that she was different, an outsider.

"Quinn," Ty murmured, cocking his head at her, and she knew he'd made the connection. "You're not Ellis Quinn's daughter, are you? Big-time movie producer?"

She smiled, knowing it looked as bitter as it felt. "That's him. He and his lovely wife, Elizabeth Raines, the actress who never quite broke into film the way she wanted. Strictly television, and oh man did it piss her off. It made great copy when they adopted me; that's what they said. How fabulous that this insanely rich couple would give a poor parentless baby a home instead of having their own. I was a prop, and they used me. For a while, I had nannies, every toy I could wish for. I traveled all over the world. But I never really had them. Then there was an oops."

"She got pregnant," Ty said. "The daughter, I've seen her. Did some awful show as a teenager."

Lily looked at him, incredulous. Ty just looked pleased with himself.

"You haven't been a teenager for, like, three hundred years. And you're not a girl. How do you know about *Totally Galactic*?" She still winced at the name of the show on which her sister had played an Earth girl who discovers she's half alien and goes to a high school aboard an enormous starcruiser. It was ridiculous, but it had made her a star for a time.

"I'm up all night, remember?" Ty said, raising an eyebrow. "Sometimes the only thing going on is reruns on Nick at Nite. Anyway, I've seen it. She was cute enough. But nothing like you."

Lily flushed with pleasure. It was stupid, to still have wounds festering after all this time. But it meant a great deal to have Ty say that.

"Yeah, well," she said, "thank you. But Ellis and Elizabeth did not agree. By then, maybe it was inevitable that they wouldn't." She sighed. "They were never around, and I wanted them to be so badly. When they were around, they mostly passed me off to the nannies. And then they told me that Elizabeth—she never wanted me to call her 'Mom,' said it made her feel too old and traditional— was going to have a baby, and I knew. I just knew that it would be a girl, and it would take my place. All the love they never gave me would belong to this interloper. I still remember, I was five years old and playing in the nursery, and the two of them had just been in to tell me their big news. I was so angry. It got bigger and bigger in my mind, and they just sat there expecting me to be thrilled."

"And I take it you showed them you weren't."

"I lost it," Lily said, blanching. "Total supercharged freak-out of epic proportions. I guess you can probably imagine the scene."

"Ruined toys, holes in the walls, things flying through the air, and one very furious little girl in the middle of it all?"

She heard the sympathy in his voice, and it was a balm to her soul.

"Yes. It was awful. A much milder version of tonight, because I wouldn't have hurt anyone, though even then I could have, and I sensed it. But they didn't know that. And to top it all off, I was yelling in another language, the same language that was coming out of me tonight. I knew I was cursing them, though they didn't. They were… well, *horrified* is too kind a word. That was it for even the pretense of me being their daughter. I had shrinks galore. My parents were always trying to have me committed. Sadly, I am boring in every other way imaginable, so that didn't work out for them. They got Rainey, my sister. And she became the center of the universe, with Daddy pulling strings to get her into the business and Mommy being a horrible influence because she was reliving her own youth through her daughter."

"She's a monster, then."

Lily smiled again, and this time it didn't pain her to. "Pretty much."

"And she grew up to look like a very large Chihuahua."

Lily burst into laughter, loud and raucous and perfectly genuine. She could see how startled he was, realized that he'd never heard her belly laugh before, and could only hope it didn't freak him out, because she couldn't have stopped it if she'd wanted to. Rainey the Giant Chihuahua. It was so perfect. And laughing made her feel good, so wonderfully alive. Normal, even, if only for a moment. She laughed until her stomach hurt and her eyes watered.

When her laughing fit finally subsided into giggles, Lily wiped at her eyes and saw Ty watching her with a bemused expression. And the look in his eyes, soft and warm, took her breath away. She doubted he knew how he looked right this moment. But she would never forget it.

It was the look of a man who could love her. Who might love her a bit already. And though she knew it was foolish and based in no sort of reality, Lily imprinted the picture of him onto her mind and onto her heart. This was how she wanted to remember him, come what may.

No one had ever loved her. Not really. But had things been different, Ty might have. And that would have to be her consolation prize.

"So you cut all ties and went your own way. Moved to the other side of the country and became a scholar instead of falling into the same trap as the rest of them. And I'm sure they don't see at all how special that makes you."

Lily snorted, amused through the sadness his comment provoked. "Hmm. Special. That would be the kindest way to put it." She shook her head. "It doesn't matter. I wouldn't have belonged there even if that hadn't happened. Not much would be different, except maybe Elizabeth would have pushed me into a few crappy acting projects as a kid too." She shrugged. "I moved on. I had to." Then she grinned at him. "All those years of shrinks were good for something, after all. I'm surprisingly well adjusted for a Hollywood brat whose parents hate her."

"I'm sure they don't hate you."

"No. They got over that a while ago. Now they're just indifferent."

"Lily." The way he said her name made her heart ache for things that couldn't be. He stroked her hair again, and this time there was nothing unsure in his action.

"They're fools. I can honestly say I've never known anyone quite like you."

"Well, I've never known anyone who drank blood and turned into a giant cat, so I guess we're even."

He smiled, and it softened his sharp features. Every time she saw that smile, Lily wound up wishing he did it more often.

"So what is it, Ty? When I said that I was having visions about the House of the Mother, you looked like you knew what I was talking about."

The smile vanished as quickly as it had come, and Lily felt a touch of sadness. But she'd wanted it to end, too, because it seemed like all she did now was scramble up the slippery slopes of her desire, her affection, for Ty and try not to fall into the abyss.

"There are stories I've heard, that the original dynasty was begun by the Mother herself. Lilith. The originator of all vampires, by way of a demon."

Her throat suddenly felt tight. Lilith. Lily.

"That's . . . an interesting coincidence. What happened to this dynasty?"

"They say she went mad. Maybe it had something to do with the demon who gave her the dark gift. I don't really know. No one talks about it. It's supposed to be bad luck to say her name."

Lily's brows went up. "Vampires are that superstitious?"

Ty shrugged. "We're an odd lot, if you haven't noticed. Our whole existence is a sort of dark magic. So why wouldn't we be superstitious?"

"Good point."

"Anyway, what you described, it would make sense that you're seeing the end of the Lilim, the very first vampire dynasty. But as I said, no one talks about them. I don't know the circumstances, and I don't know about this woman

speaking to you. Lilith herself, maybe. Hard to believe, but…
maybe. Out there, when you started speaking in another language, in another voice, I wasn't sure what was going on.
What set you off?"

"I…um…I think it was the blood. On your cheek,"
Lily said, sensing that to tell him she'd freaked out because
he'd been hurt, that she'd been ranting in some long-dead
language about how no one would take what was hers
again, would not make him hurl himself into her arms
with joy and gratitude. Much of what had happened had
come back to her now, though it was more like watching a
movie in her head than remembering things she had done.
She had watched events unfold from inside herself while
someone else had held the wheel.

That, even more than the power itself, was terrifying.

And somehow, she knew that to tell everything would
be to drive Ty away just as surely as the truth had driven
her family away. She didn't know if they had even had the
capacity to love her, and she was old enough to be philo-
sophical about it to an extent. But her destruction of the
nursery as a child had made it so she would never know if
they might, eventually, have been able to appreciate who
she was.

The desire to run was sudden, and almost overwhelming. She quashed it, but her words were still impulsive.

"Why don't we forget this?" Lily said, and saw in Ty's
narrowed eyes that he had taken her question the wrong
way. "I mean, forget this part of the trip," she qualified,
and saw his eyes become less narrow. "Anura flaked out,
and we're going to get messed up if we stay in Chicago, so
why don't we just go to your queen and get this over with?
Damien can't get inside her court, I'm guessing. Everyone

will find out one way or another who's responsible for the Ptolemy massacres, provided someone can figure out how to direct me to see what I'm supposed to. Hopefully. And then I'll head home." She smiled at him, though it cost her. "Maybe we can catch a movie. Have dinner. I'm for dating after dark if you are—that is, if you want to see me again after all this."

The yearning in his eyes, foreign and familiar all at once, took her breath away with its depth.

"Lily..." he began.

That one word was infused with as much longing and regret as any she'd ever heard. So much that she was fairly sure of what he would say. That they should enjoy the now, because it was all he would be allowed, all they could have. Silently, she cursed the highbloods for the way they'd structured their society, feudalism out of space and time. She wasn't even a vampire, but she could see how a lowblood might resent them enough to rebel, to buck the system. There were small ways to do it, like running safe houses, and large ways, like becoming a subversive, violent, amoral Shade. But Lily understood.

Her own blood, whatever it was, had hindered her in her youth. Now it seemed that Ty's blood would deprive her of the only man she'd ever connected with on so deep a level. She would fight it if she knew how.

He lightly stroked the back of her hand, a quick, tender touch that reverberated throughout her entire body.

"Lily," he said again. "I—"

The knock on the door made them both jerk.

Ty's head snapped toward the annoying sound. "Who is it?" he asked roughly, and Lily knew that the moment had been broken, irreparably and completely.

"It's Jaden," came the familiar voice. But even with two simple words, Lily could hear the strange tone underlying it.

"Rogan wants to see you. And he's got some...rather odd company you may want to speak to."

Lily looked at Ty, who seemed as perplexed as she was. He shook his head.

"Would you mind elaborating on that?"

The voice grew testy.

"Yeah, I would. I think you just need to come down. Rogan's impatient, and you know how he gets with the pacing. It's driving me mad, and I didn't have far to go. Just come down."

Then there was silence, and Lily felt sure Jaden had stalked off as quickly as he'd arrived. It was then she realized that Ty's hand had stayed on hers. The weight of it, and the symbolism in the gesture, were reassuring.

"You know about me now," she said, feeling that if there was any time to broach this subject, it was now. "Aren't you ever going to tell me what happened to you?"

"It doesn't matter. That was a long time ago." He gave her hand a light squeeze, but she saw him shut down and wanted to weep with frustration. He was only going to let her get so close. And in a bitter irony, he was one of the only people she'd ever felt she could get close to.

Ty rose smoothly off the bed, pulling on a shirt. Then he padded to the door, barefoot, and turned once he reached it to look over his shoulder at Lily. In that moment, he looked heartbreakingly beautiful. And he looked like he was walking away.

At some point, he would. That was a reality she had yet to deal with.

"You ready?" he asked.

Lily nodded. "Ready as I'll ever be," she said. But inside, she ached for what could never be. Ty had closed himself off from love. And no amount of power, psychic or otherwise, was going to allow her to breach the walls he'd built around his heart.

chapter EIGHTEEN

THE SAFE HOUSE was an ugly shell, Ty thought as they made their way down dingy and scuffed stairs, the passage tight enough that it made him slightly claustrophobic. But that didn't stop it from being genius.

The safe house was cleverly located on a dilapidated street of row houses. Junk cars parked on the street, and garbage spilled into the gutter. A block farther down, crack houses and criminals abounded. It was nothing if not convincing, and no one but an immortal should have dared to venture into this part of the city if they valued their money or their life. But Ty had to admit, Rogan was a master at his trade, which was hiding and ferrying fugitives, along with a bit of illegal this and that for fun and profit. And the construction of this particular safe house was perfect. On the outside, there appeared to be separate homes sharing walls, but on the inside, a warren of interconnected rooms and hallways stretched the length of the block. It was simple enough for the casual visitor to get around in, but only the proprietor himself was capable of navigating all of it. Rogan didn't share his mazelike designs with anyone, and Ty thought that was fairly emblematic of his old acquaintance's business philosophy: "When push comes to shove, it's every man for himself."

Ty didn't trust him. Never had, never would. But tonight, he needed him.

The old bastard would get a kick out of that.

Ty heard Lily's footfalls on the creaking stairs behind him. More, he heard every breath she took, every pulse of her human heart.

Her story was so like his, though she would never know it. To share it would open him in a way he had sworn never to do again. She would know nothing of him, in the end, but that he was Cait Sith and that he hadn't been worth the affection she'd wasted on him.

Such was the life of the lowbloods who served their masters.

He stopped at the bottom of the stairs, which were situated at the head of a long hallway. Candles glowed in sconces on the walls, illuminating tired, peeling wallpaper. Most of the rooms were dark, but the doorway to one farther down was bright with the light of many candles. Raucous laughter spilled out toward them, and Ty steeled himself for what was to come.

It had been a hundred years since their last encounter, longer since Ty had declared that he would rather serve in a respectable dynasty than scrape a living being his own master. He doubted Rogan would let him forget it.

Ty turned his head to look slightly behind him at where Lily stood, head cocked, listening intently. Her hair was vibrant in the soft light, and her skin had a luminescent glow. Tiny lights danced in her eyes when she looked back at him.

Gods, but she was beautiful.

But then, there was a reason for that, wasn't there? She carried a mark that threatened to change the rule of the dynasties, if it were truly that of the Mother. She was human, yes, but she carried high blood.

Her very existence would cause an uproar—that is, if she was allowed to live. And after watching her tonight, he was less and less sure Arsinöe would permit that.

His eyes dropped to her neck, where he noted with a pleasant little shock that she'd tied his ribbon once again. Guilt gnawed at him along with a sudden rush of desire. His ribbon. His woman.

"Rogan will know you're not my *sura*, Lily," he said as gently as he could. Still, he reached out to finger the rich velvet of the ribbon, letting his fingertips brush against the pulse that beat at the base of her throat. It quickened at his touch, and immediately his mind was filled with thoughts of her naked beneath him, his teeth in her neck while he thrust madly inside of her. It was the height of vampire passion, and he knew it would be so good with her. Better than anything he'd ever dreamed in his long life.

It took a great deal of effort to pull his hand away, to speak as though he had nothing on his mind but the matter at hand. "I can't hide most of the truth from him. He's got eyes and ears everywhere."

"I know," Lily replied. "But this is a safe house, right? Other vampires are in and out of here. They don't know who I am. All they're going to know is that I'm not a vampire. So I thought we might as well keep up the pretense. I mean, unless that bothers you."

He saw the flash of vulnerability, and his guilt only increased. Of course, it had been on a steady rise since the immediate euphoria of having made love to her had worn off. Ever since Jaden had called him on his foolishness.

"No, of course not," Ty said, feeling his chest tighten. "You're right." Then he tried for a joke, wishing for anything to alleviate the almost suffocating need he felt for her. "Just try not to kill anyone or speak in tongues, and we should be good."

Lily snorted and gave him a smile. "I'm on it."

"Right, then," Ty said, forcing his thoughts back to the very delicate matter at hand. "Rogan and I go back a long way. Don't let him intimidate you, if he tries. And don't let him grope you if he tries that either. The man's a bastard, but a clever one, and he should be able to help us."

"Why can't we just get in your car and take off?" she asked.

"I wish." Ty sighed. "But it's far too late for that. You were…I mean, I was…I couldn't be certain you were all right. You needed to be somewhere safe, and fast. The area was probably crawling with Dracul, even before the incident with you. They tend not to travel without backup. We won't get out of here without Rogan's help. He'll know this city like the back of his hand. This isn't my place, but it is his."

Her eyes narrowed. "And you're sure we can trust him?"

As though that mattered. She shouldn't be trusting *him*. He had warned her, Ty remembered. But it hadn't made any difference—and how could it, if she felt even half as drawn to him as he was to her? But he had warned her. It was cold comfort. And it was all he had.

And the selfish part of him refused to deal with it right

this second, preferring to bask in being part of a unit while it lasted.

"Well," he said, "Rogan's out for himself. But he's a man of his word, and if we meet his price, he'll hold up his end of the bargain."

"You're saying he's a man of honor."

The way she said it made him laugh. "Aye, I suppose. But don't ever tell him that; he'd hate it. Now come on."

Whatever she'd been expecting a jack-of-all trades criminal vampire to look like, it wasn't this.

Rogan McCarthy sat in the middle of a dingy living room, sprawled in a ruined recliner and holding court in the cavelike space with a bottle of red liquid parked in the vee of his legs. He was a small man, short and slight, but gifted with the supernatural good looks that all his kind seemed to share. His hair was deep brown and wavy, his features almost elfin, with large dark eyes that tipped up just a bit at the corners. He looked like he might have escaped from a fairy tale, maybe a mischievous sprite or one of the Fae's more unpredictable members. It was disconcerting. But then, she was quickly learning that with vampires, looks didn't tell you a thing. They were all beautiful, in their way.

It was their actions that were telling. But that took a bit more time to figure out.

From the demeanor of the small party gathered in the room, Lily guessed there was probably more than blood in Rogan's bottle. The laughter was just a little too loud, a little too wild, to be naturally induced. And on top of that, their eyes shone reddish in the candlelight, a color she had never seen Ty's eyes go. She heard him curse softly.

"Careful," he murmured. "They're hungry. The alcohol only makes it worse."

Though she had a vague impression of others in the room, Lily's attention was immediately caught by the two men on either side of Rogan, one immense in stature, with white hair pulled back in a short ponytail to reveal a beautifully sculpted face. Arresting, incredibly handsome, but cold. He looked like he might be a marble statue somehow come to life and escaped from a museum—and a little pissed off about having been kept still so long. The other vampire was his polar opposite, lean and dark, with café au lait skin, a swoop of ebony hair, and eyes that were dark-rimmed and liquidly beautiful despite their unnerving color.

Both turned to look at Lily, their laughter stopping abruptly as she and Ty walked into the room. A quick look around revealed ugly wood paneling, as well as faded and tattered furnishings that looked as though they'd been picked up at a series of curbs and saved from the dump. Jaden, who had managed to fade almost completely into the shadows, was in the far corner. She tried to shoot him an encouraging smile—there was something about Jaden that told her he needed as much sweetness in his life as he could get—but he was thoroughly preoccupied staring at the other person who was trying to blend into the woodwork rather than join the fun.

Lily's eyes followed Jaden's gaze, and she was surprised to see another woman seated casually in an overstuffed floral chair, as silent as the others were loud. Her hair was the color of rich chocolate woven with streaks of bright platinum, and a pair of bright golden eyes surveyed her shrewdly. She was much less drunk than the others, Lily saw, if at all. Apart from that, there was something different about her, something Lily couldn't quite put her finger on. And her guarded, suspicious expression made her nervous.

Not as much, however, as the man at the center of it all. Rogan, she saw immediately, was stone sober, his lengthened fangs exposing him as being hungry as hell. And his smile only made it look like he was getting ready to bite.

"Tynan, there you are," Rogan said, seeming incredibly pleased about something. "I had a feeling that time would make a liar out of you. Weren't you only supposed to come crawling back to me if the world ended, hell froze over, and the four horsemen of the Apocalypse were at your heels?"

Ty lifted one dark brow. "Haven't you been outside tonight?"

Rogan laughed, a deep and booming sound that Lily found surprisingly infectious. The vampire stood and strode to Ty, not seeming the least bit intimidated by the fact that he was nearly a foot shorter. He clasped hands with Ty and pounded him on the arm.

"Still a smart-ass. Ah, well, I suppose it's good to see you after all. Be better to see some of that Ptolemy money I've no doubt is lining your pockets. Lucky bastard. How are things in the land of the high and mighty?" He eyed Lily then, and she caught the calculating gleam in his pretty eyes. "Gentlemen, allow me to introduce my old friend Tynan MacGillivray, once of Edinburgh, late of the Ptolemy court." Then he winked at Lily. "And this would be his lovely *sura*, Lily. Times are good for the Cait of the Ptolemy if they're going so far as to let their more favored pets keep *suri*. Especially ones like this." He slid smoothly from Ty's grasp to take one of her hands in his and bowed to kiss it. His lips were cool against her skin.

"I do favor redheads, I must admit. Reminds me of home."

"And where is home?" Lily asked, trying very hard not to be charmed because Ty had warned her. "Ireland?" His accent was a dead giveaway, but she was curious about his origins. Ty wasn't interested in giving her his own story, and Jaden barely talked anyway. And yet the history they must have each seen fascinated her.

"Dublin born, my sweet lady," Rogan replied with a devilish grin. "Though I was in Edinburgh for quite some time. Never picked up the accent, thank the gods for that. I could barely understand Tynan when he came to me. All that rolling the words together, and he spoke mainly Gaelic besides. Stupid and impractical, even at the time. But I suppose having a Highland heritage was something to cling to for his family. You've never seen anything more pathetic than the hovel they lived in, dirt poor and covered in filth."

He started laughing, and Lily glanced at Ty. His expression was tight, grim. And yet Lily couldn't help but hope Rogan would continue, only because this was the first she'd heard of Ty's beginnings.

Still, it was obvious that even now, it pained him.

Rogan, who must have known exactly what sort of impact his loose words were having, continued gaily. "Remember when you went back, Tynan? The old witch who gave birth to you actually *spat* on the money you tried to give her! Superstitious old crone. Forked the evil eye and everything," he crowed. "I always supposed they starved to death eventually, or disease got them. Which was it?"

"Smallpox," Ty said, so softly that he was barely audible.

"Perfect," Rogan said approvingly, making his way

back to flop in his recliner and taking a swig from his bottle. "Good riddance to them."

Lily didn't know why she did it, but she slid closer to Ty and slipped her hand into his where the others couldn't see, giving it a soft, reassuring squeeze. She could feel the pain radiating from him as though it were her own, and she hadn't missed the sharpness of Rogan's grin when he'd finished.

Ty had been right. Beneath the charming veneer was a man to be dealt with cautiously. And he'd known right where to hit Ty. He'd been dirt poor and had lost his family to smallpox after they'd shunned him for becoming what he was. No wonder he was so cautious, even now. No wonder he clung to his position with Arsinöe so tightly. There was a measure of acceptance. And at least the Ptolemy needed him.

Lily still thought his loyalty was misguided. But even Rogan's small bit of information helped her understand it a little better.

Ty leaned into her, just for a moment, taking comfort in her presence. He gave her hand an answering squeeze, and Lily's heart gave a small leap. Then he skimmed his thumb down her sensitive palm before letting go, though he didn't move away from her.

"As much as I'd like to wander down memory lane with you, Rogan, my schedule is a little tight right now. You know we need to get out of town. Name your price, and I'll meet it," Ty said.

Rogan's brows shot up, his eyes rounding innocently. "Now, why would there be a price for an old friend?"

"Because there always was before," Ty said, though he didn't sound particularly annoyed by the fact. "Just name it. I'd like to be on our way. It won't be safe in Chicago for us any longer."

The dark-haired vampire laughed. "I know the feeling, my friend."

Rogan ignored him, and tilted his head to one side to regard Ty and Lily. "No," he murmured thoughtfully. "No, it won't be safe here. Nor for me, if they find you. Which they won't. I'm good at what I do."

"Aye, you always were," Ty replied with a nod.

"You *are* still working for the Ptolemy, yes?"

"I'm still wearing their mark," Ty replied, and Lily heard the edge in his voice.

"Hmm," Rogan said. "A little odd that you'd be running with Jaden, who's a wanted man, and traveling so far from where Arsinöe's settled her court."

Ty's eyes narrowed. "Your price, Rogan. You might as well just out with it instead of dancing around the matter."

Rogan let out an irritated growl, baring sharp teeth. It was the first sign Lily had seen that the man had a temper to go with his sharp tongue.

"Don't talk to me like you're my better, *boy*. I was there when you were crawling the streets half starved. I was the one who took you in until you'd learned our ways. I put clothes on your back and food in your belly."

"For a price," Ty said. "And it was one of yours who turned me."

"Yes, I remember him. Oswalt. Worthless bastard. Lost his head back at the turn of the last century, if I remember rightly. Not surprised. Think it was one he sired who did him in. Wondered if it might have been you, actually."

"Oswalt is dead?" Ty asked, and Lily could see his surprise.

Rogan seemed pleased that he'd managed to provide fresh gossip. He grinned, though there was no kindness in it. "Dead as dust. Guess it wasn't you, eh? Maybe it was Damien. The two of you were thick as thieves, and as ruthless as they come once you got your heads on straight. Did the Cait Sith proud." Rogan turned his attention back to Lily. "Your man here was an excellent hunter even at the beginning. Some are just born with it. He was one. Once he got over all the pissing and moaning about his family, of course. He'll have told you about how he came to be with the Ptolemy, I suppose. *That's* illustrious enough to brag about."

His eyes were full of challenge, and Lily shifted uncomfortably. God, she hoped this didn't turn into another fight. Ty's body was tense next to hers.

"Um...not much, really," she said, hoping it was enough to appease Rogan. "He doesn't talk about himself much. He's...modest."

Ty's exasperated glare was worse than Rogan's fresh burst of laughter.

"She's lying. She knows nothing of you, nothing of any of this," said the big white-haired man, looking bored as he sat stiffly beside the darkened fireplace. Rogan bared his teeth at him in a quick snap of temper. Lily and Ty both turned to look at him. She'd begun to wonder if the taciturn and imposing vampire was even capable of speech.

"Quiet, Sammael. You're going to upset our new guests," Rogan snarled.

The white-haired vampire seemed unperturbed. "My apologies. Habit."

He looked Lily directly in the eye, and she felt a moment of disorientation. It was, she later thought, like peering for an instant into the vastness of the cosmos and realizing just how insignificant she was in the great scheme of things. The fog cleared quickly, though, and she saw that he was not remotely sorry.

"You'll have to excuse him. Sammael is Grigori, and they're not exactly known for their manners," Rogan said a little stiffly. Then his mouth lifted in a half smile. "At least, he *was* Grigori. We're not quite sure whether they'll want to keep him once they find him. They may just want to disembowel him. Taj and I have been taking bets."

The dark vampire laughed, but Sammael didn't look very pleased. Ty just looked curious.

"What on Earth did *you* do?" Ty's eyes narrowed as he looked at the massive vampire. "I think I can count on one hand the number of times I've even seen one of your line. I've never heard of a deserter before either. What do you have to do to get kicked out?"

Taj opened his mouth, but the Grigori silenced him with a look. Then he returned his gaze to Ty. It had gone frigid, and Lily knew she was looking at something that wasn't truly human. Maybe he never had been.

"Mind your own business, cat. I think you have enough of it." Sammael looked at Lily, and the knowledge in his red-violet eyes was infinite, frightening. Again, it was like staring into an abyss. Then he looked away, and the spell was broken.

"I suppose I do, at that," Ty replied, but he still looked perplexed.

"Lovely. The camaraderie among outcasts warms my heart. Now, down to business," Rogan said, all trace of humor gone as he switched gears to discuss terms.

"Not yet," Jaden said.

Lily turned to look at him in surprise. He was so quiet that she'd almost forgotten he was standing in the corner.

Jaden was still looking at the other woman in the room with a mixture of suspicion and disgust. "I don't want her here for this."

The woman lifted one eyebrow and angled her head. She didn't look perturbed, and she really didn't look surprised. She did look like someone Lily wouldn't want to mess with. Ever. Her voice was husky and inviting when she spoke.

"That's awfully old-fashioned of you. If I were going to chase you, kitty cat, I would have done it by now. I have no interest in vampire affairs."

Lily spoke before she thought about it. "You're not a vampire?"

The woman's eyes, a burning gold that was as beautiful and strange as anything Lily had ever seen, turned her attention to Lily and made her wish she'd stayed quiet. She didn't sense any real malice, but there was something wild about this woman, even less tame than Ty and Jaden.

"No. And *you* obviously don't know how insulting that question is, or you wouldn't have asked it."

Rogan sounded bored. "Come now, Jaden. I always treat my guests fairly. And Lyra here has nothing to do with you. She's got problems enough of her own."

Jaden just curled his lip. "I didn't realize you'd gotten into the business of harboring wolves. That's a hell of a way to pad your income. Is business that slow?"

"Jaden," Lily said, mortified that he was being so openly rude. But Lyra heaved an irritated sigh and got to her feet. She really was gorgeous, Lily saw, in a very unconventional way. And tall. Though her spike-heeled boots may have had something to do with it.

"Forget it, sweetie. I'm used to it. Vamps think they're the center of the universe. But I'd rather stay warm-blooded and free than go cold and deal with all of this dynastic bullshit." Then she rounded on Jaden, baring incisors every bit as sharp as a vampire's. "You don't want me here? Good for you. Whatever makes you feel better about being on the bottom of the vamp food chain. I have more important things to do than listen to you whine."

She turned on one heel and stalked out of the room, leaving everyone staring after her silently.

Rogan frowned at Jaden. "Her money's good here, Jaden. Don't you run her off, or I'll run you *through*. She'll be a pack leader one day, if she lives that long."

Jaden just snorted. "Not with her attitude, she won't. And the wolves are supposed to stay out of the cities."

"Just as you're supposed to stay with the Ptolemy, and we can all see how that worked out. Lyra is important to her kind. That carries weight with me. I don't have many places left to hide people who don't want to be found. Humans are too nosy for their own good. Just be glad I took you in, because you don't mean a damned thing to anyone alive anymore. Dead, on the other hand, there's a reward for. Remember that before you shoot off your mouth again."

With that said, Rogan turned away from a chagrined Jaden and focused his attention on Ty. His grin reminded Lily of a shark about to attack.

"Let's take this into my office, if you're ready," Rogan said, looking pleased with himself. "Just you and me. This is going to cost you, MacGillivray. And I'm going to enjoy it." He stood and moved to Ty, reaching up to pat him on the cheek so hard it was almost a slap.

"Welcome home."

chapter NINETEEN

It was nearly daylight by the time they were done, and by then Ty had assurances of both a car and an escort out of town, but he also had a checking account with no money left in it, a list of favors Rogan expected from the Ptolemy queen in return for his help in shuttling her precious cargo safely to its destination, wounded dignity, and a blinding headache.

It was quite enough for one night. He stalked upstairs, the usual lethargy beginning to brew in his bones as the sun crept closer to the edge of his side of the world. It didn't help him knowing that Lily was in the room waiting for him, probably with questions he didn't want to answer. Damn Rogan for bringing up his family. And damn his own stupidity for having come here in the first place.

This is what he got for stepping out of line, he supposed. They barely knew any more about Lily's mark than when they'd arrived, but now he had a fugitive Cait Sith in tow and a woman whom Vlad Dracul himself wanted to "see," likely on a permanent basis. The gods must hate him, if there were any who had ever bothered to notice him.

Sometimes, on nights like tonight, he had his doubts.

He didn't see the other vampire looming in front of him until he'd nearly run right into him. Ty barely managed to keep himself from crashing into the Grigori who had apparently been lurking in the hallway waiting for him. He skidded to a halt just a breath away from the quiet giant, who stood a head above Ty's six-foot-four.

"Gods, man!" he exploded, hating that he'd been taken by surprise. This whole thing was screwing with him, screwing with his instincts, which were normally impeccable. "What are you trying to do, scare me into a second death?"

The Grigori—Sammael, Ty remembered—merely lifted an eyebrow and looked disdainful. It was, Ty recalled from his admittedly limited experience with that dynasty, a look they had perfected.

"You are not very astute for a Cait," Sammael said.

"Well, that's an interesting way to get me to talk to you," Ty replied. He was tired, damn it. He wanted to go to his room, curl up with the woman he wasn't supposed to be sleeping with, and check out of this mess for a few hours.

"I need to talk to you about the woman," Sammael said.

Ty sighed. "She does seem to stir things up wherever we go," he said with a sinking feeling.

"You need to be careful with her." Sammael's voice was deep and resonant and managed to convey a sense of urgency even though his expression remained impassive. "I do not need to see her mark to know what she is. I knew the one she came from. There is much of Lilith about her, despite the many generations between them. The blood is strong."

Ty could only stare for a moment, utterly floored. The Grigori looked back, as though he had said nothing of importance. How could he have known? And yet, there were rumors about the Grigori, about their origins. Their numbers were few, but they were powerful, and they were rarely seen out in society, preferring to keep to themselves. In America, they kept to the deserts, though whether it was the true base for them was open to conjecture. Some said there were many more of them on an island in the Mediterranean, while others insisted there was a Grigori fortress on some European mountaintop. Some said they could fly. Some said they were not truly vampires but demons. No one seemed to know for sure. No one even truly knew who led them, or if anyone did. But they all had the look of Sammael. Huge. Intimidating. Emotionless. And each bore as their mark a pair of black wings.

"You knew Lilith? The Mother?"

Sammael finally managed an expression that was easily readable: irritation.

"Did I not just tell you that? Don't ask stupid questions. What I have to tell you is important."

"Right, then, what is it?" Ty asked, fighting both weariness and mounting anxiety that the sky was going to come crashing down on him before he ever managed to get back to Arsinöe.

"Only this, ungrateful cat. She is Lilith's, and meant for more than what you're doing with her. The Ptolemy will destroy her if they discover what she is. History will repeat itself. But this time, Lilith's line will end. It was worth preserving, though we did not try to stop what happened."

"What is this? Do you mean the temple fire Lily keeps seeing?" Ty demanded. "You could have stopped all this madness?"

"We are watchers. It is not our place," Sammael said.

"Typical," Ty snorted, angry. "None of the highbloods seem to think it's their place to do anything unless it's their own ass on the line. And even then, they leave a lot of it to their servants."

Sammael's gaze was piercing. "Some. Most, perhaps. But not all. There is still honor among our kind, though sometimes found in strange places. Lilith was different. This heir to her dynasty is different as well."

Though he would have thought it impossible, the throbbing in Ty's head actually increased. He rubbed at his temple with his fingertips. "Look, Sammael, I appreciate the pep talk. But you're not giving me much to go on here. Why exactly are we having this conversation? Are you planning to fight me for her?"

That provoked a small smile from the hulking Grigori, an expression Ty hadn't imagined the man was capable of.

"Alas, no. You might be a worthy adversary, Tynan of the Cait, but you would not live. And I am curious to see what you do with what you have been given."

"I'll do what I've been trained to do. I hunt and I deliver." He sighed and gave his temple a final, irritable rub. His words sounded callous and cold, even to his own ears. "Look, I appreciate your... well, it's not exactly help, is it? But I don't have a choice. The Ptolemy are dying. And I'm tied to them, like it or not. Lily is the key to fixing it."

"Hmm," Sammael said, his face falling back into its hard lines. "One would hope you gain some intelligence before it's too late. But do as you will, cat. The boundaries between our kind were not always so harshly drawn. They may blur again while I draw breath. I will wait with my brothers and sisters, and watch."

"Yes. You did mention that's what you do." Ty shifted on the balls of his feet, impatient to be gone and possessed of a restlessness he sometimes thought would be with him for all his life no matter how hard he fought it.

When the Grigori didn't move, Ty held on to what little patience he had left and dredged up some manners. "Well. Good night, then, Sammael. Lovely meeting you. Hope you sort out whatever trouble brought you here and all that."

That enigmatic smile again. "Rogan does love a good tale. But you need not worry. I am in no trouble. I have done what I came here to do."

Suspicion bloomed deep in Ty's chest—along with a sudden fear that he would never be more than a pawn in some game controlled by those much more powerful than he would ever be.

"You mean to say you came here, lied to Rogan, just to give me that little speech?" He looked more closely at the white-haired giant, the eerie, carved perfection of him. "What are you really, Sammael? Which of the rumors about your kind are true?"

"None of them, of course," Sammael replied. "Though I have heard a few that may have had a kernel of truth in them. It matters not. We will be watching, cat. Prove yourself worthy of her, and our world will change again."

"I really wish you'd explain that."

"Yes, I'm sure you do. Good night, Tynan MacGillivray. May the darkness protect you." With that, Sammael inclined his head, turned, and walked away.

Ty briefly considered going after him and beating the truth out of him, but he doubted it would have done any good. Besides, the way Sammael had casually said that Ty wouldn't survive a fight with him rang true. He was a hell of a fighter, but the Grigori were just... eerie. Worse than he'd remembered.

Hell. He had enough to worry about without being accosted by ancient, creepy vampires spouting prophetic nonsense. He knew Lily's mark was going to mean trouble with the Ptolemy. If only because Arsinöe had never liked having rivals for attention, beautiful ones especially. Still, he refused to believe she wouldn't listen to him, to consider his plea.

Because after being basically mugged by Rogan, Ty had decided that just this once, he was due a fair price for his services to the Ptolemy crown. He wanted only one thing: to be able to keep his word, just this once. He wanted Lily to be able to go home. There were certain herbs that would make her forget, once she had helped them. Make her forget she had ever met a vampire... make her forget him. And that, he knew, was especially important. She could never be allowed to remember him, since what he had seen written all over her face tonight when she'd spoken to him had set off every self-preserving alarm he had.

Lily was falling for him, impossible as it still seemed to him. And despite what Sammael had said about trying to deserve it, Ty knew deep in his bones that such a thing wasn't possible. He was a lowblood, a liar and a killer, and such things were all he would ever be good for. He could not remake vampire society, or the strictures it placed on him and others of his ilk. But he could do his best to get her out of it and to wipe all traces of it from her memory. She could go on as she had in her tidy life—surviving.

And he could get back to the slow death that was living forever.

With miserable thoughts of living an eternity without Lily, Ty trudged upstairs.

Left alone in the little room, Lily paced like a caged tiger. Resentment bubbled just beneath the surface, right along with a fair amount of worry for Ty. How, in a matter of days, had she gone from a cozy, uneventful life as a professor to being holed up in a vampire safe house, on the run from an entire dynasty of creatures who wanted to lock her away and never let her go?

That she was being deliberately kept out of the loop right now, when this was her future, was more than a little infuriating. Granted, Ty knew the rules, the protocol, and these strange, shady people. But it would have been nice not to be stuck in this bare little room for over an hour with no company but her own thoughts, which were driving her slowly insane. Even Jaden had flaked out on her, stalking off to his room with barely a word. He'd looked like he had a lot on his mind, which Lily was sure he did.

They all did.

She paused in the middle of yet another circuit around the room and shoved her hands into her hair, cradling her head. It was then, without the sound of her own footsteps filling her ears, that she heard the soft noises just on the other side of the door. Jaden's room.

Maybe he'd throw her out. Maybe the door would be locked from his side and it was a moot point anyway. Still, the possibility of distraction from herself was impossible to resist.

Lily padded to the door dividing the two rooms and gently, quietly turned the knob.

She had to open it only a little to see that this room was a carbon copy of her own: small, functional, lit by a candle, no windows. In the middle of this room stood a man clad in nothing but faded jeans, his back to Lily as he rummaged in a small bag on the bed. His feet and his torso were bare. Just from his build and the swing of ebony hair, she knew it was Jaden.

But nothing she knew of him, nothing he had said or done, had prepared her for the shock of the sight of his bare skin.

His back was covered in scars, some white, some still an irritated pink, in a crisscrossing pattern that could be nothing but the marks of a whip. There was little of his fair skin that had been left unmarked, and Lily couldn't imagine the pain he must have endured. No wonder he had been quiet and strange with Ty; no wonder he had run from the Ptolemy.

At the thought of the dynasty's name, Lily's blood ran cold. Only a monster would inflict this on another creature. And Ty was bringing her right to the monsters responsible for this. For the first time, she began to question the validity of Ty's promise, not on his part but on the part of the one who had allowed him to make it. If these Ptolemy would do this to their own, would they really stand by their word to her and just let her walk away from them?

"It's rude to stare, you know." Jaden's voice, quiet but intense, made her jump.

"I, um, sorry, I was just…"

He turned to look at her, and she saw no surprise. Only resignation and the haunted look he seemed to wear all the time. Now at least she knew why, but knowing didn't make it any better.

"No," he said, visibly softening. "I was hoping to see you before...Well, you might as well come on in," he said, beckoning before turning back to the bag he'd been looking in. "It'll be daylight soon, and I need to be out of here before then."

Lily looked at him incredulously. "You're *leaving*? Now?"

"Best time to make an escape. Right before the sun peeks its head up. Just have to make sure you know where you can crash next, and that it isn't far, but I have my connections. You can come with me, if you like."

She could tell from his faint smile, almost mocking her, that he knew very well she wouldn't run away with him. But she was also fairly sure the invitation was sincere.

"Why are you running?" she asked. "I thought you were going to help us."

"What's to help?" he asked. "Anura has chosen to stand with the Dracul. Hell if I know why, but it's her prerogative. Which means going back to the apartment would be foolish. *Someone* will be waiting there for us, and no one we'll want to meet. Tynan won't give up hope that the Ptolemy will appreciate him for what he does for them and maybe throw the rest of us cats a bone in the process. A nice thought, but a pipe dream. And you..." He cocked his head, studying her as he trailed off.

It was unnerving, how direct his gaze was, not unlike Ty's. He was quite handsome, Lily realized. But his smiles were even rarer than Ty's. They had a hard existence, these

Cait Sith. She wanted so badly to help, but there was nothing she could do.

The priestess's voice whispered through her mind. *"Break his chains…"*

But how? Pulling an entire bloodline out of slavery wasn't exactly a one-person job. And certainly not a one-*human* job.

"I can't quite get a handle on you, Lily Quinn. You're full of contradictions." He pulled on a dark-colored shirt he lifted from the bed. "One moment I think you're just a naive girl who got hit with an ability you couldn't handle. The next, I see someone who could be a formidable force, if she tried."

Lily felt all the sting of his matter-of-fact assessment. "Neither one of those is very flattering."

Jaden shrugged. "I'm not trying to insult you. There's a lot more to you than meets the eye—of that much I'm certain. But you wouldn't be sleeping with Ty if you weren't at least a little naive. As to getting a handle on your power, that's not really your fault. I've never seen anything like it. I have no idea what it would feel like to try and control it."

"It's like trying to wrap my hands around a bolt of lightning," Lily admitted.

"Hmm." He finished whatever he was doing, then moved toward her. "Let me see that mark of yours. Ty didn't seem to want me gazing upon your virgin skin. Can't think why."

It took her a moment to realize that he was actually teasing her. When she finally did, Lily obligingly pulled down the collar of her shirt while she watched Jaden approach.

"When did you grow a sense of humor?" she asked, arching her neck a little so he could get a better look.

His fingers brushed lightly over the mark. His cool touch made her shiver.

"I have one. There's not a lot to be amused about right now, is all." He paused, then murmured, "Strange and beautiful. Like the one who wears it."

The remark surprised her. When Lily looked in his eyes again, she was surprised to see the amount of power glittering in their depths. Jaden might be quiet, but he was like every vampire she'd met so far: more than he seemed. Jaden looked at her so intently she felt as though he were searching her very soul for something. Finally, he sighed and stepped away.

"I can see why he wants you. He'd have to be a fool not to, and if you stay on this course, he won't be the last. But you're making a mistake in staying, Lily. There's a lot you don't understand about us. And about him."

"I can't tell you how tired I'm getting of hearing that."

Jaden chuckled, another rarity, though there was little true humor in the sound. "At least Ty tried to tell you, then, though not hard enough, obviously." His expression grew more serious. "I'm guessing tonight was the first you'd heard of his family. He doesn't talk about that, not that I blame him. Life was hard for him from the beginning, and it got harder for a while after he was changed. Has he told you how he came to the Ptolemy?"

Lily shifted uneasily. "No. Only that the queen of the Ptolemy saved him and that he owes her."

Jaden snorted. "Yeah. Well, she wouldn't have had to save him if he hadn't fought back during a Ptolemy raid of the local Cait Sith lair." He stopped, shook his head. "But it's not my story to tell. That one's his."

Her interest was piqued, but she refused to rise to the

bait. She hadn't exactly been going on about her own past issues, either, and Ty hadn't asked until she'd nearly plastered a city block with vampire guts. Which was fine, she told herself. Just fine. She didn't want to talk about it. He didn't want to talk about it. Which left them . . . where?

"The past doesn't matter," Lily said, her chin going up. "And I don't have any expectations, Jaden. He hasn't lied to me and pretended we have a future. And I'm not pretending we have one. If being with him anyway makes me naive, well, then I guess I am."

She hadn't realized how it would hurt to say it, that there was no future, only the now. Nor had she realized how easily Jaden would pick up on that pain. She saw his pity and recoiled from it. She'd had enough pity in her life. It had never been warranted, and it wasn't now. Still, she couldn't help adding, "Ty's different. He's a good man, even though he thinks he isn't."

"See, that's where you'll pay the price for giving a damn, Lily," Jaden replied, his expression darkening. "Ty's not a bad man. Hell, he's one of the best I've run with. Took me under his wing when I didn't know my ass from a hole in the ground and hated everyone and everything. But he's a lowblood. Worse, he's a lowblood Ptolemy-owned Cait Sith. His life isn't his own, and he does what he has to in order to survive."

"Yeah, I get it," Lily said unhappily. "I don't like it, but I can accept it."

Jaden's burst of fury surprised her. "Don't pretend it won't hurt you when he gives you to that viper and walks away!" he snapped, eyes blazing with a sudden flash of unnatural light. "And he will walk away, Lily. It's all he knows. Apart from that, this is about more than him. The Cait Sith are his family, and he thinks about them first: how his actions will affect their treatment, how staying in Arsinöe's good graces will allow him to help some of the lowest who serve the Ptolemy. She gives him more chain than most, I'll say that. But then, I was a favored little pet of hers too. And I think you saw where that got me." He shook his head, his anger vanishing as quickly as it had appeared. "Ty's the standard-bearer for the Cait Sith who have to live under the Ptolemy's thumb, Lily. To a certain extent, Arsinöe's favor of him spills onto all the Cait at court. He's a goddamned legend to the ones still out in the world who are trying to make as much of a living as they can, hoping that the highbloods won't come for them the way they did for so many of us."

Lily frowned as she digested this and remembered the scene in her kitchen. "Damien, the Shade who's after me, he basically called Ty a sellout. I thought maybe that's how he was looked at, period."

Jaden rolled his eyes. "Damien. Yeah, he would say that. Never listen to a Shade, Lily. They're professional assassins with a God complex. He thinks he's his own man? Not hardly. He has bosses to answer to, same as the rest of us. But whatever makes him feel better about the path he chose. Anyway, you wouldn't see many of our line around here to find out what they think of Ty. The Cait Sith tend to live in the Ptolemy strongholds, and this sure isn't one. You can tell their queen is an Egyptian. Fucking cat fixation. At least they give us jobs when no one else will, but the price for refusing them is steep. To the Ptolemy, my kind can only ever be slaves or prey. I'm going to see if I can get far enough away to try being neither."

"What happened? Did *she* do that to you?" Lily asked. It was urgent, so urgent that she know.

Jaden's gaze chilled, turning his blue eyes arctic, and he looked away. "She might as well have. But it doesn't matter. I won't go back. I'd die first."

"Jaden." Lily reached out, bridging the distance between them, and placed her hand on his arm. She felt how tightly he held himself, and it was her turn to feel pity. Still, it did get him to look at her.

"You need to tell Ty. Please."

"Tell me what?"

His voice was gruff, sleepy, and thoroughly irritated. Lily turned and saw Ty standing in the doorway, looking much the same as he sounded. Her first impulse upon seeing him was the same it always was: She immediately wanted to be in his arms, wrapped around him. And when his eyes met hers, she saw she wasn't alone in the sudden rush of desire.

Jaden's sigh brought her back to reality.

"I'd tell the two of you to get a room, but you've already got one. Sun's rising, brother. You ought to be asleep."

"I could hardly sleep. Rogan would have picked every valuable available off my carcass," Ty replied, sauntering into the room and coming to rest beside Lily, not touching her but close enough that every fiber of her being seemed to vibrate with his presence. He looked at the bag on the bed, at Jaden's changed clothing, and immediately his eyes hardened.

"Going somewhere?"

"What if I am? I told you I'm not going back to the Ptolemy. As I told the lovely Lily, you're welcome to come with me. But I doubt this safe house is all that safe, and I'm sure as hell not sticking around to find out. I need to get out of Chicago, ride out the storm in more neutral territory."

"Isn't that what I just paid for? Getting us out of here?"

She could hear incredulous anger in Ty's voice, slowly increasing in intensity. Jaden, however, seemed nothing but defiant.

"I'll do better on my own. Right now the heat's on you, not me. Easier for me to slip away. If I stick with you, it might not be. I can't risk the Ptolemy finding me, Ty. Try and understand that. You have something they want, and because of it I'm doubly in danger of being spotted. It wouldn't look good for you either. Best to part ways now."

"Jaden, if they came here looking for you, they'll hunt you to ground no matter where you go. What did you *do?*"

Jaden crossed his arms over his chest, glaring. "Would it make any difference? You'll go running back no matter what I say."

"They whipped him," Lily blurted out, and felt her cheeks heat as Jaden turned his glare on her. "He's got marks all over his back, Ty. I saw them."

Ty's expression softened, saddened. "No. Jaden."

Jaden bared his teeth, his fangs flashing. "And still you'll go back to her. Do you know what I did to deserve it, Ty? I mentioned to her esteemed highness that her lover had been telling everyone who would listen that we were headed to war with the Dracul, and I wanted to know if it was true. Why shouldn't I ask? The Cait are always put on the front lines of their petty squabbles. Can you imagine how it would be if there was all-out war? I thought we deserved to know whether this was really happening, so I could prepare the others." He shook his head. "She told Nero. I was whipped for insubordination, the lash dipped in a poison that will ensure the scars stay with me. She never said a word. If I'd stayed, they would have put a collar on me."

Ty's jaw tightened. Lily saw a muscle twitch in his cheek. "They're using the collars again?" He turned to Lily before she could ask. "A thousand years ago, at the dawn of my bloodline, the Ptolemy devised collars that prevented the Cait Sith from shifting back into human form. Back then, we were used as little more than intelligent vampire cats, guards and hunters whose only human trait was that we could listen and understand, think and obey. Many went mad from being bound that way—so many that the practice eventually stopped."

"For a time. No longer," Jaden interjected. "The perimeter guards are all collared and chained now, Ty. The only ones left standing on two feet are those who need their hands to serve." His voice hardened. "I know what you're thinking. You can't save them. You can't change her mind. Things have come full circle in the court, and there's nothing to be done about it. There's only highblood and gutterblood to the Ptolemy. No exceptions. You go back, you're going to find out the hard way. Let them die."

"Then many of our own die as well." Ty blew out a breath and ran a hand through his hair. "I don't know, Jaden. I never expected things would be so far gone."

"Well, they are," Jaden replied flatly. "She's not what you thought. Or what I thought, for that matter. She never was. Just another highblood bitch, lording it over the unwashed masses."

Ty shook his head slowly, sadly. "No. There was more there once."

"There is *nothing* there!"

The raw fury in Jaden's voice, written plainly across his face, was a shock to Lily's system. There were layers to Jaden, she saw, and not all of them were pleasant. The

one she saw now was all killer. Even Ty seemed startled
by the flash of temper, staring silently while Jaden continued shouting into his face.

"What do they have to do to make you lose faith in
them, Ty? They kill our kind. They make the rest of us into
pathetic shadows of ourselves. And still you defend her, telling me and everyone who'll listen to trust in the system, that
things will get better. And sometimes they do, Ty, but not
for long. And then they get worse. Every goddamned time."

Ty seemed to get over his momentary surprise quickly
enough, stepping into Jaden, so close the two were nearly
touching. Lily could feel the violence crackling in the
air and hoped, desperately, that these two would let each
other be.

"They all spit on us! All of them!" Ty snarled. "Arsinöe
at least has found a use for us, instead of leaving us to rot,
destitute, in some squalid gutter."

"It would be better—"

Ty had Jaden by the front of the shirt in a flash, lifting
him off the ground, his feet dangling a couple of inches
above it. Lily's mouth dropped open in horror. She had
never seen Ty like this, so full of blind rage.

"Ty," she said urgently, "no!" But he seemed not to
hear her.

"I have been in that gutter, brother," Ty hissed into
Jaden's face, his teeth bared, incisors long and deadly. "I
was born there. I died there. My entire bloody family died
there. Don't you *ever* tell me that the way we live is worse
than that, when you've never had to live among people
drowning in the worst sort of filth with no hope. None.
If I have to live, I'll take this." He dropped Jaden to the
floor, where the furious vampire managed to land on his

feet despite the force with which he was let down. "Go, then. I hope you find what you're looking for." Ty spat the words at Jaden before turning on one heel and stalking back through the doorway.

Lily tried to catch his arm as he passed, but he evaded her touch. She did, however, catch the quickest glimpse of his eyes. The pain in them took her breath away.

The door between rooms slammed shut, leaving Lily and Jaden looking at each other. His expression was wary, guarded, the way it had been when she'd met him. She looked helplessly at him, wishing she could fix all that was tearing him and Ty apart. That would tear her and Ty apart before all was said and done, she realized.

"I'm sorry," she said softly, stepping backward toward the door. "I need to—"

"Don't be," Jaden said, his voice cool. "He'll figure it out someday. And if he doesn't, I can't be there trying to save him. It's every cat for himself. Always has been."

Lily took another step back, pulled toward the door that Ty had put between them. Her heart ached for him, and she wanted nothing more than to be a balm to his wounds, which were old and very deep.

"Maybe you and he could get the Cait to join together," she said, hearing the desperate note in her voice. "If you rose up, demanded to be left alone. History is full of things like that!" *And then she and Ty could be together...stay together...*

"No, Lily," Jaden said softly, sadly. "They're too strong. They've taken too many. The Cait Sith do better on their own anyway. I'm used to it...and so is Ty." He hesitated a moment, then turned away. "Good-bye, Lily Quinn. I hope some god or other decides to protect you once Ty can't."

"Jaden."

He turned back to her for some reason, whether it was simply the sound of his name or perhaps the way she said it. It was impulsive, but Lily found her feet moving before her mind could stop her. Quickly, she went to Jaden and wrapped her arms around him in the sort of comforting embrace Bay had often given her but she had never quite known how to return. She felt him stiffen, and she gave him a quick squeeze before he could push her away. Then Lily stepped back, seeing his confusion. It made her heart ache. She knew what it was to be that unloved, that wary of an affectionate gesture so freely given.

"Good-bye, Jaden," she said softly. "Be safe."

Then she turned and walked quickly, silently to the door, opened it, and left Jaden exactly how he claimed to want to be.

On his own.

chapter TWENTY

LILY CLOSED THE DOOR quietly behind her.

Ty's back was to her. He stood, perfectly still, in the middle of the room. His back was rigid, his hands fisted at his sides, his head down. Defeated, Lily thought. He looked utterly defeated. It frightened her. She had meant it when she'd told him he was the strongest man she'd ever known. How had he borne all of what he'd been through and still managed to function? How had he come through losing so much, losing *everything*, without breaking?

She took a step toward him, then another, cautiously.

"Jaden's gone," she said.

"I know," Ty replied. His voice was soft, slightly ragged.

"I'm sorry he left," Lily said, flexing fingers that longed to press and soothe those rigid shoulders. "Sorry you two left it that way."

Ty laughed, a soft exhalation that was utterly mirthless. "It's the way it always is with the Cait Sith. We go our own ways. Not much good at pairing up, I'm afraid."

If she were a stronger woman, or at least a braver one, she would find Arsinöe and her worthless courtiers herself and make them pay for what they'd done to Ty and his kind. They'd turned proud, powerful creatures into servants, treated them so harshly that they no longer knew what to do with kindness; they had afflicted them with so much self-doubt that they didn't leave for fear of being unable to function outside the strictures they'd always known. It was disgusting.

"He's just afraid," Lily said. "And honestly, Ty, after seeing what the Ptolemy did to him, I am too." The idea had come to her as she'd paced the room earlier, waiting for him. Now it seemed the only way, and the words tumbled from her lips in a rush.

"I think we should go to Vlad Dracul."

Now he turned to her, but the look on his face made Lily wish he hadn't.

"You think we should what?"

"Just hear me out," Lily said, holding up her hands. "Anura went to Vlad, right? She had to have had a good reason. And there's no proof that they're the ones attacking the Ptolemy initiations, right? Just history pointing to them."

Ty's expression indicated he thought she might have lost her mind. "We're immortal, Lily. History pointing to them is no small thing. As to Anura, she makes her living on Dracul territory, and her club was just set on fire and nearly destroyed. I can see you were impressed with her, but as I told you before, she does have a vested interest in the outcome of all this."

"Why did you bring me to her if you don't trust her?"

"I don't trust anyone," Ty said.

Even if he hadn't meant to hurt her, Lily felt his words

like a knife in the heart. He seemed oblivious to it, too consumed with countering Lily's argument.

"I think a better question," Ty continued, "is why you're so determined to trust a woman you've only just met? She's a good woman, Lily; that I won't deny. But vampires, as you may have noticed, are inherently self-interested."

You're not, she wanted to say, but held her tongue. She knew he wouldn't accept it. He seemed determined to believe the worst about himself.

Instead, she kept to the subject at hand. "I felt something from her. I know it sounds crazy, but it was almost like something in me knew her. And vice versa." Lily shook her head, trying to make sense of it. "I don't understand any of this. How I can possibly be descended from some vampire goddess. How I can feel this weird connection with Anura when I know I've never met her in my life." She lifted her hands to her temples and rubbed, hoping she could keep at bay the headache she had brewing.

"I wish I had answers," Ty said, watching her from beneath thick, dark lashes. "As I told you, vampires can't have children. But you're a mortal wearing the mark of an ancient, and very dead, dynasty. You have power like I've never seen. I'm old, Lily, but I'm nowhere near old enough, I think, to know the answers."

"Is Anura?"

Ty blew out a breath, and she saw the shadow of irritation cross his face. "Anura again. Yes, she's very old, Lily. Likely she knew some of the Lilim. It's why we came to her. And why it's such a problem that she's gone and told Vlad Dracul about you." He closed his eyes for a moment, as though steeling himself, then said, "It doesn't matter.

We're out of time here. As soon as the sun sets again, we'll have to leave the city."

"And go where?" Lily asked, crossing her arms over her chest and staring up at Ty, whose expression had gone guarded. Panic began to bubble in her chest. She knew the answer. She *knew*. No matter how little she wanted to believe he'd actually do it.

"Lily," Ty began, and the tired resignation in his voice nearly broke her.

"Don't. Please don't take me to the Ptolemy, Ty. You know what they did to Jaden. Please, we can go to the Dracul, find Anura, find out the truth!"

"The truth," Ty said with a sad half smile, "is something that all the dynasties have only a nodding acquaintance with. You'll get a different story, but will it be the truth? Doubtful. One dynasty is the same as another that way, Lily. It's pointless."

Understanding hit her like a fist in the stomach.

"Even now, after everything, knowing they tortured your friend, that they're subjecting your kind to terrible things while you do their work for them, you're bringing me to them?" Her heart fluttered like a caged bird. "You would really just...just *give* me to them?"

He might have told her they had no future. But seeing it, the reality of it, was almost overwhelming. His eyes darkened with some indefinable emotion.

"I'll handle them, Lily. No one's going to hurt you. I know how to deal with Arsinöe, no matter what Jaden says. I'll—"

"She'll kill me, Ty," Lily said, beginning to back away from him, as though at any moment he might snatch her up and drag her away to the Ptolemy. "There's no way she'll let me go. I'm not a Seer. I'm not what she thinks, and when she finds out— Don't!"

She cried out as Ty's hands shot out to grip her wrists, encircling them like iron bands. Lily tried to twist away from him, but he was having none of it. Instead, she found herself pulled against his chest, his arms wrapped around her to hold her still. Struggle was useless, but Lily tried until she realized that Ty was holding on to her like a drowning man clinging to the only thing keeping him above water.

Lily stilled as his voice sounded in her ear, harsh and full of emotion. "I won't give you up, Lily. I'll find a way to save you, save the both of us. Just have faith in me," he said, and she could hear the desperation in his voice. "I have to try and make things right. But I'll never let anyone hurt you. Just have faith in me."

She couldn't imagine how hard it was for him to ask that of her. And it was that, coupled with the raw emotion in his voice, that allowed Lily to finally let go in his arms, wrapping herself even more tightly in his embrace. She buried her face in his chest, needing the steady beating of his heart.

"Ty," she said, "just don't let me go."

Desire sparked and caught fire, mixing with desperation as they clung together. They were alone in the world, Lily thought, except for each other. She'd lost almost everything. She couldn't lose him too. Not now.

Ty pulled back just enough to look down at her. Lily could see the torment in his eyes, flashing as silver as the moon, before he crushed his mouth against hers. It took her breath away, the shock of it, the sheer ferocity of it. His mouth was hot and hard on hers, taking, plundering as his hands tangled in her hair.

Lily felt dizzy, swamped by the need that crashed

through her system like a tidal wave. He couldn't tell her he needed her. But he was letting her feel it, letting her feel exactly what it was he felt for her. It was overwhelming. It was irresistible.

"I won't let you go," he murmured. Then his mouth was on hers, and she felt all the power inside of her rushing up on a wave of hot desire, a sensation unlike any she'd ever experienced.

He caught her weight neatly as she wrapped her legs around him, hauling her up against him, his hands gripping her ass. She could feel him throbbing against her, and instantly her core went liquid. Their kisses turned urgent, hot tongues, nipping teeth, as he stumbled across the room until he had her back against the wall.

Her shirt was gone. She had no idea how it had left her, but it hadn't been over her head. The bra, too, had vanished, and Ty filled his hands with her breasts as she clung to him, her thighs clenched around his waist. Her head fell back at his rough touch, as calloused thumbs rubbed over hard, pebbled nipples, and Lily moaned her pleasure.

"Gods, Lily, I need—"

"Yes," was all she said, a simple exhalation before she nipped at his ear, nibbled down the sensitive skin at the side of his neck. "Take me."

He let out a ragged groan, then disentangled himself long enough to remove his own clothing. Lily caught a glimpse of several jagged tears in the fabric of his shirt and marveled. Had she done that? She unfastened her jeans and slid them quickly to the ground, kicking them aside. Then they stood facing each other, wearing nothing but candlelight. And even as need welled and pulsed inside of her, mixing with a power that now flowed like lightning in her blood, she had to still for a moment just to look at him, the sheer feline beauty of him. Long lines, sinuous muscle, dark and beautiful and wild. His eyes were a storm of emotion as he watched her, and Lily felt all self-consciousness fall away as she stood before him.

The heat of his gaze as it traveled down her body made her quiver. He growled something in Gaelic, something that made her shiver with need.

"You look like a goddess."

"All I want to be is yours." A piece of the truth. As much as she could give him without turning him away from her.

She saw him shudder, as though her words had torn right through him.

"You don't know how much I wish you could be," he said.

"For tonight, I am," Lily said, holding out her arms, wanting whatever he could give her.

She felt herself open to him, surprised at how easily her power rose within her, unbidden, but for the first time, unthreatening. It wended its way through her like a glittering river, bringing such pleasure, such surprising familiarity, that she welcomed it. Lily closed her eyes, tipped her head back, and let the magic rush over her skin, under it, lighting her up inside the way only being with Ty did.

"Share your magic. Break his chains." It whispered through her mind, the voice with a wisdom beyond all things. And the words rang true.

She had never attempted to share this part of herself with another, but it was all she had to give him besides her heart. He had the latter already—she knew that now—though Lily would never burden him with it. But this she could share willingly, openly. If he would have it.

This magic was a part of her.

She opened her eyes again, for once at peace with the storm that raged inside of her.

"Just be with me," she said.

His gaze was hungry, so hungry. "I can't be gentle tonight," he said. "I'm not a gentle man, Lily. You'd do better to lock me out. I want you hot and fast. I want to ride you until you scream for me."

The muscles deep in her belly clenched with aching need.

"Show me," was all she said, and beckoned him. Her skin shimmered in the candlelight, illuminated from within. She didn't know how, didn't question it. All she did was want.

He came to her, and she gasped with pleasure at the feel of his body against her, his cool and silken skin against hot and ready flesh. And despite what he had said, she felt him trying to hold back, trying to go slowly. She would have none of it.

Her hands roamed over him urgently as their mouths met, as kisses tangled together punctuated only by breathy sighs and moans. Lily let her hands roam over sinewy muscle, over the rock-hard ass she'd admired every time he turned around. At last, her hand wrapped around the length of him and gave it a hard stroke.

"Please," she said when he shivered. "I want all of you. Now."

"The wall," he said, his voice barely more than a growl. "Turn around."

She did as she was told, leaning slightly forward as he pinned her hands against the wall with his own.

"Spread your legs."

He entered her in one swift stroke, filling her all the

way to her womb. Lily cried out, rocking back against him, wanting more. Her muscles clenched around him like a hot, wet fist, and he hissed like a cat at the sensation. Then he began to move, his hands drifting down until they could grip her hips. And he gripped them hard as Lily pushed back against him, urging him on. Everything inside of her was coiling tighter and tighter as Ty slammed into her, making mindless noises of pleasure that only served to feed her own. And beneath the rhythmic beat of their mating was the magic, flowing outward now, flowing out of her and into him. She could feel his pleasure as though it were her own, and the two blended together to create something Lily thought might drive her mad if it went on long enough. Her heart beat in time with his, every inhalation and exhalation made together. And still they climbed, toward some shimmering far-off peak that promised heaven itself should they reach it.

Lily rocked back against him, hearing his voice in her mind, half delirious with pleasure: *Give me oh yes give it to me give me all sweet Lily I want I want I need my Lily mine mine oh mine...*

When she came, it was blinding bright. She screamed his name, clenching around him as he shouted his own release. A flash of light burst from her as if she were a newly lit candle, powerful enough to envelop them both. Then another climax, harder than the first, blasting through her so hard that she bucked back against him. His helpless cry as he dug his fingers into her hips to ride it out with her was music to her ears. Ty grabbed her hair, snapping her head back as he continued to pump into her, and she knew what was coming, what he wanted to do.

Somehow, she knew this would be the pinnacle of it

all, a pleasure unlike any a human could ever know. And she welcomed it, welcomed that bond to him that could never be broken.

"Yes," she breathed, about to crest again. "Do it."

But he gave a tortured moan and instead dropped his head against the back of hers. Lily had only a second to feel the keen edge of disappointment before her final climax exploded within her like a dark star, nearly taking her to her knees with its force. She felt Ty's legs buckle behind her when he cried out, but he managed to stay on his feet. They clung together, Ty curled against her from behind, as the waves of sensation slowly ebbed to ripples, her power enveloping them both like a warm cocoon. She could feel him in every breath she took, in every cell of her body.

Something had changed. Something fundamental that Lily didn't understand, though she knew it with every fiber of her being. But whatever it was, understanding would have to come later as Ty began to crumple to the floor behind her, slipping from her and leaving her feeling strangely empty.

You're so close, daughter . . . so close to all that could be . . .

"Lily," he murmured as she turned, caught him up, and only just managed to get him to the bed. He pulled her down with him, wrapping himself around her, nuzzling into her hair. Then he was still, deep and even breaths the only sound in the quiet of the safe house.

"I love you, Tynan," she murmured, allowing herself to let go and drift into the oblivion of sleep.

Outside, morning had come.

chapter TWENTY-ONE

H<small>E DREAMED OF</small> L<small>ILY</small>.

She stood in a moonlit garden, clad in a simple white dress that glowed as bright as the stars above. Ty went to her, his heart as carefree as it had ever been in his long life, wanting nothing more than the pleasure of being with her. She laughed gaily when she saw him, turning so that her skirt billowed around her, and dashed off into the roses that glowed as red as blood.

"Have a care with her, brother cat. She is precious to me."

The voice stopped him cold. He turned to look at the one who had spoken, a woman shrouded in shadow. He caught a glimpse of alabaster skin, flame-red hair, and eyes that glowed as green as jade. But the darkness hid her from view.

"Lilith," he said, knowing deep in his bones that it was her.

"I am, though most would have me forgotten. They

called me monster, when I was the first, when they could not exist without me."

He could hear the anger in her voice, ancient and terrible, as well as the love she bore her kind.

"What do you want from me?" he asked, hearing Lily's distant laughter as she grew farther from him, racing through the garden. It filled him with unimaginable longing.

Lilith regarded him with shrewd, glittering eyes. They saw more than he wanted them to see.

"She has chosen you, the final child of all the many children that have come before her. I had begun to wonder if the blood would ever again be strong enough to manifest the mark of my dynasty, the mark given me by my only love. And yet the time of that rising has come round at last. Lily, of all of them, is truly my heir. So, of course, you are of great interest to me. You will help remake what was broken so long ago." She paused, arching an eyebrow. "If you are strong enough."

He knew he should tread carefully with such a creature. And yet there was so much he needed answered. His heart aching at the receding sound of Lily's voice, he took a chance.

"How is it possible?" he asked. "How can a mortal woman like Lily carry your blood?"

Even in the depths of shadow, Ty could see Lilith's mouth curve up in a bitter smile.

"Do you truly want to know of the ritual? I doubt it. But what came before and after, I can tell you. A beautiful demon, one of the Fallen, fell in love with me. From him came the dark gift of immortality so that I could be with him always. And so," she said with a sigh, "I am. No longer living, but without a true death, even now."

"Then how did the others destroy you? And why? No one talks about it," Ty said, knowing that this had ceased to be a dream, eager for the answers only Lilith could provide.

Lilith waved an elegant hand dismissively. "Petty jealousies. Desire for power and control. Fear of my Fallen lover, Seth, when he would harm none of them. I underestimated my enemies then, as so many others have in years since. At least I had the foresight to preserve *something* of what was. No matter the cost."

"So this Seth gave you a child," Ty said. Maybe Lilith was right. The sort of demonic ritual that could impregnate a vampire was something he didn't want to imagine. Such a thing would require enormous power and would be dark... very dark.

"Indeed. But sadly, it could have no part of him. Some things truly *are* impossible. There was a human man involved, of course, but he was willing enough, at least at first. A means to an end," she said, an expression passing briefly over her fine features that might have been regret. "It doesn't matter. The blood has been passed to the eldest child, always a female, down through the ages. The power has always been there, sleeping, waiting for one who could awaken it. I knew, when Lily was born, that she was the one. The first who actually manifested the mark. My mark."

"You watched her?"

Lilith's voice was sharp. "I can do little *but* watch, these long years. Though as you have seen, when I must, I can protect my own. Even if it takes everything I have." Her tone softened, grew weary, and Ty finally had a sense of the agelessness of this woman. And he felt a sort of pity for her, though she reminded him far more of the high-bloods he had known than of Lily. There was a ruthlessness about her, a knife-edged drive to preserve what was hers that he knew would slice right through anyone who got in her way.

He recognized it. Just as he recognized that the human part of Lily's lineage had been essential in forming who she was. Her softness, her empathy.

Lily was so much more than the one who had come before her, Ty realized. And Lilith knew it. Perhaps that had been the plan all along.

Lilith nodded. "Yes," she said. "I know what you're thinking. And you're right. She is more than I was. I shed most of my humanity—maybe all of it—in becoming the first of the vampires. I have few regrets, but I will always long for the parts of myself that were lost. This child, my Lily, has the strengths and weaknesses of both worlds." Lilith tilted her head, considering him, shadows playing over her face. Even here, in this place that was neither sleep nor waking, Ty saw that the moonlight passed right through her.

"You will balance each other," she said. "A good match, if you can hold her. If you prove yourself worthy of my prize."

All the years of ridicule pressed in on him, threatening to suffocate him. Worthy? He, a lowly cat?

"My bloodline—"

"Is one to be proud of," Lilith interrupted impatiently. "As are they all. Other gods, other demons, all saw what Seth had done and created their own ideas of immortal perfection through their blood. Companions, rivals, friends to me, and I was grateful. How could the diversity not be wonderful? Our differences, together, make us strong. There will always be those who would rather divide and conquer. My Lily will always need protection. But there are allies to be found in unexpected places, if you're willing enough, and wise enough, to look."

The burden she wanted to place on him was overwhelming. To be Lily's protector, her lover, her mate, to rebuild all that was lost in the face of terrifying odds... and he from a bloodline that would make the other highbloods laugh.

And yet, how could he do anything else? There was no other for him. He loved her.

He loved her. And accepting it, embracing the truth, lit a fire inside him. Suddenly, everything was clear. He knew what he needed to do, no matter how crazy it seemed.

Lilith watched him and smiled. "Awaken her blood, Tynan of the Cait Sith. It is for you, and no other. Be worthy of the gift I give to you. And beware. The danger to you is so much closer than you think."

The night garden vanished around him, and suddenly Ty was in the temple that Lily had described, full of fire and death. Lilith was before him on a platform, a goddess presiding over a losing battle. And he saw, rising behind the woman who gazed at him with terrible hope, the face of one he had never expected to see. Not here. Not like this.

"I warned her my house would rise again," Lilith said, her voice as clear as a bell above the din. "My child will begin to heal what was sundered so long ago. She has begun already. Your blood is no shame, Tynan of the Cait Sith. Power of the vampire, magic of the Fae, beauty of the cat. All these things I would welcome as my dynasty awakens. Do not falter. Be true."

He watched in horror as Arsinöe, teeth bared in a fury that was almost madness, severed Lilith's head from her body with a single stroke of her curved blade.

"Well, don't you two make a charming picture?"

Ty's eyes snapped open, screams still ringing in his ears. The first thing he registered was that Lily was still safe and warm in his arms.

The second thing was that the two of them were no longer alone.

Damien perched at the edge of the bed, watching him with the cool detachment that Ty had once thought him incapable of. But there seemed to be no feeling left in the vampire he had known. Damien was all Shade now. And he had them cornered at last.

"Stupid of you, really, to go and get involved this way. But you always did have an insufferable soft streak."

Ty tried to clear the sleep from his mind quickly to figure out how to get out of this, how to react. One of them was going to come out of this dead, and he would rather it not be him.

"Rogan sold me out," Ty said, trying conversation to buy himself some time. But if softness was his weakness, Damien's had always been a love of displaying how clever he had been. And this time seemed to be no exception.

"Not at all," Damien said with a curve of his mouth. "Rogan, or should I say, Rogan's headless body, is still tucked into bed, utterly unaware that its head will be prominently displayed on a pike as a warning to lowbloods who think to hide from justice. I'm sure it will cause quite a stir. I'm just happy I could pick up some extra cash by rolling that job into this one. Rogan made a lot of people very unhappy. Important people. And the son of a bitch never did a thing for us, so don't waste any more of your precious time mourning his passing. He's better off gone. And there's always another rat-infested safe house for those who are looking."

There was a crash downstairs, followed by shouting and the thundering of feet.

"What the bloody hell is this?" Ty asked, feeling panic begin to rise like bile in his throat. "Did you bring the entire House of Shadows this time?"

Damien's expression revealed him to be extremely irritated, if not surprised. "Shit," he hissed. "Ptolemy."

Ty stared incredulously as Lily stirred beside him, her blue eyes fluttering open first with warmth, then slow blooming panic as her gaze shifted to Damien.

"Oh God," she said.

"Hardly," Damien snapped at her. He turned his accusing eyes back on Ty. "You can thank your little freak of nature for this. She's got some friend from that hellhole in Massachusetts who's been all over the news, telling how her missing friend called her to let her know she was all right but was in some sort of trouble. The wonder of caller ID identified your location as Chicago. Not information I needed, of course. I've been following your trail all over this godforsaken city. But I would assume your whereabouts were a little bit of a surprise to any Ptolemy who knew what you'd been up to in Massachusetts."

Ty cursed and barely heard Lily murmur a name.

"Bay? You called your best friend?"

Lily's eyes were purest misery. "She thought I was

dead. I…I couldn't just leave it like that. She needed to know I'd be back. I'm so sorry, Ty. I didn't know she'd call the police. I told her not to."

The apology so clear in her voice did nothing to assuage his helpless anger, though most of it was directed at his own accursed luck. That such a little thing, a small and sneaky thing, could bring down everything for him, for both of them, seemed desperately unfair now. And that she had kept it from him burned more than he'd thought such a thing might.

He needed more time. He needed to be able to get as far away as possible before the Ptolemy realized what he had done. Because he had no intention of bringing her to them now. Not after what he had seen, what Lilith had shown him.

Damien's laugher cut through his fury like ice. He was looking at Lily with amused derision.

"You think…you think he's going to return you? Oh, Lily, *really*. Are you really so naive?" He laughed again, turning his attention to Ty. "I have to give you credit, old friend. Sleeping with the mark, convincing her that everything will go back to normal as long as she plays her part—gods, you really should have come with me to the Shades. We can use men like you!"

The din grew louder downstairs, and footsteps began to thunder up toward them.

"You were telling me the truth, weren't you?" Lily asked quietly.

For a split second, Ty was desperately afraid that she wouldn't believe him. That she would have as little faith in his word as everyone else in his long life. Then he thought of the trust she had placed in him just by staying by his side, the way she had bared herself to him last night, body and soul. His eyes locked with hers.

"No, Lily. Not now. I can't take you home. But I'll do all I can to keep you safe if you stay with me." He paused, hoping she could accept the way things would have to be. "I may have to take you to the ends of the earth to keep you away from them, but I'm not letting the Ptolemy get their hands on you."

There was so much he needed to tell her...but not in front of Damien. Not until they were free of this place. The clatter on the stairs had moved to their floor, growing louder as the Ptolemy searched the safe house.

The relief and trust in Lily's gaze humbled him.

Slowly, she nodded. "Okay," she said.

Could she love him back, he wondered? He thought she could, if they were given the opportunity to try. He'd walk through Damien to get that chance if he had to.

Damien watched the two of them, his mouth curled into a disgusted sneer.

"I should just let the Ptolemy have the both of you. This is foul," he said.

Ty looked at Lily. "If they've sent more Cait Sith to hunt us down, I can probably convince them to help us get out of here."

"Please," Damien said flatly, getting gracefully to his feet. "You think they're going to send your blood brothers and sisters after their hero? These are highbloods out for you tonight, Ty. And you know as well as I how they love a little cat hunt from time to time."

Ty bared his fangs at Damien and threw off the covers, leaping to his feet and snatching up his crumpled jeans.

"Are we going to fight now?" he asked Damien as he

slid them on, noting that Lily had followed suit, quickly and silently pulling on her clothes. "Because you might want to get on with it before the door bursts open and we have company."

Damien considered him with a typically inscrutable expression. He hadn't changed much, Ty decided as he pulled on his shirt. Damien was only predictable in his unpredictability. He might go for the throat at a moment's notice. Or he might, on a whim, lend a hand.

Maybe it was out of hatred for highbloods in general, or Ptolemy specifically. Maybe it was their long-ago friendship. But Damien chose the latter.

"Hmm. I'm being paid quite a bit of money to kill the two of you. And the Ptolemy showing up to drag you off is going to ruin that. How about this? Leave with me, and I'll try to kill you once we find a better spot. Makes it fair."

"You're a twisted bastard, Damien. What do you care about fair?" growled Ty, catching Lily's hand in his.

Damien gave a shrug. "Follow me, if you will. Otherwise, you can piss off. Have fun explaining yourself to Arsinöe." He melted into his feline form and leaped to the door leading into Jaden's room.

Ty looked at Lily. "I'm not seeing much of a choice here."

Doors slammed open perilously close to their room. The safe house had been practically empty, and the Ptolemy hunting party had picked up speed. If Damien knew another way out, they needed to take it.

"How do we get out?" Lily breathed, her eyes wide as voices sounded right down the hall now. It was the blasted speed the Ptolemy had been blessed with.

"Here, kitty kitty! We know you're in here!"

A loud bang. The sounds of furniture being overturned.

"Come on." Ty dragged Lily through Jaden's door, true fear beginning to bloom in his chest. If they were caught... They couldn't be caught, damn it, not now!

They found Damien, still in cat form and wearing an "I knew you'd come" face, licking one paw in the center of the room. He placed a paw on a knot down low on the far wall, and a piece of it slid to one side, just enough to fit a human and certainly enough to fit a cat. Damien dashed through. The Ptolemy were right outside the door.

Ty pulled, but Lily stopped short. There was an expression he had never seen before on her face.

"Come out, kitty, or it won't be just the collar for you! We're thinking we might skin you alive while the woman watches! What do you think of that, eh?" Slam. Crash.

"They're never going to stop hunting us now. I made it so you can't go back. I didn't mean to—"

Her guilt shamed him. "I don't care, Lily. We'll keep running until they give up or we find another way. I know what we have to do now. All I need is you. Now come on, they're nearly here!"

"They're too close. You'll get yourself killed for me." She looked to be on the verge of tears.

"You're worth it," he told her. Desperate to get her hidden, to get away, Ty pulled Lily forward. As he plunged into the hidden stairwell, though, Lily's hand slipped from his. He heard her voice right behind him and knew the words would haunt him forever.

"I'm not worth dying for. It's too late. Please understand... I love you."

His eyes widened in horror as the wall slammed shut

behind him, and he heard the door beyond burst open a split second later, the room filling with shouts.

"My name is Lily Quinn," he heard her say. "I need to see Queen Arsinöe immediately. I'm the Seer she's been looking for."

Ty stayed frozen, his mind reeling. What the bloody hell did she think she was doing?

Telling him she loved him, and then . . .

Saving his life. But in doing that, she might very well have sacrificed her own. And she knew it. Wild, terrified rage filled him. She was right on the other side of the wall, surrounded by powerful highbloods who would break him in a millisecond if they saw him, and still it was all he could do not to hurl himself into their midst.

"Don't be a fool, Tynan," Damien hissed in the darkness. "She's given you a fighting chance to survive, gods know why. I'd say use it. Stay, and they'll likely kill you on the spot. I hear things have gotten interesting for the Cait in your overlong absence. You're safe with me. For now."

Though his newly awakened heart railed against it, Ty knew Damien spoke true. He couldn't stay here. Shifting into his feline form, Ty forced himself to vanish down the winding stairs and into the darkness.

In the pitch-dark alley, Lily spared a final glance at the shadowy safe house, hoping that Ty was safe, that he might someday forgive her for what she had done. The only thing that eased the terrible pain of leaving him was knowing that she had bought him time to run.

In those last moments together, she'd known the truth: The Ptolemy had gotten too close for escape. So she had given Ty the only gifts she could.

Her love. And, she hoped, his freedom.

Lily allowed herself to be bundled into one of a line of long black town cars, the sort that politicians and dignitaries were always being driven around in. She tried to relax into the leather seat, grateful for the lack of company and the silent driver. But she couldn't help turning around to look, one last time, as the car began to move.

She had broken his chains, Lily thought, like the woman who seemed to be her ancestor had said. But it seemed like she was going to be standing alone after all.

With silent tears rolling down her cheeks, Lily hoped she had done the right thing.

Because from here on out, hope was all she had.

chapter TWENTY-TWO

Ty watched from behind a rancid Dumpster as Lily was put into one of the Ptolemy cars. She looked grim, and determined, and absolutely beautiful.

"Don't. Don't stand here hating yourself. It's such an incredible waste of energy, and besides, it's annoying."

Damien's voice sounded clearly in his head, only fueling the helpless rage roiling inside of Ty as he watched Lily's car pull away from the curb, followed by a small line of identical cars. It looked absurdly like a head of state was visiting this godforsaken little corner of Chicago.

"I have to go get her." He pushed the thought at Damien, who swished his tail in response and didn't bother to turn.

"Don't be an ass. It's over. You'll never get her now. Especially not once they realize she's branded with the mark of the Lilim. And I think you're forgetting that you and I have some unfinished business to attend to. Shall we?"

When the last car had pulled away, leaving the alley dark and empty, Ty slipped out from behind the Dumpster and assumed his human form. Damien did the same. That moment of vulnerability, when fur became flesh, was the opening Ty had been waiting for since he'd found the Shade perched at the edge of his bed. With the lightning-fast reflexes he'd honed so well over the years, Ty sprang in an instant. Vicious pleasure coursed through him as his fist connected with Damien's face.

Damien staggered back but righted himself quickly, then bared his teeth and hissed.

"Cheating. Not like you." He went for a right hook, but Ty, expecting it, easily ducked it.

"You don't know me anymore," Ty snarled. All the anguish he felt at Lily's decision to sacrifice herself for him, all the fury he felt for the ones who had taken her, channeled themselves into a bloodlust that knew no boundaries. And Damien, who had hunted them mercilessly, made an excellent first target.

The two vampires circled each other. Damien sprang again, and Ty grabbed him by the shirt, leaping and slamming Damien against the alley wall with incredible force. The air left Damien in a loud, pained grunt as Ty threw him to the ground and stepped back, breathing hard, waiting.

"Get up. Get up, you son of a bitch."

Damien wiped a thin line of blood that had trickled from his lip and got smoothly to his feet.

"Angry little kitten tonight, are we?"

The mocking tone tore into him. With a roar of outrage, this time Ty sprang. Damien started to spin away, but Ty, his reflexes honed from years of living with vampires who would as soon kill him as look at him, was faster. He caught Damien by his hair, then landed lightly on his feet. Ty jerked Damien's head back, exposing his neck, and brought him to his knees with a well-placed kick. The Shade went down with a grunt. Ty had his dagger out in a flash.

"Kill me, then, if it makes you feel better," Damien ground out. His eyes blazed up at him as Ty pulled his head even farther back and pressed the edge of his blade to Damien's neck. Damien's teeth were still bared, in both defiance and pain.

"Nothing can make me feel better," Ty growled harshly. "You led them right to us, you son of a bitch. They must have followed you."

"Impossible," Damien snapped, wincing as the tip of the blade dug in just enough to produce a shining crimson drop of blood. "He wouldn't have—"

He stopped himself, but he had already said enough. Dark suspicion bloomed in Ty's mind. He dug the blade in deeper, viciously pleased at Damien's soft moan.

"Wouldn't have sent them after you? Are you working for one of the *Ptolemy*?"

Damien's silent glare was answer enough for Ty. The truth felt as though it had blown a hole right through him. The terror had come from within the Ptolemy themselves. And though even the most distasteful highbloods of Ty's acquaintance would have found it unthinkable to slaughter their own, there was one he would not put it past. One who would never be satisfied with a subordinate role, no matter how close to the top of the heap he had clawed.

All the pieces clicked into place.

His voice was barely a whisper when he spoke again,

and the hand holding the blade shook with the force it was taking him to keep from plunging it into Damien's throat.

"You stupid bastard. Nero has no loyalty to anyone but himself. And he's neither a trusting nor a patient man. You really thought he wasn't having you followed?"

The truth was written all over Damien's stunned face. With a bitter laugh, Ty leaned closer to the Shade dangling from his clenched fist.

"All this work, for nothing. You've ruined my life, probably ended hers, and you didn't even get paid. I'll bet that last bit is the only thing you're truly upset about, you miserable sack of shit."

Damien's breath came in short, sharp pants. "Just kill me and get it over with."

"You'd prefer that, I'm sure. It's so much easier than what your bosses will do to you once they discover you've screwed up such a big job." Still, Ty was close, so close, to giving Damien what he wanted. A bit of pressure, and Damien's head would separate from his body cleanly. The perfect outlet for his rage…but Ty knew it would be only momentarily satisfying.

He felt the life he held in his hands. He had taken many just the same as this and had felt nothing afterward. Then he looked at the building beside him, at the darkened windows behind which Rogan's lifeless body now lay.

So much death. But Lily was still alive out there. And as long as she lived, he had a chance to right things, to start again. When he looked back at Damien, there was still raw anger, but cold calculation had begun to kick in as well. Perhaps he would give his blood brother a second chance tonight as well.

Whether he wanted it or not.

"No. You're going to help me get Lily back," Ty growled.

Damien managed a harsh laugh. "The hell I am."

In response, Ty took the blade he'd had against the Shade's neck and brought it down in a swift arc, slicing a deep wound in Damien's upper arm. Blood spattered the ground, and Damien snarled in pain, trying to jerk away from Ty. It only made Ty pull his hair harder.

"The hell you won't. It's this or I return you to your masters, Damien, with all sorts of details about your incompetence. Things that will earn you a long, painful death. And I'll get Lily anyway. Nothing is going to stop me. But your help would make it easier. And if you help me, I'll make sure you live."

"How?" sneered Damien. "My reputation will be ruined. You'll be delaying the inevitable, not preventing it. The Master Shades don't permit failure." His wound bled for only a moment, but the point had been made. Ty had no compunctions about hurting him. And he would do it again.

"I'm afraid you'll have to trust me on that," Ty said flatly. He had some ideas, but none would amount to anything if they didn't get going, and soon.

"Trust," Damien hissed. "The only thing I trust is that you'll get us both killed. Even if I go along with this insanity, two Cait Sith are not going to accomplish this."

Ty considered a moment longer, but he'd already made his decision. Damien was insufferable on many levels, but he would be an invaluable source of knowledge for what he was about to embark on. And if he turned on him, which he might, Ty would kill him with no remorse.

"We'll just have to make do. Are you going to behave, or am I going to have to remove the arm this time?"

Damien grimaced and twisted a little beneath Ty's hand, but at last he relented. "Fine. Only because it's a better death than what my masters would give me. You're a miserable bastard, MacGillivray. Far worse than I remembered. And under the circumstances, that is *not* a compliment. Now let me go."

Ty released his head, and Damien got slowly to his feet, watching him warily.

"What is your plan? Or am I not allowed to ask?" he said.

"We're going to convince Vlad Dracul to help us destroy Nero and save Lily." It sounded like madness, Ty knew. But it was what he had.

Damien groaned and looked like he was going to be sick. It was deeply satisfying.

"Damn it, Ty, why do you even care? They'll kill us, kill her. Nero will get what he wants. And believe me, he wants it all. I've never met a monster like him, and that's saying something. This is pointless!"

"I love her." Dark they were, those words he hadn't been able to say, even to himself, until it was too late. The one thing in his entire life he was still sure of.

Damien looked aghast. "I'm going to die for some pathetic sentiment? Listen to me, Ty. Two cats *cannot do this*. We would need at least a third, and even then there's only the barest chance."

Another voice, both familiar and welcome, sounded at Ty's side. "Good thing I see three cats, then."

"Jaden." Relief flooded through him and nearly brought him to his knees. This was the missing piece. The three of them could manage what he was thinking. Yes, with two other Cait, he had a fighting chance of setting this right.

If they made it through, things would change, and drastically. He was done with the Ptolemy. But so much more awaited him, if he was strong enough to catch hold of it. His blood brother's black-rimmed eyes were somber when Ty turned to look at him.

"I heard about the raid," Jaden said. "I came as quickly as I could."

"It was Nero," Ty said, and the name tasted like poison on his tongue. "All of it was Nero."

Jaden looked grim, but unsurprised. He gave a single nod. "What do you want to do?"

"He wants to die," Damien snapped. "And he'd like you to join us, no doubt."

Jaden raised his eyebrows at Damien, then turned a questioning look on Ty.

"Damien's coming with us. I'll explain on the way. We haven't got much time," Ty said. He was grateful when Jaden only nodded again. Damien gave nothing but a resigned sigh, and Ty knew he would have the help he needed from him as well. Now all he needed was luck, and time.

He hoped, for once in his life, the gods would see fit to give him both.

Vlad Dracul was not a man who enjoyed a great deal of company. Particularly not these days, when most of his visitors either wanted to kill him or were bearing messages from people who did. So he was less than receptive to the idea when Marco, his butler, arrived in the doorway of the library with the news that a trio of Cait Sith were darkening his doorstep and refusing to leave without an audience.

"Another message from Arsinöe, I suppose?" Vlad

asked, carefully marking his place in the book he'd just settled down with for the evening and setting it aside. He'd been increasingly on edge the past few weeks, waiting for the declaration of war he knew was coming. The Ptolemy queen had always hated him, but until recently, even he had not realized how deep that hatred ran.

"I don't think so, sir. They're a bit...scruffier...than her usual messengers. One looks like he's been in a fight. I made them show me their marks. The one with the black eye is a Shade, if you can believe it. The other two are Ptolemy cats, but there's something off about them."

"There's no woman with them?" Vlad asked, trying to keep his voice even. When Anura had come to him, he'd hardly dared to believe her words could be true. The mysteries and legends surrounding the long-dead Lilim were a particular preoccupation of his. Maybe it was because he'd always thought that Lilith would have been a natural ally of his. Why wouldn't an heir? And now, more than ever, he needed a reliable ally, Vlad thought, his jaw tightening.

But it seemed that whoever this woman Anura had met was, she had slipped through his fingers.

"They gave you no indication of what they want?" Vlad asked.

Marco shook his head. "No, sir. The tall one, one of the Ptolemy cats, said he'd talk only to you. I would have found a way to get them off the property, but considering..." Marco trailed off, and Vlad knew what he was thinking. Ludo had done plenty of talking before Vlad had gotten to him and told him to shut up.

"It's a good thing you didn't try," said an unfamiliar voice.

Vlad watched with interest as a rangy, dark-haired man appeared in a shadowy corner of the dimly lit room, leaning against the bookcases. Intense silver eyes watched him unblinkingly.

Marco roared an obscenity and started for the intruder, but Vlad held up a hand. At the simple gesture, his well-trained butler stilled, though his expression betrayed his unhappiness about it.

"Leave us, Marco. It's all right."

His hulking, would-be protector hesitated, his golden eyes darting around the room. "But, sir, the others—"

"Are in here somewhere, I'm sure. Consider it a lesson, Marco. Cats left on the doorstep will generally find another way in." He waved the butler off. "Go. I'll call if we need anything."

When the door had been shut, Vlad turned his full attention to his glaring visitor. He was impressed, despite himself, at how easily he'd gotten in. But then, he knew very well about being underestimated.

"Have a seat. Your friends as well. MacGillivray, isn't it?"

The other two materialized from behind pieces of furniture, one who could have been MacGillivray's brother and another who did indeed look to have been in fight, though the wounds were close to healed. Both looked to MacGillivray for a signal, marking him as their leader.

Interesting.

The ornery Cait Sith shook his head. "Thank you, but there's no time. I'm Tynan MacGillivray. These are my blood brothers Jaden and Damien. We've come because the Ptolemy have taken Lily Quinn, the woman Anura told you about." He paused. "She's Lilith's heir."

Excitement threatened to bubble over, but years of practiced restraint kept it in check. Vlad feigned polite interest. "Forgive me if I find that hard to believe," he said smoothly. "Of course, if you have proof, that's a different story."

Tynan's eyes narrowed. "You sent your thugs after her on Anura's word. Mine's not good enough for you?"

Vlad shrugged, recognizing both the temper and the pride blazing at him through those angry slits. "I don't know you. All I know is that your house is about to declare war on me. Why should I believe you?"

People rarely surprised him, but Tynan managed it when he cleared most of the room in a single, fluid leap, grabbed him by the throat, and pinned him to his leather wingback chair. No one had dared do such a thing in ages. Vlad went still with shock, torn between fury and amusement. He could have turned the tables and had this upstart and his head parted from each other in a heartbeat . . . he was pretty sure. It was that uncertainty that held his interest and stayed his hand.

"Careful, cat. I didn't get to rule a dynasty for nothing."

"I don't have time for careful either," Tynan growled, but he released his grip and took a small step back. "Lily is the real thing. I've seen her power, and she's told me about the vision she has, about the end of the Lilim. And"—he hesitated—"I had my own vision of Lilith just last night. Like a dream, but not. I understand what's happening now, but it isn't going to matter. The Ptolemy have taken Lily. Arsinöe thinks she's just a Seer and wants to use her to have a vision of your people using the Mulo against hers. Proof to launch a war."

Vlad cursed softly. "Is that what this is about? A Mulo?

She really thinks I'd be fool enough to use a Romany curse against her kind? That's about as subtle as putting my intentions on a flashing sign outside!"

"She hates the Dracul. Not just hates, but she also wants you wiped from the face of the night," the one called Jaden pointed out. "Maybe that wouldn't be enough, but she's isolated herself with a bunch of highbloods who are happy to feed her paranoia." He looked at Tynan. "One highblood in particular."

"Her people are dying," Tynan said. "It was easy to play her. It doesn't excuse half of what she's done, but she's not the source of this. If you want to avoid what's coming, we need your help."

Stunned, Vlad looked at the three of them, lowbloods with enough bravery to stand against the house that had traditionally enslaved them even when there was little hope of success. The Ptolemy were a force unto themselves.

"Say I believe you," Vlad said slowly. "What do you offer in return for what you ask? Because if I help you and fail, my dynasty burns."

"It burns regardless if you refuse to help us," Tynan pointed out. "Nero, the Ptolemy behind this, will make it happen. He's not the sort of man who leaves anything to chance. I'm sure he had a contingency plan for Lily actually showing up. And now that he knows what she is, I don't know what he'll do to her."

Hearing the concern in Tynan's voice, Vlad lifted an eyebrow. "You do this for the woman, then."

"My reasons are my own. They don't matter to you. Help us, and you avoid war and gain an important ally."

"You can promise me this alliance on the Lilim's behalf, then? Your word is binding?"

"It is," Tynan replied without hesitation.

"And if I say no?" Vlad asked, calmly folding one ankle over his knee and leaning back into the chair.

The cat's eyes flashed. "Then if your dynasty survives, which I very much doubt, you will have gained an enemy far more powerful than the Ptolemy. That is something I can *also* promise you."

The tension in the room was oppressive. Vlad had no doubt the three of them would fight him if they had to. Nor did he doubt that Tynan was anything less than serious about getting the woman back with or without his help. But of course he wouldn't have to, Vlad thought, quietly thrilling at the chance he had been given this night.

Slowly, he smiled and extended his hand, relishing the surprise on Tynan MacGillivray's face.

"Well, then," Vlad said. "Well met, brother cat. Let's get started."

chapter TWENTY-THREE

LILY WAS LOCKED securely into the most beautiful room she'd ever been in. The Ptolemy guard who had shut her in had explained, with a very pleasant smile, that should she figure out a way to escape, things would go very badly indeed for her once night fell. He never specified exactly what "very badly indeed" meant, but he didn't really have to. She'd spent three nights watching the way these Ptolemy operated.

She got it.

Beautiful new clothes had been brought for her, laid out on the bed in preparation for her arrival. All designer labels, all the right size.

It was a little scary.

Maybe she would have been flattered by the attention or excited to have it lavished on her, if she hadn't known what she knew. But no matter how warm Arsinöe turned out to be, all Lily could think of were the scars on Jaden's back, and the scars that Ty so obviously carried within himself. She didn't know if Arsinöe was responsible for those, but she'd certainly played on them.

Lily lay on the massive bed, staring at the ceiling and waiting for something to happen. She was in a beautiful old home in the middle of nowhere, in what she understood to be a favored seat of Ptolemy power tucked away in rural Maryland. Out her window, she could see what appeared to be a large river running alongside a small sand beach not far from the house. Peaceful. Beautiful. But she couldn't relax a single bit, despite how well taken care of she'd been thus far.

Something big was happening tonight. Lily could actually feel the tension crackling among the Ptolemy who'd checked in on her. It set her nerves on edge, and her nerves were pretty shot at this point anyway. But she'd been instructed to wash herself, to dress in the clothes purchased for her, to make herself fit for a proper audience with the queen.

Somehow, Lily managed it. She showered with the scented soaps and shampoos that had been provided, fascinating concoctions in little glass containers that she knew had been home blended. The smell of them was a little more opulent than what she usually wore. Heavy on the spice and musk. Still, they were better than the cheap sample bottles or, worse, guy shampoo she'd been using when she'd had a spare minute and a shower handy these past few days.

So she bathed, then dressed, little rituals that held some small amount of comfort because she was still alive to do them. In the bathroom mirror, rubbing a clear spot into the steam, Lily studied her mark. It seemed somehow more vibrant than before, glittering there on her fair skin. She sighed and covered it with her shirt, knowing it was going to cause trouble if it was seen. Serious trouble. Potentially life-ending trouble. And counting on a bout of ghostly possession to save her this time seemed like a long shot.

She couldn't think about Ty. Wouldn't think about him, even though she knew he must have lived here at times, walked these halls, spoken to these people. It simply hurt too much. And she sensed that here, tears would not be welcomed.

It would take her time, probably a lot of time, to get past the empty ache she felt in her chest right now. But, she thought miserably, even if he'd stayed with her back at the safe house, she would still be alone right now. At best, he would already have been relegated back to his spot as a servant. And at worst...

No, she wouldn't think of that. Knowing he was out there somewhere, alive, would have to be enough.

After about ten minutes of pacing the plush rug, there was a sharp rap at the door.

"Coming," she said, padding over to open it. She knew there were guards posted outside, but at least they'd let her have her privacy in the room. She hadn't been too sure when she'd caught sight of the very large, very intimidating men who'd accompanied her. But she imagined they wanted her comfortable, wanted her to think they trusted her to a certain extent.

No one had asked after Ty. Not a single question, which Lily found odd. And the one time Lily had mentioned his name, to one of her friendlier guards, the man's warm honey eyes had flashed with anger.

"You will not speak of him," he had said.

Lily had had little choice but to nod. She hadn't felt

ready to tangle with an ancient Egyptian vampire right that second.

Actually, she still didn't.

In the instant before she opened the door, Lily wondered what she would do if it were Ty on the other side, Ty come to save her, come to confess his love for her, to sweep her away to the life she wanted—a life with him. Her mouth curved bitterly. Pretty dreams. But from here on out, she would have to work on saving herself. That had been her choice, and she would have to live with it.

Lily felt an icy shiver of fear down her spine as she pulled the door open. A man stepped in, eyeing her as though she were a tasty morsel that was about to become dinner. Every single vampire she'd seen had this unnatural beauty, Lily realized. But almost all of them had left her cold. And none kindled in her what Ty had the very first night they'd met.

Damn it. She needed to move on, focus on the present. Wasn't that how *he* had lived among these creatures for so long?

"Hi," she said, hoping she sounded relaxed and friendly. "Come on in."

He was beautiful, golden-haired and flawless, with a face that would have made any Renaissance sculptor weep with joy. His hair was clipped short, but stylishly so, and he wore all black: dress slacks, fitted shirt, everything perfectly tailored. Lily was no expert, but she knew that the shoes he was wearing probably cost more than her monthly mortgage payment.

The hair at the back of her neck prickled. Her mark, which had been tingling ever since she'd set foot in the compound, began to burn. She didn't like him on sight.

"Lily," he said with a cold smile. "It's nice to finally meet you. I've heard a lot about you. I must say, I hope at least a little of it's true. Actually, you should hope so too."

He paused, and seemed to be waiting for a reaction from her. Since all Lily wanted to do was run and lock herself in the closet until he went away, she didn't say anything. The longer he stood there, the more agitated she felt. He gave a whole new meaning to the expression "bad vibes."

Looking slightly annoyed that he hadn't gotten a rise out of her, the vampire continued. "It seems we'll have a long night ahead of us. The queen would like to see you now."

Lily's eyes widened, even though she'd promised herself she wouldn't show any emotion here. "She...right now?"

The visitor's long, greenish eyes narrowed speculatively. "Yes. You announced to my men that you are Lily Quinn, the Seer, yes? Was that incorrect?"

"No, of course not. That's my name. I am what I said." Anger began to bubble beneath her fear. She didn't like being condescended to, and that was how this felt.

"Well, then, this shouldn't be too taxing for you. Unless you're hiding something you don't want anyone else to know about." He chuckled, a harsh sound. "But you wouldn't be so stupid, I'm sure. Even though you *are* a human."

Her skin crawled. All she could think of was the mark on her skin, and at her thought, she felt it go from burning to pulsing, like a second heart. *Uh-oh...that's new.* And yet somehow, it was oddly comforting.

"No, I'm not stupid," Lily said flatly.

He merely lifted a golden brow. "Arsinöe is understandably anxious, little Seer. Over two hundred of our blood have been slain now. More will undoubtedly die if we wait. She is convinced you hold the key." His expression indicated he thought otherwise.

"Come with me, if you're ready."

"Ready as I'll ever be," Lily said, hating the ugly smile that flickered across her escort's face as he offered his arm. Still, she made herself take it. She would behave, Lily decided. She would do what she was supposed to, hoping like hell that she could manage some sort of vision for these people—and that nothing insane happened that caused furniture to fly around. And that hopefully, she could negotiate a deal wherein she stayed alive.

They walked out the door and down the hall, past the doors to Arsinoë's chamber, and down a beautiful curving set of stairs.

"Remember that you will be in the presence of the queen of the Ptolemy, the last living pharaoh," her escort said with a hard look at her. "She doesn't suffer fools well, nor should she have to."

"In other words, behave myself?" Lily asked. No, she really didn't like this character.

His mouth thinned. "Yes."

"I'll do my best," she replied as they moved down a long hallway, ending at a set of gleaming double doors. She could hear the murmuring, the rise and fall, of many voices just beyond them. Her escort gave a sharp rap on one of them. The doors were pulled open by a pair of vampires who didn't look much like the richly dressed Ptolemy she'd encountered thus far. They wore severe black. One had sandy hair, one brown. Both were thin to the point of being borderline gaunt, and there was a feral gleam in their reddish eyes that Lily recognized all too well.

She couldn't see their marks, but she didn't have to. These were Cait Sith servants. And it looked like they were being deliberately kept hungry. Maybe it made them meaner. They were guards, she supposed. But there was an aura of misery about them that was unmistakable.

"Thank you," she said to each of them. She saw their surprise.

The man at her elbow hissed. "Honestly, they're just servants."

"Come in, Lily Quinn. We've been waiting for you."

Her voice was rich, warm, and welcoming. Still, Lily was on her guard as she stepped into what appeared to be the ballroom.

Hardwood gleamed on the floors. Tall windows billowed with the cool breath of night. A massive chandelier hung overhead, flickering with candles. And all around her, Lily saw the Ptolemy, their eyes alight with interest as she stepped into the room. There was a sea of them, all dressed formally, all wearing at least a splash of crimson. It was their color, Lily guessed. The color of blood. She remembered the vampires in the temple from her vision, and stumbled as she suddenly realized what she had walked into.

The warriors in the temple of the Lilim had worn crimson. It was the Ptolemy who had shed so much innocent blood. Her people's blood. She was in the middle of the dynasty that had destroyed the Lilim.

Which meant...

"Watch your footing, you clumsy bitch. The queen is watching you!"

Arsinöe stood on a raised platform at the head of the

room. Even knowing about some of the ugliness behind the beauty, even knowing that this was the woman who had effectively ended the dynasty of the Lilim with a single blow, Lily still found herself floored by her first real sight of the vampire queen.

She was, quite simply, breathtaking, clad in a simple strapless gown of pure white, the coils of her ebony hair loose around her shoulders. Her skin was gold-dusted, her shining eyes lined with black. And her mark, the very first of the Ptolemy, was singular, an ankh that glittered black and gold, embellished with intricate whorls that seemed to have been painted with pure light. She lifted her arms toward Lily in greeting, and the bracelets and rings that dripped from her shone.

"Welcome, Seer. Come to me."

Her voice was warm honey, soothing yet commanding. There was no resisting a voice like this, one that had commanded an army of vampires for longer than any human could remember. Suddenly, Lily understood why there were so many under her sway who would never think to question her power.

In her visions, she had been formidable. But in person, Arsinöe of the Ptolemy was a force of nature. Lily felt a sinking feeling deep in the pit of her stomach. She'd thought she could bargain with *this*? That she could hold her own here?

In Lily's mind, Arsinöe brought the blade down, her beautiful face contorted with rage. Lily's feet suddenly felt leaden, and her heart thudded dully in her chest.

Mother, she thought, directly addressing for the first time the spirit that haunted her. But all that answered was the barest whisper of a thought inside her head.

Free our blood.

Apparently, the sight of so many Ptolemy gathered in the flesh was too much even for a spirit as fiery as Lilith's.

That, or it was just time for Lily to make her own stand.

Or, more likely, to take the final fall.

The cats slunk across the grounds of the estate under cover of a moonless night. Ty and Jaden flanked Damien, just to be sure he didn't vanish when he was needed. Their visit with the leader of the Dracul had given Ty more hope than he'd had in a long time that war could be avoided. Vlad was as wily as Ty had heard, and not an easy man to read. But he was far more sensible than any other highblood he'd ever encountered, with the exception of perhaps Anura.

He glanced across the rolling lawn to where a silvery mist slipped through the encroaching trees. Anura had insisted on coming. There was so much more to her than Ty had known. Lily had sensed it, but she would likely be surprised at the extent of their connection. It was why Anura had run to the Dracul, why it had seemed to her imperative that a man who was a scholar of the lost dynasty understand what was at stake.

Ty understood that now and bore Anura no ill will. It shamed him, that he had been so conditioned to expect betrayal. She would prove important to Lily, if Lily decided to pursue the path that had been imagined by her forebear long ago.

It was time to awaken the Lilim, and in a way that would likely shake the highblood hierarchy to its core. But they had the backing of the Dracul, vibrant and strong. They had Anura. And soon, if they were careful, they would have the Cait Sith who dwelled here.

A soft growl was the only warning that they were about to be attacked. Ty stopped in his tracks, and the other two followed his lead.

"Who goes there?"

It was a voice Ty knew well. *"Duncan. Peace, brother. It's Ty, and Jaden is with me."*

The voice in his head changed tone immediately. *"Tynan? Hell. Go back, brother. You don't want to be here. Best to stay gone. And, Jaden, they'll kill you if you show your face inside. This place is crawling with Ptolemy tonight. They've got their Seer, and we all know that means we'll be fighting a battle for them before long."*

Ty pushed his thoughts back insistently.

"The Seer is my woman, and she's far more than they're counting on. But she needs our help. We're stopping this. And I'm freeing you and the others. Jaden told me about the collars. It's time to take a stand. This has gone on too long."

"You're mad," came another inner voice, and a pair of Cait Sith padded out from the long shadows by the trees. One was Duncan, and a younger Cait whom Ty recognized, Jake, was with him.

"We'll be cut down before we get ten feet into the ballroom," Jake continued. *"Did you not hear how many there are? And even if it were just the usual suspects of the inner court, we'd never manage it. They'd hunt us down like wolves. Free us? To send us to what kind of fate, Ty? There are, what, three of you?"*

"Unfortunately," Damien thought sullenly at no one in particular, which meant they all picked it up.

"Take me to the others," Ty insisted, and gave a low, moaning growl to punctuate it. *"We have reinforcements.*

There'll be no reason to choose between the gutter and the Ptolemy after tonight."

"*Reinforcements?*" Duncan and Jake sent out the thought in almost perfect unison, just in time for a scatter of bats to pass over them all in the darkness, heading for the lights of the manor house. They were invisible against the sky, the only hint of their presence the soft fluttering of many wings.

Duncan's yellow eyes widened, then shifted to look at the silver mist heading in the same direction.

"*Gods above, brother. What have you done?*"

"*The others,*" Ty insisted, adrenaline beginning to pump through his veins. "*I'll explain as we go. But we will not be slaves after tonight.*"

Lily stood on the platform with Arsinöe, feeling a thin rivulet of cold sweat trickle down between her breasts. She'd been unaware she had stage fright before tonight, since it wasn't a position she'd ever put herself in, but apparently, she had a bad case.

At least, if her nausea and dizziness were any indication. But then, she'd also never had hundreds of hungry vampires staring at her.

Arsinöe's hands were on her shoulders as she stood behind her, and all Lily could think of was that curved silver blade coming down across Lilith's throat from a very similar position. Her mark continued to pulse and throb beneath her shirt, and her power, dark, unharnessed, without direction, was roiling ominously within her. She could feel it, threatening to spill out in some horrible way. And then she'd be set upon, torn to pieces by a furious crowd of Ptolemy.

"Tonight, we find the source of the Mulo!" Arsinöe cried, and the crowd erupted in a roar. "Tonight, we begin the war that will wipe our enemies from the face of the night and show all the dynasties that nothing, *nothing*, can dim the glory that is the Ptolemy, the most ancient, the most powerful, the most *revered* of all!"

Their faces swam before Lily, blending into one glowing-eyed, sharp-toothed monster. What the hell did they think she was going to do? Turn into a pillar of fire and lead them to Vlad Dracul's doorstep? What if her vision didn't make any sense?

What if she couldn't even *have* a vision?

Her stomach cramped painfully.

Then the crowd stilled, going deathly quiet without even a word from their queen. It was as though they knew it was time. The air crackled with expectation. And Lily's worst nightmare was coming true. She was alone, Ty was gone, and she had no idea what to do.

The queen's voice was warm and soft in her ear.

"It's time. Do you need my assistance?"

"Whatever you can do," Lily said, perfectly honest. "I've never tried to do this before. You can help me?"

"Of course. I may not be able to See, but I have seen the process enough times to know how it's done. Listen to my voice. I will guide you."

"Okay," Lily said. What could she say? It was this or certain annihilation. She wished for something, anything, to come on its own, but all she saw, all she could think of, was the one man she knew she should try to forget.

Ty's face. Ty's eyes. Ty's voice.

"Relax." Arsinöe's voice was commanding but was as warm and smooth as rich cream.

It was surprisingly easy to fall under her sway once she let her guard down. Surprisingly easy to forget that it wasn't only the two of them in the room.

"Focus on my voice. Let everything else go."

The queen took her through the slow relaxation of each limb, the concentration on nothing but breaths. It was a little like what Lily knew of hypnosis, except that this was less about introspection and suggestion. At last, she drifted languidly in the space between waking and sleep, fully aware but utterly at peace, her busy mind quiet, waiting, it seemed, for instruction. Arsinöe gave it. And her voice rose so that the audience could hear her well.

"I seek the body that holds the curse of my people, the corpse from which the Mulo springs, commanded by another to destroy the great dynasty of Ptolemy. Open your Eye, Seer, and find where the Mulo rests."

Incredibly, Lily felt something inside of her, something that seemed to be located between her eyes, open up like a flower. Her third eye. The gift and curse of the truly psychic.

And then she saw as she had never seen before, flying over trees and mountains, rocks and earth, soaring above all that was and had been and ever would be. Joy swelled in her chest at the sudden freedom, unlike anything she had ever known.

"Seek the Mulo, Seer. You do not fly this night for your own pleasure!"

The voice was a tight snap, pulling Lily's thoughts back to the matter at hand. She drifted above the world, waiting for something that would tell her where to go, filling her mind with what Arsinöe had told her to look for. Instantly, something pulled at her, dragging her down through the

night air, past tight clusters of homes, their lights glowing
ghostly bright, through open fields that whispered with
brisk wind, and finally, into a massive and aging relic of a
house, a darkened husk without lights. She didn't want to
go in but knew she had to and allowed herself to be pulled
inside. Lily got a fleeting glimpse of sheet-draped furniture, empty halls, before being pulled down, down into
a hidden room in the moldering basement, so unlike the
aging beauty of the rest of the house.

There, on a stone slab, was a decaying corpse. The
putrid scent of it made bile rise in Lily's throat. She
gasped and gagged, the foul stench filling her lungs.

"Are you there? Do you see it?" Arsinöe's voice was
intense, urgent. Murmurs and gasps from the vampires, so
far away now.

"Yes," Lily heard herself choke out, though her voice
sounded strangely distant. She wanted so badly to go, to
fly from here, and yet, still she was pulled forward, compelled to look upon the fleshy ruin of a thing that housed
the tormented soul the queen sought. Rotting flesh hung
off of bone, lips peeled back over yellowed teeth. The
eyes, likely glued shut, had sunken into their sockets.

Then the eyelids flew open, and Lily saw nothing but
twin flames burning back at her. It *saw* her.... It hungered

Want you...eat you...

Something rose from the body, something like a black
mist with vile red eyes, sometimes shaped like a man and
sometimes a shapeless, roiling mass of hatred. It reached
for her.

Lily's eyes flew open as she gave a tortured scream. She
scrambled backward, still trying to get away from the thing
that had reached toward her, and sprawled gracelessly at

the feet of the queen. Slowly, she realized where she was, but she made no move to get up. She only sat there on the floor, trembling. The incredible hunger she'd felt from that thing, the immense and terrible power, and she'd only just escaped it.

"You saw it!" Arsinöe cried.

Lily looked up to see the queen looming over her, those deep eyes no less hungry in their own way than what she'd just escaped. "Tell me what you saw, where it was! Tell me!"

Fingers dug into Lily's arms, and she was lifted to her feet as though she weighed nothing. Then she stood, swaying slightly, before Arsinöe.

"It was so awful," Lily murmured, clutching herself tightly. "It tried to get me."

Arsinöe slapped her smartly across the face. "You stupid little bitch, I don't care what it tried to do. Tell me what I need to know!"

The shock of it had tears springing to Lily's eyes, but somehow she held it together. She would not be weak in front of this creature. She would *not*.

"There was a house," Lily managed, hating the quaver she heard in her voice. It echoed around the room as the assembled crowd shifted and murmured, listening. "It was a big old Victorian in the country. Like an estate, but fallen into some disrepair. Deserted. The furniture was all covered in sheets. The corpse...it was on a slab. In the basement. A hidden room."

"And? That's all?"

Lily didn't want to say it, much less think it, but she had to finish what she had seen.

"It...looked at me. It came out of its body," Lily said,

beginning to shake again. "It said it wanted me. It was hungry...."

The doors at the far end of the ballroom slammed open with such force that for a moment, Lily was sure it was the Mulo, come to find the woman who had disturbed its rest. And the initial shrieks and cries of the vampires at first registered as fear.

Then she realized it was outrage.

"What is the meaning of this? Get this gutterblood out of here!"

Until that moment, Lily hadn't realized what people meant when they said their hearts soared. Without even seeing him, she knew: Ty had come for her. She started forward, unthinking, her first instinct being to go to him. But Arsinöe's hand caught her arm.

"I don't think so," she said smoothly, though when Lily turned to look at the queen, she saw raw fury burning in those dark eyes.

"Arsinöe, queen of the Ptolemy! Vlad, leader of the Dracul, demands an audience! *Immediately!*"

There were shouts and curses at the demand, delivered in a full and throaty voice that was clipped and cool, British but with a hint of his Romanian homeland. It wasn't Ty, Lily realized, and her heart plummeted as quickly as it had risen. Still, it was something unexpected, and she couldn't contain her curiosity. It was a wonderful distraction from abject terror.

Lily still craned her neck, watching to get her first glimpse of the man Arsinöe hated so much. There was quite a commotion at the back of the room, and she couldn't see.

Arsinöe hissed a breath out. "Let him come to me. Maybe he wishes to surrender preemptively."

There was a ripple of nervous laughter as the crowd parted. Lily watched, fascinated, as the most reviled vampire leader strode toward them. With his name, she'd expected the movie cliché: dark widow's peak, slashing brows, maybe a bow tie and a cape. Instead, what she saw walking toward them was a tall, fit man with pale blond hair and ice-blue eyes she could see glowing all the way from where she stood. He wore an expensive-looking suit, charcoal gray, with a dark plum tie over a black shirt. The severe colors set off his fair looks beautifully, which she was sure he knew.

His features were fine, dashingly aristocratic, with a slightly stubborn chin and large, deep-set eyes that betrayed no emotion as he ascended the platform. He glanced at Lily, then fixed his attention on Arsinöe.

"I don't recall inviting you, Vlad. The only animals allowed here are servants."

He gave her a thin smile. "How amusing. I see I've interrupted you trying to pin your dynasty's troubles on my people."

Arsinöe stepped toward Vlad, and when she did, Lily stepped back. Whatever this was going to be, she was pretty sure she ought to get out of the line of fire. She took another step back as Arsinöe glared up into the face of her nemesis.

"In fact, you're a little late. The Seer has just described a house I know very well. It was mine, after all, before you bought it and then let it fall into disrepair. There, the corpse of the Mulo rests. A Gypsy curse only your kind knows, hidden in a house you own. If there were any question you were responsible, and there was little, there's none now. You chose a poor battle to fight, Vlad Dracul."

Lily felt something brush against her ankle as she took

another step back, toward the curtains that hid a small stage.

"Please," Vlad snapped, his voice resonating through the room. "You may hate me, Arsinöe, but I'm not a fool. How fascinating that a Mulo sits in an abandoned house of *mine*, just waiting for you to discover it. How lucky that it's a curse everyone associates with *my* people. If you'd received a poorly typed confession note with something that looked like my signature on it, would you take that as proof as well? You would use any excuse to get rid of us!"

Something brushed her ankle again, harder this time, and Lily looked down. It was hard to contain her gasp as she took in the sight of a huge black cat, winding around her legs. It could have been any of them, she told herself. Anyone.

But the silver eyes that looked up at her were Ty's.

It was all she could do not to throw her arms around him. He shook his head very clearly, back and forth once. *No.* She looked away from him only with great effort, but she understood. Exhilaration mingled with fear as she glanced around, looking for signs of other Cait Sith, other Dracul...other *anyone*. Surely these two couldn't have come alone!

Arsinöe was shouting furiously up into Vlad's face, and the crowd moved restlessly as they strained to hear, discussing amongst themselves whether it would matter if they just killed the leader of the Dracul tonight.

"You slaughter my people!" she cried, and Lily noted that she seemed truly anguished over it. She certainly had feeling for her own blood. It was everyone else's that was the problem for her, Lily supposed.

"Lies! I have come tonight because I have proof that

your people are slaughtered by one of your own. Stop this madness before one more drop of innocent blood is shed. Hear me out, Arsinöe."

That shut her up. Arsinöe gaped at Vlad for a moment while the crowd erupted in furious disbelief.

"Bastard," Lily heard her say softly. "Whatever sick game you're trying to play, I want no part of it. Get out of here. None of my people have the power, nor the sickness of mind it would take to do such a thing."

Vlad sighed, and for a moment, his features softened, making a sharp and handsome face into that of an angel. His words surprised Lily, but she didn't harbor the same prejudices as Arsinöe toward him, and the idea of an inside job made as much sense as anything. In fact…she wondered….

Her eyes sought Nero, who had been hovering near the platform, but he had vanished. It gave her a very bad feeling about all of this.

"I have the Shade who was hired to kill Tynan MacGillivray and Lily Quinn," Vlad said. "Come here, Damien."

A cat leaped out of nowhere to land on the stage, prompting hisses and filthy insults. The cat, for his part, looked unconcerned. He glared at the crowd for a moment, then stood and became, with a shift of movement and light, a man.

It was Lily's turn to gasp. She hadn't ever wanted to see Damien again. The memories brought back by seeing him were nothing she wanted to be reminded of. But she felt Ty pressing reassuringly into her leg, and she stilled, trying to focus on his warmth, the comfort he was trying to provide.

"Damien Tremaine, Your Majesty," Damien said,

sweeping a mocking bow at her feet. "Hired by Nero of
the Ptolemy to destroy the Seer before she ever got here,
along with the hunter who brought her." He paused with a
mocking little smile. "Obviously, I had some difficulties."

Arsinöe didn't look convinced—she looked outraged.
"How dare you bring this creature into my court and pay
it to spout its lies!" she shrieked at Vlad. "I will never
trust the word of a Cait over my own blood! Where is
Nero? I demand he come up here and defend himself!"

There was an awkward moment of shuffling and mut-
tering among those gathered. Damien raised one well-
arched brow. "Hmm. Seems to have found something
better to do all of a sudden."

The queen curled her lip at Damien, who looked
equally disgusted to be in her presence.

"You impugn Nero's honor and the honor of my house."

Very clearly, so that everyone could hear, Damien
said, "Spare me. He's probably filling the room with poison gas as we speak. Then he'll take all our heads and
wear them as accessories. He killed a Gypsy girl for the
curse and then threw her away like so much garbage. And
she was far from the first. He'd even decided to keep your
Seer as a pet instead of killing her, hiding her from you
so he could do Gods-know-what. You have no idea what
he is."

"If he's tried to run, he won't get far," Vlad said, then
inclined his head toward Lily. "And you, Arsinöe, are
holding the heir to an ancient dynasty against her will.
You'll need to let her go now. She needs to be presented
to the council."

Arsinöe began to laugh, a throaty roll that would have
been beautiful except for the edge of madness to it. "The

little human? She's nothing. She needed my guidance for a simple vision. You're mistaken, Vlad. And if you have been foolish enough to surround this house with your soldiers, then you'll have war no matter who is responsible for the Mulo—this I promise you!"

"Arsinöe. He's right."

That voice was the most beautiful thing Lily had ever heard. Then he was beside her, tall and lanky and dark. He didn't look at her—not yet—but kept focused on the queen. She stared at him as though he had just stabbed her in the heart, and Lily saw then that she did care for him. Not in a healthy way, certainly, but the sort of hurt written on her face was a good indicator that when it came to Ty, Arsinöe was not made of stone.

"You . . . you brought the Dracul here?" she asked hoarsely.

Ty looked at her a long moment and then nodded. "I did."

"But . . . *why*?"

"Because I don't want to see this destroy you," Ty said. "And because I'm in love with the woman you've locked in here with you. Listen to the Dracul, please, Arsinöe. They are not your enemy."

Lily couldn't have moved if she'd wanted to. She felt glued to the spot, and all she could hear was that he was in love with her. Had he actually said that? She wanted to hear it again. And again after that.

"Tynan," Arsinöe said softly. "You went to Vlad? You profess to be in love with this insignificant slip of a thing? A *human*? You betray me," she said, her voice growing steadier as she looked at Ty accusingly, though no less full of pain. "You betray us all."

"No," Lily said. She stepped forward again. "You betrayed Lilith. And I am hers."

Unafraid now, she bared her mark to Arsinöe, who went sheet-white. "Demon child," she muttered, and incredibly, began to back away. "Seed of the demon, *abomination*!" she shouted, lifting her hand to point at Lily in horror.

It was eerily like watching her berate Lilith in her visions.

A column of smoke appeared by Lily then, slowly taking the form of a woman. A beautiful, dark-haired woman with luminous eyes as ancient as the stars.

"Hear me now, all of you," Anura cried, and the cacophony of the crowd fell to silence at her rich voice. "Lilith, the Mother, was no demon, and neither was her child! It's true, Lilith enlisted the aid of the demon to conceive," Anura said. "But there is no demonic taint in her line. Those were lies told to destroy her, and all who followed her."

Arsinöe looked aghast at Anura's appearance.

"Have we been invaded by every gutterblood in the area?" she asked, sounding shell-shocked. "Anura, you're a traitor to your own dynasty. You willingly tainted your blood with that of a man who was little better than an *animal*. And yet you expect me to believe this nonsense!"

"I do," Anura said calmly. "Because I was there. I delivered the child that Lilith conceived by a human man, aided by her demon love, for a price she will pay for eternity. It may not have been a path many would have chosen, but it was her choice. And this is the descendant of that daughter, the child of her blood. She is no demon seed. She is half human, half vampire. The ritual saw to that."

"You," Lily said softly, suddenly understanding. "You were the one who took the baby from the temple."

Anura's smile was radiant. "Lilith was as my own sister. Our lines have ancient ties, little one. I promised to protect the babe. That was the promise given by the Empusae, to care for the human children of Lilith until the dynasty could be reawakened. But time and carelessness lost the carriers of her blood. Still, I believe that same blood brought you back to me."

"Blood is destiny," Lily murmured.

"For the love of Sekhmet," Arsinöe snapped.

Her people were in an uproar, shouting epithets at Lily, at the Cait Sith, and threatening the Dracul with slow, deliberate dismemberment. Arsinöe shoved Vlad aside and strode to Lily, who held her ground. She wasn't afraid anymore. Whatever happened, she knew these people had her back.

If blood was destiny, if it truly was, then it had brought her to the people she was meant to be surrounded with. But to reawaken an entire dynasty, to create something that important when she was only one human with a mark that was singular in all the world...how was she supposed to do *that*?

And yet, even as she asked herself the question, she understood.

Break his chains. Free our blood.

"No house can stand alone," Lily said softly as Lilith's voice whispered in her head. Blood might be destiny. But there were always choices.

Arsinöe tore Lily's shirt down the front with a single swipe of her hand. Lily didn't even have time to react before Arsinöe was inches from her, glaring at the mark that seemed oddly illuminated in the candlelight.

The queen bared her teeth. "She would have created chaos. She created a child with a demon, whether you share his blood or not. Where we seek to preserve our lines, she reveled in tainting hers. Lilith's actions were worthy of death then. And I refuse to see her madness continue." She looked to Ty, who moved to place himself in front of Lily.

Lily stayed him with her hand and a meaningful look. She saw all of his raw emotion, so close to the surface, stamped onto his beloved face.

"You don't need to save me this time, Ty."

"What if I want to?" he asked roughly.

"I'm going to kill you both," Arsinöe hissed. "That should solve all of our problems."

That was when Lily saw it, rising behind the vampire queen like the shadow of Death itself. It was a patch of pure darkness, only vaguely man-shaped, with red eyes that spoke of an ancient hunger. And no one could see it but her.

Nero had sent the Mulo. And in all the confusion, he intended to kill the queen.

Lily heard her own warning cry, even as Arsinöe drew the same glittering, curved blade she had seen in her dreams since she was a child. The Mulo opened a gaping maw filled with jagged, sharp teeth, a rotting hole still flecked with bits of blood and skin. And it gave a furious, ravenous wail a split second before it struck, its only warning, and far too late.

But it was not coming for her, Lily realized.

She didn't think, didn't even have to try. For the first time in her life, the power inside of her burst through her as naturally and easily as breathing. There was no struggle, nothing held back behind some invisible wall.

In that moment, she was all Lilim. And there were no voices, no alien sensations of another sharing her body. This was all her.

Her own scream filled her ears as she threw Arsinöe aside. There was a bright burst of pain as she did so, but Lily had no time to consider what it might mean. The Mulo was inches from her in all its vile fury, and denied of its target, it turned its attention to the next thing in its path: her.

It was as she wanted it. Lily didn't shrink back as it lunged at her. She reached for it, though it had no visible substance, and caught the sides of its foul mouth with hands that thrummed with white-hot light. It screamed at her touch, thrashing from side to side as it tried to get away. But Lily, possessed of a strength that she had never known but always felt, just out of reach, hung on tighter. She pushed the energy into the Mulo, pulling to the sides as she did so, burning it even as she tore the shadow in two.

The ballroom was filled with horrified screaming; her ears were filled with it—it came from the dying creature that should never have had this second life.

With a final, deafening roar, it surrendered to the inevitable as Lily rent it in half. There was a flash, the stench of ozone, and she watched the tattered wisps of shadow that hung from her hands flutter rapidly in some unseen breeze before vanishing completely.

She had done it. She'd finally managed to use what was in her for something good, to harness what she'd never been able to. Even if it was only this once, Lily thought as pandemonium erupted around her, with Ptolemy fleeing for the exits and dozens of men and women she'd never seen before pouring in through the windows, shoving through the doors, it had been a big once. She'd stopped a war. She'd saved the Ptolemy, though whether that was all so great was debatable. She understood what she was, how she had come to be. And she had a man who loved her. Who had announced he loved her in front of one of the scariest vampires in existence.

It really didn't get more devoted than that. And all she wanted to do was wrap herself in his arms and go someplace quiet and dark, to tell him how she felt, how she wanted nothing to do with this dynasty business unless he was at her side.

Lily turned, finding it odd that the room seemed to spin with her. Everything seemed to be moving too slowly. She saw Jaden (*Jaden!* she thought with a burst of pleasure) hurl Nero to the floor, a feral snarl on his face, and raise his blade. She saw Vlad rush toward Arsinöe, who was staring at her own knife, which seemed to be dripping with blood. Damien watched her with something like pity in his eyes.

She stumbled as she turned and felt Ty catch her. She would know his touch even in the most impenetrable darkness, Lily thought, a faint smile on her lips. Why was it getting so dark all of a sudden?

"Lily," she heard him say, and she looked up into his eyes. "Stay with me. Lily, please…please…"

His eyes were the stars, the moon in the sky.

Then she was gone.

chapter TWENTY-FOUR

HE WATCHED HER DEEP, even breaths as she slept. He monitored those carefully, half convinced that at any minute, her chest would cease to rise after a fall. That she would vanish from him as stealthily as the ghost that had once haunted her, never to return.

The door behind him opened, throwing a bit of light into a room that was furnished with an ornate canopy bed draped in taupe and cream linens, a carved bombe chest, a towering wardrobe carved with the faces of cherubs. It was all a bit much for Ty, but he knew antiques when he saw them, and this room was worth a fortune. He was hard-pressed to care at the moment. About anything, including the Very Important Person who moved quietly to his side to study Lily's still face.

"She's lucky. I don't know how Arsinöe, of all people, managed to miss internal organs. It could have been over right then. Still, she lost a lot of blood. It's lucky there was so much chaos, really. Not everyone would have been able to resist the scent."

Ty glanced up at Vlad.

"Lily saved the woman's life, and she still took off as if the hounds of Hell were nipping at her heels. Not a word. Just that odd expression." He sighed, ran a hand through his hair. "At least no one batted an eye when every last Cait Sith stormed out of there. The Ptolemy will have to wait on themselves for a bit, I think. Might be good for them."

Vlad eyed Lily speculatively. "You're sure she'll take them?"

Ty nodded. "You could do a lot worse than the Cait Sith as a foundation for a dynasty. I suppose you could do a lot better, too, but the woman seems to have a thing for strays," he said. "No, they need her. And she wouldn't turn them away. She has a big heart."

His brothers and sisters were taken care of. That, at least, he had seen to. Things had indeed become bleak as Nero's hold on Arsinöe had increased. He'd brought out the worst in her, but Ty could blame no one but the queen herself. The worst had always been there. He just hadn't wanted to see it. How he could have so badly misjudged the queen, he didn't know. She seemed so brittle to him now, so contrived. So unlike the warm little creature he had been alternately infuriated and infatuated with, the one lying here now. Too late, he understood the difference.

One had judged him worthy despite his mark.

The other had found him worthy without ever considering his mark at all.

Now it might be too late. Despite Lily's words to him before she'd given herself up to the Ptolemy, Ty knew, better than she, how much things had changed. She would be shouldering a great deal of responsibility, and thousands of years of history. Would a woman who now needed to choose a mate, a partner with whom to reawaken the oldest and greatest of the vampire dynasties, truly consider a lowly Cait Sith? Especially when every single council member would argue against that choice?

Perhaps not Vlad. But Ty was certain the Dracul would be happy to volunteer if Lily rejected him.

Vlad pulled up a chair, seemingly oblivious to the fact that Ty wanted to brood and mope in peace. He'd already irritated Anura out of here.

"So how is she?"

"Lily?" Ty shook his head. "No change. I'm glad you had a doctor around to sew her up. But like you said, she's lost a lot of blood."

"He would have been happy to give her some from our supply. But as I told you, her blood isn't...normal." He paused. "You have to make the decision, Ty. All of us agree. It's your right."

Ty sighed heavily and scrubbed his face with his hands. "Yeah. I know." And damn him, damn him for having wanted his teeth in her even when she'd been dying in his arms, her blood soaking his shirt and beckoning him, *begging* him to drink. The scent of it lingered on her, though she'd been sewn and bandaged, her wound cleaned, her clothes taken to be burned.

He felt Vlad eyeing him. "Her mark is beautiful. I'd never imagined I would see a true mark of the Lilim, much as I've studied them. And your Lily looks a great deal like Lilith herself."

She did. And Vlad had been obviously fascinated with her from the moment he'd seen her, to the point where Ty was seriously starting to consider starting his own war with the man. But...Vlad had treated Ty and his broth-

ers as though they were equals instead of some random
lowbloods banging at the door. He had listened. And as it
turned out, the man was a formidable strategist.

Ty supposed he was officially a traitor. Funny how it
felt like doing the right thing, after all these years.

"So was Lilith really just a power-mad demon queen?"
Ty asked. He'd been mulling the accusations flung back
and forth, wondering where the truth lay. It didn't matter to him. Lily was perfect, as far as he was concerned,
demon ritual or not. But he did wonder.

"According to popular legend, of course," Vlad said,
settling himself more comfortably.

After two nights of Vlad's company, Ty could tell when
the Dracul was about to lecture on one of his pet subjects.
For such a formidable vampire, the man was just a little bit
of a geek sometimes. Damien seemed to like him. Damien
and his encyclopedic knowledge of bloody *everything*. For
a man who'd been in such a rush to get back to his life of
intrigue and assassination, Damien didn't show any signs
of leaving anytime soon, even though Vlad had paid him
twice what Nero had owed for the job. His reputation was
secure. The Master Shades would be pleased...if he ever
went back.

More than once, Ty had had to fight the urge to beat
them both with an enormous book and shut them up.

"I never believed it," Vlad continued. "There was
no one left to tell Lilith's tale but her enemies, or those
unsure enough about the truth to stay quiet. That tends to
make for a pretty skewed story. Her way of running her
dynasty has fascinated me for years, as I told you. The
inclusion. There weren't as many varieties of lowbloods
back then, and likely a few that have since died out. But

she included them in her court, in her decision-making.
The Lilim were not simply their mark. The actual mark
was only a piece of the dynasty's identity, and not a necessary one. 'No house can stand alone,' she's purported
to have said in some of the oldest texts I have, not that
you'll hear that anywhere else. The vampires love their
caste system. Or at least, the ones who can keep it in place
do. But her words resonated with me. The Dracul are not
perfect, but I'm trying to push the envelope without having my head cut off for going too far. Small steps." He
grinned. "And now, a new ally. New blood. It's just what
we need, though the other dynasties are going to fight it."

Ty looked back down at Lily. She didn't stir, but for
those steady breaths. And she was pale, so incredibly pale.
He sighed.

"All she wanted was to go home."

"You and I both know that's impossible in any case,"
Vlad said gently, his smile fading. "She likely won't wake
up at all unless she is turned. She's not going to open her
eyes and tell you to bite her, Ty."

Ty jerked his head up to stare into Vlad's grim face.
Vlad nodded.

"She's lost too much blood. Morgan, my doctor, told
you, she's not asleep; she's in a coma. Being turned is
the only way out of this for her, and it's the only way her
vampire half will ever be fully awakened. If the situation were different, I would take her myself, but"—he
paused—"she's already chosen you."

Ty grimaced. "She walked away from me. And she
was probably right to."

Vlad raised a single pale brow. "If I'm understanding
things correctly, she thought she was saving your life. But

I'm sure she'll be happy to beat that into your thick head if you give her a chance." He gave a thin smile. "I'm afraid that's all I have in my grab bag of relationship advice."

"And the fact that I'm a gutterblood Cait Sith? You don't see a problem with me...tainting her?"

Vlad simply groaned and got to his feet. "Spoken like a true Ptolemy. Look, Ty, I'll tell you what. I'll come back in half an hour. If that girl is still at death's door, I'm throwing you into the street and taking her myself. And if you persist in disparaging your bloodline, I'll throw in some creative torture just to make you forget all that angst for a while. All right? Good. I'll be in my study if you need anything."

Vlad turned on his heel and strode from the room, shutting the door quietly behind him. Ty stared after him for a long moment, trying to decide whether he thought the man was amusing, a prick, or both. He was leaning toward the last.

But the man had made some good points.

Ty turned back to Lily, silent and still, and noted her breaths were shallower. He grabbed her hand. It was like ice. She was leaving him. He could feel it, had tasted the bitter edge of his own death on his way to entering this new life. Panic bloomed in his chest, constricting his breathing.

"Lily," he said, "stay with me. Please, *mo bhilis*, stay with me." He paused, the words so close to pouring out. Finally, he let them, knowing he had nothing left to lose. She was all he had—and all he needed.

"I don't want to live without you. I love you, Lily. Please stay. I love you."

He felt it then, the faintest squeeze of her hand. And in

her weakened state, for the first time, he could hear what
was in her mind.

Ty…love you.

He had his answer after all. Perhaps he had known it
from the beginning. Even that very first night, something
in him had known she was his.

He slid into bed beside her, stretching out along the
length of her. Her warmth, her wonderful warmth, was
fading fast. He could feel it ebbing from her. Some of it
would never return…but enough would. And she would
be with him.

He hoped she would forgive him for this, the dark
gift she had never asked for. Her birthright, though it had
nearly ruined her life. An eternal kiss from a vampire
who would never deserve her.

Ty rose above her, brushing her hair tenderly to one
side. Even now, he could smell the lifeblood that flowed
ever more sluggishly through her veins, the intoxicating
scent that caught him and refused to let go. His fangs
lengthened, sharpened. He hadn't wanted her to see this
part of him, lest she think less of him for it. But she had
bared her soul to him. She deserved to know all of him as
well.

He nuzzled her neck gently, marveling at the silken
softness of it. He could smell Arsinöe's soaps on her, like
the ghost of a bad memory. But the natural oils of her skin
combined with the spices to make the scent somehow
her own, utterly Lily. Then he did what he had longed to
do since the first time he'd seen her under the stars: he
opened his mouth, sank his teeth into tender flesh, and
drank.

The taste of her, wild and sweet, burst into his mouth

and rushed through his system, flooding it with the old, undeniable hunger, the drive to drink until there was nothing left. But more, it filled him with Lily's essence, the taste that was singularly hers among all humanity. She was like nothing, no one, he had ever known. Drinking from her was as close to heaven as his tattered soul had ever come, and he reveled in it, lifting her to him, hands tangling in her hair.

Against his chest, her heart stumbled, paused, stuttered softly.

It was time.

He pulled his teeth from her reluctantly, fighting the instinct to drain her dry. But one look at her banished any lingering urges. She had gone from pale to sheet-white, the two red pricks of his teeth the only color on her skin. Quickly, Ty took a nail, extended it into a claw with little effort, and sliced into the tender flesh of his wrist. As blood welled dark in the cut, he pressed it to Lily's bloodless lips.

"Drink, sweet," he urged her, feeling a surge of guilt that he had never felt more alive, while she lay there slipping through the veil of death. All she needed was one swallow, one tiny drop to enter her system. "Drink. Stay with me, Lily. Can you hear me? Be with me forever. I love you." It was so easy to say now. And she couldn't hear him.

Or maybe she could. There was a faint, tentative swallow. Then another.

The relief was so great he nearly wept like a child. She would not leave him. Not tonight, not ever, if he had anything to do with it.

He began to feel the pulls at his wrist, stronger now as his blood entered her system and the true change began.

The pleasure of the experience surprised him, beginning as a tingling at the site of the cut he'd made and slowly becoming more intense, pulsing with each sip. Her tongue lapped at his skin greedily, and his breathing quickened.

Now is not the time, he told himself. She wasn't strong enough; she might not even want him that way anymore.

Then she pulled her mouth from his wrist and dragged his lips to hers.

He grunted in surprise, which quickly turned into a moan as she wrapped herself around him.

"Lily ... woman ... weren't you just dying? Take it slow, sweet, take it—"

"Don't want it slow. Want you. *Now*."

She was tearing at his clothes, surprising him with her ferocity.

"But, don't you think—"

"Just shut up and let me take you. Do you know how much I missed you?"

It was difficult to argue with her request. He helped her where he could with the clothes, allowing her to set the pace, stunned by the intensity of her energy. Then she was against him, her skin so incredibly soft, cooler, yes, but the heat they created between them would be more than enough.

Lily rose above him, a pale goddess in the darkness, her hair like fire. And her eyes, he saw, burned like blue stars. As a human, she had been beautiful. As a vampire, he realized, his breath catching in his throat, she was stunning. And she was his.

With his cat's eyes, he could see her mark, still glittering green, the pentagram, the snake. But encircling them, as though in a protective embrace, were the arms of the cat. He reached up tentatively to touch it, torn between pleasure at the symbol that bound them and regret that he hadn't been able to give her a mark that meant something in his world.

She watched him and seemed to understand.

"Yours is the same now," she said, brushing her fingers over his collarbone. Then she grinned, the humor in it thrilling him deep in his soul.

"My blood was stronger. That freaking ankh is gone. You're mine now."

More beautiful words had never been spoken.

"You should know I love you, Lily Quinn," he said.

"I love you, too, Ty. I'm sorry for leaving you like that. I couldn't see any other way." She shook her head. "I thought I could do it alone. But I needed you. I'm always going to need you."

"Hey," he said softly, dropping his hand to trail over the curve of her breast. "It got us here. And I want to tell you everything. All the things you wanted to know about me. No more secrets between us."

"Agreed," she said. "But there's something we need to do first."

She sank down onto his rigid shaft before he could answer, and then he couldn't think. She was so hot, so tight. All he could do was arch up beneath her and give a strangled moan.

"Yes," she gasped, her head falling back.

Then she began to move. Lily rode him beyond thought, beyond reason, until both of them were shuddering at the edge of release. And in his single lucid thought, Ty knew how to take them over the edge. He grabbed her hips, flipped her so that she lay beneath him, and thrust deeply into her, making her moan.

"Bite me," he growled, then sank his teeth into the side

of her neck. Pleasure washed over him as he moved inside her. Then he felt her teeth, newly sharp, pierce the sensitive skin of his own neck, and he was immediately caught up in an explosion of pure, hot sensation. He thrust into her again and again, taking, being taken, fused together so completely that he was no longer sure where one of them ended and the other began.

Until together, they hurtled over the breathless edge into dark, wicked bliss.

Later, they held each other in the big bed, tangled together. Lily rested her head on Ty's chest as he talked about his life: the poverty of his upbringing, the rejection of his family when they discovered what he had become. His companions, and the different paths they had chosen, none of them particularly good. And finally, the reason for his allegiance to Arsinöe.

"It was a raid on a Cait Sith safe house, much like the one we were in, though the cats used to stick together a bit more in those days." He stroked her back absently as he talked, and she listened to the rumble of his voice.

"The Ptolemy used to flush them out occasionally, for sport, I suppose. Some would end up enslaved; some would be killed. Then the house would be torched. I don't know how many times I'd barely escaped one of those raids, but eventually, my luck ran out. I'd been working for Rogan, smuggling, stealing—bit of this and that. He was out, of course. Bastard always was when there was trouble. About an hour before dawn, the Ptolemy came. Small contingent, but it was enough. They had a merry time, looting, pillaging, raping a couple of the women who couldn't get away. I told them what I thought of them." He smiled wistfully. "I was full of myself then, thought a few lowbloods standing up could change the world."

"I bet you kicked his ass," Lily said, snuggling against him.

Ty snorted. "My mouth was a lot bigger than my ability in those days. I was flat on my back with a blade at my throat in under a minute. Figured my time was up. I was almost happy it was," he said, his voice dropping. "But then I heard another voice. Arsinöe's voice, telling them to clear out. You could tell she was angry. Over the years, I saw her get really furious from time to time over the lowblood hunts, but usually she looked the other way. It never really stopped." He shook his head. "Anyway, she told the vamp with the blade at my throat—Jeremy, his name was—to stand down. She helped me up. Stretched out her own hand and helped me up. Apologized for the cretins she was responsible for and offered me a job. Told the rest not to lay a finger on me under penalty of death."

Lily frowned. "Weird. That sounds almost compassionate."

"Aye. She could be, then. But things are changing, and those changes have made her brittle, somehow. The Dracul being accepted into the Council was a big blow to her. She likes the old ways best. I just didn't realize how much. All I knew was that she made Jeremy drop the knife and gave me a chance at a life that was better than I'd ever had. For a long time, that was enough for me."

"And now?" Lily asked, already knowing the answer but needing to hear it.

"Now I want more. I have more," he said, pressing a kiss to her head. "I have you. And you're saddled with me, whether you want me or not." He sighed. "The rest of the freed Cait Sith too. I still can't believe you want us all. We're an unruly lot."

"It's whether they want *me*, not the other way around," Lily pointed out. "I understand what I'm meant to do now, but building a new dynasty is going to take some time. I'm going to need a lot of help. And they're going to have to be patient. Things aren't going to change overnight. But if they want it..."

"Most do, Lily," Ty said, soothing her, rubbing circles on her back. She could feel him even in her blood, *their* blood, always a part of her. The intimacy of it was something she didn't think she'd ever grow tired of.

"My people have been spit upon for a long time, or used up and tossed aside. We've always had one another, but to be able to be a part of something bigger, to be valued—hell, to not be called gutter cats anymore, even—it's worth more than you think to them. And to me."

"As long as you're with me," Lily said softly, "I think we can do this."

"We can," Ty said gruffly. "I will be with you. I always will be."

She curled against him, savoring the slow and steady beat of his heart. He couldn't know, couldn't possibly know what he had given her. Power coursed through her like light, like blood. When the change had sparked fire in her veins, Lily had understood herself in a way she had never been able to. The inner struggle she'd become accustomed to living with every moment of every day had fallen away at once and become peace. Ty's dark kiss had opened the night to her like a flower, and in it, she saw herself as she truly was. She was Lilim. She was Cait Sith. She was his.

Lilith had been right, and so was Ty, in his way. She had broken his chains, and he had in turn been the key to unlocking all of her darkest, most wonderful secrets. Finally, she was free.

So thinking, she rose on her elbows to look at him, tousled and well loved.

Her blood was her destiny. But so was he.

THE REBORN LILIM

LEADER: Lily Quinn-MacGillivray
ORIGIN: Lilith, the first vampire, now merged
with the blood of the Cait Sith
LOCATION: Reemerging in the safety
of Dracul territory
ABILITIES: Lethal bursts of psychic energy;
can take the form of a cat

Acknowledgments

I owe endless thanks to the following people:

Selina McLemore and Latoya Smith—for the enthusiasm, support, and being such a pleasure to work with. This book is the culmination of a lot of dreaming. Thanks for bringing it to life!

Kevan Lyon—for being an awesome agent, and for always telling me, "We'll get there." Well, here we are. You're the best!

Cheryl Brooks, Marie Force, Loucinda McGary, and Linda Wisdom—what on earth would I do without the four of you? Laughs when I need them, understanding when no one else can, and of course, the flying monkeys. Your friendship is golden.

And of course, I couldn't do any of this without my amazing family. Thanks, now and always, for continuing to put up with me. Not a day goes by that I don't realize what a lucky girl I am. Love you!

The world of night still isn't safe . . .
A new threat looms, and under the
cover of darkness ancient enemies
will form a forbidden—and
passionate—alliance . . .

═══════════

Turn the page for a sneak peek
of the second book
in the Dark Dynasties series.

Midnight Reckoning

Available in January 2012.

chapter ONE

Tipton, Massachusetts

O<small>N A NIGHT</small> when only the thinnest sliver of a crescent moon rode the sky, at a time when even the most adventurous humans had fallen into bed and succumbed to sleep, a solitary cat padded in and out of pooled shadow as he made his way across the deserted square in the middle of town. He was large, the size of a bobcat, with sleek fur the color of night. His coat shimmered as he moved, gleaming in the dull glow of streetlights in between shadows, and he moved with speed and grace, if not purpose. Eyes that burned like blue embers stayed focused on the path ahead of him.

The cat had gone by several names in his long life. For more than a century now, he had been simply Jaden, or even more simply, "cat." He would answer to either, if pressed, and neither if he could get away with it.

Tonight, in the night's seductive and silent embrace, Jaden answered to no one but himself.

He took his time as he made his way through town, savoring the stillness of it, the blessed lack of humanity with all its noise and emotion and complication. He paused in front of the darkened windows of a beauty salon. Jaden let his gaze drift over the sign, which read CHARMED, I'M SURE, and then lifted his head higher to smell air that was heavy with moisture and ripe with the promise of rain. Summer was making its way to this little corner of New England, though he knew that even in early May the frost could arrive on any given night to give the season's fresh blooms a deadly kiss.

Deadly kiss, Jaden thought, swishing his tail. Yeah, he knew all about those. When you were a vampire, especially a lowly shape-shifting cat of a vampire, deadly kisses were sort of your stock in trade.

And damn it, so much for a late-night walk to clear his head.

The shift came as easily as breathing to him; in a single heartbeat, Jaden stood on two feet instead of four. He stuffed his hands deeply into the pockets of his coat and continued on down the street, glaring at the ground in front of him as he went. Though he'd spent years silently seething at the Ptolemy, his highblood masters who had treated "pets" like him with little mercy and even less respect, these days he didn't seem to have much anger for anyone but himself.

He now had what he'd always thought he wanted: friends, a home, and, most important, his freedom. The Ptolemy were not gone, but they were cowed for the time being, and his kind, the much-maligned Cait Sith, had been chosen for an incredible honor. They were to be the foundation for the rebirth of a dynasty of highbloods that had vanished ages ago, only to resurface in the form of a single mortal woman who carried the blood.

The seven months since Jaden had helped that woman, Lily, make a stand against the Ptolemy had passed quickly. And though it had been considerably less time since the Vampiric Council had given Lily's plan its grudging blessing, Jaden was now really and truly free. Whether it had been a wise decision, Jaden couldn't say. The Cait Sith were an unruly lot at best.

But he was grateful, as were the rest. And that had to count for something.

Jaden rubbed at his collarbone without really knowing he was doing it. There, beneath layers of clothing, was his mark, the symbol of his bloodline. Until recently, it had been a coiling knot of black cats. But a drink of Lily's powerful blood had changed it, adding the pentagram and snake of the Lilim, now encircled by the protective arms of the cat. It meant new abilities he was still exploring, newfound standing in a world where he had always been beneath notice. It should have meant hope, Jaden knew. After all, for the first time in his long life, he was not a pariah. He could be his own master. It should be everything. And yet...

The empty places inside him still ached like open wounds. Something was missing. He just wished he knew what it was.

A soft breath of wind ruffled through his hair, bringing with it a whiff of scent that was both familiar and unfamiliar.

Then he heard the voices.

"There's no place to run to now, is there?" That was a gravelly male voice, reeking of self-satisfaction. Its owner gave a low and vicious chuckle. "You're going to have to accept me. I've caught you. It's my right."

A female voice responded, and a pleasant shiver rippled through Jaden's body at the low, melodious sound of it.

"You have no rights with me. And chasing me down like prey isn't going to get you what you want."

He was almost certain he'd heard that voice before, though he couldn't place it. What Jaden *could* place, however, was the scent that had his hackles rising and the adrenaline flooding his system.

Werewolves.

Jaden's lips curled, and he had to fight the instinctive urge to hiss. Not only were the wolves vilified by vampires as savages, banned from their cities under penalty of death, but as a cat-shifter, Jaden hated his uncontrollable physical reaction to the smell of their musk. He had two options: fight or flight. It was less trouble to run. But this was his territory now, vampire territory. And these wolves had a hell of a lot of nerve coming into it.

Jaden was moving before he could think better of it. His feet made no sound on the pavement as he headed for the parking lot behind the building. And as he slipped into shadow, he listened.

"You can make this easy or hard, honey. But you're going to have me one way or the other. And there's not a damn thing you can do about it."

A low growl from the female. A warning. "I'm not about to take a backseat to some social-climbing stray. I don't want a mate."

The male's voice went thick and rough, as though he was fighting a losing battle with the beast within. "My family is plenty good enough for an Alpha's daughter. You should be glad it's me, Lyra. I won't be as rough as some. And you and I both know there's no way the pack is ever going to have a female Alpha. There's too much at stake to let the weak lead."

Lyra... The pieces clicked into place, and Jaden's stomach sank like a stone.

He did know her. And that brief meeting had put him in one of the fouler moods of his unnatural life.

Memories surfaced of a Chicago safe house, full of vampires in hiding, in trouble, on the run. And it had also been a hiding place for a female werewolf with a sharp tongue and a nasty attitude. Rogan, the owner of the safe house, had mentioned something about Lyra being a future pack leader...right after Jaden had demanded she leave the room.

Lyra had gone, though she hadn't taken the slight quietly. And now she was here, in the seat of the Lilim. It was almost inconceivable. Jaden wondered briefly if Lyra hadn't hunted him here to finish their brief altercation. That would be like a werewolf, brutish and nonsensical. But no, Jaden realized as Lyra and the male who was accosting her came into view. Lyra seemed to have bigger problems than any grudge she bore him.

Jaden kept to the shadows, melting into darkness as effectively as he did in his feline form. He now had a clear view of a tall, overmuscled Neanderthal who was wearing the typical smug sneer. A predator. Jaden had gotten very good at identifying them, being that he was one. Lyra he saw only from behind, but he would have known her anywhere. Long and lean and tall, with a wild tangle of dark hair shot through with platinum that tumbled halfway down her back. He let his eyes skim the length of her, suddenly apprehensive—hoping that his reaction to her the last time had been some kind of sick fluke. It had been easy enough to dismiss then. Being under constant threat of annihilation could do strange things to a man. But he knew it had fueled his anger at her presence in the safe house.

And now, just as before, the sight of her sent desire cascading through him in a wild rush like no other woman had provoked in him.

Jaden's sudden arousal mingled with a punch of bloodlust, creating a tangled mix of wants and needs that had his breath beginning to hitch in his chest. He moved slowly, walking the increasingly fine edge between man and beast as he struggled to stay concealed. He remembered more than just his brief meeting with her, no matter how he'd tried to block it all out. He'd had dreams—bodies tangled together, biting, clawing, licking . . .

He couldn't truly want a werewolf, Jaden told himself, appalled. Apart from being forbidden by both races, it was just *wrong*. Wasn't he screwed up enough?

It was a relief when the Neanderthal provided a distraction from his thoughts. The male moved like lightning, and far more gracefully than his bulky form would suggest. A hand shot out, snatching something from around Lyra's neck. He dangled it in front of her, a silver pendant hanging from a leather cord. She tried to snatch it back, but the male held it high above his head like a schoolyard bully.

"How *dare* you."

"It's just an old necklace," he said with a smirk. "If you want it that badly, come and get it."

Jaden could hear the helpless outrage in her voice when she spoke.

"My father—"

"Isn't here right now, is he? No one is." The Neanderthal shifted, crooked a finger at her. His stance said he knew he'd won. "I've got a hotel room. Or we can do it right here. Your choice."

His grin was foul. She seemed to think so too.

"Like hell, Mark."

Lyra's muscles tensed. She was going to run. What choice did she have? But the other man knew it. And while she might be fast, there was no way she could match his strength.

Jaden hissed out a breath through gritted teeth. He was no hero. He might be nothing more than a lowblood vampire, a gutter cat with a gift for the hunt. But even among his kind, there were unspoken rules. And something in Lyra's voice, the hopeless outrage of someone railing against a fate she knew was inevitable, struck a chord deep within him. He had spent centuries being pushed and pulled by forces he couldn't fight. No one had ever given a damn what *he* had wanted, not from the first.

Gods help him with what he was about to get in the middle of.

Lyra spun, leaping away with a startling amount of grace. The man lunged almost as quickly. His hand caught in all the glorious hair, fisting so that her head snapped back. Jaden heard her pained cry, heard the man's roar of victory. Then his hands were on her, grabbing, tearing...

One look at Lyra's eyes, wild and afraid, and nothing on earth could have prevented him from stepping in. Jaden sprang from the shadows with a vicious snarl, bloodred fury hazing the darkness. He landed directly in front of the grappling pair, fangs elongated and bared. The shock of his appearance gave Lyra the opening he'd hoped for. She twisted away, but not quickly enough. The male she'd called Mark took her down with a quick clout to the side of the head before whipping back around. Jaden watched, an odd twist of pain in his chest, as Lyra gave a single, shocked sob and collapsed to her knees.

Still, Jaden had gotten part of what he wanted. Lyra could no longer be used as a shield.

Recognition dawned in Mark's eyes a split second before the instinctive hatred did. Then another set of fangs were bared. Eyes flashed hot gold. The werewolf gave a guttural growl and reached for Jaden, long claws already extended from his fingertips. Jaden hissed as he stepped out of reach and waited for his chance. Jaden knew from experience that a wolf would always go for brute force over finesse. And against a vampire, it was almost always the wolf's downfall.

This time was no different.

Mark lunged, swiped. Jaden ducked easily and extended claws of his own, drawing first blood across the vulnerable belly. The thin ribbons of blood darkening his T-shirt seemed to incense his adversary, and he launched himself at Jaden, only to find himself with a face full of asphalt. Unable to help himself, Jaden laughed, though it sounded nasty and hollow to his own ears.

"Hmm. I think someone's going home alone tonight."

The werewolf dragged himself off the ground, face bloodied now, and growled at his tormentor. "Get out of here, bloodsucker. This is wolf business."

"Really? Looks like garden-variety jackassery to me,"

Jaden said, watching Lyra out of the corner of his eye. She had shifted to a sitting position and was holding her head in her hands, staying very still. Jaden didn't know how badly she was hurt. It was so like a wolf to try to win a woman by damaging her. Regardless, it was time to run this bastard off and give Lyra what care she needed.

He tried to ignore the way his heart began to stutter in his chest at the thought.

"Leave now," Jaden said, his voice soft, deadly. "Or I kill you."

Mark snorted. "Skinny piece of shit bloodsucker like you? I don't think—"

His words were cut off abruptly by two kicks, one to his gut and one across his thick head. At that, he went down like a ton of bricks with only a soft grunt for a response. This time, he stayed down. Jaden glared down at him for a moment, only barely denying himself the extra kick he wanted to give the wolf, just for good measure. But the stupid bastard should feel lousy enough when he awakened facedown in the parking lot in the morning. While it would be momentarily satisfying, killing him was nothing more than a messy waste of time.

And despite his disturbing attraction to Lyra, Jaden had no interest in getting the Lilim into a pissing match with whatever scruffy pack of werewolves this loser belonged to.

Satisfied that they were now, for all practical purposes, alone, Jaden moved to Lyra's side and crouched down beside her. A light, intoxicating scent drifted from her, making his mouth water. Apples, he remembered. Sweet, tart apples, with something earthier beneath. Strangely enough, he felt no urge to run, to hiss and spit. It was a good thing he hadn't gotten this close the last time. He might have done something really stupid.

Though he supposed his current actions qualified.

"Lyra?" he asked, trying to keep his voice low and soothing. He wasn't sure how successful he was—he was way out of practice at damage control. Usually, he *was* the damage. "Are you all right? Do you need a doctor?" Wolves were self-healers, he knew, but it could take a little longer, which was dangerous when the wound was severe.

She said nothing, not moving a muscle, and Jaden's concern deepened. He reached for her, momentarily overcome by the urge to make even the simplest physical connection. But his hand stilled in midair when she finally lifted her head to look at him. And whatever he'd expected to see—fear, confusion, even a little gratitude—none of it was in evidence as he looked into Lyra's burning, furious eyes glowing fire-bright in the dark.

"Don't even think about touching me, *cat*," she said. "I can take care of myself."

THE DISH

Where authors give you the inside scoop!

From the desk of Vicky Dreiling

Dear Reader,

While writing my first novel HOW TO MARRY A DUKE, I decided my hero Tristan, the Duke of Shelbourne, needed a sidekick. That bad boy sidekick was Tristan's oldest friend Marc Darcett, the Earl of Hawkfield, and the hero of HOW TO SEDUCE A SCOUNDREL. Hawk is a rogue who loves nothing better than a lark. Truthfully, I had to rein Hawk in more than once in the first book as he tried repeatedly to upstage all the other characters.

Unlike his friend Tristan, Hawk is averse to giving up his bachelor status. He's managed to evade his female relatives' matchmaking schemes for years. According to the latest tittle-tattle, his mother and sisters went into a decline upon learning of his ill-fated one-hour engagement. Clearly, this is a man who values his freedom.

My first task was to find the perfect heroine to foil him. Who better than the one woman he absolutely must never touch? Yes, that would be his best friend's sister, Lady Julianne. After all, it's in a rake's code of conduct that friends' sisters are forbidden. Unbeknownst to Hawk, however, Julianne has been planning their nuptials for four long years. I wasn't quite sure how Julianne would manage this feat, given Hawk's fear of catching *wife-itis*.

After a great deal of pacing about, the perfect solution popped into my head. I would use the time-honored trick known as *The Call to Adventure*. When Tristan, who can not be in London for the season, proposes that Hawk act as Julianne's unofficial guardian, Hawk's bachelor days are numbered.

In addition to these plans, I wanted to add in a bit of fun with yet another Regency-era spoof of modern dating practices. I recalled an incident in which one of my younger male colleagues complained about that dratted advice book for single ladies, *The Rules*. I wasn't very sympathetic to his woes about women ruling guys. After all, reluctant bachelors have held the upper hand for centuries. Thus, I concocted *The Rules* in Regency England.

Naturally, the road to true love is fraught with heart-break, mayhem, and, well, a decanter of wine. Matters turn bleak for poor Julianne when Hawk makes his disin-terest clear after a rather steamy waltz. I knew Julianne needed help, and so I sent in a wise woman, albeit a rather eccentric one. Hawk's Aunt Hester, a plain-spoken woman, has some rather startling advice for Julianne. Left with only the shreds of her pride, Julianne decides to write a lady's guide to seducing scoundrels into the proverbial parson's mousetrap. My intrepid heroine finds herself in hot suds when all of London hunts for the anonymous author of that scandalous publication, *The Secrets of Seduction*. At all costs, Julianne must keep her identity a secret—especially from Hawk, who is determined to guard her from his fellow scoundrels. But can he guard his own heart from the one woman forbidden to him?

My heartfelt thanks to all the readers who wrote to let

me know they couldn't wait to read HOW TO SEDUCE A SCOUNDREL. I hope you will enjoy the twists and turns that finally lead to happily ever after for Hawk and Julianne.

Cheers!

Vicky Dreiling

www.vickydreiling.com

♥ ♥ ♥ ♥ ♥ ♥ ♥ ♥ ♥ ♥ ♥ ♥ ♥ ♥

From the desk of Jane Graves

Dear Reader,

Have you ever visited one website, seen an interesting link to another website, and clicked it? Probably. But have you ever done that about fifty times and ended up in a place you never intended to? As a writer, I'm already on a "what if" journey inside my own head, so web hopping is just one more flight of fancy that's *so* easy to get caught up in.

For instance, while researching a scene for BLACK TIES AND LULLABIES that takes place in a childbirth class, I saw a link for "hypnosis during birth." Of course I had to click that, right? Then I ended up on a site where people post their birth stories. And then . . .

Don't ask me how, but a dozen clicks later, my web-hopping adventure led me to a site about celebrities and baby names. And it immediately had me wondering: *What* were these people thinking? Check out the names these famous people have given their children that virtually guarantee they'll be tormented for the rest of their lives:

Apple	Actress Gwyneth Paltrow
Diva Muffin	Musician Frank Zappa
Moxie Crimefighter	Entertainer Penn Jillette
Petal Blossom Rainbow	Chef Jamie Oliver
Zowie	Singer David Bowie
Pilot Inspektor	Actor Jason Lee
Sage Moonblood	Actor Sylvester Stallone
Fifi Trixibell	Sir Bob Geldof*
Reignbeau	Actor Ving Rhames
Jermajesty	Singer Jermaine Jackson

*Musician/Activist

No, a trip around the Internet does *not* get my books written, but sometimes it's worth the laugh. Of course, the hero and heroine of BLACK TIES AND LULLABIES would *never* give their child a name like one of these. . . .

I hope you enjoy BLACK TIES AND LULLABIES. And look for my next book, HEARTSTRINGS AND DIAMOND RINGS, coming October 2011.

Happy Reading!

Jane Graves

www.janegraves.com

From the desk of Paula Quinn

Dear Reader,

Having married my first love, I was excited to write the third installment in my Children of the Mist series, TAMED BY A HIGHLANDER. You see, Mairi MacGregor and Connor Grant were childhood sweethearts. How difficult could it be to relate to a woman who had surrendered her heart at around the same age I did? Of course, my real life hero didn't pack up his Claymore and plaid and ride off to good old England to save the king. (Although my husband does own a few swords he keeps around in the event that one of our daughters brings home an unfavorable boyfriend.) My hero didn't break my young heart, or the promises he made me beneath the shadow of a majestic Highland mountain. I don't hide daggers under my skirts. Heck, I don't even wear skirts.

But I am willing to fight for what I believe in. So is Mairi, and what she believes in is Scotland. A member of a secret Highland militia, Mairi has traded in her dreams of a husband and children for sweeping Scotland free of men who would seek to change her Highland customs and religion. She knows how to fight, but she isn't prepared for the battle awaiting her when she sets her feet in England and comes face to face with the man she once loved.

Ah, Connor Grant, captain in the King's Royal Army and son of the infamous rogue Graham Grant from A

HIGHLANDER NEVER SURRENDERS. He's nothing like his father. This guy has loved the same lass his whole life, but she's grown into a woman without him and now, instead of casting him smiles, she's throwing daggers at him!

Fun! I knew when these two were reunited sparks (and knives) would fly!

But Connor isn't one to back down from a fight. In fact, he longs to tame his wild Highland mare. But does he need to protect the last Stuart king from her?

Journey back in time where plots and intrigue once ruled the courtly halls of Whitehall Palace, and two souls who were born to love only each other find their way back into each other's arms.

If Mairi doesn't kill him first.

(Did I mention, I collect medieval daggers? Just in case . . .)

Happy Reading!

Paula Quinn

www.paulaquinn.com

From the desk of Kendra Leigh Castle

Dear Reader,

It all started with the History Channel.

No, really. One evening last year, while I was watching TV in the basement and hiding from whatever flesh-eating-zombie-filled gore-fest my husband was happily watching upstairs, I ran across a fascinating documentary all about a woman I never knew existed: Arsinöe, Cleopatra's youngest sister. Being a sucker for a good story, I watched, fascinated, as the tale of Arsinöe's brief and often unhappy life unfolded. And after it was all over, once her threat to Cleopatra's power had been taken care of in a very final way by the famous queen herself, I asked myself what any good writer would: what if Arsinöe hadn't really died, and become a vampire instead?

Okay, so maybe most writers wouldn't ask themselves that. I write paranormal romance for a reason, after all. But that simple, and rather odd, question was the seed that my book DARK AWAKENING grew from. Now, Arsinöe isn't the heroine. In fact, she's more of a threat hanging over the head of my hero, Ty MacGillivray, whose kind has served her dynasty of highblood vampires for centuries, bound in virtual slavery. But her arrival in my imagination sparked an entire world, in which so-called "highblood" vampires, those bearing the tattoo-like mark of bloodlines descended directly from various darker gods and goddesses, form an immortal nobility that take great pleasure in lording it over the "lowbloods" of more muddied pedigree.

Lowbloods like Ty and his unusual bloodline of cat-shifting vampires, the Cait Sith.

Now, I won't give out all the details of what happens when Ty is sent by Arsinoë herself to find a human woman with the ability to root out the source of a curse that threatens to take her entire dynasty down. I will say that Lily Quinn is a lot more than Ty bargained for, carrying secrets that have the potential to change the entire world of night. And I'm happy to tell you that it really tugged at my heartstrings to write the story of a man who has been kicked around for so long that he is afraid to want what his heart so desperately needs. But beyond that, all you really need to know is that DARK AWAKENING has all of my favorite ingredients: a tortured bad boy with a heart of gold, a heroine strong enough to take him on, and cats.

What? I like cats. Especially when they turn into gorgeous immortals.

Ty and Lily's story is the first in my Dark Dynasties series, about the hotbed of intrigue and desire that is the realm of the twenty-first century vampire. If you're up for a ride into the darkness, not to mention brooding bad boys who aren't afraid to flash a little fang, then stick with me. I've got a silver-eyed hero you might like to meet. . . .

Enjoy!

Kendra Leigh Castle

www.kendraleighcastle.com

Find out more about Forever Romance!

Visit us at
www.hachettebookgroup.com/publishing_forever.aspx

Find us on Facebook
http://www.facebook.com/ForeverRomance

Follow us on Twitter
http://twitter.com/ForeverRomance

NEW AND UPCOMING TITLES

Each month we feature our new titles
and reader favorites.

CONTESTS AND GIVEAWAYS

We give away galleys, autographed copies,
and all kinds of exclusive items.

AUTHOR INFO

You'll find bios, articles, and links to personal websites
for all your favorite authors—and so much more.

GET SOCIAL

Connect with your favorite authors, editors, and
other Forever fans, and share what's important to you.

THE BUZZ

Sign up for our monthly romance newsletter,
and be the first to read all about it.